THE EVOLUTION DISTURBANCE

What if Charles Darwin was wrong?

Andrew G Davies

Contents

Dedication

For anyone who is carrying the weight of a hidden or chronic disease. Also, for anyone who is labelled as 'different', society doesn't fully understand how special you are.

Acknowledgments

Special Thanks

To my family & friends, too many to individually name.

Author Biography

In 2011, at the age of 46, I was diagnosed with Multiple Sclerosis (MS). Although I had heard of MS before, I lacked a comprehensive understanding of the disease and its symptoms. A year later my employment was terminated due to ill health. Despite my illness, I continued offering marketing consultancy to small businesses across Merseyside. In 2015, I was honoured with a prestigious fellowship from the Chartered Institute of Marketing (CIM).

I was born in Liverpool in 1965 and am commonly known as Andy. Childhood was an educational experience, the area we lived in presented numerous challenges. Despite these obstacles, I grasped the notion that better opportunities awaited. During my informative teenage years, I was introduced to my first (very basic) computer. It was an affair with technology that lasted throughout my working life. During this period, I also discovered my aptitude for selling products, which naturally led me to the field of marketing.

Writing, whether in the context of formal proposals or academic settings, has always brought me great satisfaction. During the later phases of the Covid-19 global pandemic, I informed a few colleagues of my intention to produce a book. The Evolution Disturbance has taken over four years to develop and 18 months to write. I am immensely proud of this work, it describes episodes of my life including the strains of living with MS. Above all, it will take the reader on a journey of discovery that starts and ends with, what if?

Preface

What is the Evolution Disturbance?

Quite simply the evolution disturbance is the practical conclusion of a scientific hypothesis. Future generations will proceed to prove the science which will both rewrite our history and achieve a unified future. It is a significant claim and will be observed through a seismic phenomenon that will alter our evolutionary trajectory. Interestingly, as I write this, it serves as clear evidence that the event has already taken place, indicating its significant success. Science and technology coupled with human ingenuity will one day prove there are no barriers to what we can achieve. The term 'disturbance' is used to soften its transformative impact, a more accurate choice of description would be 'reengineered'. Danny believes this choice is carefully considered and certainly premeditated. Reengineering implies the outcome is universally beneficial as the original 'evolutionary plan' carried flaws within its build. This insight into our past and our future will challenge everything we currently believe. In summary, we are now able to comprehend the reality concerning the creation of our own universe and the nature of consciousness within humanity.

This is not so much science fiction, instead it's part-fiction based on known science.

Was Charles Darwin wrong?

He is primarily known for the 1859 publication, On the Origin of Species. This set him apart as the architect for the theory of evolution by natural selection. Darwin's explanation for evolution was accurate, although it was influenced by the scientific limitations of his era. What he couldn't witness, or even begin to imagine was a world that proved this wrong in the case of one species. Charles Darwin would have been astonished to observe a world in which all of humanity collaborates toward a unified objective. Eventually, every question we ever had will be answered, every conceivable padlock will finally be opened.

Join me on an exceptional journey into an era where science and technology reign supreme. Time, space, and matter are applied to unlock the disturbance that altered our evolutionary path. Although, our journey begins in the darkest depths imaginable; Danny has been planning his elaborate and intricate suicide for well over a year. Some might incorrectly presume this would be the closing scene and an end to his seven-year battle against MS Multiple Sclerosis. But his fight was with an entity far more divisive, his adversary deployed destructive armaments that threatened to destroy his life, or so he presumed.

Everything altered course for Danny during a few short weeks in the summer of 2018. Envision a perfect utopian landscape without wars, nations, governments, religion, or suffering. He observed a perfect state of peace and harmony. Through advanced technology we can barely imagine, he is presented with an amazing and repeatable window of opportunity. Peering 2,034 years into the future is both daunting and captivating. It presents significant challenges while offering remarkable opportunities. Was he intentionally selected, and can he successfully fulfil his role to become a guiding light that will shape the future? Will free choice prevail over destiny, and do individuals truly possess free choice?

This could be perceived as your idea of heaven or hell, for some it will simply say utopia, and for others it will mean complete anarchy or complete perfection.

"The book to read is not the one that thinks for you but the one which makes you think."

Harper Lee

Chapter 1
Planning

I strained my neck while looking over my left shoulder, all this in an attempt to see the time. The green digital display on my clock alarm was slightly blurred but it confirmed 05:35. Then, as my senses began to register, I could feel the chill in the air on my face and right shoulder. I could hear Jane in the shower as she moved about, it made the water bounce and splash in a random rhythm which woke me further. Our bedroom backs on to the bathroom, consequently I can hear every sound. Typically, every Monday, Thursday, and Friday it's the same routine as she gets ready for work. Her alarm, which is next to her side of the bed goes off at 05:15. It partially wakes me, although it almost catapults Jane to attention and she's up, out of bed and ready to start her morning ritual. By the process of elimination, I figured out it was Thursday. By this point my awareness had fully kicked in, it was Thursday 1 November 2018. Also, with this realisation, I opened my eyes completely and began to stare at the artexed ceiling, my undivided attention focused on one point. It's always the same obscure and abstract detail that captures my gaze. I continuously stare at this sole point as it helps me gather my thoughts for the day, and plan what needs to be done. But even with this focused approach I will no doubt forget around 80% of those plans as soon as I walk downstairs.

This was no ordinary Thursday though, today was going to be a day like no other, a day that you can only experience once. Consequently, it had to be big, and it had to be loud. This was meant to be my final day on this planet, and for me, at that time it was the best thought out plan, and the only option available. For the past 11 months I had carefully and meticulously planned every element of my suicide.

Everything I had planned pointed towards this particular date, this cold dark Thursday would change everything for me and those around me. It doesn't take a genius to work out that it didn't happen, because you are reading this now tends to give it away. How I got to this point, now staring up at the ceiling with an alternative plan and a new agenda is nothing short of incredible. What changed my mind is simply mind-blowing, please join me on this newfound spirit for life and I guarantee you won't be disappointed.

I understand more about mental illness now, how changes and events in your mind along with chemical imbalances can throw everything into a whirlwind. If unchecked, these can quickly develop into a raging and uncontrollable hurricane. Reality and rational thinking became blurred, the determined focus that used to serve me well eventually turned on me and created a creature that threatened to consume me. There were several individual things that helped me out of the blackhole that gripped me tightly, and with an unforgiving power. With every wrong decision I made, its grip tightened. As part of my preparation, I listed my top 10 favourite things, these were everything from movies, songs, bands, food, places etc. well you get the idea. As I compiled each list and enjoyed them one last time, I realised how deeply enjoyable they were. It wasn't just the taste of a beautifully crafted red wine, or song lyrics that stirred emotions of happiness, sorrow, or anger and the angst of a teenager in love. Nor was it movies that told such brilliant stories full of twists and turns. Or the happy memories of birthdays, family gatherings, bad dad dances or simple walks with the dog on holiday in Scotland while Jane prepared a meal back at the lodge. A quote perfectly sums this up when Louis C.K. said, "What happens after you die?", "Lots of things happen after you die – they just don't involve you."

Well, what helped change my mind, in part was the fact that I wouldn't get to see what came next. I also learnt that the phrase, 'this is it', is utterly perfect and accurate in its simplicity. We have one life, and it should be enjoyed and savoured for what it is. Because, as your lights go out for the final time and you think your last thought, that's it, then nothing. Your brain is dead, there's no power source to supply it, and one thing is certain, there are no second chances. I considered this notion numerous times, what will be my final thought. It's hard to say with complete accuracy, you may want to rehearse the final words you speak and who you want to hear them, but as for your final thoughts. Will they be of happy memories or faces of those you love. Will they be of remorse for things you didn't do or say. will they be of repentance for things you did during your life. After several months of contemplation, I knew what mine would be.

All the things that gave me such pleasure would end with my last breath. I would never again have conversations with friends that would have us laughing so much that our ribs and cheeks would hurt long after we said, 'see you later'. And on the flipside, I would never have conversations that developed into debates that turned into friendly arguments, which inevitably turn full circle into us laughing once again. Storytellers and actors that I admired would continue to create masterpieces that I would never see, and the list goes on. But most of all I would never see my beloved Everton FC win the Premier League. For those of you who follow or have awareness of English football will know that this is highly unlikely. For too long now Everton have been mediocre at best. Sadly, we must constantly watch our rivals' winning tournaments and acquiring the best players from around the world.

Even now, I find it almost impossible to think what it would have been like for my family and friends. I don't think you can ever imagine what something like this would have done to them, the blame they would take on would live with them forever. It was my despair, it was my pain that would have eased, but in turn every ill that I felt would have been forced upon them. The thought of this still haunts me, and I often wake up in a cold sweat. They would have countless unanswered questions, they would be loaded with guilt, and with the constant thought they could have done more to help.

The problem was that I hid my pain too well, every time someone asked if I was OK, my automatic response was, "Yes, I'm fine." I hid everything behind laughter and light-hearted banter, the mask I adopted concealed all the pain and sorrow I carried. It was all my fault; I didn't let anyone beyond the protective wall which was erected as means of self-preservation. The recurring trouble was that I should have opened-up, asked for help or just found someone to talk to.

How this would have affected Jane, Toni, Georgina, and her girls would be enormous and truly devastating. Jane and I have been through so much together, every challenge that has been thrown at me, or rather us, has never daunted her. I now see how this would have destroyed Toni, our beautiful and caring, intelligent, and courageous daughter. And, at a time when important life decisions are being made. I am sure both Jane and Toni would blame themselves for not observing changes in my attitude and approach to life. Still, as I have said, I concealed everything far too well. This would undoubtedly be the same for my sister Georgina. She probably knows me better than anyone, I would have hurt her simply by not talking to her about my troubles. The list would extend through other family members and friends, each one asking could they have done more, each one sharing a huge weight of guilt.

The events that happened, and primary motivation for the change took place during a couple of months in the summer of 2018. What pulled me out of the blackhole that had consumed me, can only be described as mind-blowing. Months of planning and readiness were rendered completely worthless. Although, I will always be grateful for their intervention and for everything they gave me. I was given the unique opportunity to witness the future of humanity and the Earth we inhabit. It's a perfect world, imagine if you can, a world that has…

NO more Wars, NO need for Nations, NO Religion,

NO Intolerance, NO Lies, NO Disease,

NO Injustice of any kind, NO Governments,

a place where there is NO Greed,

NO Crime, and NO Suffering.

This could be your idea of heaven or hell, for some it will simply say utopia, and for others it will mean complete anarchy or complete perfection.

Whatever your current beliefs are, or maybe what you have been told throughout your life by those you trust, or by those in power, it's your choice whether you think this could be true or not. But please remember, those in power over us have a vested interest in maintaining the status quo. There was a time when the phrase, 'religion is the opium of the masses' summed up perfectly how control was maintained, and this remains the case in far too many regions around the world. Move forward a period and you will find that TV and Shopping are now challengers for the top slot. Every Sunday you will see queues of traffic waiting to enter the retail parks that now outnumber churches.

Watching TV for hours upon hours has numbed our brains and sanitised our intake of culture. This brainwashing is not happening, it's already happened. Infants are given screens to watch and distract them from normal and basic emotions. Dummies or pacifiers have been replaced by mobile phone and tablet screens. I can still picture John Lennon making a remark that they (The Beatles) were, 'more popular than Jesus'. It was made in an interview, in which he argued that the public were more infatuated with the band than with Jesus, and that the Christian faith was declining to the extent that it might be outlasted by rock music. John Lennon's home in Liverpool is now treated like a shrine. Hundreds of thousands from around the world flock there each year to visit this small, ordinary, 1950's semi-detached house.

Now social media and the overwhelming abundance of media in all its forms helps to keep us in our place. It's also like a drug that numbs and sedates our brains as we stare for hours mesmerised by the screens on our phones. While we are in this state, we are unlikely to want more and question less, those in power couldn't be happier. For those who want to keep us neatly in our place it's a win-win, the content is increasingly created by the culture it feeds. We are encouraged to follow the path of our parents and for countless generations before them. We are told we can make a better life by working hard, paying taxes, living our lives to defined borders of education then work, then family, then more work, then retirement and finally death. The cycle is self-perpetuating as we are encouraged to breed during our fertility period, and all while continuing to work and pay taxes. If we look around, we can already see the next generation entering the food chain and maintaining the class system where it has always been.

If you are living with the luxury of free choice, and able to read this freely, please appreciate what you have. Millions of young girls are banned from all forms of education around the world. The reason is simply because of interpretations of a so-called holy book.

I was given the unique opportunity to see a world that is free from all the cruelty, immorality, and corruption that we continue to tolerate into the 21st Century. I have battled with myself repeatedly, as to whether to write this, never mind going on to publish it. Fanatics will undoubtedly see this as an attack on their religion, this could cause extremists to act as they often do. Even where we find less rigid nations and regions, whoever challenges their beliefs is automatically an enemy. Forget for a moment that contentious subject, the list above also states no more wars, no need for nations, no suffering, and no disease. If you were shown a place where this is true, wouldn't that be our idea of perfection. Theists may be happier if we referred to such a place as heaven. Once again, I urge you to imagine a place on earth that delivers such perfection, and I ask you, whatever your beliefs are, isn't this worth striving for.

What I witnessed will never leave me, and the gifts' I was given will also stay with me forever. If like me you have an open mind along with a trust that science is there to be proven and challenged, then you're in for a treat. For those who don't have either or both, then I invite you to turn to Chapter 9 titled: 62.87 Theory. In this chapter, science is given the opportunity to state its case and disprove most, if not everything we currently accept about the universe and the creation of mankind.

I know there's a lot to take in, and it could have all been very different if my original plan was seen to completion. The planning really started in late 2016, but it was really throughout the subsequent year when it all came together, and it was 2018 before I began the readiness. I know the thought of suicide sends shivers down the spine of most people, and they could never imagine themselves in that position. Well let me tell you, you are the lucky ones, it can be all consuming as I can testify to, I spent the best part of a year designing plan after plan. I would spend weeks in deep thought as I ruled plans in and then out, considering what would work and which ones were futile. It had to be spectacular as this would be my final statement of defiance. This was my overwhelming objective; I can see now how it blinkered all rational thoughts and formed part of my great depression.

Twitch

Lists were prepared in my mind; I would often just drift back into the creative part of my brain. Ideas would form, as they did, they would tussle with what remained of the rational part. Eventually, after days or even weeks ideas would be given a green or red light depending upon its credibility. The primary list included three things that were not negotiable. Firstly, no one else must be physically hurt during the event. Secondly, it must be visual, and in this it had to be spectacular and grab people's attention. And finally, above all others I must get my message heard and by as many people as possible.

Getting my message heard had driven everything up to that point, it had to be clear, and it had to be enormously loud and visually impressive. Now people may think the reason for my suicide was due to my MS. In 2011 I was diagnosed with Multiple Sclerosis. Like many people, I had heard of MS and that it was a particularly nasty disease, but that was it. I didn't know anyone with MS, and I knew nothing of how people get it, or how it develops. All I thought I knew, was that it leaves people disabled. I remember seeing the odd runner wearing orange tops in the London Marathon collecting money and presumably raising awareness for the charities that supported sufferers.

It started, coincidently on a Thursday in March 2011, I returned home the night before from a business trip where I had spent 3 nights away. This wasn't uncommon, and I will explain more about that later. Anyway, on the Wednesday night I felt really tired, and my left leg was aching. The next morning, I could feel a soft twitching in my cheek just below my left eye. At first Jane couldn't see anything. Then after about an hour, she looked again and could see a noticeable twitch, it seemed to have its own relatively fast rhythm. Jane was more worried than I was, in order to keep the peace, I agreed to get an appointment with our GP. Luckily, I was able to get an appointment later that morning, this was uncommon as you can normally wait much longer. I drove the short distance to the village and parked up in Sainsbury's car park. By this time, I felt increasingly tired, and the twitch felt stronger.

At the surgery, I waited patiently for around 20 minutes, continually looking at the large TV screen that hung on the wall. Advertisements rolled by, advising me to lose weight and to give up smoking while pregnant. When my name appeared, it would tell me which room to go to. I could feel my eyes becoming more tired, I was woken by the sound 'bing-bong', my name appeared along with the message 'please proceed to room 2'. As I entered the room, the doctor gestured for me to sit down, as I did, she asked me to tell her what had happened. I immediately noticed how pretty her eyes were, they were a mesmerizing pale blue with green flecks.

As I relayed the events of the morning she simply nodded and asked me to perform some basic tests. I was aware that my speech was laboured for some reason, and I remember feeling more anxious. The actions she wanted me to perform involved blowing my cheeks out, following her finger with my eyes. She then proceeded to shine a light into my eyes, first one eye, and then the other. Without her giving any observable reactions, we then progressed to questions being fired at me. My mind went blank, and I found it difficult to get my words out. She could tell that I was increasingly confused and agitated. With this, she called through to reception and asked them to call for an ambulance. The realisation hit me, there was something seriously wrong here. I felt reassured that I was going to be looked after, she put her hand on mine and said, in a calm voice, "Try not to worry, it will be okay".

The following nine days seemed to blur and distort into periods of sleep, followed by a few hours of obscured consciousness. And 'wow', could I sleep now, prior to this I used to survive on four, or maybe five hours per night. This was even the case when I was driving down to London which would take over four hours from our home in Warrington. Warrington was always described as a strange town, it nestled quietly between two rival cities, and never said much. I always thought that sleep was a luxury, but I found that routines were hard to break. Even when I was awake, I would try to keep my mind as free as possible. Anything that could tax my brain seemed to cause a range of problems including slow speech or difficulty getting some words out. Understanding or processing what these medical experts were saying would leave me informed but not necessarily any the wiser. Each day there seemed to be different doctors coming to see me, they would ask me more questions and perform the same or similar tests. Then there were the continual blood tests, junior doctors would end up with blood everywhere, and the number of bruises would go up daily. "Is it alright for us to perform a lumber puncture?", calmly announced a young doctor, is deflective age had him looking like an 18-year-old student. Trust me, if anyone even suggests a lumbar puncture, run as fast as you can, they hurt, a lot!

I didn't know at the time, but they initially thought it was a stroke or a bleed somewhere within the brain. This was ruled out with a CT scan, which I had on the first or second day, this also excluded a brain tumour. I found out later that Jane was kept informed when she came to visit twice daily. I can see how this must have been for Jane, one day we had plans for holidays, weekends away, friends to meet, restaurants to try, concerts to look forward to. Everything changed, and it will never be the same again. I would have to adjust, and Jane would have to accommodate these changes. Our family and friends would have to understand. It's a big ask for each individual person, and as a collective they would have to rally around and work as a team.

Finally, on the eighth day I was taken for an MRI scan, throughout this stay in hospital I was in a single room, rather than a ward with three other people. This helped me enormously, noise and bright lights seemed to make my symptoms worse. As I was wheeled back from the scan and helped into the room, the door was left partially open which meant I looked out onto the nurse station. Around 20 minutes later, I could hear one of the nurses in a slightly raised voice calling, "I have the consultant radiographer on the phone, they need to speak with the consultant for Mr Daniel Thomas". Presumably, the same nurse must have placed a call to find him. I then heard her say to a colleague that 'serious abnormalities' had been reported. I remember laying on the bed with the palm of my hands resting on the cool metal restraint bars. Over the past couple of days, I had noticed my hands continually tingled with unrelenting pins and needles, I searched for anything cool which would relieve the sensation. This was just the latest in a growing string of highly unusual symptoms that I noticed and began to report.

Within less than half an hour, a doctor who I hadn't seen before came in and introduced himself as Professor Paul Mularkey. He had another doctor with him, who I had seen previously, but there were countless doctors, and far too many tests, hence I couldn't recall his name. He asked me how I was feeling and what I understood had happened. I reeled off the list of symptoms which included the twitch on my face. This remained in its intensity, it was relentless, and continually in my field of vision. I was still feeling slow and confused, which also meant my speech would slow down and be laboured. Weakness in my legs was compounded by a lack of balance, this resulted in a couple of stumbles and near missed. But most of all I just felt wiped out and sleeping way more than normal. It was a long list, and with each one he nodded, it must be something they perform in training, nod, and look serious, but not too serious as it would induce fear.

My fear had been in overdrive ever since I overheard the phone call from the radiologist. This Professor explained that all the tests they were running indicated there was indeed a problem. The MRI scan had helped them to identify the 'abnormality', essentially, it showed clear Demyelination. The words came out of his mouth, and I definitely heard them, but very few of them registered as meaning something. He continued explaining that it showed damage to the protective covering to the myelin sheath that surrounds nerve fibres which are found in the brain and spinal cord. He finished this brief explanation by telling me, when the myelin sheath is damaged, nerve impulses slow or even stop, causing neurological problems. Eventually, the thunderbolt came with a finale that would change everything, as he said the next few words my whole body dropped. The announcement shuddered by entire being, without hesitation, "Demyelination is known better as Multiple Sclerosis, or MS". Those two letters MS would continue to invade my waking hours and thoughts for years to come. I could be sitting quietly sipping a coffee months later, and from absolutely nowhere, those two letters would barge their way forwards and demand that I recall segments of that first conversation. Two weeks later, Jane and I attended an outpatient's appointment with a specialist neurologist. The doctor was accompanied by a specialist MS nurse, they reiterated what we had previously been told. Worryingly for me, he sounded delighted when he announced the MRI scan lit up like a Christmas tree.

Revenge

My final act of defiance on this planet would have to be staged, and be completely clear, it would have to hit hard and with all the power I could muster. When I received my diagnosis, the hospital will have informed my GP surgery, and presumably the doctor who initially saw me. A couple of days after returning home from hospital, my own doctor called out to our home. The conversation was very relaxed, and she tried her best to reassure Jane and I that it wasn't a death sentence, and it didn't mean I would be confined to a wheelchair. I think the main advice she gave us was about taking time for the news to settle in, and try not to worry, but this was easier said than done. The 'taking time' element was also given to us, as she signed both of us off work for three months. Like most people I hadn't been off work ill for anything like that time, I think the longest I had been off was a week when I had shingles about a year before this incident. Now I had a ridiculous amount of time to fill, but without the usual demands and routines of work.

Little did I know, after being extremely supportive and accommodating to begin with, my employers at the time would sack me within a year. For this reason, and the way I was subsequently treated over the following five years, I wanted revenge, or to be more accurate, I needed it. I wanted the world to know the pain and misery they caused me. I was just a line on a spreadsheet that had a value next to a pound sign, their goal and objective was to reduce this by as much as they could. They didn't care, and I don't even think they thought about the impact it would have on a fellow human being. They managed to de-humanize the entire process.

On 20th December 2012, I received a letter which announced that they were terminating my contract after nine years, the reason given was casually mentioned as 'unable to carry out duties due to ill health'. They didn't even wish me a Merry Christmas, which would have been a nice touch. This solitary act would trigger a chain of events that consumed most of my waking hours for the following three and a half years during the tribunal case. I sued my employer for unfair dismissal along with disability discrimination. By the end of this, I was emotionally wrecked and physically exhausted. Almost every day I had to battle through my ongoing MS symptoms, but I had to get up and stand up for what was right. I was more than just a line on a spreadsheet, more than just a number.

I would later find that my real enemy wasn't just my employer and their spineless and two-faced owners. On that chilly late-autumn Thursday in 2018, my anger would be solely directed at a firm called Stowama2 HR PLC, or S2 as they are known, and the tactics they used throughout the case. For them it was purely down to win or lose, how much will it cost and what will be the optics along with the narrative. They're nice words, and both seem to be slowly sneaking into our language with various meanings. Both optics and narratives will simply refer to whatever the results are, they need to consider how will they appear to potential clients, but more important, their investors. Ultimately, their efforts will be focused on manipulating the results to ensure they do not look bad. They will use an array of language to make sure people interpret it in a way that would minimise or eradicate any backlash. This part of the manipulation is called 'positioning', they will do their upmost to play it down, twist the story, and in most instances they win. They also have very deep pockets, paying people off, and tying uncontrollable elements into non-disclosure agreements, and all to protect their good name.

Stomama2, with their company logo that stood 30 foot tall, S2 gleaming proudly in front of their monument to success. A 12-storey office block of reflective and glistening smoked glass adorns and beautifies their European HQ. Home to their corrupt directors who enjoy privileges such as their named parking spaces in front of this tower of underhanded tactics and blatant lies. It is these people and their shrine to money that would receive my focus and my interpretation of justice and revenge.

It had to be them because my employer ceased trading just six months after I received my termination letter. My research revealed that their share price valued Stowama2 HR PLC, with assets over £2 billion. They also had various companies dotted around the World, with dozens of trust funds that also showed how they will avoid taxes by any means. I couldn't help but think, if I was treated in such a disgusting way, then there will be many others who received the same treatment. This ignited my need for justice, I was on a crusade to do as much damage as I could, and to highlight my case and the treatment I received. I hoped that it would give others the encouragement to pursue a claim and to fight as hard as you can. As I look back now, I can only see that the succession of previous governments has actually made it harder, if not impossible to take a rogue employer to court. Over the years they have reduced the number of tribunal courts, while increasing the costs to begin a claim. It's just another example of the rich protecting their own.

The Plan

But how do you even make a dint into this colossal giant of a business, especially one that's extremely corrupt and well protected by lawyers. They even have a Digital Reputation Manager to protect their good character and enhance their appearance to onlookers. If there was ever a bad review it would miraculously disappear within days if not hours of being posted. There you have it, you can see the magnitude of my challenge, over the course of the previous 18 months I would set out to hurt them as much as I could. Initially, I simply had ideas that I would explore only in my mind, thinking would they achieve all the goals I wanted. They were quickly discarded if they failed under analysis, meaning they did not tick all the boxes required. Although if there were elements within the idea that had potential, I would store them for future consideration. Unfortunately, MS affects my memory, therefore I knew early on that I would have to be more organised if this was to succeed. Our home was usually littered with post-it notes reminding me to do things or remind me where things are. Most of these notes are for future events like phone the doctors, pay a bill or remember the window cleaner is due on Thursday, which means Pete will be here today and he's going to expect a cuppa and a chat, which is more of a piss-taking exercise regarding football.

I would have to be more organised about this, Microsoft Excel in my opinion is a work of beauty. Funny thing is, I don't mind being referred to as a nerd by friends. A few years ago, a close friend gave me a mug that stated this proudly, 'I Love Spreadsheets', this instantly became my mug of choice. Spreadsheets rely on accuracy, if data is entered correctly, you can do wonderful things with it. I could easily waffle on for hours on how you can sort and view information, set queries and what ifs. I can handle most things, but my sister Georgina has been a Data Analyst in a bank for over 40 years. She loves her job and doesn't really see it as work, well that's commitment, and a wonderful thing if you obtain satisfaction in this way, especially when you consider how much of your life you give to it.

Anyway, a new spreadsheet was created with its own password, in cell A1 I entered, Main Objectives for the downfall of S2. In column A, the headings started with: Newsworthy. Column B continued with: Highly Visible, and the headings continued with; Sudden, Ability to be Vocal, Embarrassment Level. The next set included, Stowama2's Involvement, Planning & Delivery, Impact on Others, Longevity and finally, Ability to See It Through.

As possible ideas came into my head, I evaluated them using the checklist and a point scoring system, 0 to 5, five meaning it satisfied my needs. Some would never work; some I knew that I couldn't see through. Selfishly, I wanted my death to be as quick and as painless as possible, but when you then evaluate this need against the others they failed. It needed to be visible which ruled out things like hanging, overdose, and toxins intake. Visible options such as jumping off a bridge or high buildings would impact others unnecessarily. Others were ruled out instantly if they put other people in danger. Throughout this period of evaluation, I was misguided when considering the likely impact on Jane, Toni and the rest of my family and friends. There were two sides to my actions, and I initially failed to see the devastation that would inevitably be caused to the people I love. What would they think of me taking my life in this way, in such a public display. The final two columns were without doubt the hardest and with each plan this is where they failed.

Suicide is a selfish act, and I now understand that, but at this time my focus was taken elsewhere. What I learnt during those couple of months in the summer of 2018, changed everything for me, and showed me how wrong I was. I would urge anyone who is contemplating this for any reason, please, please STOP! There is no set of circumstances that are worth ending your life for. Anything that you are going through, anything you feel you are enduring now can and will be resolved. If you or someone you love or know is considering this, then please ask them to simply read chapter 17 and specifically the section headed: Every Life Matters. Specialist organisations are there to help anyone who may be contemplating suicide. All you must do is reach out and ask for help, the statistics show how many men and young people are tragically taken in this way. I am not able to provide specific help, all I can do is tell you my story of how events altered for me and what I learnt.

Thursday 1 November 2018

Eventually, a plan was developed that ticked most of the boxes, I knew I would never have them all, but with this plan I would achieve the most critical ones. It started with finding a storage unit, it needed to be local and one that allowed 24-hour access. Ideally, they wouldn't ask me too many questions regarding its use. In January, I visited a few local self-storage units, fortunately I found the perfect one that had 50sq meter units which were arranged in rows of around 20. Each one stood adjacent to the next, the beauty was they were all located outside of the main building which housed around a further 2,000 of various sizes. They also took in deliveries for people who rented their units, this also suited my needs. Online shopping then helped me out as you can purchase things anonymously. Over the next couple of weeks, the storage unit accepted five deliveries for me, and all without question. Each delivery contained 30 plastic liquid bottles, large enough to hold around 5 litres. This provided sufficient containers for my needs, I figured 150 litres would do the job. The other items needed were relatively easy to pick up including 30 extra strong carrier bags, and a pack of large cable ties.

With the hardware secured, the two remaining tasks were just as easy for me. Robust research these days is made as easy as online shopping. I created a few more spreadsheets to organise the information I needed. Each one was saved using a different password, and I stored all the passwords for this project in a word document, and yes you guessed correctly, this had its own password. With laptop ready, over the next 3 months I sourced all the information I could find. Once I had found the various names, I then set out to collate individual data for each person identified. In addition to the standard information of name, business name, email address, I needed to acquire contact phone numbers for each one, this was a little harder to source. Fortunately, LinkedIn provides a lot more information about the company's my targets worked for. Using creative phone calls to their offices, I was able to obtain landline and mobile numbers. Social media contact points are obviously simple to find, although I had to go a couple of levels further to extract the information needed. A few more columns on their group's spreadsheet gave me their usage, frequency of posts, and shares etc.

I then turned my attention to the email content, using a standard body of text which described both what was happening, and what I wanted to say took around five revisions. In the end I was happy with the content and could move on up to the next thing. These just needed top and tailing to suit each set of contacts, I would also use the main points of the email to create what I was going to post on social media. Once again these were modified to suit each social media platform, Facebook gives you a couple of thousand words, but Twitter is really restricted. Because of this, I also created a website using a domain name that I purchased for less than £10, Stowama2-thetruth.com. The website itself took around three weeks to develop, it had a really cool looking header image, I blended their logo into an image of the tribunal courts in Manchester. I added the words 'The Truth about Stowama2' as a heading. And for a finishing touch, I added a montage image that I created of the two sisters who owned Stowama2, along with the three directors who had lied and covered up those lies with money.

They thought money could fix any 'difficulty' they had in business, they wrongly thought it would work with me, I had a different plan. I recalled a poignant saying, 'there is only one thing more dangerous than a foe with unlimited resources, and that's an enemy with nothing to lose'. Therefore, with the various plans made, and the checklist checked and double checked, I was ready to execute my revenge. As I lay there looking intently at that single point in the ceiling, I had a final choice to make. A final opportunity to execute the plan or retrieve the memory sticks, diaries along with various sketch pads that were also kept in the secure lockup. I knew what my decision would be, and with a faint smile that accompanied the thought of irony, irony that both futures were housed together in a secure metal box. The future you are about to hear could have easily been destroyed forever, and I would have only been remembered for the explosive exit that might have been.

Later that morning, I got ready and made my way to the storage facility, it had brightened up, but there was still a chill in the air. It would have been a perfect day for my trip over to Leeds on the M62, a journey that I knew well. There I was, stood outside B22, the number of the 50sq meter box, under my arm was three sketch pads, six notebooks, and in my pocket were the world's most valuable memory sticks. Making my way back to the car I took a moment to contemplate what might have been, what could have happened and how it was intended to play out. My saving option is that I now understand that I was in a crisis, if it was to happen again, I knew I would have to find somebody to talk to. That's all it takes, and I now understand that we just need the ability to talk.

START

The plan for Thursday 1 November 2018, was to leave our house in Warrington at 13:30, and drive the 15 minutes to the storage facility. I was grateful that in the end, I didn't have to write the letter to Jane, my amazing and supportive wife of 30 years, along with our beautiful, caring, and talented daughter Toni who was going to turn 25 in September this year. Putting pen to paper to explain why I felt this was the only option open to me, the only way that I could have the justice I hungered for, was without doubt the toughest thing about this whole exercise. I would have to name individual family members that I loved and cared for. Doing so, I would have been able to see their faces, I would recall them, and each one would be while they were smiling. Anytime I speak to someone on the phone, their image appears in the second layer of my memory, and they are always smiling. Then there are friends that have stuck by my side through the hardest of times. I feel sorry for some of them as my regular updates were often painful for me to say, never mind them having to listen.

I allowed a further 30 minutes to load up the car, I wasn't happy that this had to be done in daylight, but there was no choice. The drive to Leeds is a little over 65 miles and providing there was no unforeseen incidents should take 1 hours 40 minutes. I rehearsed the route three times previously as I checked out access and places to park. The plan was to park discreetly around the corner from Stowama2's office block, there I would have made the final checks and waited for it to get darker. At 16:30 the plan was to drive around the corner and park up directly outside the entrance to their lavish office building. Ideally, I would block the reserved parking bays which housed either the Bentley or Maybach with their personal registrations. These were obviously designed to illustrate their importance and to prove how extra special they are. I would then wait with the doors locked, waiting for a passer-by or security to tap on the window and tell me parking was not permitted there. Handing them a letter through a small opening in the window, I would then gesture for them to look in through the tinted rear window. There, they would see the back seats full of plastic containers.

18:30

The note I passed to them simply read, 'my name is unimportant to you at this time, I am sat outside in a blue 4x4 car with the engine running'. The second line of the note said, 'Every inch of the interior and boot space is filled with fuel. At 18:30 I will ignite everything, all that will remain will be a burnt scar on the side of your building for all to see. To help avoid this, I want to speak directly in person to either of the owners, Petra Smythe or Anita Smythe. They must be accompanied by either Dan Wilson or Calum Wright, whichever have the bottle to come and talk to me directly, there must also be a TV camera broadcasting our discussion live.

At precisely 18:30, stage 2 of the plan would kick in. I knew they would not be willing or able to meet any of these demands. The only point of the notice was simply to allow them sufficient time to clear the area of workers and the public. Stage 2 also involved 2,273 emails being sent to the news desks, editors and journalists of every newspaper, TV, and radio channels I could find, in both UK and US. Software that I use took care of this and I had pre-tested every email address to ensure it didn't go into Spam or Junk. Another piece of software allowed me to schedule 5,612 social media posts to the same people and organisations who received emails. Additionally, I arranged to send emails and social media posts to Stowama2's competition. Every email, post and image contained a link to the website that would provide them with all the evidence needed to hurt or at the very least embarrass Stowama2 HR. Using another piece of paid software, I scheduled an informative and slightly cryptic SMS text message to be sent to the mobile number I had for everyone on each of the various lists. It simply read, 'Check your email for breaking news about Stowama2 HR PLC.'

This is where the definitive planning ends, and my imagination kicks in. As I sat calmly in the car, I envisaged people leaving the front of the building, scurrying to their safe registration points they had practiced many times before, but never thought they would be used. In the distance, I would hear the various subtleties in siren tones between police, paramedics, and fire engines that quickly grew louder until they would be accompanied by an array of blue flashing lights. Previous scouting missions had revealed the locations for the nearest base for each of the emergency services. Although, I could not factor in the proximity of any vehicle that may have been close by on the day. Phase 3 would then kick in 20 minutes later, a further 5,612 social media posts would be sent. This one provided a link to a live broadcast from my car, each one would be told that it would start at precisely 19:15.

I couldn't predict what each of the emergency services would do. I presumed the police would take the lead and ensure everyone was at a safe distance. Curtsey of DVLA records they would quickly be able to trace my identity from the car registration, and from there obtain my mobile phone number. Earlier in the day, I would have replaced the personal greetings message to announce what I was doing, and that at 19:15 they could watch a live broadcast which would explain everything. There would not be much more I could do but wait, therefore, I had created my final playlist. Ten songs that have either inspired me, engaged me, or simply made me feel happy within myself, which I know is a difficult thing to achieve. I had timed each of the ten tracks, if I pressed play at 18:03 the final song would finish at 19:10. Songs by Paul Heaton, Paul Weller amongst others would have energized me sufficiently to pick up my phone, give a slight glance as to how many missed calls I had and then begin.

Dozens of rehearsals had brought me to this point, all the preparation, all the planning, the countless hours researching and building lists had all come to this. With my phone mounted on the steering wheel and the last tune still going through my mind, Going Underground by The Jam. Don't be fooled by the title of the song, do a little research, and you'll find wonderfully crafted lyrics by Paul Weller. It's not about death, it's not about giving up, rather it's intended as a wake-up call directed towards those who fail to see what's happening.

You choose your leaders and place your trust

As their lies wash you down and their promises rust

You'll see kidney machines replaced by rockets and guns

And the public wants what the public gets

But I don't get what this society wants

With the words and the tune slowly fading, I look up and see myself on the screen, as I do so, I offer up an open invite to anyone who has found the link. By this time, I would have strapped my left wrist to the steering wheel and taken some of the strongest painkillers I had. There could be just one or two people watching, then again there could be millions as the social media posts had sufficient hashtags and mentions to ensure they would be seen and shared. Hopefully, looking beyond the screen of my phone, I would find members of the public, all holding up their phones in a way that showed they were also broadcasting live the dramatic scenes. They could be live streaming just as I am, the only difference is that I hold the cigarette lighter in my right hand, one soft twist and it would all be over. The person filming me, waiting for the outcome, and growing impatient thinking will he, or won't he. It depends on the person whether they want their name attached to the footage as it is shared across the planet. While someone is waiting at traffic lights in Brazil, Hong Kong or anywhere, when they look at their news feed to see some nutter threatening to blow himself up, just to seek revenge on his employers. Would you watch it, would you comment or just give it a like, hug or laughter.

Would I have the bottle to quickly pull back my thumb, who knows. I know for certain that the first three to four seconds there would be this incredible heat that would hit me from behind. There would be a futile nanosecond, as I automatically reach for the door handle in a useless bid to escape. Once that passes, there will be nothing, no sound, no light, no thoughts just complete nothingness. This would be followed by complete silence. Essentially, the lights go out and the only thing remaining would be the complete carnage my family and friends would have to endure until their dying day. The other thing would be the pictures and stories, and of course that video that toured the planet more times than Virgin Atlantic. The unmistakable unknown will be whether my efforts would achieve the objective I planned and wished for. Would people be interested enough to investigate my back story. Indeed, would anyone care that some guy from a smallish town in England wanted to make a stance.

In truth, I knew as I stared up at the ceiling I would not go ahead with this plan. Earlier in the year I learnt the value of life and the perfection of everything we have. What I saw, and what I documented in those memory sticks and notebooks has the potential to change the course of mankind along with humanity. Maybe if I put a picture of a fluffy kitten playing with a beagle puppy on the front cover and on social media posts it will get noticed.

I knew that today; I would be sorting through the notebooks, along with the various sketch pads. I would also be rewatching each vlog that I made. Will anyone believe me, will I be silenced by those it will offend, the truth is nobody knows. I am not setting out to deliberately offend, nor am I putting everything together to become a celebrity. From the final visit in July, and the subsequent events of that day in August, I knew what I must do. I was definitely not going down the route of a human car bomb, but I was unsure what to do regarding the gift I had been given, and the insight I now have.

Options

What I am about to tell you is almost unbelievable, and for that reason I am giving you an option. You can continue reading what happened next and enjoy my testimony of events; alternatively, for those sceptics amongst you, please feel free to bypass the evidence strewn story. Retaining your neatly fitted blinkers and with deafened ears you can ignore an alternate view of creation. We are all far too reliant on what we are told, we rarely question those who we are told to trust. In fact, most people don't really want the truth. They just want constant reassurance that what they believe is the truth.

Most religions function on fear. The phrase, 'god fearing' always made me wonder, if you don't believe, or dare to question then you will be punished for all eternity. As children we are indoctrinated to believe the religion of our parents or education systems. The belief of 'choice' is then typically governed by where you were born. In Europe and in the US, it will be a form or 'brand' of Christianity, whereas in parts of Asia you will follow another brand. All of the 4,000 or so religions currently in existence were created by men. The one I am most familiar with was created some 2,000 years ago. This was a time of almost zero education, with beliefs that were based on limited knowledge and understanding. Such as, the earth being flat, the belief that the sun orbited earth, with no understanding of things like gravity. Information was spread through stories, and it is incredibly sad to see that these stories are permitted to continue to blight our development. If the bible had revealed facts regarding our world and the universe, such as the structure of a molecule or the number of galaxies, then I would been inclined to investigate further. Instead, it's full of archaic rules and hatred for many things. I believe and I can only hope that The 62.87 Theory lays down an alternative option for the 21st Century and beyond.

The 62.87 Evolution originated as a theory, and it is this theory, which will eventually be proven by science, that states creation in its entirety was not in the hands of a godlike fantasy. Therefore, anyone wishing to bypass the introduction to this, and how I obtained it then please direct yourself to Chapter 9, titled 62.87 Theory. After reading this you are free to declare it as, 'The biggest load of rubbish ever.' Although, shouldn't we then categorise this as a work of elaborate fiction, and place it alongside all other similar stories that make the same claims. Although, it should be argued that The 62.87 Theory does provide scientific evidence to substantiate its claims, but others are merely stories. There's a great saying; Science will admit when it is wrong, whereas religion will kill to prove it is right.

I make a very bold claim that this is the first book to provide evidence for the creation of everything. Because of this, those previously mentioned may feel the need to ban it, making sure their children's eyes are never poisoned with this blasphemy in print.

"It's easier to fool people rather than it is to convince them they're being fooled."

Mark Twain

For those brave souls that remain, I invite you to proceed to the next chapter titled, From Russia with Love. I can hear the American contingency shrieking now, "Not only blasphemy but he's also a communist". Saying that, most wouldn't have read this far, therefore, here's another spoiler, it's about the World Cup in 2018.

Let's consider your options in a way that grants you having a choice of which rabbit hole to pick. Do you take the red pill, and read how a theory, that's so magnificently colossal that it changed humanity forever. A theory that took scientists many years to agree its validity and claims. Which backed each claim up with stringent science and rigorous scrutiny of its supporting data. Unlike unsubstantiated and unrealistic claims, this came complete with scientific evidence which insisted it must be continuously contested.

As humanity and science evolved, a further realization became evident through subsequent findings. Before you completely dismiss this, think for a minute what it also delivered. The list shows a utopian existence for all, and without unachievable catches. Forget that it says, 'No religion', wouldn't you grab with both hands all the other benefits. For those who have answered no, sadly, I can offer no further words to convince you otherwise. Although, before making your final judgment please try to read chapter 9 with an open mind.

Or do you bravely take the blue pill and continue with the rest of the book. Come with me on this journey and uncover the most remarkable series of events. Thursday 7th June 2018 kickstarted these events that gave me a brief, but extraordinary view into the future for humanity. A future with abundant riches, a few of which are also listed below. If you have a free mind, and a trust in science in all its forms, please join the minority who rightly question outlandish claims. Could the universe with its immense size and complexity be created in just seven days. Were we humans created in a way the bible and other religious books claim. Is there really a heaven and hell or are these merely created to satisfy and give comfort to the living. We must be allowed to question everything and seek proof for any claims made, and that includes religion in all its forms. Please enjoy my tale of discovery. Whether you believe me or not, how can you decide without knowledge.

One pill could be described as extremely sweet, the other could be the polar opposite and the bitterest pill you have ever taken. How you describe them is your choice, but you should taste one to be certain.

After all, who wouldn't want a better place for future generations and a future that delivers perfection.

*****

For individuals who are still uncertain but have a desire to satisfy their curiosity, please refer to page 135. This section towards the end of Chapter 8 introduces the theory. At this point, a quote from Arthur Koestler precisely encapsulates the necessity for the theory.

Chapter 2
From Russia With Love

Firstly, thank you for choosing a pill, whichever one you selected you are brave to have stayed with me as I tell you the events as they happened. Maybe you chose the red pill which took you straight to the 62.87 Theory. There you will have learnt the secret to humanity, along with the creation of the universe, pretty massive hey. But how did this come into my possession, well you're about to find out as you join those who chose the blue pill. It's a perfect world, yet it's staggeringly detached from what we must endure today.

I spoke to an old school friend recently on the phone, we meet up now and again, but he now lives and works in Cumbria. It's a bit of a challenge to meet up on a regular basis due to the distance and other non-important things. He was probably wondering why I had been quiet recently. Anyway, it's impossible for us not to laugh every time we catch up as we recall events of our school days together in the 1970's and 80's. Our recollections were not all rose tinted, we were both born and educated in Liverpool before we both moved our separate ways as our working lives began. Unbeknown to us at the time, surviving school was an education in its own right. The area of Liverpool where we both grew up was and still is, what politicians would call 'deprived'. We would prefer to class it as rough and challenging, getting out of there was a challenge but I don't think either of us would have had it any other way. Friends stood by you if there was ever any trouble and let me tell you we had a knack of finding trouble at times.

Fortunately, we both loved football, we both could, and should have turned professional but for one thing. Granted it's a big thing called… talent, or lack of it in our cases. Once football is in your veins from a very young age, it almost becomes a part of your DNA.

The other main attribute we possessed was a cracking sense of humour, although being funny by itself is good, for us pair it was all about speed. Sarcasm, and sharp observations coupled with a killer speed certainly gave us the edge. It certainly got us out of some awkward situations with potentially painful outcomes; although, it could land us in hot water too. There was a knack to using it in a class full of kids, some teachers would allow a degree of brevity. But, for some it would result us in enduring detention or worse.

We had a tight-knit group of friends as we entered our teens, with these friends we shared the third and without doubt the most important thing for me, and that is music. Music surrounds me daily, in the car, while getting dressed to go out, and when relaxing. Saturday evenings are often spent watching a concert on YouTube, or just letting their algorithms select the next video we watch. Since we recently invested in a Smart Speaker called Alexa, I have had enormous enjoyment creating playlists and listening to albums and bands I may have missed. I don't know about you, but we have had to rename ours, we now call her Doris when referring to it in conversation. Too many times she would pipe up when you least expect it with, "I don't know that". Also, if you haven't tried it yet, say, "Alexa, I love you", well it made me laugh.

It was around May 2018, when the TV adverts started building up to the World Cup in Russia, which kicked off on June 14th. They were expecting and preparing for violence and disturbances between the supporters of rival countries, as a result it was also making additional appearances on the main news. Now and again they also spoke about the chances of England, and the next crop of hugely talented, but over-paid prima donnas with ridiculous haircuts and arms that were filled with tattoos. Typically, England do well during the qualifying stages and friendlies, but as soon as it becomes serious, the talent and teamwork fades and it's just another let down, plus another spoiled summer.

England were in Group G, along with Tunisia, Panama, and Belgium. I wanted to watch the Belgians play as most of the team played for clubs in the Premier League. I would have to wait until 18th June for our first game against Tunisia, on the same day Belgium would play Panama. Group F was another I was looking forward to, Sweden, Mexico, South Korea, and Germany. Throughout my life of watching international football, Germany and penalty shootouts go hand in hand, but never in our favour. Other teams I was looking forward to seeing were Spain and Portugal who were both in Group B, France in Group C, Croatia in Group D, and of course the mighty Brazil, who just ooze talent and were in Group E.

Thursday 7th June 2018 began like most days, it was exactly one week before the start of the World Cup. Jane was in work which meant if I was feeling OK and my MS symptoms allowed me, I usually dropped her off at our local train station. Thankfully, it was a good day, although my left hip was tender which I put down to just sleeping awkwardly. The day panned out as normal, after the trip to the station at 07:35, I would return home, then a cup of tea and some muesli along with my first lot of medication, these are primarily to manage the pain and stiffness in my legs. Currently, nine are taken in total in the morning, eight at lunch time, and a further nine when I go to bed. These can be topped up with the odd paracetamol here and there. Each one comes with its own set of side-effects, many of them include drowsiness. One of the medications I take for pain is also an anti-depressant, I sat and perused the information leaflet once and the noted side-effects read, 'may cause patients to consider self-harm and suicide'. Maybe best not to mention this one.

In the morning, I managed to get a bit of work done for an article on USP in marketing. I had undertaken bits of consultancy work, copywriting, and blogs since 2014. This was a couple of years after I was forced out of my role as Marketing Manager in 2012. The company deemed that I was surplus to requirements, I was simply a broken cog in a well-oiled machine. It took a couple of years to adjust to my new life, and my new normal. Although, I don't think you can ever fully adjust, and accept a new normal, there are simply too many hurdles to jump, and minefields to navigate. There's no guidebook given to people in my situation, I know we are all different, and each set of circumstances are unique to the individual. I once attended a three-part self-support course on 'how to manage a life limiting illness', it surprised me that I lasted until the end of the first session, but I remember the coffee was nice. I once thought of creating a guide, and calling it, MS for Beginners, I would ensure it would be an absolute guide.

The thing I miss most in relation to work is the banter between work colleagues, plus the social aspects that came with it. I used to spend a couple of days per week working from home, but I still felt part of the team, along with being valued. It's having a sense of purpose and worth, you can never underestimate how crucial this is. The other thing that hurt me was the lack of money, overnight I went from having a good salary with a healthy amount of disposable income, to nothing, or what felt like nothing. I had to deal with having to claim benefits and sick pay. This didn't just impact me, it will have also had a huge impact on Jane, Toni, and the rest of our family. We had plans, ambitions that stretched far beyond our working lives. At the age of just 41, I was effectively thrown on the scrap heap. I joked that my mid-life crisis didn't involve a little red sports car, and a trip around the world, as most do. Instead, I got a wheelchair and a list of medications that would put a small horse to sleep.

This is something the medical professionals overlook, they see you as an NHS number, an MRI scan and a 15-minute appointment. Most of them fail to see you as a person that has just lost everything, well may be not everything, but around a 90% loss to what I previously had. Soon after my initial diagnosis a few leaflets arrived, these primarily likened MS to a battery. The battery only had a certain amount of energy which could be adversely affected by pain, lack of sleep, fatigue, heat, humidity, and of course the tasks I was attempting.

07-June-2018 15:31

After lunch, I relaxed listening to some music, I asked Doris, I mean Alexa to play songs I might like. It's hard to pick fault with the selection she usually presents to me, and I always have the option to skip any I didn't like. This routine now happens about three days per week, typically the days when Jane is in work. I was feeling good, after an extended break of around two hours I returned upstairs to continue. I noticed the clock in the bottom right corner of my laptop screen, it read 15:15 along with the date. I thought I would finish checking through the article, email it and then treat myself to a coffee, my eyes closed as I pressed send at 15:31

The next thing I remember was hearing my name being called by a voice I didn't recognise. I think I was confused by how they were saying my name, it continued, "Daniel", "Daniel", and for a further three or four more times. I then felt I was waking but there was a strange sensation all over my body, it was like being hugged by the largest marshmallow that enveloped every part of me. I could feel it between my fingers and toes, my armpits seemed to lift upwards and outwards. It gradually took my entire weight as it moulded around my legs and arms. My neck felt supported, and my shoulders dropped in sheer relaxation as a warmth spread down my back.

Throughout this sensation I stopped hearing my name, it was replaced by a different voice telling me to open my eyes, and a different voice again said, "It is alright Daniel, you are safe, just open your eyes for us". The third voice was definitely female, it was much softer, and I began to place the position of this voice as being on my right-hand side. I was beginning to get my bearings although for some reason I couldn't open my eyes. Panic began to set in, thoughts began to race around my head, was I in hospital, why couldn't I open my eyes. With this increasing panic, I tried to move my arms, they still felt suspended, but I was unable to move or flex my arm at my elbow joint. Likewise, my legs wouldn't move as I instructed them, every direction I tried there was something or someone holding me down. No wait, correct that, it wasn't holding me down because I still felt suspended, although every attempt to move was futile. I began to kick out and struggle, but the more I tried, the more it encased me.

Eventually, with the increasing panic my eyes opened slightly to let the light in, it was a sharp brilliant white light. The light stung the back of my eyes, it was like the flash from a camera, the intensity was the same, but it was continuous in its ferocity. The female voice grew louder, "It's alright Daniel, you are safe, just open your eyes for us". I desperately wanted to shield my eyes, and although I was squinting it didn't seem to help. Moving my hands was useless, it was like they were being restrained by elastic. I felt I could move them upwards, but with a soft restraint I couldn't shield my eyes. Reluctantly, I tried to calm down, as I did the sensation of being hugged deepened and my breathing, well I just realised that my breathing had remained the same throughout this experience. This only added to my overall confusion. As the various sensations continued, I felt more relaxed and tried to open my eyes further. With each blink the sharp white light etched a halo pattern of blue and orange concentric shapes within my vision. I began to blink with a greater frequency, slowly with each one I was able to register more and overcome the pain.

Throughout this time, I didn't scream or shout, it was just one more thing to add to the confusion. I struggled to take everything in, was I in hospital, was I dead, where's Jane and Toni, where am I, all of these questions run furiously through my mind and at a speed that shocked me. For the briefest of moments, I allowed my emotions to cascade, I felt a terror hit me and rush through every sinew of my being. I was hurtling down the rapids being bounced and thrown from side to side. But just as quickly, I was able to regain my composure, I focused on my breathing which helped settle me. For the first time I was able to get some words ready, as I spoke those words, "Where am I?". As I said the words everything about the actions felt weird, it was my voice, but then again it wasn't. How can I explain this better, when you actually speak the words, you also physically hear the sound. I am unsure whether there's a delay or not, but this time the voice was different, it was more like my thought voice. What made it even worse, as I looked down slightly, I couldn't see my face or lips move to deliver the words. By this time my vision became clearer, and a male voice said, "Everything is good Daniel, when you are ready, we will explain what is happening, do not worry, you are perfectly safe". As these words reached me, it felt counterintuitive, although I did feel more relaxed, safer and while the hugging sensation softened, it also became warmer.

As I continued to blink, I found myself looking at three people who sat around 12 feet from me, I remember repeating, "Where am I?" a further two or three times. This was immediately followed by, "Who are you?" My eyes were unable to focus on one thing, they scanned from left to right as I tried to place my surroundings. Eventually, I concentrated my focus ahead of me before trying to place anything else. There were two men sitting to my left, and a woman sitting to the right. The floor was a dull grey colour which formed seamlessly into the seats they sat on. Everything else in the room seemed to be emitting light, that's why it was incredibly intense. It was difficult to capture any more detail about the three, in front of each person was what looked like three translucent computer screens per person. I could see through these screens, but they partially obscured everything else, that was apart from their head and shoulders. As I looked closer, I could see there was a large amount of activity on each screen as they flashed with an array of colours.

I was brought back from glaring at the activity on the opaque screens, the male in the centre slowly stood up and spoke. As he introduced himself as Trynes, his voice was most definitely calming. He told me I was completely safe and that he would explain everything. Gesturing to his left, he introduced the female as Helena. As he did this, she also stood up and smiled, nodded once, and then sat down again. I don't know how or why, but I knew information about them. Something, or someone was seriously messing with my brain. Trynes is aged 45 years and 32 days, his position is Observation Manager with the Try-neural Evaluation team. I knew if I concentrated, I would obtain more information about him. Just like the fact that his full name is Trynes-MOncrast-21, I decided Trynes was sufficient. Likewise, the female is named Helena-StomHunjar-A1, again Helena would do just fine. She is aged 33 years and 245 days; her position is Lead Psychoanalyst also with the Try-neural Evaluation team, and coordinator with the 62.87 Evolution Ethics Mandate P211 Team. I didn't know what any of this meant or how I was accessing it. All of this was adding to the overload of information my brain was accepting; I felt really dizzy and wished this dream time would end.

As Trynes remained standing, I was able to take in what he looked like. He looked to be in his mid-thirties rather than 45. He was slim but not skinny, clean shaven and his complexion looked radiant, you may say that he had been on holiday recently. I then noticed they all wore the same clothes, the guy in the centre had a plain light blue t-shirt, the way it fitted him suggested the material was heavier than a standard cotton. The other two wore plain grey t-shirts, and all three had a white circle motif which measured around 20cm across. It was actually the first thing I noticed; it looked like it was made of plastic, but as the light caught it, it reflected hundreds of colours all bouncing and clashing with each other. It was like a prism, although the reflections seemed to be focused on me rather than in a random pattern.

Helena had shoulder length brown or auburn hair; she looked very pretty without being too good looking. I know that's a poor description, but I couldn't liken her to anyone famous or recognisable today. She was naturally pretty; I suppose it was her cheekbones and the shape of her face that gave her this flawless beauty. I know there are algorithms for working this out and measuring this type of thing. Her complexion and skin tone were also perfect, I wouldn't say she had makeup on, but I am no expert. Her smile was equally as pretty, perfect teeth, but not the false tip-ex white fake ones you see too often on reality TV shows. She took too much of my attention as I missed the name of the remaining male who also stood up, smiled, and sat down again. Each smile was genuine but only to a point of procedure.

Throughout these few seconds of introductions my eyesight cleared more. Once again, I asked "Where am I, what am I doing here, please tell me what's going on?", as before, I knew I was asking the questions but weirdly it wasn't my voice, I couldn't feel movement in my face. I remember trying to move my arms again, it was useless as there was something softly pulling them back every time. In fact, I couldn't see my hands or my arms. Instead of panicking I remained calm, I knew I wanted to become more aggravated, shout louder these questions in a pointless hope of getting an answer. There were countless things running through my mind, but I couldn't form the words, I wanted to shout but I was unable.

The recurring thought that railroaded wildly through my brain was that I was in hospital, and something was seriously wrong. I now understand what having a split personality feels like, or having two personas at once, one screaming and raging while the other one was calmly listening. I could almost see the other version of me in a sort of secondary vision, this made the whole sensation even stranger. I must have looked startled or concerned as the male in the middle sat down and began talking again. This was only the second or third time, but as with the others, I found myself focusing on him over anything else including my own thoughts. He then told me that I was going to be perfectly safe, and they just wanted to ask me some questions. As he began saying this, I could see increased activity on the translucent screens as before. I didn't notice, but I must have taken my focus off him and glanced down to the screens. He also looked downwards, he asked if these were distracting me, I calmly said, "Yes". As soon as I finished the word, they all became invisible, although the hands of the two people either side of him seemed to be moulded around something, and I could see their fingers frantically twitching.

I must have appeared calmer as he continued to speak. He opened with the statement, "You are going to find a lot of this hard to believe". If ever there was an understated message, I don't want to hear it. Anyway, he continued to explain, 'at this moment they just wanted to ask me some questions'. He told me I was in a semi-conscious state, and if anyone saw me, they would just think I was asleep. Then came the killer blow as he told me that they inhabited Earth 2,034 years in the future. I didn't know if they were waiting for a response, but strangely, or maybe understandably, I couldn't think of a reply that warranted further discussion. I mean, it's not every day that someone tells you that you are speaking to a future generation. He continued to tell me I would always be safe, and they would only come to talk to me when it was completely safe to do so.

At that time, he didn't tell me how they communicated, or how they knew it would be safe, and I didn't even think to ask.

I listened intently, and remained calm as he told me there would be 'no experiments', they only wanted to talk to me about what life is like in the 21st century. He expanded on this to say they wanted to know what childhood I had, what relationships were like, along with work and all aspects of life. As he spoke, I tried to figure out the accent he had. It wasn't American which made me think it could have been Canadian, but some of the words he pronounced has a hint of Dutch. He then told me there may be other people who would want to talk to me and asked if this would be alright. He could have asked me anything because I was becoming very tired, therefore, "Yes" came out slightly softer than before. He then concluded what he was telling me by adding that I wouldn't be able to remember anything of the conversation we had had. They finished by all thanking me for my time and continued with the reassurance it would all be safe.

07-June-2018 16:05

As I woke, still in my office chair it took a moment to understand my surroundings and the time of day. It seemed darker which made me think it was much later in the evening. My laptop had gone into sleep mode, as I moved my index finger over the touch pad, I immediately noted the time 16:05. It must have been the bright light that I had just been exposed to, but a few more blinks and my eyes adjusted fully. I then clicked on Outlook; my last email was sent at 15:31. I seemed calm as I recalled what I had just dreamt about during the time I was asleep for 34 minutes. But what if it wasn't a dream, it all seemed too clear. I was beginning to get a headache type pain across my forehead and around my temple areas. I remember feeling very tired, but I was conscious I had to pick Jane up from the station in Warrington at 17:35. As I made my way downstairs to make a coffee, slowly more of the dream came back to me, the only thing I could think about was the voice and how calming it was.

I got to the station carpark early and instead of listening to music as I normally do, I just sat there quietly recalling parts of the dream, but I couldn't get my head around the fact that it felt incredibly real. As Jane got into the car she asked if I was okay, I thought it best not to tell her what had happened, I mean where and how do you begin. Later in the evening I couldn't stop myself from reliving what had happened during the 34 minutes I was either asleep or in this semi-conscious state. There must have been more said, but as he told me I wouldn't be able to remember. On my tablet I opened a Notebook App and began to write as much as I could recall. I also began to think that if it really did happen what would be the questions they would ask. Why me, kept recurring. I then thought I had to draw a line under the day, stop thinking about it and simply put it down to a dream, that is unless it happened again.

"Religion is like a blind man looking in a black room for a black cat that isn't there, and finding it."

Oscar Wilde

Chapter 3
Routine

The next morning started as every other day does when Jane's in work, although Fridays do feel different. I don't know why that is any more, weekends now simply mean I have a different set of routines to follow. I still get that feeling around 19:00 on a Sunday when you contemplate the things you didn't achieve, and the plans you should have made. That's usually accompanied with the deflated feeling that Monday will soon be here, and the roundabout of routines will start again.

One of the many things that MS has taken from me is spontaneity, everything we do now must be planned in advance. Gone are the days of receiving a phone call inviting us out for Sunday lunch or planning a weekend in the Lake District. Any plans we now make always come with the caveat that things could change with little warning, if I am feeling unwell, we must make the difficult phone call and recurring explanations. Eventually, the invites become scarcer, I still joke that 'the only thing, which is predictable with MS, is that it's totally unpredictable'. Those days of just going out for the day and seeing where we ended up, or short notice hastily planned weekends away are a distant memory. As are the evenings that start with little planned and end up with a fun filled night, with long-lasting memories of slightly embarrassing events.

It had also been a long time since I found myself waking up and staring at the same spot on the ceiling, the one that aided the detailed planning of my day. It was unusual as I didn't start the day with either planning for the events of 1st November or gathering items for it. I was surprised that I had a relatively good sleep, and I didn't dream of Trynes, Helena, or any other part of my previous dream. Little did I know at that time, but I would never dream again, ever. I still can't work out whether that's a good thing or not, what's the point or purpose of dreams. I did ask Alexa who instantly understood the question and told me, 'One widely held theory about the purpose of dreams is that they help you store important memories and things you've learnt, get rid of unimportant memories, and sort through complicated thoughts and feelings'. Well, if that is the case, will I miss out on not having this ability or maybe, I will compensate in other areas.

The daily ritual played out as normal, but I couldn't stop returning to the thought of that dream, and I began to question myself. If I was asleep or in a semi-conscious state for over half an hour, was there more stuff that I couldn't remember. Everything I completed during the morning seemed meaningless and undertaken at a very slow pace. Normally, when I feel like this I turn to music and a latte. About a year ago we purchased one of those coffee machines that recreates Costa coffees. They're okay, but if they could get the taste to resemble the aroma that's generated, it would be an absolute winner. The music of choice that day formed part of my preparation for the events planned for November. Creating shortlists of my favourite bands was proving harder than I first expected. I had completed some of the 'really like' bands, but the real gems were testing me which was a good thing as I was listening to more.

After lunch I waited eagerly to see if I would fall asleep either naturally, or by some other means which would result in a further insightful dream. Nothing happened for the remainder of the day. The Friday evening ritual began as normal. After picking Jane up from the station in Warrington, and listening to her moaning, either about how busy or quiet it had been. Along with the office bitching and politics of who wasn't talking to who, lasted the entire journey home. It would continue while she got changed into something more comfortable, removed her makeup and poured a glass of wine. Within a couple of large sips, the tone changed, and I could physically see her shoulders slowly relax. I joined her with a glass of red cranberry juice. I would have the odd drink of alcohol, but it did nothing for me, although for Jane the first bottle would be followed by at least one Vodka.

Nothing much happened on Saturday, there was a lot of news about the World Cup and England's chances of winning, which varied from abject confidence to the importance of team choices. Sunday was very relaxing which suited me fine. We planned to have a call with our daughter Toni who is in her final year of her degree at the University of Edinburgh. She was ecstatic when accepted into The Royal (Dick) School of Veterinary Studies, and she enjoys every aspect of university life. We were immensely proud as it was the highest ranked veterinary school in the UK, and the one she set her heart on. Her work ethic is brilliant, and she loves everything connected to animals of all shapes and sizes. We knew from an early age that this would be her ideal career. As a child she only ever wanted animal toys, she would wrap fabric around them to replicate a bandage. At the age of five we got our first dog, a beagle named Oscar. The pair of them were inseparable for many years, he just wanted to be with her and protect her at all costs. I remember saying to her, if you can find a job that you love, you will never do a day's work in your life. I had enormous confidence that this will be the case for her.

Every time we speak to her is an absolute joy, and we can't wait to hear about all the things she is doing and planning. During the call she told us about her plans for the remainder of the summer which involved spending some time at home. Jane was delighted beyond words and the two spoke about where they would go and who they would see. Toni always worries about me, we communicate via WhatsApp messages throughout the week, and I think she knows when I am having a good or a bad day. When I was first diagnosed it devastated her completely, and overnight it turned her world upside down. We tried to protect her from much of what was happening, although she showed a maturity beyond her years. In the end we decided that we would be honest about everything and answer truthfully all her questions. It's amazing how resilient kids are, she would often take time to digest information, but once she had figured it out, it didn't faze her.

Stupidly, I had convinced myself a long time back that my plans for November would ultimately benefit her. The last thing I wanted was to be a burden on Jane or Toni. I didn't want them to be forced into a place of caring for me. I wanted to maintain my dignity and have the ability to choose how and when I wanted to die. What I learnt during these next few weeks changed my outlook on suicide, and the long-term effects of such actions. Now I could be a spokesperson for suicide prevention, what I gained should be given to anyone contemplating taking their own life. Chapter 17 headed: YOU CAN'T REVERSE THE RIPPLE EFFECT and specifically the section: EVERY LIFE MATTERS has more about this.

As Sunday passed and the hours seemed to go faster, I found myself thinking less about what had happened, and I tried to convince myself it was a dream, although everything about it felt very real and perfectly clear. Especially the pain I felt in my eyes caused by the incredible light, even then if I closed my eyes, I could still see the negative impact marks that remained. It must have been a dream, albeit strange and tremendously vivid. I allowed myself time to capture every detail of Helena's face, her eyes were distinctly real to me.

Three Questions

Monday came around quickly, and the routine began with Jane's alarm half waking me. Whatever the time was, my body was screaming it was too early and craved more sleep. Once the bathroom was free my routine here would start. It started with a shave; the electric razor had seen better days and took ages. Next was a shower, today was a good one as we had fresh towels. Once dressed I made my way downstairs, this was an increasing challenge because MS causes muscles to tighten. Then during breakfast came the morning array of medication with tablets of various colours and sizes. I forget what I take some of them for now, Jane spends around half an hour on a Saturday refilling my daily tablet dispenser. If we are running short of any, I reorder them via an App on my phone. Yes, that's the Rock & Roll lifestyle we have now. For about four years after my initial diagnosis, I would have to inject myself daily, they're called Disease Modifying Therapy DMT. MS is an autoimmune disease; the injections reduced the likelihood of a relapse by around 30%. My life changed enormously when I had multiple relapses in the first and second years after my diagnosis.

The remainder of the morning continued as normal with a bit more writing and the odd email chasing clients for money. After some lunch, I settled down to rewatch one of my top 10 movies, as with my choice of songs by bands, shortlisting movies was becoming a nightmare. I settled for an old classic that would be high in my rankings, Cool Hand Luke portrays the coolest person to ever walk the planet. Paul Newman plays a prisoner that lives life at his own pace and with his own set of morals. If you haven't seen it, I urge you to give it a play and you will see what I mean… Cool! Another to grace my top 10 and of a similar theme would be The Shawshank Redemption. This is beautifully written and acted. It tells the perfect story of someone being wrongly convicted, and then eventually obtaining his own form of justice.

I probably watched a little over 20 minutes, when as before, I could feel a sensation of being hugged tightly, this covered every millimetre of my skin. It slowly expanded between my fingers and even beneath each of my fingernails. I could feel it slowly progress around my arms, as it did it softly lifted me upwards. It seemed to track down my spine until it supported my entire weight. This time I could feel very faint electrical pulses, they began in my fingers and moved slowly up through my arms. There was no discomfort associated to these electrical pulses, and they continued to track slowly alongside the warm and uplifting sensation. As the sensation tracked down my legs, I could also feel it softly spread up my neck and over my face. As it followed the contours of my face it slowly entered my ears, the initial sensation of warmth didn't distract me as it covered my eyes which were softly closed.

Suddenly, this calm tranquil state was harshly interrupted by a piercing light that initially glowed a pale electric blue. That was before it began to sting every cell in the back of my eyes. I blinked furiously, but to no avail, at the start each slither of light came with the same searing pain. A faint thought flashed briefly to tell me this couldn't be a dream, well certainly not a recurring one. I had no idea how long I was in this state, I continued to blink until the pain slowly subsided, but it didn't halt. Eventually, as my eyes adjusted, I could make out the shadowy outlines of three seated people. "Hello Daniel, how are you today?" said Trynes who once again sat in the middle, and as before Helena sat to his left. He didn't wait for a reply, he gestured to his right and a tall gentleman stood up, he must have been 6 foot 6 inches easily. "We are joined today by Xendar", he nodded, smiled, and then sat down.

Just as with the others, I knew the spelling of his name, and his age was 47 years 65 days. Somehow, I was able to read his full name as, Xendar-Prakanish-26. This came to me along with his position which was Project Leader of Try-neural Evaluation Team, and key coordinator to the 62.87 Evolution Ethics Mandate P211 Team. He wore the same type of clothing as the others, but the colour of his t-shirt was different, it was #4A206A, and this made his plastic circle stand out more. It glistened the same as the others, it could be, or more accurately, it was mesmerising, I quickly looked away. I also noticed that they all wore the same-coloured trousers, which were dark blue. The multicoloured circles that adorned each t-shirt seemed to scream for attention.

My focus was regained by Trynes who spoke again, "Hello Daniel, how are you?" I was able to get my bearings quicker now, and my eyes seemed to adjust to the bright lights emitted from every surface within the room. I also noticed the wall to my right was now opaque, the shapes of people walking by caught my eye for a second, I answered sharply, "I am okay, but I don't know whether this is all a dream or what?" Trynes told me it wasn't a dream, and that they understood how it might be confusing, I thought to myself there is no way you could ever know. As I thought this, Trynes said if I had any questions, they would be happy to answer them. I paused for a couple of seconds and asked the first of three.

Question one was relatively simple, I asked, "How are you able to talk to me if you're 2,000 years ahead of me?" As he began the explanation, I found my focus intensify, and I absorbed everything he said. He told me there are two things that will begin to explain this for me. The first part relates to a small probe called a Chrono-Diverse-Transponder, or CDT for short, which they sent backwards through time, and to an exact point in time. This CDT device entered my body through a vein in my neck, it then remotely traversed to an exact location within my brain. As soon as he began to explain this, I noticed the two other people sat up straight, and their fingers began to move and twitch faster. I was going to jump in with another question, but I found myself still focused on his voice. He continued, "what you are seeing, and hearing is real, and we are 2,034 years ahead of you. The CDT device allows us to communicate with you by means of both audible and visual stimuli, we can see and hear you as you can with us".

My brain went into complete overdrive when he explained the next part. Previously, they had created a fairly standard website, and through embedded code they can maintain a link to the device. Via technology we have today, they instantly upload and download data in real time. It's ridiculous to think, all of this is available, and maybe the reason I was chosen is because I have a 600Gb fibreoptic router with a super-fast Wi-Fi connection. Maybe I should have been worried that this may rack up a huge bill from my internet provider. It sounds simple and at the same time preposterous to think, but I can appreciate how this could work. As he was talking, I noticed that in the lower half of my vision I could make out words and imagery, but I had to park the thought temporarily.

My face must have looked a picture as he explained the next part, which weirdly remains the first part of his overall explanation. He then told me the CDT device sent out a microscopic communication antenna, which then entered my central nervous system. This antenna gave them direct access into my brain, it is this device package that allows them to communicate with me in real-time. Incredibly, what I am seeing is like a video conference call, but unlike Skype or Zoom there's no lagging. I immediately joined the dots in my mind, and as I did, I could visualise the schematics with all the references and technical names for all the parts. It was the strangest sensation ever. Not just understanding how they did it, but seeing it in such incredible detail.

The second part of the explanation started with Trynes developing a soft grin, it was the first time I saw any resemblance of real emotions or feelings. 'Reverse Time Travel' he explained, is all about finding a specific point in time. His face lit up as he told me, every molecule, every atom no matter what type, and in whatever state it may be in, it can only exist in one place and at one moment in time, it's all unique. They had established that these unique instances leave a trail, and if you overlay the tracks of these atoms against a specific timestamp, you are then able to pinpoint all these variables. For this to work, you must first identify its geographical location within the solar system, if you like, its coordinates. Critically, you need to know where that particular atom is, or was, and at a particular moment in time. This is where incredibly powerful computers are used to build a representational model of certain molecules and atoms against a unique timestamp. In my instance they knew exactly where I would be on 7 June 2018 at 15:31:55.05 as I pressed send on an email. As he paused, I was just about to ask how they knew I had emailed someone at that time. His pause ended as he told me they had been monitoring my digital traffic to ensure I would be in a safe position and location.

By this time my head felt like it was going to implode or explode, either seemed inevitable. As I began to think about it more, the problem resolved itself, I could once again see the drawings and designs of how this works. Granted, I didn't know what any of the language or mathematic symbols meant. Additionally, even though the schematic drawings rotated in 3D form before my eyes, they didn't tell me much that I could understand.

Space and time can be navigated in the same way that we use super telescopes like Hubble and Webb. They can see what the universe looked like around a quarter of a billion years after the Big Bang, or to give it a more scientific name it's actually a primordial singularity. This is when the first stars and galaxies began to form. If you re-engineer telescopes like this to look for specific points in time, in this instance it's just over 2,000 years.

Let me put into context how difficult this calculation is. The earth rotates once every 23 hours, 56 minutes, and 4.09053 seconds, it's called the sidereal period. The earth's circumference is roughly 40,075 kilometres, the surface of the earth at the equator moves at a speed of 460 meters per second, or roughly 1,000 miles per hour. The earth travels some 584 million miles in its orbit around the sun, and we are travelling at a speed of around 67,000 mph (107,000 km/h). This collection of events provides us with gravity, although it also makes calculating where an atom was on a given day and time incredibly difficult. Adding time to a set location simply adds the fourth dimension. Later I would find out more about this section of science, but for now, I was happy with an explanation I could partially understand.

Before I could hit them with my second question, Helena spoke for the first time, "We know there is a lot to take in Daniel, we can revisit any part of this in the future", her voice matched her beauty perfectly. My focus was reluctantly returned to Trynes as I asked my second question, "Why have you picked me, if you want to know things there will surely be millions of people more suitable than I could ever be?" Xendar began to speak, as he did my focus moved slightly towards the right. Before he answered this question, he said he would help me understand things better. Telling me that I was communicating through my thoughts, and that I wasn't really speaking, made sense somehow. I was forming speech in my mind which I then delivered. This differentiated thought from actual speech, although by now I knew I was not actually talking. He told me other thoughts were also being picked up via sensors, as soon as he delivered this, I became self-conscious about my attraction to Helena. Xendar explained that I obtain and visualise additional information through these sensors. He gestured to the plastic looking circle. This is called a Heptadecagon-interface Refractor Transmitting Prism or HIRTP. It's a device that enables thought communication, and data messaging between other prisms. He also told me that this device produces the terminals or screens they use along with many other related tools.

To be honest, I was more fascinated with this technology than time travel. I guess I probably understood this better, and it was more believable. I looked blankly at Xendar, he hadn't provided a clear answer, therefore I wrapped it into my final pitch. Looking straight at him, I asked, "What is it you want from me, and why did you pick me?" Xendar explained that I was not selected for any specific reason, although I did meet some essential criteria. To ensure suitability, he told me, they had been tracking possible subjects, but I was not selected for any specific reason. At that time, I had no reason to doubt them, accordingly I readily accepted it.

He paused and smiled again, without changing the tone of his voice he said, "We can communicate in thought, although you may find it better to form the words". I wanted to test what they had just told me, I merely thought, 'OK, but what are you hoping to get from me.' He accepted the challenge, I then picked up on his thoughts in reply, he said, 'We can communicate in this way, your thoughts can only be interpreted by one person, you don't possess the power beyond that. Additionally, you will tire quicker if we were to continue.' It was my turn to smile in acknowledgment.

The question remained hanging like an unwanted guest, what did they want from me. Well, Trynes took over the floor and told me they simply wanted to ask me some questions about life in the 21st Century. Which bizarrely he referred to as the first, the first 21st Century. This seemed innocuous enough, but I did begin to wonder why they felt the need to do this. Trynes also told me they would never try to contact me on consecutive days, and they would always ensure it would be safe. He expanded on this as he tried to reassure me, "Please don't worry, we are not invading your brain we are merely opening a new 'CDT event'. You can stop this at any time just by telling us", he said in a very calm voice. Helena sprung in quickly and asked me if I would like to continue to take part in the experiment. I said "Yes" without hesitation. Helena continued to explain, I would not be permitted to communicate with anyone about what was happening. Additionally, they could not tell me how many CDT events there would be, and most crucially of all that I would not be able to remember any information, communications, or scenes after a couple of days. I was confused as to why she told me this, they must have known that I was able to recall events and conversations from the other day. But I guess the real test for this was yet to come.

They were correct in that I wouldn't be able to remember things about these CDT events. Well to be more accurate, the closure of this particular one. I couldn't even tell you much about anything that happened after I awoke or the remainder of the day. This is not unusual, my MS means I can forget things for a period of time, or things could be eradicated permanently.

"I would rather have questions that can't be answered than answers that can't be questioned."

Richard Feynman

Chapter 4
Brain Power

On Tuesday morning, I woke up refreshed after a relatively good night's sleep. Jane wasn't in work today hence there was no early alarm call, and the morning routine was less defined. She had planned to go shopping in Manchester for the afternoon with her sister. This would usually mean grabbing a meal later with several drinks, a late train back, and me having to pick them up at Warrington station. The benefit of this would normally mean I would have another day were I can take my choice of working, planning, or obtaining items for November. Although this was the first time, I knew I wouldn't receive another CDT event. The news continued to carry various stories around the World Cup which started with the opening ceremony on Thursday. Normally, I would be waiting for the start with eager anticipation, but my head was filled with too many questions along with various scenarios of what may happen the next time there's an event. I also agreed to call them events in my own mind and how I would later record them.

Since the last event, I couldn't stop thinking about how they were able to read my thoughts. In turn, I placed a fair amount of thought about how to get around this, but I couldn't see a solution. Other things baffled me too, as they were talking to me, I was able to obtain a huge amount of additional information, along with diagrams that explained everything in detail. Why was I able to access this if I was unable to use it. The most annoying thing by far, was that I was only able to recall a limited amount of the conversations we would have had. I based this on the fact that the information I recalled was low when compared to the time I was asleep. I also developed a plan to capture any information that I could remember after each event, furthermore, this would have to be non-digital. They told me that they were able to monitor my digital footprint to ensure any contact would be safe. Considering this I knew I would have to be regimented in how to recall the information and store it for future use.

Stopping myself with a shuddering realisation, I was in the process of ordering some pen drives along with a ring-light from Amazon. They could be monitoring every keystroke, every piece of data, and every web browser page I viewed. This would call for me being extremely conscious every time a device was in front of me. Retaining the routines I have would be key, if these deviated, they may suspect me of using that time to record the events.

Back in 2001, I landed a job that really excited me, I knew I would be exposed to customers that would challenge my skills at that time. The Sales & Marketing Director I would be reporting to was well known within the industry, hence, I would be learning from the best. One of the key skills I learnt from him was the importance of getting to know your client. He had an extensive database of information on every client he had contact with. Everything from which sport they followed and teams they supported, their marital status, if they had children, their names and ages were all recorded. As he opened each conversation, he could chat sociably about how their team was doing, and what plans they had for holidays with the kids, which always meant using their names. It was a lesson that I carried with me throughout the remainder of my career, and one that I could use now. His name was Richard Spencer, he could speak five languages fluently. I would sit dumbstruck when I was with him on a conference call, he bounced between the various languages and all with precision and dexterity. I often wondered what happened to him, it wouldn't surprise me if he had burnt himself out by the age of 50. Unlike another colleague from the same time, he had an economical method to work, which basically meant he would do as little as possible. He was also reoccupied and fascinated by the benefits of fruit.

Considering all these factors, I knew I would have to record everything, or as much as I could remember offline. I had a small but adequate digital video camera, and a trip to the local PC store would provide me with some memory sticks. I also had some spare notebooks and even a couple of sketchbooks, each would help me meticulously record information or images that I could recall. What you are now reading comes from these, although the most important was the vlogs that were made shortly after each event. I also created a master spreadsheet that allowed me to catalogue all the material on one tab, and on another I created a plan to ensure I maintained my normal routine. I had no idea how long this would continue or what I would be able to ask, and for that matter what they truly wanted from me.

The remainder of Tuesday did play out as predicted, I was feeling very tired in the afternoon, this resulted in time spent listening to music while sleeping, but I found it almost impossible to switch off from the events that had happened, and pondering what is yet to happen. Around 20:00, I received a giggly phone call from Jane asking if I could pick them up from the station. The number of shopping bags would be an indication of the ratio between actual shopping and drinking. Whichever it would be amusing as she would tell me the conversations they had, and the outcomes of people-watching they had done. If this was ever to be an Olympic event the two of them would be in the medal positions every time.

"Fulfilled Childhood?"

Wednesday arrived and the countdown was almost complete, but unlike every other major footballing final, this one didn't give me the same buzz of excitement. There was only one reason, and it was beginning to frustrate me, I announced to myself that I would just take each CDT event as it happened. In the afternoon I pottered around, there were a few things Jane had asked me to do which I had been putting off for a while. Thinking this would help take my mind off things, I dived in. Around 15:15, I sat down for a well-earned coffee and a game of online chess against a couple of friends, one being Dave, who is my old school friend. We started playing about three years ago, shortly after I set up a WhatsApp group called, 'The Chess Moaners Club'. Periodically, we would either gloat over a well-planned take or scream when a stupid miss meant the loss of a queen or other strategic piece.

It was a warm day, and I was feeling tired, when you combine these two it only means one thing… sleep. As soon as I sat down my eyes closed, I couldn't guess how long it took before I felt the strange but comfortable sensation begin. It began with my shoulders and neck becoming relaxed with a weird tingle and a feeling of weightlessness, it then slowly moved down each arm until it reached my hands. Once in my hands, the sensation intensified, and I felt it penetrate my fingers. Simultaneously, the same feeling began to track down my spine, it then wrapped both legs and supported my entire weight. As with the previous occasions the sensations followed the same routes, although now I observed more.

For the briefest of moments, I was content and satisfied with the feeling, although this was shattered when a bright light suddenly burst. It was like looking directly into the sun, I was absorbing its light and heat at the same time. The only way to relieve the pain was to accept it and begin to blink. My blinking became furious, the stinging pain was so intense that I could feel tears running down my face, but I instantly knew this couldn't be real. Softly at first, which then grew louder, I could hear my name being called along with the instruction to blink. Eventually, the rapid blinking eased the harshness and allowed me to concentrate my focus on the three shapes that sat in front of me. It was Trynes who greeted me and as before he sat in the middle, Helena sat to his left, and Xendar to his right.

Remembering the action plan, which was made yesterday, I tried but failed to guard my thoughts before speaking. As I did this, I explained that today was Wednesday and there was a risk that Jane may find me. Trynes reassured me that if she did happen to find me, I would appear to be in a deep sleep, she would be able to wake me, although I may be confused for a while. When I asked them how they knew it would be safe for them to open a CDT event, Trynes told me they knew I was online at the time and that I was in a stationary position. This led me to ask a couple of related questions, it turns out that the device now connecting them to my brain, also provides them data regarding my overall state of mind. They were unable to monitor things like my health, but they knew when I was resting and obviously when I was connected to a device such as a PC or phone.

It didn't take them long to begin to ask me questions, each one was evidently given a lot of thought beforehand, they were carefully structured. The first one was probably one of the strangest, Helena asked, "Did you have a fulfilled childhood, and did you feel like you were accepted?" I could have understood if they'd asked if I had a happy childhood, but fulfilled, and accepted, seemed odd. As I began to answer, I found myself comfortably speaking, rather than thinking about the answers ahead of my response. I explained that I was born and brought up in a relatively poor part of Liverpool, and my early childhood was extremely happy. There were few boundaries, and whilst I developed friendships, they seemed to fade as quickly as they began. The task of education was not enjoyable for me, and I found certain subjects beyond me, although I would excel in others. As I thought about the question while recalling the odd story of my childhood through voice, I concluded that my childhood up to the age of around 11 years was not fulfilled.

The 'accepted' part of the question phrasing also required more thought. As I once again allowed my speech the freedom to continue, I recalled more about childhood events that had scarred me. I wouldn't class us as poor; we always had the necessities like clothes and food, but at the age when fashion mattered, we were always outcast from the cool kids. It may have been worse for Georgina, but as you enter your teenage years, I think you automatically become self-conscious. The short answer to the question of fulfilment would have to be 'no', but this would be primarily based on material objects that were beyond my reach. As I think about it now, the answer would remain 'no', in every other sense. I didn't feel loved as a child, but that was probably my own fault in many ways. I also felt that education in the traditional form didn't work for me. I was never encouraged by either family or teachers to focus on my strengths.

As I entered my middle to late teens, my circle of friends grew tighter, and more protective of each other. Our inner circle consisted of just five, Dave being one of these. In school we were friends, but outside of those boundaries we were mates. There is a fundamental difference between the two that only a 'scouser' would understand. Your mates are close, and most often closer than family, there are unwritten laws of trust that exist within a group of mates, especially at that age. As a group of five we did almost everything together, this was helped as we shared the same interests and passions. There were two staples that were beyond all others, music and football. Both took up most of our time, playing football and just hanging around would be interspersed with finding the odd bit of trouble, there was never anything serious and most often it was in the pursuit of a laugh. Alternate Saturdays would be spent at the home of football, Goodison Park to be precise. We all had season tickets and the excitement to each home game would build from the previous Saturday, although you would get butterflies from around midweek. For away games we would all gather to listen to radio commentary and the half time results for other games, and all while drinking beer.

Our other shared passion was music, and again to be precise, The Jam. To this day I still boast to people when talking about music that I saw them play live twice. They were the first band I saw live, and it really did change my life. Our love of music, and the variety of brilliant bands around during that time of post-punk, new wave, coupled perfectly with our quest to obtain alcohol for spontaneous parties. If we were unable to find a vacant home, then our local park became a steadfast replacement. Strong lager mixed with cider provided our escape route, and a space for the safe experimentation we needed. As Paul Weller sang, 'life is a drink and you get drunk when you're young', we took that as a direct action. I almost forgot there was a third bond of acceptance into our group, that being fashion. Here again, Paul Weller was to lead a certain youth culture into a Mod look, this was also influenced by music of the 1960's. As I continued with my reminiscences, I noticed the fingers of the three people who sat opposite me twitching furiously. Xendar adjusted his position while remaining seated and I glimpsed the translucent displays projected by his Heptadecagon-Prism thing. One of the two screens appeared to display what looked like data flowing in refreshed columns and heart traces. This halted my conversation, and I began to think again rather than speak.

Percentages

My recall ended at this point; as a result, I can't remember whether I answered this question completely. Helena then spoke, this time I noticed more of her features, she had short brown hair that was pushed behind her ears. As I noticed previously, I couldn't tell if she was wearing makeup, but to my untrained eye I would have guessed not. There was no need to try and improve on her flawless beauty. The other noticeable features apart from her perfect complexion were her eyes, they looked oriental in origin and shape, they were also a deep mahogany brown. She had perfect teeth with a natural lip line and shape, the resemblance of soft dimples added to her natural beauty. Her question startled me, "Is there anything else you would like to ask us?" Once again, almost without hesitation I asked the next question I could think of, although I could have probably worded it better, "I can't get my head around this whole thing, if it's real, and I think it is now, how is all this possible?" Before they could answer, I continued, "I know you said about reverse time travel, but the technology is just incredible".

Xendar shuffled in his seat again before telling me that it all started with the digital age, the point in time that they were now visiting. I had to take a moment to think about this, did he mean our time, 2018. He explained that the human brain is far more powerful than we currently think. It would be a couple of thousand years of further development before humanity and our brains would reach their combined optimum performance. Very early on in his explanation he mentioned the 62.87 Theory for the first time. He didn't elaborate further, but he said this gave the whole of humanity the drive and purpose for its future, and the ultimate objective. I remember, as he said these words the other two beamed with pride, I could see in their eyes that this was immensely important to them.

As Xendar continued, he stood up and once again I could see how tall he was, both men were clean shaven with very short, cropped hair, probably a #2 with clippers. Even though his uniform was loose, I could see he was athletic and there was no way he looked 47, if anything he looked early to mid-30's. Anyway, he started telling me that our brainpower began to expand beyond the normal realms and measurements expected within the rules of evolution. This was tied to a precise period of time, the dawn of the digital age. Seamlessly, a display screen appeared to his right, and as my eyes moved, I could focus on it clearly. A diagram of a brain appeared along with a readout of data. He explained, if you were to look back just nine generations of humanity within the developed world, 86.4% of the population would have been tolerant of just 6.5% of available information.

I must have looked confused, or in need of further clarity, he provided more detail of what he meant by this statement, and the meaning of being tolerant. Essentially, it means they were able to absorb available information and use it within their daily lives. As an example, this is gathered from sources such as vocabulary, education, and daily tasks. As my eyeline dropped I could see all the data that supported this, along with the locations around the world, ones they classed as 'developed' at that time. When you break this down, it becomes more understandable. Today, education is available to a large proportion of the world's population, and this is driven by similar standards. To a certain degree, understanding of logic and problem solving would reflect education levels.

Rollback just three generations using the same parameters and we note the crucial percentage only increases to 13.6% of a population stat of 91.3%. The next two parts of his explanation really got me thinking. He explained that in the non-developed world even in our time, the percentage hasn't raised beyond 10%. Importantly, he added that although we see these results our brains maintain the same capabilities. As Xendar spoke my peripheral vision was being bombarded with supporting data, charts, and analytical reports. If this wasn't enough, the finger twitching of Helena and Trynes caught my eye, as I looked closer, I could see their eyes furiously scanning from left to right, interspersed with up and down movements. He continued, but his speech pattern now slowed, maybe he could read that I was struggling to keep up. Just one generation before yours (being our parents), the rate of tolerance merely grew to 14.9%, from 6.5% nine generations before. This sort of made sense, as a result I allowed him to continue knowing that I had the opportunity to ask further questions.

As he prepared to deliver the next sections, the display screen changed into a 3D illustration of the brain that hovered between the both of us. I remember him gesturing with his right hand, palm upwards, which then slowly moved towards me. As he did, he said, "And your generation saw one of the key triggers being exercised to expand your brainpower enormously". I didn't understand what this meant, but I took it that it is our generation that has transitioned into the digital age.

As with the majority of what you are reading here, these are my own recollection of the conversations we had, and this part will be clearer if I explain it. Xendar explained that it's all about multitasking, along with the ability to use tools which are at our disposal. The first part began to interest me as he explained it. If you think about the information we are currently exposed to, and compare that to previous generations, we begin to see the gap. In the mid-19th century, education, vocabulary, and the use of tools will have begun to improve significantly on the previous century. Even then, around 25% were illiterate and the skilled workforce was still very low. Factory work became more common, although the working conditions in factories were harsh. Hours were long, typically ten to twelve hours a day which contributed to their low score.

My lower peripheral vision began to produce a range of data and charts. One stood out for me; I recognised they also rated the populations general IQ. It's worth remembering that the data they used was gained and driven from the developed world at that time, I could see the scores for every country. Xendar then moved on to show the same data and comparable scores for the 20th century. The average individual alive today would have an IQ of 130, whereas in 1910 the average would be just 70. With the creation of the digital age, we need to measure our brain's power and associated IQ differently. Our parents may have been able to read a paper, while listening to music and answer a basic question posed to them. I was born on 4th May 1966, I was around 14 or 15 years old when I was first exposed to the most basic of computers. Computers and the advancements in technology have been with me throughout my life, and until the past year or so, I have been able to grasp anything new. To begin to consider our development in brainpower, just think about what most of us are now able to do in our daily lives.

As I am writing this paragraph it won't surprise you that I have music on in the background. I am forming words through a complex keyboard with numerous commands, and even more complex applications such as Excel, which I love dearly. I am currently using significant parts of my brain to recall the events and place them in a context that you hopefully understand. If I didn't have music, I may have a quiz on TV, I would be conscious of the questions and shout out the odd answer. Even as we relax in the evening, I could be playing online chess while Jane would be playing word puzzles, the TV maybe on and we would both be following the programme. I know that I would also be thinking about what to write next, while Jane is also messaging her friends and family on a different application. Humanity has never been exposed to this much change in a ridiculous short period of time. It's not surprising to hear that our mental health is suffering in such a way and with marked results. We are unable to see what comes next for future generations, as technology advances our brains, and how we use them will continually be playing catch up. What I witnessed in 2018 was a perfect world, what I concluded was the journey to arrive there could not have been easy, and I see why it took over 2,000 years. It is evident that we are now using our brains more effectively, and they are being forever pushed to achieve more. Computers are advancing at a faster pace, but I fear that humanity may lose control if not extremely careful.

23.37% Can Split Their Brain's Activity

What Trynes showed me next, amazed me beyond anything I could possibly think of. Firstly, he explained how the Heptadecagon-interface Refractor Transmitting Prism worked. At the age of seven all children are fitted with a read only device that links the optical lobe and associated eye movements to the HIRTP. When activated by the brain, data is transmitted and can be stored separately for later recall. Information is always transmitted in priority order by GAPS, this was the first time they had mentioned this. GAPS is their Global Application Priority System; it works with other controlling computer systems that enhance the lives for everyone. HIRTP pre-sorts the data for the individual based on complex algorithms, it sorts data and determines what the user needs to know. Computers are working directly to maximise the brain's power beyond the control of the individual. Is that frightening, well I'll let you decide.

The next thing he told me also raised a partial smile from his two colleagues. For this part, I remember vividly the words he used, "Those with higher intelligence levels are now able to split their brain's active use". As he announced this my automatic response came, "What?", I asked. He defended this by telling me that some 23.37% of the population can achieve this. It works in a similar way to how we can now multitask with various devices. These people with a higher intelligence can hold a conversation or take part in one meeting, whilst at the same time conversing with others in text formats. They used the words text formats; I think this was done with the knowledge that I would be able to relate to it. He then demonstrated how this works, we continued to talk, well to be more accurate, he continued to explain how it worked. By now the 3D brain had been replaced once more by a standard display. As he continued to talk, I could see he was communicating with Helena in text form, as with our text or WhatsApp messages each person was represented by their name and colour. Well, if this hadn't just blown my mind, the next part of the illustration completely shattered it. Trynes then joined in, each person was either talking, listening while all three were communicating. Although it got even better when they all stopped typing, and the screen continued to fill. For my benefit, one of the messages informed me that they were all now communicating through their own HIRTP device.

I must have looked completely dumbstruck as this example played out, if I had been awake, I am sure my mouth would have opened wide as my bottom jaw dropped and demolished as it hit the floor. They proceeded to tell me and show me a game they use to practice these skills. NICC stands for Neuro Imagining Common Contest, as I watched them illustrate the game, I was instantly hooked. They told me about the global structure of NICC, and how players are seeded. When major competitions are played, billions around the world watch the top players to understand how they perform some of the moves. For viewers, while watching these titanic games they also see readouts of their calculations, and gameplans are viewed in real-time. People will discuss moves and strategies just as we admire quality footballers, the only difference is that while they may be admired, they don't have celebrity status as everyone is equal. Children are not permitted to play until the age of 13, they are able to begin mental exercises along with the basis of moves and strategies.

Let me try to explain the structure and how the game is played. Firstly, you have the game area, this is a virtual cube, the size of this is determined by the ranking score you have obtained. Games are played between players with similar rankings, although these are not visible to the other player. Each player has either two or three catching spheres, the top ranking 6.51% are the only ones permitted to play with four. The object of the game is to pass the saga between your spheres, simply passing the saga from one to another. Your opponent is merely trying to intercept your pass and capture the saga, this is known as an I-T. Once your opponent has the saga, he has a set time to pass it to one of his other spheres, once again this period is determined by the players ranking. The longest period permitted to make a saga pass is five seconds, for the elite player this can be as short as 0.75 of a second. Up to now it sounds easy, but not so quick, as the game, the cube and the various spheres and sagas are all controlled by the brain or mind whichever you prefer. Two players are connected to the tournament's control system, they sit in specially augmented seats that hold the player in a suspended state. Interestingly, the name saga is taken from Sagittarius A*, which is in reference to our own Galaxy's supermassive black hole.

As the game starts a visual display wraps them in a 360-degree cocoon. Their seats which suspend the player spin and rotate as they strategically manoeuvre their coloured spheres to safe positions. Meanwhile, their opponent who is in a similar position is also moving their spheres to locations they believe will be able to intercept the saga as it is thrown. Still sounding easy, again, not so quick, each move, and all anticipated moves are all based on mathematical calculations and coordinates.

For example, if you wish to move the sphere to your right, your brain is making those calculations and changes in split-seconds. The faster your opponent moves their sphere to engage a successful catch of the saga, your reactions need to be as fast or faster to complete a T-I. It's also made harder as certain players can perfect moves that launch the saga to one position, while already calculating the move for the next receiving sphere. The scoring is equally baffling, a successful catch awards a certain number of points, but the faster it is then released increases the score for the next one. Although as with almost every game, speed brings its own element of risk.

As Xendar finished this explanation, I thought my peripheral vision would have exploded or overheated with the sheer amount of information, data, images, and facts. I wanted to pick up on one thing he mentioned about the way Heptadecagon-interface Refractor Transmitting Prism could send information that would be stored and could be called on later. By now I couldn't have taken any more information onboard, this session was exhausting, and I thought later this is the reason why they never open up an event on consecutive days.

My eyes physically ached as I slowly woke, this ache accompanied a raging headache too. Within a minute of me gaining my senses, Jane walked into the room shouting, "I have been calling you!" She must have known from my look of amazement that I hadn't heard her, or that I had been asleep. As she calmed down, the question came, "Have you been asleep?", a quick look at the clock suggested I had indeed been out for the count. Jane knew by now that MS fatigue can hit me without warning and leave me looking like I needed a further eight-hour sleep, despite only just waking up. My fatigue is made much worse by heat, and especially humidity. On really bad days, I can struggle to move, it can feel as though heavy weights have been tied to my limbs. Add to this, the feeling like elastic bands pull in the opposite direction. And don't forget to add a high level of pain that descends just to make sure you know there's no escape.

This event would have to be recorded in the best way possible, later that evening I set up my camera ready for the morning. I also spent that evening scribbling notes of the key events that I had observed along with the ton of information I had been given. Instead of answering questions I had, they simply gave me more to think about. Another dilemma that I tried to resolve was whether to tell someone about what had happened. I knew it should be Jane, although she may read too much into what it could do to me, she would switch to protection mode.

Chapter 5
Amazing

Despite today being the start of the World Cup, I couldn't seem to gain excitement by the prospect of this much football. As it was Thursday, I had my default routine for the beginning and the end of the usual working day. What the remainder would bring puzzled me. Whilst I focused on my usual spot on the ceiling, I lay awake listening to Jane getting ready for work. The usual planning for November had already taken a firm back seat, events over the past couple of days had seen to that. As a result, my planning today involved recording everything I could remember, drawing as best I could the scenes I witnessed, and of course thinking about questions I could ask them. This is the one thing that baffled me more than any other, they have opened up to me and showed in great detail the world they inhabited. Conversely, they told me I would not be able to remember events after a period. Are they instructing me to record the events, and if so, why.

I proceeded to set up the camera on a tripod, the lighting in my office/bedroom wasn't the best but it would suffice. Each recording would start with the day/date along with some background information. Then, I simply allowed myself to speak into the lens, it was as if I was talking to a friend and telling them this amazing story. Editing would not be permitted as I would have to use my laptop, the fear of them gaining access was now a constant consideration. It was crude but I merely stopped recording if there were parts that needed to be corrected or explained better. As I began this, I worried that they may also be able to track what I was doing through the device which sat there in my brain. It took the entire morning until I was happy that I had recorded everything, or at least everything that I could recall. Over lunch I began to sketch some of the images I had seen and named each one by date. I was worried that I would soon run out of memory space on the camera. This left me two options, either buy more memory cards or find a way to save them securely on a laptop with the ability of cloud storage.

Eventually, I convinced myself that watching the opening ceremony of the World Cup would be worthwhile as it was a one-off event. There I was, at 15:30 I sat with a coffee and was pretty much underwhelmed by the events at the Luzhniki Stadium in Moscow. Vladimir Putin gave a speech about how much Russia loved football and how welcoming they would be. I was moved by the book 1984 and Animal Farm when we read it in school, although I could see both the value and the harm that comes with a communist state. Over the years, I have become increasingly intolerant of politicians and anyone with power, it seems that it's in our DNA to always be susceptible to corruption and greed. Putin will have been delighted that they beat Saudi Arabia five nil, but I couldn't help thinking he would have wanted more goals.

Even during this first match my mind was rushing 100 miles an hour through questions and scenarios. I wanted to know why I was allowed to see such amazing information within my lower peripheral vision. Why allow this, and then tell me I wouldn't be able to recall any of it. It all seems mysterious, and simply to be thought of as mysterious. Of all the questions I could ask, I decided my next question would have to be, what life was like for them and what did planet earth look like 2,000 years from now. Obviously, I didn't know how long this would continue, I planned to ask what I thought would be the most insightful and beneficial questions first.

Later that evening, Jane pointed out that I looked very tired and was worried that I was overdoing things. Reassuring her that I wasn't, I agreed to take more breaks. This was a valid point; the effects of MS can hit without warning and leave me almost lifeless. Until a few days ago, the sleep that I would have in the afternoon would help to replenish my batteries, now they are the equivalent of running a marathon while doing complex mathematics. I knew this would have to be resolved somehow, but right now it was almost impossible to switch off. A few days later she gave me a 'get out of jail card' when she said, "You're looking even more tired now you're watching every game on TV". It's true, to start with there are three games held per day as they work through each of the various groups. For a lover of the beautiful game, it's brilliant, and for me it would prove to be the perfect cover.

Initial Questions

Friday morning kicked off with the usual routine once more, I surprised Jane as I got up shortly after her. A refreshing cool shower was the perfect way to start a day, I am not yet brave enough to go all the way with a cold one. Jane looked at me quizzically, this was out of character, but I was genuinely keen to get on with the day. After dropping her at the station, I diverted my usual route, ending up in my favourite café in the village was much needed. I sat in extreme comfort as the sun increased its strength, whilst also watching people rush in and out. People watching can be a huge reliever of stress, although perhaps mornings are not the best. It's difficult sometimes to read their body language, and they often lack interaction with others. There was a pleasant background hum of sound that allowed me to think without distraction. In my trusty notepad that accompanies me everywhere, I made my list of subject matter, items I thought best to investigate. There was no premeditated order to these, I simply thought they should be topics to ask about.

#1 Space Travel: I added this first because we have only recently begun to understand and explore Mars. Also, one of the few positives about humanity is that it's always seeking to know more and explore further. By now, I wondered how far we had gone, and what amazing things have been found.

#2 Creation of Everything: I could only hope and pray they have ditched the lunacy of religion, yes folks that's irony for you. Maybe they have found the answer to the largest of all questions, maybe there isn't a simple answer. I chuckled to myself at the thought that it could actually be 42.

#3 Education: evidently, science and technology had served them well, reverse time travel, as wild as it sounds has been successfully deployed. The link I made, presumed that education must be at the centre of everything they do. If not the centre, then surely it must have a high level of importance.

#4 Science & Technology: for this topic alone, I can think of many questions. I would need to consider carefully what I ask and structure questions to be precise. If, what happened in the last CDT event continues, where they offered up much more information than I expected, then I can only absorb everything they give me.

#5 Government & Politics: probably a 'no-brainer', if they had survived over 2,000 years, they must have figured this out and changed the way societies operate.

#6 Reproduction: I stopped myself to reflect; they may tell me it's all changed and there's no need for it. I guess the question of sexuality links in with this.

#7 War & Peace: I could only hope that humanity could see past its differences.

The list continued, although with these next topics, I merely hoped that we would have sufficient time, or they would be covered by other topics and answers. Wealth & Finance, Countries & Borders, Crime & Punishment, Employment, Life Expectancy; I wondered what their life expectancy would be, considering how young they looked when compared to their true age. My list continued, Nature & The Planet. They obviously sorted global warming, although we may have completely messed the planet up and they are now living elsewhere. In no particular order, Family & Friendship was the next heading, I would hope they valued both, but who knows. Travel & Transportation, Nutrition & Farming, I had to ask how they fed themselves. Sport & Entertainment was my final entry, I sat there and pondered this one, and it wasn't long before my mind went into overdrive. I had already seen NICC which challenged the brain but surely, they must have other sports. As a football fan you would hope that it would continue forever.

As I wound up my break, and after a second coffee, I thought that maybe these would be the wrong questions. Surely, I should be asking how to cure and eradicate cancer along with hereditary and chronic diseases such as my own MS. Like the thought of telling Jane, which was quickly discounted, how would you even begin to tell anyone, never mind the medical profession. Can you imagine how this would sound, "By the way, here's a cure for all known cancers". Which would be swiftly followed by, "sorry, I can't tell you how I know all this". Additionally, I doubt they list astrophysics in the phone book, there's another age reference gag. Plus, if I started asking too many in-depth questions, they may instantly trigger alarm bells and know that I had been speaking about this. For now, everything would have to remain the same, and I would take each CDT event as they occur.

Valued

Once I returned home, I caught up with some emails that I had been putting off. I started to get a twinge of excitement in anticipation of the Portugal vs Spain game later. There were two matches before this, but I was happy to catch up with the highlights of those later. As I sometimes do, I made some lunch and decided to watch the news instead of listening to music. I kept closing my eyes in an effort to bring on the next CDT event. I mustn't have waited long as once again the feeling of weightlessness accompanied with a soft warm pressure began to cover my body. Soft electrical charged particles danced over my skin, randomly trickling downwards before disappearing. This weightlessness is difficult to describe, yes, I am floating in a way, although it feels much deeper than just supporting my physical weight. This time the tingling sensation began at my shoulders and intensified as it reached my hands and fingers. As expected, my awareness was then shaken as a beam of light penetrated my eyes, it seemed to burn and scorch. I began to blink rapidly, with each movement my eyes slowly adjusted, although traced patterns of light and colour remained throughout. My focus was then drawn to a soft voice that relaxed me. Eventually, I could make out the shapes of the three figures that were seated in front of me.

Helena greeted me and told me that her and Xendar were joined today by Staten-temrazenka44, and she gestured to her left. Instantly, I obtained the spelling of his name, I probably focused on this for too long. I think it's because they use digits, hyphens along with names that were unfamiliar to me. I knew I would have to shorten his name to Staten, but I liked the number 44, hence Staten44 it would be. Although I was slightly distracted, I had sufficient time to see that his role was Director General of the Try-neural Evaluation team, and Liaison Director of the 62.87 Evolution Ethics Mandate P211-2 Team. This meant he was Helena's boss by the looks of things, his age was 62 years and 167 days, again there was no way he looked anything close to this. He looked to be average build, and I would have to say noticeably stockier than the other men I had seen. He wore the same uniform, although his was a very dark grey. He was certainly mixed race, which was noticeable, only because Xendar and Trynes would probably better be described as white European. As with the other men, he had very short hair. As he spoke his voice matched his years as it was deeper than Xendar'.

"Hello Daniel, I have heard a great deal about you from my colleagues, it is a real pleasure to meet you", he said. His tone of voice seemed more genuine and relaxed than the others, and he actually smiled a genuine smile as he finished. Before they asked anything else, I jumped in and asked if they could call me Danny, I told them that's what most people use. As I did, they all nodded in acceptance. Without any further indication, Helena hit me with the next question, "Have you enjoyed your working life, and did you feel valued?" I was in the process of forming my answer, but while doing so, I remained conscious of my own thoughts. Ahead of delivering my response, Staten44 interrupted my preparation and asked me if I was comfortable to answer their questions, and if I needed anything to make each CTD event more comfortable. I was taken aback by this as it seemed more personal and caring. Telling them I was happy to answer any questions they had; I noted a slight alteration in their shoulders which indicated relief. Continuing, I also told him directly about how overwhelming the whole thing was, but I felt privileged to be given the opportunity to take part.

Composing myself, I seized the opportunity to mention the entry into each event, and the incessant bright light that pains my eyes. He looked unphased as he told me that this wasn't real, it was just a byproduct when they initiated the Chrono-Diverse-Transponder, and the boot-up sequence triggered these symptoms in my brain. Obviously, I wasn't really blinking, there was no brilliant light, but the sensations along with the feeling of weightlessness was my mind coping with the foreign body. He told me that I would be able to overcome it, I just needed to tell myself it wasn't real. I have heard people preach to me in the past that MS is all in the brain, and I should be able to overcome the symptoms. A pain management consultant once told me that he had examined an MRI scan of mine, he was amazed at the number of lesions within the pain receptor part of the brain, as a result, I guess they are right. What people don't see is the pain, the spasms, and the lack of sleep caused by both. They don't see me having to self-catheterise four times per day, or the ongoing constipation caused by the medication. They don't see the uncontrollable mood swings, or the depression which is probably not helped by sometimes only seeing two people in a week.

With this news that they must boot-up the device, I knew they could not monitor my thoughts outside of an event. This meant I could make more notes and more importantly more detailed vlogs. Although, I later questioned myself about how they knew it was safe to begin an event, could they be lying to me. During the event, I made a conscious effort not to think about this as I immediately began my answer to Helena. I began by telling them of a newspaper delivery round I had when I was about 12 years old. It meant I was able to earn my own money which inevitably went on buying singles. As I delivered this opening, I could see their fingers twitching furiously again. My peripheral vision pinged to life with a question, 'Please define singles?', this was a first. I paused for a moment and made a quick mental note to be more clear or more specific in my answers. I explained that singles referred to 45rpm vinyl records, music, songs that were released by bands. Each one would cost around 70 pence at the time, with this added information their finger twitching slowed. At around 14 to 15 years of age, I got a Saturday and holiday job in a local electrical shop. They sold and rented TV's and video cassette recorders, VCRs were the latest technology, but very expensive. I was passionate in my explanation of how much I loved this job and the people I worked with. I was fascinated by technology, in 1980 aged just 14, I got my hands on my first ever computer, the Sinclair ZX80.

Once I had finished my A levels in school, where I attained a 'A' for Art, I faced the choice of what career to take. Some of my friends went to university, and for most of them they would have been the first generation to have this opportunity. Most would enter manual jobs, the lucky ones at the time would have learnt a trade. As I said this word 'trade' I knew I would have to be more specific, a trade referred to something like an electrician, plumber, plasterer, bricklayer or even a mechanic. With training they would become qualified, this meant they should always have employment of some sort. For me, it was easy, by the time I left school I was earning commission on everything I sold. I was not just hungry for money; I was absolutely starving. Instinctively, I taught myself a few techniques of how to talk to customers. With these self-taught skills, I found selling easy and more profitable.

The owner of the company must have also witnessed this, and for the first time ever paid for me to undergo a three-day residential training course. It was this course that illuminated my future career, and ignited a thirst for knowledge of marketing, branding, and the techniques of selling. Since this first exposure to selling, I have had various roles, each one proved to be a steppingstone and progression upwards from the previous one. Each one paid me a commission on sales or sums invoiced, it was this arrangement that gave us the lifestyle we had. That was until in 2011, when it all came crashing down.

Within my summary, I told them about some of the intricacies of the work, and how I created marketing strategies that were highly complex, but each delivered results for our clients. Through this, I did obtain job satisfaction, and I hope I have instilled this into Toni as she now embarks on her career. Whilst the rewards were good for me and Jane, in return I always gave 100% effort. This often involved working away from home, very long hours with missed holidays and weekends away. I also told them of the people I worked with and relationships that were built up over many years. I remain friends with a few of them, although having a chronic disease segregates the real ones from those who merely benefitted from the association. I summarised Helena's question by stating that I did enjoy my working life. This enjoyment and associated rewards lasted throughout my time and within various firms. Overall, I did feel valued, and this instils a deep-seated feeling of fulfilment. I ended by stating that this was certainly true until my last employer sacked me shortly after my diagnosis. It was with this closing part I noticed the finger twitching went into overdrive once more.

Incredible, That's The Only Word

Throughout my lengthy response, I glanced images on the opaque screens that were projected in front of Helena, Xendar, and Staten44. Like heart monitors, I could see data readouts and scans that traced repeatedly. All the time their hands and fingers remain poised over invisible spheres, they twitched sometimes softly, and other times frantically as though they were trying to keep up with something. During my ramblings they didn't interrupt again, I continued to briefly tell them what happened after I was forced out of my last paid position. Essentially, I had been doing bits of consultancy, preparing marketing strategies for much smaller firms than I was used to. These were all close to Warrington, which meant almost no travelling, plus, I was able to get a true sense of achievement once they saw results. Furthermore, I told them about some of the articles I wrote for some trade journals and alike. I had planned to create an online marketing course for small business owners and start-ups. What I found was the original concept of marketing and branding, did not lend itself to this particular sector. My plans for November superseded the creation of this, maybe now I can return to it.

Once I completed this final addition, all three of them thanked me. Helena wanted to know if they could ask further questions next time. Once again, I said yes without hesitation, and I asked if I could be shown more of their lives, and the planet as it is now. Despite my previous planning and preparation, I blurted out, "Can you show me what life is like now, in your time?" Staten44 stood up and took a step closer, his voice remained calm and immensely relaxing. I remember him saying, "Well that would take a very long time, why don't I take you on a tour?" Stupidly, I tried to nod in approval until I remembered thinking, 'that would be great'. As he began to speak everything in front of me fell away and I could see dozens of huge semi-reflective, semi-translucent spheres that stretched as far as I could see. His voice, calm and deep told me that these are our colony pods in the E-1 quarter. My lower peripheral vision ignited with information, names, grid references, populations, purposes, and schematics. His voice continued, as he explained that these pods are where they lived, worked, and met socially.

My view then soared upwards between two of these glistening spheres, they were connected at various points by cylinders which looked like walkways, but they must have been 300ft in diameter. As we reached the top, I could see there must have been close to 500 of them, although some were smaller, but each one was connected in the same way. My view then spun me around, maybe this would have been a good time to mention that I get motion sickness. Anyway, from the top of the sphere closest to me, I could see they all sat beside a very large river that meandered into the distance. Beneath me, each sphere on this side of the river sat in beautifully maintained gardens. In the distance, I could see they were bordered by woods and more landscape. Walkways zigged and zagged throughout the gardens, I could make out lakes and people walking through them in pairs and groups. Staten44 told me that 45% of their power requirements are generated by high-performance cells within each reflective pane. Each sphere is located to bounce reflective light onto its adjacent sphere. My secondary, or peripheral view showed me detailed drawings and calculations of how this worked. Light is absorbed by these outer cells, and streamed throughout each sphere, I could only look on and think how amazing this was.

As I hovered above the sphere closest to me, Staten44's voice asked me if I would like to see inside, as yes entered my thought, we descended headfirst into the centre of the sphere. He took pride in telling me this particular building is the controlling pod for this region, it has a staggering has 2,314 floors. This put into context the sheer size of each one. He continued to impress me with facts, I guess he could sense how excited I was. Every structure within the colonies is manufactured from electrically streamed mineral quartz which is silica and oxygen. He simplified this by telling me it's simple sand, and what you see is glass. He went a bit too far with his explanation, I was shown how the molecules are charged, and this adjusts their state. This changes each molecule from a solid, into a liquid, and then into a solid once more. It also means that none of the physical structures are permanent, I saw this previously when seats materialised from the floor. Within my lower peripheral vision, I could see the chemical compounds along with the construction techniques, and how GAPS integrates everything, for everyone. This is the second time I had heard mention of GAPS. Continuing further, he explained, each sphere provides our living quarters which are tailored for our family units. I then saw various rooms that resembled a plush flat with seating areas and connected rooms. Each space is ergonomically designed by GAPS to meet the needs of the people using them.

Staten44 went off on a tangent and explained that GAPS provides them with everything they need. It is like having a smart application that figures out exactly what each person wants, and more importantly needs. It knows their preferences and organises every aspect of their day. GAPS also monitors their health and wellbeing, if added nutrients are needed then GAPS provides them. Likewise, if exercise is needed, GAPS will make time in the day to fit this in. They refer to GAPS as a life enhancement tool, I wasn't sure if a computer system could organise every aspect of my life better than I can. Although, if you think that it monitors the individual and ensures their health is in a prime condition, then you can see how it may work. I think if it managed every aspect, then isn't the individual just an extension of the computer system.

We returned to the inside of the sphere, Staten44 called this the core as it resembled an apple, which it was obviously modelled on. As we descended through the core, he told me what activity was undertaken on each floor. I didn't understand most of what he described, although I was able to pick out certain terms, such as research and development, but even this was drilled down into sub-categories. Other floors included phrases like forestry management, oceans and seas, atmosphere control, GAPS programming, and dozens more. As we descended further, we came upon floors that covered power management, and around ten floors that covered space, although he didn't expand on what they performed here.

We then stopped and hovered at the 922nd and 921st floors, he told me, this is where the research I am involved in takes place. It was huge, I could see through corridors where people walked, and offices filled with display screens along with machines that resembled MRI scanners. Below these floors came around 40 to 50 floors that had been assigned to the 62.87 Evolution development. These included one that stood out which he called, Multi-Dimensional Tri-Complex Cell Creation MDTCCC, these words and letters wrapped around the balcony of the core, it was noticeable as it was the only one named in such a way. Three floors were dedicated to; Future Intelligence Neurological Expansion Development FINED, Staten44 told me this is where he is posted.

As we lowered, I saw a floor which stood out as I recognised the words, DNA Programming. I instantly formed the question, 'What happens here?' I knew he could understand my thoughts, but this time he chose not to explain it further. What he did tell me, was that there are 23 facilities of the same magnitude across the planet, these are all dedicated to complex DNA Programming. It's evident that it must be a big deal, and I wondered why he was not explaining more. Another floor within this section was named Preceding Human Analysis, but I struggled to see how these would all be connected. We then slowed our descent once more, and I recognised a name which took around four floors, Chrono-Diverse-Transponder Research. Around 20 floors further down came further names that sparked recognition, Astronomy and Astrophysics, although they were interspersed with dozens that had no meaning to me. We quickly arrived at the ground floor which took my breath away, not from the speed of decline, but the space and the thousands of people milling around. There was a huge white stone in the centre which had BTBT chiselled into it, people sat in what looked like cafes, I could see them chatting and smiling.

In an instant we were outside, and Staten44, with a buoyant spirit in his voice said, "Would you like to see more?" Without waiting for an answer, we were off again. With this, came an avalanche of information as my lower peripheral vision began flickering. What you see here is the site of the third colony to be commissioned, there are now 16,721 sites across the globe, housing 13.625 billion people. He continued to impart facts and figures. They are completely self-sufficient and their primary role beyond their 62.87 work is to maintain the planet. Each colony sits on the smallest footprint possible; they are surrounded by enriched land. Beyond all of this, it is maintained in its natural form. In your time, Staten44 told me you spread across the land and destroyed it, for the past 1,634 years we have been returning it back to this untouched state.

Now we streamed across the land, the speed was incredible, but I was able to see colonies that looked like silver gems on a sea of lush green. I gazed upon ripples of reflective blue from rivers, lakes, and then seas. We zigzagged over the land through mountains with snow covered peaks which tracked into rivers and over waterfalls.

'Incredible', that's the only word I could think of to describe it all. I saw the planet in its natural state, as untouched by human hands as it could be. We stopped at one colony which looked to be around five times the size of the one we had left only minutes before. I could hear the pride in his voice as he said, "This is the place of humanity's second beginning". I thought this was an unusual term to use, as it sounded almost biblical, which made me smile. At the centre of this colony stood a park called The Home of Advancement, in a region they called Precious. At the centre, one building had its name emblazoned in gold and spread over two impressive doors, History of Development and Advancement. It was a huge white building, and without doubt, it was the tallest single building I have ever seen. I was unaware at the time, but I was allowed to enter and view everything within it. At that time, I had no idea what they were preparing me for, or what was to come. If I'd have known this, then the word incredible would not suffice, in fact there is no word within our language to cover it.

I seemed to blink, and then without notice we were off again. I obviously recognised the shapes of certain coastlines, and I made educated guesses of countries and even regions. It was made harder as all the usual landmarks that litter our capital cities were gone. I recognised the cliffs of Dover as we travelled north from where we started. As we continued in this direction and skirted west, we passed over Ireland. Passing over smaller islands, our speed began to reduce, this came as a relief for my visual sensors. I couldn't be 100% sure, but I recognised the coastline of New York, although without the statue of liberty it looked different. Continuing inland we came across another huge colony.

I seemed to blink a few times more, and suddenly we returned to the room and joined Helena and Xendar again, they both smiled, and Helena asked if I enjoyed the journey. I remember trying to gather my thoughts enough to respond, but I think my mind was still racing. Then Staten44 told me that I would be able to see and understand more about their lives in the coming weeks. I logged this statement but didn't give it a further thought. In her usual single-toned voice, Helena said, "Hopefully, you will have seen how we live and work, you will see more and be able to ask more questions".

Suddenly, everything went black, as I woke up, my mobile phone was ringing. In panic and frustration, I dropped it as I tried to answer. It was Jane to tell me that she was leaving early as it was Friday. My usual routine was interrupted slightly, I quickly realised that I had been asleep or more accurately in an 'event' for almost two hours, the longest by far. Reality grounded me that evening, Portugal played Spain, and it lived up to the hype that surrounded it. Spain was mesmerising but couldn't finish effectively, miraculously it ended in a three three draw. In the earlier games Uruguay beat Egypt one nil and Iran beat Morocco by the same score, but there was nothing to write home about. Even as I watched the game, I was frantically making mental notes of the key events and wondered when I would be able to record the next vlog.

Chapter 6
The Journey

As Friday night slipped softly into the early hours of Saturday morning, increased light was greeted by a dawn chorus from awakening birds. All I wanted was to sleep. The CDT event that happened yesterday continued to race through my mind with unbelievable clarity. For the first time, I was able to match some of the data that accompanied the images. Most of it didn't make sense, schematics overlayed complex calculations, and what looked like computer code blurred it even further. But the images became more vivid as I played them over and over, I knew this would frustrate me later as my sketches would not do them justice. I must have had around three hours sleep before Jane woke, as we both lay side by side; she told me of her week in work along with what we had planned for the day. I didn't even try to get a word in, what could be said about all of this. I desperately wanted to share everything, but I knew she wouldn't understand it fully. This came with the risk of potentially derailing aspects in my own mind. Additionally, I didn't want to jeopardise this, as now it was becoming more and more addictive.

As Jane planned her day it gave me a three-hour window courtesy of a hair and nail appointment. With this news I gladly took her grocery shopping in the morning. After lengthy debates over what to eat later plus what to have for our Sunday lunch, around 14:00 I was ready. With camera set up, I waxed lyrically covering every detail I could recall, both what I saw and what Staten44 had told me. As I thought of him, I could feel myself liking him more, it wasn't just that he showed me things, it was his relaxed demeanour. In contrast, the others that I met seemed to be always on guard, scared of what they may say or do. Also, their use of language seemed odd, unlike Staten44 who just spoke freely. As I thought about this, I noticed they all had the same accent, which probably wasn't that unusual as they were in the same colony, although I still couldn't place it.

As I spoke about the various floors within the spherical building, more clarity came into focus, and I was able to recall more facts. It had floor names like Stage 7 Oceania Repossession. Another one stood out as I had seen it before, 62.87 Evolution Ethics Mandate P211. This came to me repeatedly within my peripheral vision, it was within the job descriptions for all the people I had met. Other names meant less than nothing, but I was able to recall them, Chrono Embryonic Cell Interruption, Endothelial Cell Enhancement, and Astrocytes Exponentiation. There were also some that seemed familiar at the time, and I later learnt more about them, Try-neural Implant Evaluation, Try-neural DNA Development and Try-neural DNA Deployment. There were also six floors dedicated to various aspects of the Chrono-Diverse-Transponder; I knew this was responsible for the CDT events.

The surprising thing for me was that I was able to pronounce these names and without hesitation, and all from my own recall. I also began adding further facts about the various colonies I had seen, their populations, each one seemed to be classed as a centre of excellence for the various activities or scientific research they were involved in. Much as we have today, most of the colonies were based around the coastal areas of countries, or along extremely long and wide rivers. I remembered that we didn't go over the equator or either of the frozen polls, I presumed that they had rebalanced global warming, but as with many things, I couldn't be sure.

As I concluded the filming, I knew my next question had to be, how did humanity progress to this. I knew this one question must take precedence over the others I had only recently formed. The news is often littered with articles concerning the devastation caused by global warming. Whole regions can be destroyed because of catastrophic floods, or wildfires that reek uncontrollable havoc. Lives and homes are lost with near untold misery and long-lasting consequences. Famines are endured by millions, while pop stars are in the news for getting married again, and spending tens of thousands on flying people out to their revoltingly lavish bash.

I managed to enjoy some of the four games on Saturday, including France who beat Australia two to one, Denmark who beat Peru one nil. Croatia looked comfortable in their two nil defeat of Nigeria, although they are a one-man team, and I can't see them going too far in the competition. Argentina who was once a fearless and formidable opponent, could only manage a one all draw against Iceland. I had a soft spot for Iceland after their performance in the Euros, this extended to their fan base which is highly impressive considering their pocket-sized population. Sunday rolled around slowly, and it was nice that it was incredibly relaxed. In the afternoon, we had a video call with Toni, her energy could be felt and seen in her face. With pure excitement, she told us about all the things she had been doing. Her passion was for small animals, this passion was breath-taking sometimes. We forecast years before that her probable career path would end in this direction. Although, we had no idea where she would go after her studies, we didn't know and were probably too scared to ask. Near the end of the call, she announced that she would be down to see us next Sunday and Monday. On the Tuesday she would have to leave early to travel down for a conference in Oxford.

Personal Relationships

I finished Sunday by watching the highlights of the games that day, Jane thought it very strange that I hadn't watch them all live. The TV was on, but I wasn't really concentrating, and she could see I slept through most of the action. It was a day for unbelievably funny results, Germany lost one nil to Mexico which was a huge shock, but it showed that they were not as strong as they used to be.

Brazil could only manage a one all draw with Switzerland who looked quite good. And in the final game Costa Rica lost one nil to Serbia.

Monday began again, as does every other Monday, I may sound like I am always moaning about these routines, but they have certainly helped me. I work better when I don't have to worry about other unimportant things, routines have set times and activities for me. With nervous anxiousness and with butterflies in my stomach, I waited for the next CDT event to start. I must have looked at the time on either my PC or phone every 20 minutes. Up to now every event had been in the afternoon, considering this, I tried to keep myself busy until lunchtime. That's how my morning played out, although I did play around with how to word the next question. Right enough, dead on time, I fell asleep about 10 minutes after I finished my lunch. I looked down at my phone at a boring Facebook video, an advert popped up and that was it, I was asleep.

Remembering the advice that the brilliant light was not actually real, and that I should be able to overcome the effects. The warmth uplifting sensation began, and it felt extremely good and immensely relaxing, if this was the only entry into an event, I could have multiple events without question. It felt like my entire body was not just in weightlessness, but more, I didn't have any mass, and therefore, absolutely no weight. The soft ripples of delicately charged particles danced over my skin again. Sadly, it was only the warm appetiser before the stark cold Japanese delicacy called fugu, or blowfish. Not that I have encountered a blowfish, but I hear the pain is intense. Within seconds the screeching pain burnt bullet holes through both eyes. Frantic blinking only scattered the shards of razor-sharp light into every light receptor I had. These specialized neurons are found in the retina, they convert light into electrical signals that stimulate physiological processes. Mine were working overtime, there was only one signal they screamed, and that was 'Pain'.

Eventually the blinking paid off, but with my blurred vision I could only see the outline shapes of two people. "Good afternoon, Danny", it was Helena, and I felt instantly at ease. As my vision began to clear the outlines rendered to confirm it was of course Helena, along with Trynes, who was absent from the last event. I remember he spoke at the very beginning and said in his monotoned voice, "Hello Danny, I am here to observe this event". We exchanged some niceties before Helena hit me with another carefully crafted question, "Have your personal relationships always been happy and fulfilled?" Before I thought too much about the loaded question with the words, 'always and fulfilled', my reply and my words flowed freely as I began to tell them about my relationships as a child. I explained that our mother was very protective, and I am sure very loving, but due to many things she didn't shower us with frequent displays of affection. Explaining as best I could, parenting is often learnt from previous generations. I assumed for this reason along with the absence of other role models we were brought up as she was. We always felt safe and protected, this would not always be the case for friends of mine.

I then moved on to my relationship with my sister Georgina who is three years my senior. When we were very young, I must have been like a new toy doll for her to play with. I remember being comfortable and safe as I was always by her side. As we grew up, we inevitably grew apart in the sense of games we played and school friends we had. You can add to this our general social circle, but I guess that's harder to define. Obviously, I loved football which to a youthful girl was just dumb, now I can't think of what she did during those times or the friends she had. At home it would be different, there in the sanctity of our home we were free to play boardgames and alike. Music was the main thing that divided us as we grew up and it's still there to this date. I remember her liking bands like The Bay City Rollers and The Osmonds, and you know what they say… the 70's was a decade that fashion forgot. Well, if evidence was needed, you can Google either of these, although I warn you in the strongest terms possible not to do this. Punk burst on to the scene with bands like the Sex Pistols, The Clash, Buzzcocks, for me and my friends at the time it was like the loudest wakeup call ever. Then of course came The Jam and everything changed, it was no longer about shouting loud, it was about saying something even louder. If you talk about relationships, then I have had a very long and extremely happy love affair with music. I had a passionate, but all too short love affair between, May 1977 and December 1982 with The Jam. To this date I have never tired of listening to their songs and I feel as passionate now as I did back then. A social media post recently summed this up perfectly, in school, the cool kids listened to The Jam, today, the really cool ones still do.

I then thought it best to focus on Jane and Toni, I know I am going to get it in the neck as I now have to say I love them more than The Jam. Of course I do, Jane has been my rock for many years, when I received my MS diagnosis it was a life sentence for us both. Those two letters haunted both of us for years after the death-knell, but I think now we know how to live with it. Anyway, enough of that for now, Jane and I met when I was 20 and she was 17, I don't know if it was love at first sight but there was a definite attraction from day one. I worked alongside her mother which may have been awkward, as she thought I was still a bit wild having only just escaped my reckless and partly irresponsible teens. By this time, I was more focused on earning money. From our early days of going out together music and watching live bands was a shared passion. As we frequented different places our group of friends grew larger and we became very good friends, or to title them properly mates.

We remain friends with a couple of them to this date and they have become more like family.

My relationship with Jane has obviously changed over the years, we used to hold hands comfortably in public, but we were never over the top in showing our affections. My love for Jane has changed and after 27 years marriage it's bound to have. I would do anything for Jane and of course Toni, these are the two most precious people in my life and it's difficult to articulate my love for them. As with the other day, I kept catching a glimpse of the translucent monitors with their flicking images of streaming data and tracing lines. Each time I did, for the briefest of moments I lost the track of what I was telling them. Their fingers also twitched frantically throughout this entire time. Returning to my response, I tried to explain that the word, 'fulfilled' is difficult to quantify. What may have been happy does not automatically mean it was also fulfilled. There are things I personally wanted to see and do with my life, although having a chronic disease tends to shatter them. Presumably, the same must be for Jane along with other people in my life. There is a saying, that you should never have regrets, or something like that. I can't but help to have regrets, and even anger that my life and ambitions have had to be curtailed. Does anyone have a completely fulfilled life, do you.

My response was summed up by telling them of my heart bursting love for Toni. As a child she constantly amazed us with her results, be that academically or in the various sports she took part in. She was always happy, and we had immense joy and laughter as she grew up. Toni was always popular and had a fantastic network of friends. Even through her teenage years she never once let us down, she excelled at everything she focused on. When her grades met the threshold for her chosen university, she was happier than I had ever seen anyone, if only that joy could have been bottled. Returning momentarily to that word fulfilled, maybe without even knowing it,

Jane and I always tried to ensure her childhood was just that. We couldn't ask for a better daughter, and we know her life will be a journey of discovery and amazement. The physical contact I missed as a child and inwardly craved was given a backseat for many years. Toni fulfilled that gap a thousand times over for me. Toni was often the middle piece of a three-way mega-hug; she was the bond between me and Jane. Finally, I told them why she got the name Toni, I explained that it's often the first question people ask, and if that's not an icebreaker, then what is.

World Change Movement

As I concluded my response, I could see Helena smile, although Trines' face didn't change throughout the whole time. Helena then looked at her monitors and said we have another question, "You didn't mention your farther in your previous response, is there a reason?" I paused for a moment or two, then told her that I didn't really know my father too well. When I was born, he had just turned 50 years old, and I am sure for him it was a gap too far. I have very few childhood memories of times with my father, my strongest memory is running to meet him as he walked down the street when he finished work. After this, the lasting memory I have is him sitting reading the newspaper every night and watching TV. I am sure he loved us, but there was never any physical contact, no hugs, no kisses, and no guiding hand of support. I wanted Toni to feel the love I have for her; I wanted her to constantly know how much she was loved. We would often just sit and listen to music; I think she knew these were special times for me. It's one of the good things she has inherited from me, music follows her everywhere. We had our own special song, The Mayor Of Simpleton by XTC. Please find the lyrics and it will become apparent why I used to sing it to her. We also loved to walk together with our first dog, he was a beagle named Oscar, and she loved him very much. They had a special bond, the only one you could have between a young child and a sweet natured dog. Now, I miss the walks incredibly, and the special times we all had together.

Even during this short addition, I could see their fingers twitching frantically, their eyes scanned the translucent screens in front of them. They were completely captivated by the activity, not just on a single screen, but by three of them. Trynes said they may return to this topic again, I had heard that before, but nothing came of it. Helena asked if there was anything I would like to ask. This was quickly becoming the norm; they ask me a question and then it would be my turn. This time I was ready and with a large intake of breath, I asked, "I have seen the world you have, and it looks amazing, but how did we get from what I see now to what you have?" Trynes looked at Helena and with a nod of approval she stood up. It was the first time I had seen her stand; she looked amazing, her quiet beauty matched her physique. You could tell she kept fit through sport or exercise, her figure even though it was hidden by lose clothing was demure. She was the type of person who knew she was good looking, although it would never use it in a negative way.

Helena took a step forward and a screen appeared to her left, just as it had with Staten44 during the last event. Her soft voice still had a strong element of boring monotone. Unlike today, she didn't attempt to mask it, maybe they were oblivious to the audible tone. She started by telling me that the question has thousands of answers, "People can easily have the answers, however, what they choose to do with information cannot be controlled". I sort of understood what was meant from this opening statement. She continued, "It's easier if we take you back to the beginnings of the WCM", hesitating for a moment, possibly realising I needed more, clarity was added, "World Change Movement". I was told there were 36 founders of the movement, gathered from around the world, these people came together to form a new beginning. As I was told this, one line stood out as she stated, "It would be a world that would be free from all the turmoil that had preceded it". As these thunderous statements registered, my mind began to ask question after question. I had to reign it in otherwise I would be in danger of missing key parts.

Helena went on to tell me that these visionaries brought together invaluable skills in engineering, project management and the vast array of sciences. Each one had a shared and common goal. These 36 pioneers formed plans for the first colony and the rules for each colony member. Initially, these relatively ordinary people gave up promising futures to create the foundations of the movement. They knew they would never see the fruits of their labour, but they had a belief that future generations would benefit from their sacrifices. A ridiculously simple slogan was used to provide their identity, BTBT which meant Build Today for a Better Tomorrow. Thereafter, every generation knew it was also their goal to build upon and continue the unselfish work that had preceded them.

The WCM developed plans that illustrated how free energy would begin to release humanity from the commercial chains it had endured for many decades. WCM showed that through the right investment free and clean energy was easily achievable. Sadly, many countries that could have adopted this gave in to various establishments, however, two others agreed the plans and they became the first two states to merge. Initially, no one could foresee this outcome, but by sharing infrastructure and resources they soon became incredibly strong. As Helena's voice continued my internal prism drive started to receive an incredible amount of data. With free energy she told me, they quickly became a mini superpower, their economies grew strong and the WCM had its first home, although there was still much to achieve.

The Charter

I was not expecting this much information, but it wasn't really answering my question, nevertheless, I was happy to let her continue. She then told me, the blueprint for the first colony would be home and a place of work for 7,324,160 people. Colony 1A would be 100% self-sufficient, it was funded by the wealth gained by everyone who bought into the ethos and the rules by which all would live. One wealthy philanthropist also committed to become a member and took his place alongside the next. She made a sidenote which I thought was strange, this individual and their family all signed the charter which stated everyone is equal within the colony. By this added statement she may have had some understanding of wealth and what it meant to that individual and their family. What they were abandoning was probably luxury, power, and status, but they will have seen the long-term benefits.

While Helena was talking, the screen depicted everything she was telling me in exquisite 3D form. 16 years after the first colony was incepted, the rules by which everyone lived became the first charter. This time was significant as history told them it was when the 62.87 Theory was first published. This '62.87 Theory of Evolutionary Change' was the catalyst for everything. A mental note was added, this would assist me to ask her to reveal more about this phrasing. Helena then revealed the charter, as each one appeared on the screen just like a PowerPoint presentation, she added dialog if it was needed.

Science must never be used to extend human life beyond its expected lifespan.

Helena added, care can be provided where euthanasia is not elected. As she said this my thoughts could not be contained, did she really say euthanasia. She then said more boldly, "I will explain this in more detail in a moment". I held my thoughts as she continued.

Humanity must care for the planet and all living creatures that inhabit it.

I thought this would be self-explanatory, although she added that humanity is responsible for maintaining the planet and all lifeforms in a near perfect state. 'Near perfect', I thought, which then allowed her to add, natural events can alter the eco-systems in certain areas.

Science must never be used to create new lifeforms or recreate extinct lifeforms.

I presumed by this point that they had the ability to create new lifeforms, but why would you want to create something new. Helena added, all scientific research connected with this was strictly forbidden.

My inbox or whatever they called it was being inundated with information and a huge amount of data. I could see Trines' eyes frantically scanning from left to right and his head simulated these movements. His fingers also moved feverishly, they seemed to be without rhythm or meaning. Helena for once stumbled over a couple of words, her usual monotoned voice waivered a little and she looked nervous. With her regained pose she continued with the list and the PowerPoint presentation.

Humanity must never create life on other planets within the universe.

I also thought this would be self-explanatory, but she went off on a tangent explaining that Elsorn planets and Dexential planets where experiments, although they provided negative results. Also, the philosophy for creating life should always be beyond the powers of humanity. Once again this would have had me asking dozens of questions, but I managed to park them.

Anyone may enter the New World Order and its colonies, providing they live in accordance that benefits humanity.

When Helena got to this point, and she read through the information, the phrase, New World Order raised an eyebrow from me. After all the new names they had for things, World Change Movement and New World Order seemed quite predictable. Anyway, she told me that the New World Order has its own rules which governs how primary colonists shall live. Confidently, she boldly told me this would all become clear.

Every colony member will adhere to the three stages of life as set out in the life plan.

As this point came onto the screen, it slowly morphed into three silver spheres that rotated on their own axis. The first I was told is Education and Enlightenment, the centre of the sphere turned a blue green and opened like a chocolate orange to reveal 12 parts. Each of these 12 parts then glistened a different shade of blue and each segment had its own topic from what I could see. The first 30 years of a colonists' life plan involves education to the standard agreed by their principal mentors. Before she had finished saying this, there was an answer ready for me. Every young person is allocated three principal mentors, they will help guide that person for the first 30 years of life. They provide support, both within the family unit and in their life journey. Life planning, emotional support, peer support, contribution planning, and fulfilment are all topics the mentors will assist with.

I had even more theoretical questions than I seemed to be getting answers. Comfortably though, I was happy to relax and listen. The next sphere came to life just as the first did, the warming orange glow that came from the centre preceded the opening. Once more 12 parts opened, and each with a variable shade of the sphere's primary colour, each segment had wording engraved within it. The second stage lasts for a further 30 years and is known as Replenishment. I thought this was an odd name until she explained more. These 30 years are where a colonist will work for the benefit of the colony and the 62.87 Evolution. Work, I was then told differs from what we may perceive, it's all about giving back. Each colonist will have a chosen classification and operate within this. Classified roles could be in the sciences, education, exploration, sports, arts, the list goes on. During this phase each colonist will also endeavour to give back to the planet too.

Helena didn't expand on this, once again I tried to focus on listening. The final part takes colonists from their 60's to their 90's and beyond. It's known as Fulfilment, and this is where colonists can relax and enjoy everything the planet has to offer. Colonists are given complete control over their lives, some may continue in the classified roles they had, at least for a period. Some people will devote more time into providing mentoring roles or work within the various evolutionary paths. Many will simply tour the planet seeing first-hand any of the 18,265 sites of natural interest and wonderment. I remember joking, or should I say trying to, when I told them that this is known as retirement, although only a few have the energy or money to see anything like that.

Next came the part I wasn't expecting as she told me about the Closure Phase. This is where a colonist, in agreement with their family unit, will agree a life termination. I clarified this, and it was what I thought… euthanasia. I was told that this is in fact a happy period, although the person will obviously be missed. Instead of it being a sad event, almost everyone will take the opportunity to recall their many achievements and what they contributed to BTBT. There is no rule for when a person must terminate, they rationalise this as the population within the colony is strictly controlled. Subsequently, it is their duty to allow the next generation to begin and continue the BTBT philosophy. She was very stern, and her choice of words were very precise. Prior to termination there are gatherings between friends, family, and their replenishment colleagues. They are always a happy time and the person leaving the colony can access support from mentors. When she spelt it out like this, I could see the logic, and it must have been happening for 'possibly' thousands of years, therefore it's expected. Still not sure, but who am I to talk, as I planned my own exit in just a few months.

Before she continued, there was a momentary pause, this was accompanied with a sideways look over towards the door. Before she continued with the next point and before I could think too much she immediately said, "There are three more after this". The screen then reappeared as the spheres melted away, this allowed the next bullet point to join the others.

Every colony member is equal without exception.

No matter what their chosen role, each person who lives within the colony structure is equal to the next. I thought this was straight out of the communist handbook and could never work in practice. That was until she told me, every colonist and their families have everything they could possibly want or need. GAPS ensures that everyone in the colony is valued in whatever replenishment they do. It's important that we maintain a perfect equilibrium in every area of our lives. Everyone has a fulfilled, happy, and rewarding life. It then clicked why they are asking the questions of me, or was I overthinking this.

Suddenly, the screen that had taken up most of my view dropped away and there were three men standing behind where Helena and Trynes sat. They stood behind a semi-translucent green mesh; I could see they all wore white clothing as the mesh hovered around 2 feet from the floor. Trynes stood up and said clearly, "Sorry Daniel there has been a disturbance, we will have to terminate this event now".

I woke up suddenly, I was very confused, and my head was banging. I couldn't seem to focus, no matter what I tried I was in this state for at least two minutes. I was trying to also control my breathing, it slowly began to calm from several frantic gasps for air, to a steadier pace. Eventually the confusion lifted, but there was a pain that seemed to be emanating from somewhere within my right eye. It was now 16:30, I had to check this a couple of times, it meant I was consumed within the CDT event for about three hours. Was it the duration of the event that left me wiped out or was it the intensity. As a result, I knew I couldn't pick Jane up from the station as I really didn't feel safe enough to drive. The phone call to her at work explained this and with an understandable reluctance she said she would get the bus. This added about 45 minutes to her journey, but it wasn't the time that was an issue, it was the school kids and other people she disliked.

"Trust the science" is the most anti science statement ever.

Questioning science is how you do science!

Chapter 7
Truth

By the time Jane had made it home, it had gone 19:00, understandably she wasn't in a good mood as the scheduled bus hadn't arrived. I had to explain that I had fallen asleep and woke suddenly with a headache and a pain in my right eye, this also accompanied blurred vision. Taking no chances, she phoned the NHS helpline who took all the important information including my ethnicity and marital status. We had to make our own way to the Accident & Emergency department at Warrington Hospital, where we spent the next six hours. Oh yes, we had a fun filled evening, which dragged painfully slow into the night. I underwent the usual blood tests, blood pressure tests and urine sample. We then sat waiting for them to figure out what had happened. This gave us an impromptu bout of people watching with the added interest of guessing their ailment. Eventually, the diagnosis was handed down, it was a TIA, a Transient Ischaemic Attack, or mini stroke. This was caused by a temporary disruption in the blood supply to part of the brain/eye. In my instance there was a small bleed in the back of my eye. They gave me medication to thin the blood and told me that I would be contacted by the TIA clinic.

Wearily, at 03:20 Tuesday morning we returned home. My headache was worse, despite the near-constant light shining, the discomfort in my eye had eased. Jane now had something else to worry about, and I received the standard lecture on doing too much during the day, and 'not switching off'. This is a recurring line for her, 'not switching off', I can see her looking at me, she instinctively knows that my mind is running on the spot and out of control. It's true, and I know I should try and relax, but with everything I have going on it's almost impossible to do that.

Incredibly, I felt refreshed the following morning, Jane let me sleep in until 09:30 which is a rarity for me. I promised her no work, and that I would rest all day. That minimal activity on my part started with a catch up on the highlights of the games I missed yesterday. Fortunately, I had recorded the whole of the England game. I spent the evening before trying not to hear the result, it reminded me of the TV show, 'What Ever Happened to the Likely Lads', and the episode called No Hiding Place. Anyway, Sweden beat South Korea one nil, in our Group G, Belgium beat Panama three nil, I really enjoyed the game, this reinforced my belief that they would go on to win the trophy. In our game, also in Group G, we managed a two to one win over Tunisia, although the critics were not complimentary over the win and demanded more. That's seems to be a theme with England, start slow, get better, build our hopes up, and then crash and burn when it gets serious. That crash and burn is typically characterised with the loss of a penalty shootout. England always seem to play it out in the most frustrating style with a penalty overshooting the bar, and ending up in row Z.

Questions Without Answers

Between small catnaps of sleep, I obviously couldn't get my mind to switch off from the events of the previous day. I knew that I should have been more concerned about the TIA, but the hospital consultant played it down, as a result, I was able to park that. The issue that wouldn't leave me was the thought that it may have been my last CDT event which caused it, but we had an enormous amount of unfinished business. I still had many questions to ask, and I was sure they hadn't finished experimenting on me. The questions spun around my head like an enormous whirlpool; I found it hard to focus on one at a time. There was a solution, on my phone, this being the only device I was allowed that day, I opened a new notebook item.

Q1. They must have known there was an issue with a bleed when they halted the event. Okay it's more a point than a question, but they must have been monitoring my brain. If they deemed this to be serious, they may not begin another event.

Q2. What if that was my final event, what would I do with less information than I wanted, or more importantly, needed. I tried not to deliberate on this too much and thought 'what would be would be'. But who was I kidding. I wanted this more than anything I have ever craved.

Q3. This led to another related question, I have a small device stuck in my brain which isn't going to be invented for around 2,000 years. My question must be, how were they intending to remove it. This is something else that I was happy to park for now, but I had to find out.

Q4. Why me, and what do they want from me. This question started to get into the biggest issue of all, I was nervous to ask something like this in case it brought things to a close. For a moment, I did contemplate how it would all end, but I had no way of guessing the correct scenario.

Q5. Why am I able to recall this incredible amount of information when they told me I wouldn't. Yep, another big question, although I quickly discounted it, potentially asking this, may also bring on closure.

Q6. Over the past two weeks, I have not had spare time or the inclination to focus on 1st November. I have been distracted that's true, but I had to justify what my targets were. Much planning and preparation had gone into my act of revenge, I couldn't lose sight of that now.

I drew a line under my questions and thoughts at this point. As the day went on there was a fog that lifted from my consciousness. With MS, sufferers can get brain fog, I normally get it when I am tired as in now, or with high humidity. By late afternoon it was clear that this was no ordinary clearing of the symptoms, such as slowed speech, laboured thinking, coupled with constant amnesia and fatigue. For some unknown reason, I was able to quickly consider a problem and generate a resolution. Now, this wasn't just why do England start slowly; I watched the news and articles about random things that I had no interest in, they quickly became understandable. With this newfound understanding came solutions that seemed simple and practical.

The remainer of the day concluded with me watching football. For a change Jane insisted I watch while she prepared one of my favourite meals. It's not for everyone, but chicken fillets stuffed with haggis and wrapped in Parma ham is nothing short of delicious, although Toni would obviously not approve. This is accompanied with a peppercorn sauce and a couple of chips; it was fantastic and not normally a midweek meal. Returning to the football, Japan beat Columbia one nil, there were a few good players in the Japanese team, and it was an okay watch. Senegal beat Poland by the same result, Idrissa Gueye who is an Everton player scored the first for Senegal. That concluded all the opening games, we then returned to Group A and Russia beat Egypt three one, few would doubt that Putin would have had a few billion Rubles on the result.

Unexpected

I slept well again on Tuesday night and woke even more refreshed than the day before. Jane had to go back into work as she was covering for a colleague's holiday. Apparently, she had told me last week, but as usual I didn't listen. I had one or two other things on my mind last week, but I didn't fancy an argument that I know I could never win. Anyway, it gave me time to record the next vlog and make supporting notes. The pain in my head along with the accompanying discomfort in my eye had all gone. Surprisingly, the tasks that would have taken maybe an hour to do, seemed easier and less demanding. As instructed, I did take it easy late morning, but as usual, I couldn't stop my brain from riding on an out-of-control juggernaut, that was speeding perilously towards a blind bend.

The three matches today didn't really look much on paper, after lunch and whilst in a relaxed state, I revisited compiling the list of favourite bands, songs, movies etc. Today, I focused on bands, second to The Jam must be Paul Heaton who is one of the finest lyricists ever. Paul Weller's writing was 'of that time', charting the mood of the late 70's, and early 80's. He said when The Jam split up in 1982 it was the right time, looking back I can now see what he meant. Mr Heaton took over for me in the mid-80's with The Housemartins. They retained a strong political stance, and his ethical compass was certainly aligned with mine. He also had an alchemist's touch when adding some belting tunes. As I sat there relaxed listening to tracks from Blondie, and yes Debbie Harry was my first ever crush. Other great bands include and on their own merits; The Undertones, The Police, Ian Dury, The Clash, Elvis Costello, Buzzcocks, Madness and The Specials also sneaked in with a couple of well-crafted tunes. The Stranglers had a sound all their own, as did OMD and both had strong themes for songs too.

As I sat in the garden with a coffee in the warm afternoon sun, listening to a playlist I created a while back, it was inevitable that I would fall asleep. What I wasn't expecting was the uplifting feeling that heralded another event and the burning light that would heap more pain on my already blistered eye. I tried to hold on to the relaxing and uplifting feeling that once again spread across my body and suspended me perfectly. Then came the voice, and the request to open my eyes, I knew this would have to be done to gain more information, and wow, did I have some questions for them. "Hi Danny, can you open your eyes please", It was Staten44' voice that greeted me, and I must admit I was happy to hear it was him. Somehow, the intensity of the light seemed stronger and directed to the most painful part in my eye. I blinked furiously and with different beat patterns to see if that helped. Eventually, I was able to keep them open although I blinked faster than I would normally.

Staten44 sat in the middle this time, he was flanked by two other men, both of whom I had not seen before. Courteously, he introduced them, to his right was Vans-tem-Iraldic-6, as soon as he introduced him, his name along with added information appeared in my vision. His age was 57 years 267 days, he was Director of the Ethics Mandate P211 Team along with Liaison Director of the 62.87 Evolution. Like Staten44, he was the Liaison Director of this 62.87 Evolution, and they both wore the same-coloured uniform. He was much stockier than the other two, not overweight, but he looked like he enjoyed food over exercise, and there's nothing wrong with that in my book. Staten44 then introduced the person to his left, it seemed unusual, and I remember the words perfectly as he said, "Danny, allow me to introduce Olin-AA02 to you". A few things seemed odd, firstly his name was incredibly short, but none less unusual. Secondly, the only information that I could see in my lower peripheral vision was his title, which was simply, President of Section P211. His age also appeared as 67 years and 67 days. For once he actually looked his age, and although his hair was short, his was predominantly grey. I knew each name would have to be shortened to make life easier, therefore, Vans-tem6 and Olin would fit perfectly.

Olin and Vans-tem6 both made eye contact with me, they gave a beguiling smile as they were introduced. Staten44 then explained that the previous CDT event was curtailed due to unforeseen circumstances, well that was one way to put it. Genuinely, he asked how I was feeling, and he assured me that the bleed was not caused by the device which sat uninvited in my brain. He asked me if I wanted to continue, I could tell by the tone in his voice that this was something they wanted as much as I did. I took a little time before I answered, which gave me time to read their body language, which supported my assumption.

Before we continued, I told them I had some questions, and they were keen to hear them to put my mind to rest. They said they were aware of an issue as they detected a change in blood pressure within a certain part of my brain. Vans-tem6 spoke for the first time, once more he stated that the device used to engage with them could cause no medical issues in the subject, by that he meant me. I didn't ask what would happen to this item once they had finished with me, and you can deduct from this I didn't ask when they would end. As to my fourth question, 'Why me and what do they want from me', I wasn't sure if I should be asking these questions in fear, they would pull the plug and move on to their next subject. It was too late; my speech overtook my thoughts, and it came out as a half-babbled splurge. Vans-tem6 had the floor, while he did, he told me they were conducting other CDT events across the globe at various times. "People were selected based on a criteria matrix", he told me, but once again I thought it best not to delve too much. As predicted earlier, I didn't raise my final question about my ability to recall more information than expected by either party. I was receiving mixed messages, and mixed signals. I think they knew how much I could recall, and for some reason they were happy with that.

We then settled into our established routine or so I thought, they ask me a question then it would be my turn. Although, today it was different, maybe because the two either side of Staten44 had the same level of authority. The questions came one after another and fortunately, I decided to answer each one without a great deal of thought. The first came from Staten44 who asked, "Do you consider yourself trustworthy?", I replied yes, "I would, but I always try to understand what trust is being asked of me". I continued, "trust is a two-way street, trust must be earned and not simply expected. Also, I think you must consider it in context, if someone will be protected by the trust asked, then you would lean towards yes. On the other hand, if that trust could be used to hurt or damage someone then I may decline. The other thing you need to consider with trust is the consequences of going against the trust". As the three sat there around 12 feet away from me, I could see their hands cupped over invisible spheres which allowed their fingers to twitch rapidly.

The second question came from Vans-tem6, he had a deeper voice than the others, but once again I was unable to distinguish their accents. His question was just as peculiar, "Are you a fair person?' I must have looked frustrated or maybe it was the tone of my answer as I explained. "Fairness is also something that must be earned the same as trust. I would trust someone and be equally as fair to them, that is until I feel that person did not deserve either. If they broke the trust that I gave them, or I found them to be unfair towards a person, then I would be guarded in the future". I concluded this answer by saying, "these are common decencies, I would hope that I surround myself with people who share these". As I delivered this additional piece of information all three grinned. There was a momentary pause, to which I added, "I like to consider myself 'fair', but these are traits that should be asked of the recipient, what I mean is, I can't really judge myself. I may think that I have acted fairly, although others may have a different opinion." There was no visible change of expression on the three who faced me, although I could see their fingers go into overdrive.

The final question came from Olin, he had a softer voice that matched his age, and I guess stature. "Danny are you an honest person?", as he spoke, he gave a partial smile, I also noticed a glint in his eye. I thought for a moment and simply said "Yes". I told them that honesty and integrity should go hand in hand as far as I am concerned. I continued with a simple statement, "I value honesty above all other things, if you don't have true honesty, then all other values become worthless and unimportant." I made eye contact with

Olin, and I detected a small but telling grin. Vans-tem6 thanked me for my answers and just as he did, Olin interrupted and asked me if I had told anyone about what had happened to me. I told him straight, "No, I had not told anyone, not even Jane or Toni". I then elaborated, "This wasn't just because they had instructed me not to, it was simply that I couldn't begin to think of a way to explain it". I then pushed back and said, "I had been truthful to them throughout all their questions, and I believe I would be fair and trustworthy". I returned the question, "Have you been the same with me?", this brought a noticeable level of discomfort in their body language. Staten44 told me that I would probably recall more of the event than they initially expressed. In retrospect, they hadn't lied to me, it's just that I remembered more than either they wanted or expected. I wasn't sure which of these was the case, but at least everything was now in the open.

With this newfound level of trust, I thought it was the best time to ask the bombshell of a question, which could also be described as the largest ever elephant in the room. Well here goes, "Is there a reason why you are allowing me to see the world in which you live?" Now this really made them uncomfortable, as I delivered it and saw the reaction, I thought 'this is the end'. Olin stood up and took a couple of steps forward, he wiped the sides of his face with both hands and stood silent for a moment. With a more sincere tone, he told me that a select few have been given greater detail and greater access. The reason he told me was to evaluate trust, honesty, fairness along with other traits. At this stage there is no other agenda he said, I merely accepted this on face value. I softly said, "Thank you", and prepared myself to deliver the next question.

As Olin turned around to retake his seat, he stopped suddenly, turned once more to ask another precise question, "Danny, are you respected?" He broke for a second, and then delivered an additional part, "What I mean is do people respect you as a person?" I didn't read anything into this immediately, as a result I answered as best I could. "I hope people respect me as a person, but no one is perfect", I told him. "I am respected in my work as I have reached a high position with the experience to show for it.", I stated calmly. I then hit back with a killer statement which has worked for me before, "Trust and integrity have to be earned, not through words but through deeds and actions, if I want respect, it's not something I would have an agenda to seek". As my words finished Olin turned back and with the slightest nod of his head, he returned to his seat.

Unfinished Business

Before we continued, Staten44 said he would finish the remaining few points on the charter. I was pleased that he offered this up, firstly I preferred his voice, and secondly, he seemed to provide more detail. Taking a couple of paces forward, he prepared himself. A screen appeared with the previous bullet points listed. As the next point appeared, I instantly thought that this would be covered by the one above, which said, 'Every colony member is equal without exception'.

Each member's contribution to the 62.87 Evolution is equally beneficial.

Staten44 explained this point further, essentially, the entire colony only operates as a whole and one that has a perfect equilibrium. Science may lead the search for answers to the Evolutionary Patch, but they are nothing without the weight of the colony behind them. Every scientist appreciates the efforts of every colony member, no matter what their chosen role. Mutual respect is given between every fulfilment role, it has always been this way and always will. At this point my mind went back to the novel Animal Farm, communism will always fail as we give in to greed and power. Unlike when Helena read through the points, Staten44 took a question. I told him, "I can see how this would potentially work, but where, and how are decisions made?"

He smiled, and it was a proper smile this time. He told me that everyone makes decisions, everyone has their say in how the colony is run. They also have their say regarding the direction and management of the 62.87 Evolution, and how they proceed forward. I must have looked puzzled at this, consequently he went into the detail that was lacking with Helena. Every colonist can vote on every decision that is made within the colony, no matter what it is, or its gravitas. There are key decisions that everyone must vote on, these could relate to major scientific innovations or ethics issues, and some space exploration missions. Then there are more local issues or matters relating to their chosen area of replenishment. Colonists who are seeking approval for something beyond their normal remit can debate its value and offer a vote. Likewise, a department may request a vote in the same way. GAPS ensures everyone is aware of issues that impact them, or they have an interest in. Following a vote, all decisions are final and accepted without question, although they are free to resubmit a further counter proposal.

As Staten44 delivered this I could feel myself nodding and smiling as everything made sense, once again my peripheral vision was being loaded with an incredible amount of data. I don't know what prompted me, but I asked a question, "I can see you, but what do you see when you look at me?" At first, he answered with a remark that usually unsettles me as it often comes from the mouths of politicians, "That's a good question." He then told me that they see a perfect version of me, much like an avatar, only they can read every gesture and thought with perfect clarity. I didn't ask more, and he continued to the next point.

The colony will provide unconditional care for those who choose to live outside of the colony.

As soon as this popped up, I felt instantly confused as I thought the colony was everything. He told me that there are people who never wanted to join the colony system, and they respected this. They live a poor existence from the land, they have little in the way of effective medical care. Continuing his explanation, colonists go into these communities and provide compassionate care and medical aid when and where it's required. This prompted a further question, I asked, "Who are these people and why would they not want the perfect lives you have". Staten44 looked down for a split-second and said, "These people are fearful of science and have ancient beliefs. They remain in certain parts of the world that offer little nourishment or protection, and they believe we are their enemy". I must have looked bemused until he expanded, "They live in belief that their gods will one day save them. Each year a few thousand will seek entry into the colony, following the debriefing process they can be admitted"

Science in all forms must adhere to the ethics code governing its development and use.

As this final bullet point appeared, I thought once again it was straightforward, although he gave a summary. Each area of science has its own declaration and governance process. He explained further, the 62.87 Theory laid out the initial science that spurned the concept. There was a particular addition that he added, I instinctively knew this had colossal importance when he said, **"The author provided conclusive proof in the form of previously unexplored scientific awareness"**. Staten44 added, "years later after extensive and rigorous debate it was unanimously accepted by the scientific community. Since then, it has been our mission to fulfil the theory through scientific advancement, and with protocoled experimentation". He rambled on further about how science if unchecked, can be extremely harmful, that is why every scientist knows the importance of the code.

As he finished, the screen melted away and he took his seat once more. Olin stood up again, he hit me with something I wasn't expecting, but every fibre of my body tingled with excitement and anticipation. He announced, "We are going to provide you with unlimited access to the 62.87 Theory along with the experiments." He told me that science had searched for answers regarding both the beginning of the universe and the creation of mankind. The answers were unpalatable for huge numbers, that was until science proved without question their truth.

Staten44 asked me to brace myself and to accept everything. Nothing could have prepared me for what came next. A gush of warm air enveloped me, it came at me simultaneously from all sides. This was accompanied by a warmth that touched every living tissue within my body. Electrical activity pinged and surged over my skin and weirdly within it. A storm of incredibly vivid coloured lights headed towards me at phenomenal speeds. It was like being thrown into a kaleidoscope of colours and lights that weirdly became part of me. As they surged past me and through me, they began to blend in the back of my eyes. It's difficult to explain, but I felt an inner peace.

Knowledge and understanding of 'everything' will now open before me. I knew it was all there, I felt its grandeur and power. I was like a small, frightened child looking into an abyss that held the key to everything. The entire experience lasted for about 10 seconds, as it ended, I could still feel small pulses of electricity throughout my body. Strangely, I felt almost refreshed by the experience, I then simply smiled my acceptance to the three people who sat there patiently. Consciously or not, the act of smiling seems to be an acceptable currency for both parties. Staten44 told me this event would end now and politely asked me if I wanted to continue. "Yes", came as easy as ever. I didn't have time to add anything else, the lights dimmed, and the false warmth I felt within the CDT event was replaced by a genuine belt of heat from the sun.

Chapter 8
The Gift

Wednesday ended as strangely as it began, especially when you consider the unexpected centre. I picked Jane up as usual from the station, although she was extremely nervous that I was driving too quickly after the TIA. I managed to reassure her with the falsehood that I had rested all day, and the only exercise I had was making cups of coffee while watching the football. As it had been a day of unexpected events, we decided to get a takeaway on the way home which suited me as I was particularly hungry. For some reason, I felt very calm all evening and whilst my mind was racing at an almost uncontrollable and dangerous pace, I was able to pick out events and study them in detail. I was able to instantly see solutions, as we watched the 22:00 news they spoke about issues to which I instantly found remedies. My mind raced through processes and efficiencies of things I had no real interest in. That night I slept well, and although Jane was in work again and obviously worrying, she seemed to accept that the TIA was a minor event. The only exception to the bewildering events of the day came with the football. Portugal beat Morocco one nil, the Portuguese reminded me of our English players, always underperforming when it came to major tournaments. In the other games Uruguay beat Saudia Arabia by the same result, while Spain matched the underperformance with the same result, beating Iran one nil.

The Thursday routine began as normal, although there was a problem with the shower which kept going from hot to cold. Between yelps as it went from the correctly set temperature to episodes where it dipped by a chilling 7 degrees. As I got up to tell her that it was due to the water pressure, she had had enough and exited early with traces of conditioner still in her hair. There was still an awkward feeling as I drove her to the station, it seemed, for an inexplicable reason, that I had caused the dips in water pressure. She kissed me goodbye at the station and told me to take it easy, as she walked away, I could see her greet a friend and begin to laugh as she recalled the events that had happened. I knew that a text mid-morning with a kiss and a smiley face would bring her around.

Added to my normal routine today was a trip to the chemist to pick up my repeat prescription for pain killers. I joke that I take enough in one day to bring down a horse, but it's possible. I take 1200mg of Pregabalin three times a day, a friend once took 100mg for severe neck pain and slept almost constantly for 24 hours. This is just one of an array of medications I take daily. This diversion took me to Sainsbury's on the way back. It triggered my usual frustration and anger levels to skyrocket through the roof. I have a blue disabled badge which allows me to park in designated areas and on double yellow lines etc. As I drove into the car park, I was followed by a huge and expensive Mercedes 4x4 SUV, this was driven by a suit wearing pretentious knob. I watched as he parked as close as he could to the shop doors, as he paraded into the store with a red tie and blue pinstriped shirt my anger grew to a level that demanded an outlet. As he returned opening the car from his key-fob some 30 feet away, I exited mine and said to him, "You forgot to display your blue badge". I expected the response, and sure enough it came, as he replied, "I was only in there for a minute". My outburst was cool, calm, and measured, and by this time two other people were in earshot, "The thing is that you want the benefits of a blue badge, where I have a blue badge and would give anything not to have one", I said. As his mouth opened, he searched for a reply, although mine was quickly followed up, "You can gladly have mine, as long as you take my disease with it". I finished, "by the way, my disease is Multiple Sclerosis, and I wouldn't wish this on my worst enemy". Hopefully, this would have the desired effect and make him think twice in the future. I didn't want to purposely embarrass him;

however, I am sure it would play on his mind throughout the day. There again, it probably wouldn't, which may be an indication of his attitude.

With a clear head and a revitalised energy, I quickly created my vlog, although there were huge sections I couldn't articulate properly. I know that I have observed a great deal, or to be more precise I had been given access to much more information, but I couldn't find the key to unlock it. The morning was also interrupted by a friend who called around with Eddie his dog. He is a rescue dog from somewhere like Romania or Moldova. There's a charity that rescues them and brings them to the UK to find forever-homes. This poor little dog doesn't know how to play with toys and his only motivation is understandably food. He likes coming around here as there's a plentiful supply of treats. I once asked him why he called the dog Eddie, and his reply was that it would get people talking and feel at ease, a bit like why we called our only child Toni. We enjoyed a coffee together and discussed everything from politics to the price of fish. I really like those conversations where neither party has an agenda or an alternative opinion that is only there as a rebut to mine. I have another friend who I value as a friend, although he takes pleasure from an argument where he takes an opposite stance, merely to argue rather than debate.

The remainder of Thursday went by in a flash, my brain's thoughts were uncontrollable at times, but all pretty much the same in that I focused on processes and efficiencies. This attention to detail extended to me making a drink. I analysed every part from switching the kettle on with exactly the correct amount of water, to getting the milk on the way to picking up the sugar. I was doing this whilst also thinking about what Jane had told me the night before, she told me how frustrating work was when it comes to invoicing a job. It was a new kind of anal thinking that I had not witnessed before; to be honest it worried me slightly.

When I picked Jane up from the station, she commented on how well I looked, she claimed the credit for this as she had told me to rest. When we returned home, she was amazed that I had prepared tea, setting the table correctly and even cleaning up. What I didn't tell her was that her amazement was completely shadowed by mine as I couldn't recall doing any of it. That evening, as with the past couple, Jane was busy either preparing for the visit from Toni or talking 'at' me about it. I must admit, I was excited as her, the thought of just hugging her again and seeing her beautiful smile in person rather than on a screen gave me butterflies in my stomach, if I could only collect them and keep them forever. That night I slept well again, and my sleep was only interrupted by very painful spasms in my legs that lasted for about 20 minutes. My MS symptoms include chronic pain, it is one of those invisible symptoms that is also difficult to explain. My right foot used to feel like it was being plunged into ice cold water, if you want to replicate this, please feel free and you will see how excruciating it is. Another bizarre symptom was under both feet, the feeling like I had a square shaped block under the arch of the foot. This one is more difficult to replicate but equally as painful.

Jane's talking continued through the football, for some reason it didn't cause the normal level of discomfort. To be honest, my mind was rushing around solving problems and finding solutions to all manner of things. Today introduced some of the major contenders into the competition, teams that promised much and possessed the firepower to succeed. Youth teamed up with experience which tantalised the appetite. We started with Denmark against Australia, I had a liking for the Ausie's as back in the day, Everton's own Tim Cahill was also their star player. Australia managed a one-one draw; France entered the affray with a tame one nil defeat of Puru. Argentina was beaten by three goals to nil against Croatia. In

Argentina we find another once great team that seem continually destined to fail on the world's biggest stage.

Straight To The Point

Friday started with extreme excitement, hopefully we would have another CDT event later, I couldn't begin to entertain a thought that it wouldn't happen. Jane was equally excited as it was only two more sleeps until Toni arrived. And now we began our final routine for the week, although this week would see the dawn of something different as Jane would declare 'here comes the weekend'. As I checked my emails and responded to some boring requests, I found time to email Jane with the resolution to her invoicing dilemma. I didn't expect the response I received some 45 minutes later, it was perfect for her, and she would take the credit for showing it to her line-manager. Her email finished with the line 'I didn't think you were listening, thank you'. To be honest I wasn't listening that intently, but it was easy to see where the failings were. As I sat down for lunch, this time I broke my usual habit, as it wasn't accompanied by either music or a movie.

I remember looking down at my phone, it was 14:14, then my eyes slowly closed, and a warm uplifting sensation covered my entire body. My spine tingled; I could feel each vertebrae loosen as it detached from its surrounding tissues. This same feeling spread downwards, through my legs, then onwards through my ankles and into my feet. At the same time the feeling spread upwards, my neck became released from all the tension I felt. Eventually, it expanded into my shoulders, I was then completely relaxed, and my body was no longer mine. My consciousness became engaged once more and my excitement level jumped a notch as I heard my name being called. Although, before the joy of seeing the amassed greeting party there would be the pain. I thought back to a previous conversation, this is all in my mind, the sensations I am feeling, they're not real. Sadly, it was useless, the bright beams of light burnt searing holes in both eyes, although my right did feel worse. Rapid blinking gave little relief, but I knew it would make things better. As I began to open my 'imaginary' eye lids more, figures slowly became more defined. It was Helena, she seemed to know the pain was easing and said, "Hello Danny, how have you been?" I blinked furiously to finally reveal four people sat in front of me, once again it was the three men from the last event. Olin and Vans-tem6 were back once more and the fourth person was Staten44. Each one nodded politely and smiled, as I focused on them a stream of information entered my lower peripheral vision.

Vans-tem6 stood and took a couple of paces forward, he told me that they would like to ask some more questions, they thanked me for being open and honest to this point. He then hit me with the first question, I immediately suspected that it had been structured with a great deal of thought. "When you were diagnosed with Multiple Sclerosis, how did that feel, and how did it impact your family life?" Wow, that was straight to the point, they managed to pick the one event that changed everything for me. Unlike on a game show when the host proudly boasts that £50,000 is a life changing sum of money. With a gleaming smile and a sparkling suit, our slime ridden host prods the winners to reveal how this will affect them. The camera turns to focus on the winners who tearfully state it will help them enormously; the winnings will buy a new car and a family holiday. Alternatively, it may be used to help with the purchase of a new home. Each time I witness these events I cringe, and I can't help myself from shouting at the TV, 'having a diagnosis of a chronic disease such as MS is <u>truly</u> life changing'.

How did it make me feel? I began by telling them how I ended up in hospital for nine days, and the various tests they performed and the specialist doctors I'd seen. When the death-knell finally came there was an element of relief to know that there was a reason for the increasing and worsening symptoms. Also, the name given to it wasn't cancer, I think people fear the treatment more than the actual tumour found. To begin with, I didn't associate the disease with any life changing conditions. This quickly altered as I defied the expert's advice and began to read information about MS online. The internet is a wash of material, the advice was correct in parts, some of the articles weren't helpful as they promised incredible cures. Through proper channels and official websites, it was evident what the disease can do and what people must deal with. My own doctor came out to the house shortly after I was discharged from hospital and signed both of us off work for 3 months. She said we both needed time to come to terms with the diagnosis. Quickly I became obsessed with the thought that I would end up in a wheelchair or worse. F

Throughout this first part of my response, the four people who sat before me paid attention to every word, this changed somewhat, for the next part I could see their fingers twitching rapidly. I had three distinct feelings during this initial period, the first was absolute fear for myself along with Jane, and especially Toni. I didn't want them to have to alter their lives to accommodate my illness, an illness that I didn't ask for or want. This fear started in the pit of my stomach and sometimes I did feel as though I was going to vomit. I don't know how, but I sort of calmed myself down each time it happened. The second emotion was anger, it was the sort of anger that has the hairs on the back of your neck stand on end. I had nobody to blame and no one to vent my anger on. This emotion stayed with me the longest. I was angry at everyone who came close to me during those early times, more often than not it was Jane. I did my best to hide it from Toni, but she was old enough to gauge when it was safe to approach me. Even as I relayed these two emotions, I could feel myself recalling the feelings. It was during this time that Olin looked the most engaged, the others seemed more occupied with the opaque screens that sat in front of them. Any time I paused slightly, Helena looked up and over towards me, it was momentary as I quickly began again.

I took a deep breath before I delivered the third part of my answer. The final emotion I felt was relieved or almost happy with the diagnosis. I explained further, my life had come to resemble a hamster in a cage with only a running wheel for company. I felt imprisoned in this cage and forced to run in the wheel just to survive. I was going nowhere, yet if I didn't turn the wheel 5,000 times and at a constant speed I would be penalised. Looking up, I could see four confused faces. Either they didn't know what a hamster was or indeed a pet hamster, or analogies were doomed to fail. I thought I needed to elaborate, but as I did, following vigorous finger twitching over the invisible balls their faces told the story that they finally understood. Focusing once more, I continued, I felt my life was no longer my own, they talk about the work life balance, well mine was totally unbalanced up to that point. Weirdly, I looked at the diagnosis as the opportunity to redress the balance, although I never told anyone that. Summing up I guess I was on a true roller-coaster of emotions. Sadly, it took the worst of events for me to finally escape the prison I found myself in. It took a devastating diagnosis for me to break away from the numbers. It was numbers that imprisoned me, chasing sales figures, reporting statistics to clients, paying the mortgage while having enough for a holiday. If only more people could see this, the happier we would be as a society. It's too bad that many only see this happening when it's already happened.

As I finished my answer which took longer than I initially thought, Olin thanked me and said, "You have been very helpful". I was confused by this, but didn't give it too much thought, I considered I was getting more out of this arrangement than they were. It then opened the floor for their second question. It was equally considered and structured as the first one. It was delivered by Vans-tem6 who also stood as he asked, "Can you describe the love you feel for your daughter Toni, and what lengths would you go to protect her?" Now this was a 'wow' question, but once again I took a deep breath in and began my response. I told the gathered party of three men and one female that it's almost impossible to articulate the love you feel for someone that you brought into this world. From the day she was born and every day since, I simply can't believe how fortunate I am, sorry, 'we are' to have created a perfect human being. Every time I hug her the bond grows stronger, and over the years, we must have shared millions of hugs. You can never hug someone enough, I think, because that was missing from my childhood, every day and with every hug I was ensuring history would not be repeated. I think the love you have for a daughter can never be matched, a father's role is to nurture and protect. When that child is a daughter, it is undoubtedly unmatched anywhere in nature.

I finished my response with a sigh, not of relief it was over, more an outpouring of emotion that temporarily drained me. As I looked up again, I could see that they had all relaxed further into their seats, although the reflections of each screen that sat before them showed intense activity. Then I remembered the second part of Vans-tem6' question, I started again, although this was extremely brief. As to protecting Toni, I would do anything to protect her from actual harm. Sometimes we must be hurt in order to learn from that feeling. For example, ditched boyfriends, having to stand up to bullies, losing a friend, or the death of someone close, and even the loss of a pet. However, when it comes to physical harm, there is nothing I wouldn't do, including sacrificing my own life to protect hers. I have had probably the best years of my life, giving up the remainder isn't a question that needs consideration. It would be a simple statement; I would do anything for Toni. I find it weirdly interesting that people often state that they would sacrifice their own lives to save a loved one, although would they readily do the same and commit to 'take' another person's life. Once again, I sighed as I finished and with a look of contentment I looked straight at Vans-tem6. He smiled as a signal of understanding and retook his seat alongside the other three.

The Ripple Effect

I asked if there were any more questions, Olin told me that there wasn't, but they may return to these subjects again if that was ok. I couldn't see how I could provide any more detail, but it was my turn now. I told them about my mind racing and being able to find solutions to any problem that was put before me. Staten44 remained seated, he told me that I would soon be able to rationalise my thoughts, whatever this meant. Explaining further, he told me that I was initially advised that I would not be able to recall anything of an event, but this was obviously not the case. The 'ability' I had been given will help me and I would soon be able to selectively use it during future CDT events, and thereafter to build a better understanding. He sort of emphasised the word 'understanding', the whole thing left me confused. I took the opportunity to dig a little further, I asked if other experiments had also reached this point. I remember he looked sideways at Olin who nodded slightly, he then told me that I was the only one who had gone this far and been given such detail. I wanted to clarify this, but I was learning that time is precious, and I trusted an element of what he said, 'I would soon be able to selectively use it during future CDT events, and thereafter to build a better understanding'.

Olin stood up and took three steps forward, he cleared his throat with a gentle cough. As he did a display screen joined him to his right, "Danny, we are going to give you three essentials to life, three keys if you like". I didn't know it then, but what came next revolutionised my life and opened an incredible number of doors. As he began the first part, he told me to have an open mind, by this time it was wide open and ready for anything. As he started to explain the first one, the screen to his right turned green and a heading appeared. In contrasting colours, The Ripple Effect emerged in the top centre of the display. Olin explained that everything within the universe is linked by fields we haven't yet discovered. Reverse time travel is only made possible through the three intertwined occurrences, they are Time, Space and Matter. The screen then displayed the process of calculating an exact point within the universe at precisely the correct time, "...doing this allows matter to be moved", he told me. All I knew is that it looked incredibly complex, and yet it all made sense. It's not just reverse time that is dependent on this, future time operates to the same rules, but to date, "...they have not been able to calculate these accurately", I was told.

Olin continued, this ripple effect is everywhere, every action creates a reaction. If you were to bump into someone and they lost something of value. That bump was innocuous to you; although, it may go on to change the course of that person's life. The consequences will always be incalculable to you, you may have said, "Sorry", and meant it. You will be unaware of what other events may have happened during that person's day or life up to that point. Importantly, you can't alter or adjust your life in case this type of incident may happen, but you can always be mindful and ensure the ripple effect in that case is not counterproductive. This puzzled me at first but as I gave it more thought, in time it began to resonate more. The next part of his explanation linked in and made sense too. What is said cannot be unheard, every communication we have or send can impact on others in ways we can't calculate in advance. Positive or negative, they are a direct reaction to your action, but don't stress too much as negatives can be required, although it's how they are delivered that matters here.

All of this sounded very deep and Buddhist like, but what he then showed was a world where this isn't just possible, it actually works. The screen illustrated a world where everyone is mindful of this and genuinely caring about their fellow colonists. This place was as close to flawlessness as you could possibly wish for. There is no need for greed as everything you could possibly want is supplied. Every person is born into this perfect world where perfection is given freely, they don't understand the concept of lies. In fact, every flaw that you can think of has been irradicated from our DNA, that's obviously biologically untrue, but a fair measure of what life is like here. Mentors guide children and young adults through this world and each one is told the value and benefit of everything they are given. They are also told and shown the importance of everyone's value to the 62.87 Evolution and the rules by which they live.

He ended by illustrating a very simple, but effective example of the ripple effect, hey (they do get the use of analogies.) It concerned something hugely monumental in a person's life, it would, without question impact on others. The decision to have children or not, the choice to take a life, or the choice to take your own life, all will have an irreparable impact on others. We don't know or can't calculate how these things will change history. The analogy he fired at me seemed to be dragged from my darkest and deepest thoughts. If a person were to take their own life, it would certainly have an impact on other family members along with their wider network of friends and associates. This negative impact could be short-lived during the understandable grieving process, it could sit with them for many years, reoccurring constantly. They may choose to submerge the impact in the darkest and immersed recesses of their mind, but it will always be there. The worry is that the negativity could be affecting them in unknown ways. It may manifest itself partially suppressed to the outside world until such times that they break.

What I learnt from this is that 'too late', is just that, once the act has been committed it can never be reversed. A comment or an action works the same, here it is on a monumental scale. Thoughts of how the ripple affect propagates and indiscriminately impregnates others should be explained to anyone thinking of taking their own lives. Olin continued his explanation as he elaborated further. An action no matter how large or small could, for example, prevent or delay a pregnancy and unbeknown to all concerned is that child's potential would be unknown. As Olin whittered on I couldn't help but think that his choice of subject wasn't just random, it was selected for a reason. I had put a huge amount of thought and planning into 1st November, and my reason for doing it was too important to be side-lined now.

Now, if you're still with my train of thinking and I am sure you are, what they have opened and shown me will have an impact and a reaction from me. As soon as I fell asleep on Thursday 7 June, just 15 days ago they began a ripple effect with unknown consequences for me and obviously for them. Whichever, if you think about my future opportunities and actions they will have a direct impact on their space, time, and matter in their year 2073 PD Post Digital. Incredible to even consider, are they aware of my future actions that ultimately shape their current being, they must be. I don't know about you, but I need a very strong coffee at this point, or maybe something much stronger. Even typing this, at precisely this point, I am possibly reshaping the future of mankind, and it's all because they opened a looking glass which has allowed me to view what they have. Are they taking the biggest gamble ever waged, or do their skills extend to counting cards, I have yet to find out.

Ownership & Responsibility

The second gift or life lesson they gave me was unexpected, but no less important than the first. As Olin began to introduce the next section the screen developed an orange background, and as before the heading stood bold and centered at the top. He split his explanation into two parts and took the latter word first. We must all take responsibility for our failings and learn from them, a complex diagram of the brain's workings showed how we accept and adjust following failure. It's true, as a species we learn quickly from our mistakes and sometimes we must accept these to build better. Firstly, we must free our minds from all forms of superstitions and rituals related to teachings such as religion. As he declared these, I said that the latter was very easy for me, and I didn't rely on the first. I remember him smiling and telling me that in this age we used this more than we thought. It goes beyond religion and into other habits we acquire as we learn and develop, things like luck and coincidence must be treated as they are. We must accept that random events happen, trying to find links to comfort us is as ridiculous as picking a god haphazardly. As he said all this, I acknowledged that you can't pick and choose.

Once this registered, I could see that even I clung on to the odd one or two. My lucky number is 22, although having that dictate my choices is just as random as any other number. Along with the stupidity that all people born between certain dates will all share the same traits and characteristics. By the way, I have never bought into that. We can also urge ourselves into wishing for a big lottery win on the basis that we would do much with the winnings. Or that we deserve the high pay-out because our lives have been incredibly 'shitty' of late. The reality is that it's all random, even if you wear your lucky pants while having your fingers crossed and ensuring you didn't walk under any ladders and saying good morning to a particular type of bird. You, like everyone else, will have a 14 million to 1 chance of winning the life-changing sum.

Olin turned to explain the first part of this section, 'ownership'. Instantly, I could see how they were both linked. When we have achieved something, we should celebrate it. Just as we need to own our responsibilities and learn from them, we also need to accept credit for our achievements. These are particularly noticeable when we tie religion into the equation. On that point he then confirmed to me something I have trusted in for most of my life. "Danny, I can tell you now that there is no god, or a god like creature, everything associated to this wanting belief was created by mankind", as Olin delivered this, I glanced over to the other three seated people who all smiled as they knew what this meant to me. They know this simply based on all scientific reasoning, although it's the same scientific knowledge we have today, it's just conveniently ignored by many. I saw a T-shirt once that said, 'Religion' and below it said, 'One day we will find a cure', credit to the creator of this.

Anyway, he then told me something that amazed me, although on reflection it shouldn't have. Our universe is in its second generation, although this could even be more, our big bang was the pinpoint of a mega black hole they called Evantis246. Their scientific research indicates this mega black hole or singularity took over 72 billion years to consume everything that existed before. The universe that existed in the same space previously was gone, and eventually gave birth to the one we see today. They know this because the tracks they used to mark time, space, and matter have an underlying trace that shows a previous universe. The notion that a godlike creature who created everything in such a short period is just ridiculous. As I was told this my shoulders dropped slowly in pure satisfaction, but there was not even a trace of surprise.

Later as I thought more about Olin's statements, I noticed people's use of them, and on each occasion, I told myself that I must avoid using them and try to correct others. Watching the football recently, I observed some players crossing themselves as they enter the stadium in prayer to their particular god, for what, a good outcome for them and teammates, and a bad outcome for their opponents. Bizarrely, one of their opponents was doing exactly the same thing. Then if they happen to score a goal, once more they perform a ritual of thanking their god for providing them with the skills necessary to achieve the result. Just as peculiarly, we don't see them also asking the question to that same god if they miss a penalty or inadvertently score an own goal. The player should take ownership of the skills they have honed since they were a child, and the hours they would have spent every week of their lives training and obtaining a level of fitness needed to perform at the very top.

I also watched a bakery show where contestants were required to provide showcases of their skills. As one 'would-be baker' placed her items into the oven she declared, "It's in the hands of the gods now". When she finally takes out her sweet bakes and they are a triumph, who gets the instant credit as she also affirms, "God and my dear dead grandmother were looking down on me today". Conversely, if it was a complete car crash of a pudding, does she say, "God had it in for me today". In these instances, god can never lose, just as, when a child falls down a mining shaft and rescuers have been spending day after day, night after night trying to dig a shaft to free the little boy. They always seem to be young boys. Anyway, the whole village, then the country and through social media the entire world send prayers to save him. Alas, 13 days later he is pulled out dead, therefore… we are comforted to know that 'god moves in mysterious ways'.

It appears that god cannot lose. Before I leave this topic, I saw a post on social media (which was verified) and I wanted to share it here with you. It demonstrates the corrupt side of religion and certainly Christianity, although they are all guilty in one form or another. It showed one of those US mid-west evangelic types who implore their viewers to get out their credit cards and give as much as they can. This particular one had found a novel way to increase revenues with the marketing line 'Jesus will return to earth, but we haven't raised enough money yet'. With that sort of tact, they are on to a money-making scheme till eternity. Every religion has its own sort of cost to its devotees, whether that's measured in financial terms, unpaid services or the best one sacrifices and disadvantages.

Those sacrifices and disadvantages range from sexual pleasures to certain types of food and beverages. All of these to please a deity that simply doesn't exist, and the next chapter and its contents disclose everything you need. There is a saying that, 'money is the root of all evil', there's probably a very good argument for this. But we must repeatedly ask ourselves, why do churches and religions continually ask for monetary donations.

Language

Before he finished, Olin hit me with the third and final strand to an improved life, and free us from the straps of the previous dark-aged millennia. Language and our use of language is learnt from our elders, in recent years I have noticed that language and the use of new words and vocabulary tools have changed significantly. He explained that language for them had become less cluttered with improved descriptions. Once again, at first, I must have looked puzzled or gave an internal reaction that they picked up on. He elaborated by showing me a long list of adjectives and how standardisation has been adapted for each one. Many of them shared descriptive measurements, once I saw this it all made sense. Essentially, it removes the possibility for them to be personalised and graded incorrectly. I instantly associated this to our own current use of language and how we describe or measure something which is not standard. If I thought a response to this book was good, another may describe it as awesome or some other descriptive measures. To the listener, their interpretation of good, awesome, or even terrible is a personal measure based on their own experiences. They have simplified the measurement of expression and to a scale that is tangible to the subject they are discussing or rating. Fortunately, they provided me with various examples which also appeared on the screen which helped. If I were to rate a film for example the standard options available are restricted to; extremely poor, very poor, poor, average, good, very good, and extremely good. The listener would know in advance that a rating of good for that genre of film is based on a given percentage.

They continued to provide me with a huge number of examples where streamlining language really helps. Even the expression 'huge' as a fixed number banding where the exact number is not known. You can see how this works and after much thought I can see how it is beneficial. They moved on to the next part of language which has helped change their mindset for the better. Figure of speech, 'If you're lucky, fingers crossed, god I hope not', are just a few examples where we use speech that has been passed down to us, but its use can mask ownership and responsibility. They also lean on superstitions that are also inherited and meaningless. One area that I successfully changed is the use and various phrases from religion, that has been easier in the verbal context, but a lot harder in thoughts. Saying god or Jesus along with any variations as part of an expletive also forms part of this mind change. Having practiced language change in conjunction with all the other things I have now been exposed to, does free the mind, it also allows me to be more focused.

One item you may want to consider is a word with such importance within our language, although its use is totally absurd. The word 'love' can be misused in many ways. I openly declare my love for Jane and Toni, and for me this is an expression of a deep-felt feeling, although the word itself doesn't do that emotion the true justice it deserves. On a TV talent show, although I would argue such a programme shouldn't be aired without there being a disclaimer of false representation. Annoyingly, one of the judges will declare, 'I love you', after listening to the voice of a contestant for only a few minutes. The audience will applaud in solidarity and heartfelt agreement at his gushing sentiments. Two acts later the same judge will declare the same level of love for a different contestant. What fascinates me is what will happen when the judge returns home later that day and guess what… yep, he declares his love for their partner and children. I know this is a 'soft target', but we evaluate our appreciation in an unregulated manner. We as the audience don't really know the true and accurate measurement the judge has really apportioned to each contestant. We can't simply love everything to the detriment of other worthwhile feelings. A Paul Heaton lyric summed it up perfectly, '…we're so busy loving it, we've forgotten to hate.' For the purpose of illustration, I suffered immensely while I watched a very popular celebrity strewn dance show. In just one episode I counted 67 references to the word love. In almost every occasion, other more descriptive words of meaningful assessments would have been available. This is merely one example of lazy language.

Finally, for this section are the other things that confuse our lives and stop us from taking responsibility. They can also cloud our judgment, although you will see that they are all a load of crap and have no scientific evidence to prove they work or are true. Other things I don't believe in, besides god, good luck/bad luck, fate/destiny, karma, having a calling, synchronicity, the soul, bad omens/good omens, spirits, ghosts, energies, demons, angels, horoscopes, immortal beings, with the exception of Paul Weller, homeopathy, reincarnation, crystals, the law of attraction, and chakras. None of these have a place in the 21st century or beyond. It's also good having a bit of fun with anyone who actually believes any of this stuff, simply ask them to provide verified scientific evidence that it either works or exists and I will happily go along with you.

Allow me one final point relating to our use of language and the term luck, or to be more specific, good luck. I think it could be an unintended insult to wish someone 'good luck'. In the context of an exam, the individual will have studied extensively, often they will have spent many hours revising, yet someone deems it necessary to wish them luck. As mentioned, luck has no basis of scientific fact, therefore, it's irrational to indicate that 'luck' in a random sense will be a factor towards the result. Take the example to its potential conclusion, if the individual passes the exam, do we then attribute an element to luck and state, 'You were just lucky'. Of course not, we are more likely to congratulate them for the hard work they gave towards their studies. Instead of using the word luck, simply replace it with a word like 'trust'.

Introduction To The Theory

As Olin returned to his seat, I could see he was less mobile than the others. I could also observe other features, such as, his greyish hair was short and noticeably thinning on the top. He looked either mixed race or certainly southern European, his voice mirrored the others in dialect and pattern, but I was still unable to place it with any certainty. His face was more rugged with a complexion that was good without being too imperfect. He looked worldly wise, now I know that's a personal interpretation, but he did. As he sat, Helena stood and moved closer towards me. I remember what she said perfectly, "Danny, we are now going to give you another key, this one will prove to be the most valuable. With this key, you will unlock the 62.87 Theory, you will also see how this became our evolutionary path, and which proved the disturbance factor". She paused for a split second before adding, "The evolution disturbance". Those words were life changing for me, they did unlock a theory along with my understanding for the future of mankind. It turned out to be a future with no limits. I absorbed each word, they were very precise with their use of language, the evolution disturbance provided them with a revised evolutionary path.

Helena asked me if I understood the meaning of the word evolution, of all the possible questions there could be, this caught me by surprise. I was understandably guarded with my response, and I figured she was hopeful of a negative reply. I wanted to hear their definition, especially with the thought echoing and reverberating, 'evolution disturbance', therefore, I answered simply and with a soft voice, "Not completely". She began with a hint of excitement. Initially the theory submitted was so enormously ground-breaking and against all other proposals. She reiterated a previous declaration, the author provided conclusive proof in the form of previously unexplored scientific awareness. Once this was accepted, it took a further 16 years to validate the findings beyond any scientific doubt. Once this was established beyond any further argument, the whole of mankind accepted it, she announced proudly.

Continuing, she explained, as each element of the theory became better understood and science caught up with each part, humanity knew it had to change. That mass change coincided with the development of more colonies and with greater wealth and strength behind the World Change Order, which underlines the World Change Movement. To deliver each part of the theory, humanity would have to have a common goal, with a single point to aim for. Every person within the colonies and members of the World Change knew they would probably never see the end result. This is where BTBT originated, Build Today for a Better Tomorrow. It drove the initial concept of the New Evolutionary Path and brought humanity together.

Helena returned to her meandering explanation, evolution by its standard definition as you would expect it, states that in biology, evolution is the change in the characteristics of a species over several generations and relies on the process of natural selection. The theory of evolution is based on the hypothesis that all species are related and gradually change or improve over time. I could feel my head nodding in understandable agreement. The 62.87 Theory stated that the evolutionary path for homo sapiens was interrupted by an external force. The look of shock/surprise I felt must have been evident for them to see. Helena gave me the briefest of moments to absorb this, did she really say that our evolution was, 'Interrupted by an external force'

Her expanded explanation soon followed. Although we did not evolve from any of the apes living today, we share characteristics with chimpanzees, gorillas, and orangutans, these are collectively known as the great apes. We evolved from Homo heidelbergensis, the common ancestor we share with Neanderthals, who are our closest extinct relative. I got the feeling she was ready to explain everything, and in minute detail, however she was interrupted by Olin who brought on a swift closure. He took the floor and stated clearly, "You will find, understand, and appreciate what the theory gave us". This stern statement was at odds with the accompanying soft gaze. Craving more, I simply said, "How so?"

In a measured response he told me that the theory would be the saving of humanity and the planet we share. With my newfound skills for observation and ability to process information quickly and find resolutions, I was ready to access the theory. He told me all the files needed for this had already been downloaded to me. Once again, I must have looked or gave off the signals of confusion. If I concentrated on accessing information, I would be able to open the files, my mind now worked like a huge filing cabinet.

To test this, I closed my eyes, shadows of headings were visible, and within each one lay the information I needed. Now this is where it gets really weird, as if everything I was seeing was totally mundane and normal. He advised me to avoid reading the information contained in each document and instead focus on understanding it. With an all-knowing smile he said, "Don't worry Danny, you will see what I mean", the quizzical look came and went. I found a level of trust and belief in what he told me. I was excited and nervous as to what this newfound skill would reveal. Would it supply me with all the answers to the questions I was starting to develop. My gaze then turned back to the others who sat their quietly and with an air of contentment coupled with satisfaction on their faces. Olin announced that they would be ending the event now, he reassured me again that all the answers would come, and to be patient with the access I had been given.

I awoke again, reactively checking the time on my phone, with a second look it displayed 16:16. It felt like I had been inside the event for much longer, the information and conversations I had were incredibly intense. I made a mental note to ask them about this next time, then I realised they hadn't asked me if I was ok to be contacted again, something else to worry about. I remained stationary, gathering my thoughts, a couple of things didn't sit right about this last event. Olin who seems to be the most senior of the three men delivered the three keys to a better life, which I fully understood. The most important part, accessing the theory behind the 62.87 evolution disturbance was initially left for Helena, who was clearly the most junior in rank. Another item that puzzled me, then hit me like an out-of-control formula 1 car on ice, and with a blindfolded driver. If the ripple effect is as monumental as it obviously is, my knowing everything, and what I am about to access, means the future will undoubtedly change.

This means, or could mean, their future may not exist. Depending on what I choose to do with the knowledge I now have, or I may have, 'will' change everything. This is more than weird, and ridiculously monumental if I were to get it all wrong. What I have seen so far is a perfect world where humanity has finally got through its growing pains, its rebellious teenage years have passed and finally created utopia for all mankind. Maybe this is a test for me, I could probably end this now by not accessing the files regarding the 62.87 Theory. Perhaps, I shouldn't do anything until the next event if indeed there is going to be one. Suddenly, another racing driver hit me on a blind bend. Toni was coming over on Monday, because of this, I would not be free to access an event. In the end I decided I was going to sleep on it, but then who was I kidding, I wanted the knowledge more than anything.

What follows in the next chapter is my attempt to relay to you the 62.87 Theory. I extracted this information from the files that are now stored somewhere in my brain. I have added some background explanatory notes that I hope, and trust will help you with the understanding. I spent most of the following day accessing the 62.87 Theory, I justified it to myself that having the knowledge and doing something with it would not impact on the future whatever that may be.

"The best way to keep a prisoner from escaping is to make sure he never knows he's in prison."

Fyodor Dostoyevsky

Chapter 9
62.87 Theory

Which coloured pill did you select.

Well, that doesn't really matter now, you're here and that's the main thing. When I say it doesn't matter, of course it does really. Those who skipped a major part of the book will read this in isolation, and without the enlightenment the others have gained. If you favoured the blue pill, you would hopefully read this chapter with open eyes and appreciate this in the context of the events that have happened so far. For those who have omitted the previous chapters, I hope you will read this critical piece with a fair and open mind. It's critical as the theory, from an unknown author, provides the blueprint for humanity's path forward. It is this theory that will divide science and our current structure of societies. This divide will exist until it is ratified by science and accepted as the truth. It will be difficult for some to accept as it destroys their currently held beliefs. Once you have understood this chapter you will be able to argue for or against its claims. Following this, I hope you will return to chapter 3, where I continue with an explanation of how I was given this precious charge.

For those who opted for the red pill, I surmise you will have already made up your mind and will read this chapter with the sole purpose of ripping it apart. Proving to yourself and others that it is a joke, and a danger to the free world. You may think that it's a glorified brand of communism. This will give you another reason to buy every copy available, then proceed to collect every copy you can find, from every school, every library and every person's hand. Place a wooden stake in the ground and rejoice together around the funeral pyre as they are burned. Well, if nothing else it will boost up my 14% market share.

Before I get to explain the theory as best I can, there are a few things to understand and appreciate. Once these are with you, it will make better sense and help put things in context further. Recently, I saw a promotion on Facebook for a t-shirt which made me chuckle, I may have given it a small laugh in recognition, but the post added a few of their own laughing emojis. In letters that filled the front area it said, 'I can explain it to you, but I can't understand it for you'. Now that's not meant as a put-down in any way, but a warning some of this gets a little heavy. Around 76% of people will understand the theory after a single read through. I have complete confidence in your ability to fully understand this, so read on and open your mind to another way of thinking. Don't worry if you fall into the group that require a second read. Those who find themselves in this group should be proud, it simply means your learning style differs slightly. Why would you be classed as proud, well that's because you've owned it and not conformed merely to 'fit in'.

The word 'generations' as a plural are used a lot throughout this book. We sometimes use the term generations as a measure, but like many things we can only think of them in single numbers. Looking backwards, our great, great grandparents may have worked down a mine and fought in the first world war. Historical events help us to calculate the context and appreciate the measurement. Looking forward, we may refer to something we have built stating it will last for generations. We also use this term as another measure. A good example, in question form is, 'Do you consider that we have a better education system than our parents had?' We also want better things for our children and their children, but again we find it difficult to see too much further down our gene line.

This chapter will probably be the most divisive for some. It finally proves beyond all doubt that there is no god or gods. In my early teens I began to question the stories I had been told as a child. I went to a Church of England school; this meant a drip feed of mild brainwashing had begun. Fortunately though, it was never forced with a strong determination. I was also fortunate that my parents never really sat on one side or the other. An art teacher that I liked would make some insightful quips at paintings that depicted scenes from the bible. When I was studying for my A-levels, which would place me aged 16 to 18, we would take time to just sit and chat with him. He never told us to either believe or not, and most of the arguments against religion came from the three of us who were studying. I think that was the intended purpose, with free unencumbered minds you are allowed to question everything. I also remember that he constantly carried around a mug of tea, although many knew this contained something much stronger.

The theory relies on scientifically proven research, please don't worry if this subject was beyond you during your school days. I have endeavoured to translate the theory from pure understanding, it is best viewed or thought about as three components or elements that constitutes the whole. Each component is divided by scientific research, although they are all connected by the result. The primary conclusion is that our evolutionary development suffered a disturbance, and it was interfered with at a point in time. Essentially, human evolution was re-engineered to serve a specific purpose, it is this intention that we need to understand.

You must be sceptical about what you hear, it's only right that you are. A scientific theory is an explanation of an aspect of the natural world. There's a great saying, always listen twice, first what's being said, then who said it. I later discovered that the theory had its origins in a much-ridiculed hypothesis of an evolutionary change or disturbance. Any scientific claim must be repeatedly tested and corroborated in accordance with a scientific method. This must be applied using accepted protocols of observation, measurement, and evaluation of the results. The 62.87 theories were repeatedly tested over dozens of years, every set of results continually validated the claim.

In summary:

Before I continue any further, I would like to provide a synopsis of the theory. What follows is the supporting information I found within the various folders. These were provided by the author to explain or validate the claim. I am not a scientist nor am I here to promote the claims, I am only here as a chosen voice for them.

In my opinion, the quote by Arthur Koestler effectively encapsulates the fundamental principles of the theory and provides a rationale for its necessity.

"The evolution of the brain not only overshot the needs of prehistoric man, it is the only example of evolution providing a species with an organ which it does not know how to use."

Arthur Koestler

What If Charles Darwin Was Wrong?

'The author provided conclusive proof in the form of previously unexplored scientific awareness'.

The 62.87 Theory used the findings of Charles Darwin, which simply proved the theory of evolution and how a species progresses and improves through generations. But, and here's a big but. His work, On the Origin of Species which was published on 24 November 1859 was based on observed evidence at that time. What Darwin could not have foreseen was the evidence I observed some 2,193 years after its publication. I doubt if Darwin would have believed his eyes, or maybe, just maybe it's what he truly envisaged.

The key to unlocking everything within the theory asks us to look forward, and much further than we have ever dared look before.

Once we consider this it becomes starkly apparent that the human species has not followed these same rules. Evidence of the turning point for humanity was primarily when we adopted organised farming, and of course the digital age. Both occurred far too early within our overall evolutionary progression. Among all the possible theories for this, the theory finds that intervention from a third party must be responsible.

Here's where the 62.87 Theory really comes into its own. The author provides evidence that categorically proves how this fracture with Darwin's laws, and the intervention occurred. Hold on to your seats while I explain how the intervention was caused by non-other than humanity, if you like…ourselves.

Before you burst a blood vessel screaming that Darwin cannot be wrong. Human evolution was interfered with at some point and by a partially unknown method. The theory goes on to prove that the normal evolution of human brains was given an implant of modified embryonic cells. These not only accelerated its development of intelligence, but they were also either pre-programmed with certain events, or they were susceptible to them. I was able to witness how the entire force of humanity, along with the science they possess some 2,034 years from now strive for a single objective, which is to solve this problem.

The 62.87 Theory provided the solution to the task, but not the capability, future generations would solve this and bask in the glory the achievement would bring. The author knew that humanity would benefit enormously whilst on this road to discovery. The solution was neatly split into three distinct paths. The first being to develop the cell structure that would be implanted into early humans. This cell structure would need to carry further important steps, and these are:

1. Proceed to multiply throughout humans in an organised method.

2. Carry pre-programmed code to instigate certain events at set times or be triggered by external means.

The next two parts spurned completely new areas of science, the first being the reason I am now able to bring this to you. They needed to create a vessel that would transport the cell structure and complete the impregnation of early humans. They had been able to create the means of reverse time travel. Through CDT technology they successfully moved a device backwards in time, this went on to place a probe into my brain. Subsequently, through current technology we were able to communicate. I know all of this sounds mad, crazy perhaps, but think about what we have been able to achieve in the past 40 years. Since the birth of the digital age, our world has changed enormously. Just think what we could go on to achieve at the same or expanded growth rate, and in 2,034 years. They have mastered time, space, and matter to their own benefit, what could be next.

The third new area of science relates to selecting the optimum time to undertake and complete the impregnation of the cells. This is possibly their most difficult challenge, as they are dealing with the unknown, and a time that cannot speak directly to them.

And finally, somewhere either in the 62.87 Theory or within other documents or stories, they have taken it upon themselves to create something so groundbreaking that it almost defies description, but more about this later.

To protect their future, and that of the planet along with the universe, they created laws which encased science and technology. This alone sounds crazy when you say it aloud, but I understood the need. As they hurtle down the road of creation, I found it went against one of their primary rules. I may be missing something, but this sounds wrong, anyway it's important for you to know and understand. A summary of their monumental challenges are here, in the triad definition:

1. **Create the cell structure & pre-programmed DNA.**

2. **Create the means to transport this precious cargo.**

3. **Identify the optimum time for deployment.**

Well, that's the introduction done, the remainder of this chapter explains the hypothesis.

As we know, Charles Darwin defined evolution as to 'descent with modification', the idea that species change over time, give rise to new species, and share a common ancestor. The mechanism that Darwin proposed for the evolutionary path, is neat little thing called, natural selection. If you consider the food chain, in the wilds of Africa and specifically now the restricted savanna area, the lion is depicted as being top of the chain. Lions are a top predator in the savanna, top predators can also be keystone species, or species that are essential for keeping the ecosystem balanced. Lions control the population of primary and secondary animals. Without them hunting the grazing animals, the population of grazers would grow out of control, the knock-on effect can be catastrophic for various fauna and flora that require this balance.

The continual evolution of lions has been halted now because of humans, and the indiscriminate spread of civilization over the past couple of centuries. In just a couple of hundred years, we have irreparably damaged this chain that was perfectly balanced. It took millions of years for the lion as we know it today and its predecessors to evolve to this grand position. It's important to remember that their evolution is intrinsically linked to the development and evolution of other animals, along with the vegetation, which is the fuel for everything above it.

Trusting that you accept Darwin is correct, and it was clearly explained and proven to you in school. For those who question this because of their beliefs, we can see evidence of this everywhere we look. Naturalists and zoologists produce highly detailed TV series that show us this evidence in amazing detail. Instead of questioning proven theories they should turn that quizzical eye on their religions that dismiss even the dinosaur age. The demise of dinosaurs perfectly illustrates how fragile a range of species can also be.

At one point, the majority of people thought that the Sun revolved around the Earth, that didn't make it true. At one point the majority of people thought that the Earth was flat, that didn't make it true. Today, the majority of people on Earth believe in various gods, and once again, that doesn't make it true. Arguing that something is true because a lot of people believe in it is a logical fallacy called, an 'appeal to the people' (argumentum ad populum), or argument to popularity. Something doesn't become true because many people believe it. The idea must stand on its own merit and be proven by science.

Humanity may have halted or interrupted the evolution of many species; their costs has propelled our own evolution into overdrive. That's the disclaimer part done and dusted. Before I hit you with the theory which simply developed the concept of re-engineered evolution, I just need to talk about numbers.

That's how the author's files explained Darwin's law's and how they function. It also states how they have been irreparably damaged by humanity. The next section follows humanity's possible development into the future. Numbers are vital to the theory, and it's crucial that we truly understand our place within them.

The universe is around 13.7 to 13.8 billion years old, and our galaxy, the Milky Way formed around 13.61 billion years ago. Most galaxies began to form around 10 billion years after the formation of the universe. Our solar system, with our centralised Sun developed around 4.6 billion years ago. And we know that Earth, being one of the eight planets in our solar system formed some 4.543 billion years ago. Now these are all enormous numbers and it's incredibly difficult to comprehend that amount of time. Even if we drew a timeline, it doesn't make it easy to relate to our own existence. Here's the bit to get worried about, in around 5 billion years, the Sun will run out of hydrogen. But don't worry too much as our star is currently in the most stable phase of its life cycle. Conversely, because of humanity and the spread of civilizations that are disobediently polluting and choking our planet, Earth is currently in its most unstable period.

Astronomers estimate there are about 4 billion stars in the Milky Way alone. For everything else we can only have an educated guess. Currently, we can only observe an estimated 15% of the observable universe. This 15% could be a wild exaggeration of the fact, what we can actually see is a tiny element of what's really out there. We have deployed super telescopes like Webb and Hubble; but even these have vast limitations on what can be observed. Considering this, there are 400 billion trillion stars in the universe, and to give that its correct term 400 quintillion. Again, like time it's a number that's difficult to get your head around. These are enormous whichever way you look at them, and it's easy to be scared to think that we are on one planet orbiting one of those sparkling lights. Putting that into a decimal format it's 4 followed by 23 zeros. It may also help you get your head around this if you think of it this way. Current estimates claim there exist roughly 30,000 stars for each grain of sand on Earth. This number will undoubtedly increase as we discover more galaxies with more powerful telescopes. Some people find these numbers too enormous to comprehend. For me, it's invigorating and leaves me desperately wanting to know more.

Putting all of this into a further context, we need to ask, how big is a billion. If you were to count to one billion, and start one, two, three, four and so on until you reached ten, and then started again, one, two, three, four etc. That's one count every second for every minute of the day, day and night. It would take a ridiculous 31.8 years to reach one billion. Also, if you think of the world's richest people who individually own hundreds of $billions. That's not just ridiculous, it's disgusting.

You may have seen this passage before, but it sums all of this up perfectly. If the Earth formed at midnight, and the present moment is the next midnight, 24 hours later, modern humans have been around since 11:59:59pm, which can be shown as just one second before the lights go out. The author of the theory used these numbers along with others I just didn't understand. I hope this is all registering so far, the author then moved on to relate further sets of numbers to our own evolution.

The enormity of space is often measured in light-years. Simply said, light travels through interstellar space at 186,000 miles (300,000 kilometres) per second and 5.88 trillion miles (9.46 trillion kilometres) per year. To put all that into context, if you were to travel at the speed of light it would take you 1.3 seconds to reach the Moon. It would take you 8.3 minutes to reach our Sun, and incredibly you would have to travel 2,000 years to reach the edge of the Milky Way. 90 billion years would get you to the edge of the observable universe.

Approximately 300,000 years ago, the first Homo Sapiens, anatomically modern humans arose alongside other hominid relatives. These modern humans, our direct ancestors originated in

Africa within the past 200,000 years. As we formed and developed in accordance with the evolutionary path Darwin set out, 'descent with modification', the following can be seen. Around 12,000 years ago we developed from the 'hunter gatherer' phase, to planting seeds. Although, this was not the case for all regions across the planet. Language in very basic forms had longed helped the species to organize groups, and the population began to expand rapidly. The world's population today is 1,860 times the size of what it was 12,000 years ago, when it stood around 4 million. And, as I write this, the population of the planet currently stands at 7.59 billion. That's a rapid expansion that may put a further dimension on to the theory of Charles Darwin. We quickly became the dominant species, that is despite our physical limitations. We did, however possess certain attributes like superior intelligence and dexterity.

The author painted a clear picture with numbers, the main being that our species could exist on this planet for billions of years. We look back on time and see thousands of years as large numbers. The three or even four-dimensional picture I saw allowed me to look back on time from the reverse end of a multifunctional telescope. What I mean by this is that time must be viewed as a whole, and that means stepping forwards millions, if not billions of years, and then looking backwards. We are not familiar with this concept; it takes time and training to accomplish it freely.

Most people don't really want the truth. They just want constant reassurance that what they believe is the truth.

I have mentioned a few times the importance of the digital age to the development of humanity, and where it could possibly take us. Numbers showed us our place within the universe and the timeline that governs and defines everything. We have just stopped crawling on all fours and took our first baby-steps into our journey of discovery. Now begin to put all the pieces together.

The Digital Age

Another Charles, Charles Babbage was also a genius beyond his years as a mathematician and inventor. He is credited with having conceived the first automatic digital computer during the mid-1830s. These were plans developed for the Analytical Engine, at that time there would have only been a handful of people that would have understood what this meant. Today, computers are unrecognizable from his designs of the Analytical Engine or even from the huge computers of the 20th century that occupied vast rooms, such as the Electronic Numerical Integrator and Calculator.

Texas Instruments first used a microchip in Air Force computers and the Minuteman Missile in 1962. They later used chips to produce the first electronic portable calculators. I remember as a child in the 1970's having a Casio calculator and entering the number 37818, then turning it upside down to show the word. In the summer of 1980, my own life changed forever when I got a Sinclair ZX80 computer. My sister and I would spend hours methodically typing in lines of basic code to create a game that we then stored on a separate audio cassette and recorder. If you're younger than 45 please do a bit of research to see what we went through, but the results were worth it, at the time that is. Sometimes, 1980 seems like yesterday for me, I can see personally the development of computers and what we have been able to achieve by having them. Computers have changed every aspect of our lives, for good or bad, but what we can't do, what we can't stop is their progression. Computers are not a life form, but they too abide by the theory of Darwin to a point, albeit they soon may create their own improvements, and independent of us.

Now take one very small step forwards and we move less than 40 years. Our current blindfolded view of time and future planning doesn't really expand more than a few decades, or at best a few hundred years. We are proud of ourselves when we create a new trainline or powerplant that will see its use into the next 30 to 40 years. To appreciate the power we now hold, look at your mobile phone, laptop, or even the information that is instantly available simply through voice. I can ask my smart speaker for the temperature in Moscow or the size of Neptune, or indeed any other random question you can think of. As soon as I have finished the question, a voice that I understand perfectly, not only tells me the answer, but also offers additional information to me. Firstly, it's the computing power to recognise my individual voice, with any accent I may have. It understands my question, it then retrieves the correct information, or as best that can be found. The answer is then spoken to me in a completely legible voice. These devices can now operate connected equipment and devices around our homes or offices. They were first introduced in 2014 in the US and 2016 in the UK. Move on a couple of years and they seem to be everywhere, sales reached a record high of 146.9 million in 2019, up 70% from 2018.

Our lives are changing, and we are increasingly reliant on this sort of technology. Now, let yourself go for a moment and think what computers could do in another 40, or even another 400, and for that matter 4 million, even 4 billion years. What will our lives be like, what further developments can be achieved. With computers, our evolution and development has radically changed and broken forever what Darwin observed in nature. No wonder really that our bodies and minds are in turmoil. Simply put, we may not have been designed to accelerate this quickly. Our mental health and the fuel we consume through food is having an untold amount of damage, and it's damage that may never be reversed.

Numbers have already shown us that human life could exist on Earth for close to 5 billion years. 5,000,000,000 years means that since the birth of the digital age, the one that we created, we have potentially only witnessed 0.000000000008 of its potential lifespan. Please retain that open mind when I tell you that in the summer of

2018, I was allowed to communicate with people 2,034 years in the future. You would think that I have finally lost my mind, and it simply couldn't happen. Incredibly, it didn't stop there, I was allowed to view in graphic detail what Earth looks like and how civilisations function in the future. It is a utopian existence, and one I now crave.

We now need to place both of those two periods of time onto the same counting period. 12,000 years ago, when humanity first handled farming tools and 1979 when computers first began to change our lives. These are the two starting points, the finishing point could be, let's say conservatively four billion years from now. If you analyse these figures, the first noticeable thing will be that you would require a microscope to look for the delta between the two. Secondly, as we are unable to even comprehend what computers will be capable of in the future, we would be unable to create a meaningful graph. That's not to say we couldn't speculate, although the safest bet would be to draw a vertical growth path over four billion years. Each generation of computers are currently intertwined with our own development. But what happens when you extract humans and allow computers to develop at their own rate, and we merely tag along for the ride.

The introduction to this section provides a synopsis or summary of the theory. Remember these are my words and not theirs. You should remember this is my understanding of the information available within the downloaded files. As I dive deeper into the files more, I know that further information will be sourced and brought to light.

62.87 The Basis of the Theory

Previously, I explained that our lifespan can best be traced back around 300,000 years, this is when the first Homo Sapiens developed. Although, it took a further 100,000 years before modern humans, as we would recognise them originated in Africa. Since our earliest identifiable point, our evolution has outpaced everything else around us. Language and our use of tools aided this acceleration. In certain regions around the world this progression and development has either slowed or increased at an extraordinary rate. Importantly, we can only associate true intelligence in our species around 12,000 years ago, simply because farming requires planning and organisation. It's far more than just planting seeds and hoping for the best.

Farming requires a societal structure to support it. The structure requires a great deal of organisation to function effectively. When and where to plant seeds, when to harvest, and who produces the food. Further support is needed to manufacture the specialised tools, where to store the reaped grain, how to mill the grain etc. Since our scientifically re-engineered evolution sparked to life there has been no stopping us, although our increase has not been universal. If you look at places like Somalia where water remains the only currency between life and death, and millions of children and babies die in excruciating pain each year from malnutrition. In these places, in these areas human development has almost halted. We tend to look away when we see TV pictures showing their plight. Without a date stamp, we could easily be fooled into thinking these were images taken around 6,000 years ago. Travel just 6,000 miles to the heart of London or any other developed country. There we see the extremes of luxury and wealth, where it is measured in garish watches and handbags that cost the equivalent of a nurse's annual salary.

As human societies began to spread across the planet, over thousands of generations modifications could be seen and recorded, and all in accordance with Darwin's laws. Modifications in things like skin colour, facial features, hair colour, and eye colours and even physical size could all be seen and noted. These are simply adaptions to suit the climate and what the natural world provided them. These are evident as we spread to the four corners of the world. Other traits can be noted which were crucial to our development, these primarily relate to problem solving. If you look back over the centuries and map geographically where most discoveries and inventions where made, it makes for interesting reading. Everything from gunpowder to the steam engine, antibiotics to powered flight. The correlation is clear, as you move further from the source of humanity's beginning in Africa, our development accelerated. There are, however, certain fundamentals that have remained, and these are crucial.

Once we began to farm, the population expanded to create further variations along with separate languages and defined borders and countries. As we continue our timeline, certain individual characteristics became unified such as numbers and counting. Individual dialects, along with their own alphabets can also be noted. During these thousands of years, we grew further apart and warring factions grew larger and more lethal.

As we draw closer to our time in history, there are two defining moments, pinpoints that caused a shockwave across the civilized world. The first resulted in a seismic ripple effect that changed humanity between 1760 and 1840. The industrial revolution produced mass quantities of goods and equipment, and with each new invention humanity took increasingly greater steps forward. The second, should be evident by now, the birth of the digital age that happened, amazingly in our lifetime. In thousands if not millions of years' time, mankind will look back to this birth of the digital age. Future generations will be able to look back and see your involvement during the very birth. Recordable history in the form of data will show how it shaped our lives, and unavoidably, for every human from this day forward.

Another unifying system is our global measurement of time and seasons. Just as our ancestors redialled and reset the clock to BC and

AD, in the future, they reset their clocks to 1979/80. The birth of the mass digital age was seen as the turning point. Sadly, it would be many centuries before we saw beyond our divides, and finally reunited to rebuild humanity. Irony popped its head up here too, the digital age is set to free us in ways that we can't even begin to imagine, although this period of our history is also leaving black marks in the record books. It will be many more centuries before our individual societies finally come back together after thousands of years of growing apart.

Some people mistakenly believe that we use almost all our brains power and ability. It's correct to say that it's a myth, future science will show that we currently use around 40% of the brains productive power. We have only just started to test and expand our brain's power and true potential. There is a whole section on this subject in a previous chapter, plus more to follow within the groundbreaking evidence. You will see that we can do much more with our brains than we ever thought possible. This is not a sci-fi idea of how to make a movie more popular or challenging. This is part of Darwin's law that he, or for that matter we, could never imagine. Where our brains will take us in the future cannot be calculated or foreseen, and when I say future, I mean millions/billions of years from now. Remember I said that we have only just taken our first baby-steps in the equivalent of mankind's life on Earth. What will happen when we begin to walk and eventually run free. Maybe that's for me to discover I have no idea.

The Bombshell Moment

It's mind-blowing to even consider for a moment what the author claimed within this complex and intertwined set of theories. When I began to appreciate them, my first and understandable reaction was to completely refute them. I argued with myself that it would of course be feasible for these seismic occurrences to have happened naturally. If you like in accordance with a form of evolution or natural selection. If the human brain, along with the crucial trigger points were indeed externally influenced, then human ingenuity really does have no limitations. Allow me to explain further, it may help visualise this before you explain it to others. Just as I was allowed to communicate with our descendants or lineage some 2,034 years in the future. Extrapolating their use of advanced science and technology which allows them to bend time, means that future generations, breeding more advanced science and technology will be able to bend time even further and importantly reshape human history. It's a self-perpetuating cycle of improvements, advanced generations righting the errors of previous ones.

I haven't asked them yet, but is it possible that Albert Einstein, Nikola Tesla, the Wright Brothers, Alan Turing have all been contacted via future development in CDT technology. We could even travel further back in time when we find other outstanding visionaries such as Galileo Galilei and Isaac Newton among many others. What about Bill Gates or Elon Musk in our own time, only they know.

What this means is that our current development is inherently dependent on future technology. You and I owe everything to future intelligence, without their science and technology we would still be, well who knows. I did try and warn you that an open mind would be essential for this part. This, however, is merely the entrée. What came next and what I was shown really knocked me sideways, I think I accessed it with my mouth open. It probably illustrated the gigantic rift between them and me, it probably had them thinking that they selected the wrong subject for their experiments.

Accepting that our current and future intelligence is due only to an external influence may be almost impossible to understand. When I began to access the files regarding the next section, I ran out of question marks in my own thinking. We now move on to the creation of intelligence, and the constituent parts of the cells that would be implanted.

62.87 THE FIRST COMPONENT:

Create The Cell Structure & Programmed DNA

The challenge was to create a section of pre-programmed DNA/RNA that would sit within a cell structure. Our ancestors would then be impregnated with this cell structure that has travelled backwards through time. The human brain as we know it today will then be created. Somehow, it will sabotage and invade the existing brain only to recreate the wonderful organ as we know it. This future man-made cell structure will need to integrate with the hosts existing DNA. Scientists will need to ensure that the hosts immune system also accepts this invasion,

And there you have it, the most outrageous science experiment there will ever be. Although, to be more accurate, the most successful science experiment ever. Proof of its success is evident within every human who ever had the thought, **I wonder if**.

Deoxyribonucleic acid (DNA) molecules are made up of two strands that wind around each other to form a double helix, they carry the genetic information that controls an organism's development and function. Every living thing needs to grow, develop and reproduce, the code or instructions to do this are contain within these DNA molecules. These instructions are present inside each cell and are inherited from the parents to their offspring. The DNA molecules are extremely long and hence without the right packaging, they cannot fit into cells. Because of this, DNA is tightly coiled to produce formations referred to as chromosomes. Every chromosome has a single DNA molecule. In humans, there are 23 pairs of chromosomes that are present within the nucleus of the cells.

Our brains, which weigh around 3 pounds in the average adult, and that have a highly tuned system of cells, neurons, glial cells, and nerves, are the most developed organs out of all species. They have an incredible network of electrical activity that controls everything we do, from breathing to blinking, speech to walking. It's an organ that controls its own energy source through oxygen enriched blood. Even if the body is injured it takes measures to protect itself above all others. It's constructed using around 60% fat, with the remaining 40% coming from a combination of water, protein, carbohydrates, and salts. Following the deployment of the re-engineered DNA cells, each generation of brain will improve on the previous one until. Well, we don't really know what the end product will look like and, dare I say it, be capable of.

'Following publication of the theory, all strands of the scientific community concluded that an external source had implanted an embryonic cell cluster into early humans.'

Whichever future generation created the implant, they did so knowing how much credit would be owed to their ancestors. The theory initially mapped the critical early trigger points, although as all good science should, it invited further scrutiny. They instructed future generations to argue and challenge every point, and with each generation and improvements in technology, further trigger points would be established. One aspect that cannot be underestimated is the required integration and acceptance by the host. I know first-hand what it's like to be invaded by an uninvited foreign body, my own CDT device is evidence. Unfortunately, medical trials would be difficult if not impossible, they would be dealing with numerous patients with the inability to communicate.

Now before we have all the different brands of religion claiming this for their own. This book and all the revelations within it, is not a rule book of how you are to live your life, or rules that teach us morality. What I witnessed, puts every religion to shame. It's about working to a common goal, where freedom and all those amazing attributes of a society I listed at the beginning of the book mean more than any other fairy tale.

Key Requirement #1: Thought & Language

To begin with, science needed to support the claims of the author by establishing the primary trigger points. Proving these were indeed external would help rationalize and focus future work. Triggers began when humans created, and began to use specific tools, use of those tools would initiate greater dexterity and improved control between brain and hand. It was around this point that they believed **structured thought** entered our brains and our abilities. I would find out later that this remains an unknown to them, and something the second part of the theory mapped out.

Think about that voice in your mind that is currently reading this. Your voice or thoughts enable you to understand, sort, organise, and remember segments of this sentence. It also enables you to relate this to the paragraph. You are also gathering this into other thoughts, as you read this you may also be thinking that the use of grammar is very poor, or everything this guy is saying is beginning to make sense. As I am writing this my mind is picturing you reading this. How thoughts can travel and how unique are our thoughts. Also, your thought voice is different from your spoken voice, why is that.

Because I have now mentioned this, it means it will gain a higher ranking within your memory and subsequent recall. These thoughts or voices help us to control everything we do. 95% of our decision making is done within the subconscious part of our brain, your decision to want that next coffee when offered is more often a swift decision. Our central nervous systems are built to operate without direct thought. This frees up space within our brains to think. In a stable mind it can do great things and achieve incredible accomplishments. But in an unstable mind the voice can cause havoc and destruction. Contemplate this for a moment, somewhere in human history, the first thought would have formulated and eventually be replicated by others.

Was that thought pain, thirst, or hunger, whatever it was, it would have been the first-time language meant something more than a simple grunt. Early humans would have developed subtle differences in sounds, those would be used to identify things around them. Language and intelligent thought, only occur in one species. Humans are unique as our vocabulary knows no limits, the theory stated that the structure and development of our brains could not have achieved this without either an external factor, or programming from an external source.

It is evident that our thoughts can now understand and solve extremely complex problems, couple this with language and you have the beginnings of education. In the beginning, this would have been the cornerstone of our development and improvement between generations. Although this would have been extremely slow and almost stagnated for periods, that was until we come across the external triggers, which were referred to earlier.

Recognising items, and the processing of things like constructed dialog allowed mankind at that time to navigate the world around them. We make sense of the world through thought and language. Let me explain, if I said think of a red cup, you can picture a red cup, you can read the words red cup to form language, the words can be spelt out in your mind. Here's the most important aspect to all of this. We now understand what a red cup is, this means we can explain it to others. This function alone sets a staggering distance between us and all other creatures. Each aspect of thought is now wired into our brains. Our ability as a species to master thought and language has happened in almost the blink of an eye. The same must be said for our development into the digital age.

The theory claimed that creating thought and associated language would be the most difficult of triggers to design and install, either within the embryonic cell cluster or within the programming of the DNA. It took many years to prove that our brains were designed and eventually manufactured in this way. Somehow, the miraculous cell cluster would be implanted into early humans. Proving it is one thing, creating it is a whole different ball game.

I almost forgot to add the section that linked consciousness and thought to memory building and how that relates to the ability for dreaming. Now whilst we are not the only mammals to dream, we use dreams to sort information that we have recently learnt. This storage also considers the format that enables us to make this retrievable and with speed. I did say this wasn't going to be an easy task, but once humanity accepted it, the entire weight of the scientific community drove it forward. Creating programable DNA was going to be a tough enough ask, and when you add all these other challenges it was made millions of times more so. Science had long been able to modify DNA to remove unwanted and harmful elements such as hereditary abnormalities.

Feelings and emotions are personal to everyone. Some people may fall in love quickly, others may choose to guard their emotions. Once again, we are not the only mammal, or indeed the only living creature that displays emotions. We are continuing to learn more about our neighbours, I don't mean that in a traditional way, in this instance, the term neighbours refers to other living creatures. Loosely engineering the ability to develop feelings and emotions would also be a monumental challenge. Ensuring the cell cluster would generate this hardwiring element within the brain would take coding into a new realm.

Key Requirement #2: Hand Eye Coordination

Hand eye coordination doesn't sound much, and we treat it now as a given. Creating this highly complex skill proved to be anything but a given. Think for a moment what is essentially required. Earlier we praised our basic smart speakers and how they can understand our request and perform elementary tasks, such as play music or turn on a light. Expand that performance power by many millions and you begin to approach what is needed.

Ernő Rubik, a Hungarian architecture professor, invented the Rubik's Cube in 1974 as a teaching tool to help his students understand 3D geometry. A 1981 guide to solving the Rubik's Cube written by a 12-year-old English schoolboy – You Can Do the Cube – sold 1.5 million copies. Max Park of the United States holds the record for the fastest time to solve a 3x3x3 Rubik's cube at 3.13 seconds. There are many astonishing facts around this six-sided puzzle, what's important here is the brain power to not only complete the puzzle, but the coordination of hand, eye, and brain, and with remarkable speed.

This skill when incorporated with others are a key differential between us and other mammals. It's also a learning experience that improves with practice. If we were to give this 'toy' to earlier generations, and even with a simple tutorial, in many situations it would soon lay dormant. Manual dexterity, along with processing speed has improved beyond all measurements. As I sit here typing with barely two fingers, I know Jane can perform touch typing. That is to say, she has mastered a skill to type without looking, but this is further enhanced as she can convert speech to text, and at the speed of normal speech.

Thought and language, hand eye coordination along with many other skills would have to be hard wired into the DNA they were developing. This strand of science also had to incorporate, memory and recall. I had recently taken delivery of a huge array of uninvited filing cabinets that sat somewhere within my brain. My hosts instructed me how to access these, although, typically not in an intuitive way. Designing key components of the brain's function, then coding them into a few cells sounds beyond our capabilities. Each cell would contain its instructions for life within a single DNA block. This incredibly complex set of demands may also not have the benefit of trial and error, but more on this later.

While the first strand of the theory dealt with understanding the pre-programmed trigger points and key requirements. The second component faced an equally daunting mountain to climb. Here they had to create the DNA itself along with the cell structure that would deliver it. This new arm was called Multi-Dimensional Tri-Complex Cell Creation MDTCCC, yep it rolls off the tongue, but don't get hung up on the name. What they were charged with was creating cells that would be implanted into a species that had only just separated from other similar but less equipped ones. Scientists in their tens of thousands worked endlessly within this new area, breakthroughs were followed eagerly by everybody across the globe and in every colony.

I was shown huge laboratories with banks of equipment that resembled CT or MRI scanners we have today. These were accompanied with hundreds of display screens and people gathered in glass walled rooms. I was told that there are 923 facilities of the same magnitude across the colonies, each one was working to develop their own areas of the Tri-Complex element. When I was shown these, I was also told about the 'Tri' part of the theory and the science that supported it.

The second part of this three-way harmony of science and technology would have even a tech savvy person questioning a grip on reality.

62.87 THE SECOND COMPONENT:
Means Of Transportation

The second task would call on other new areas of science and technology. I had witnessed first-hand how they were able to bend time, there is a little more on this at the end of the chapter and a whole lot more later in the book. A Chrono-Diverse-Transponder CDT was at the cutting edge of their technology. In just 70 years they had progressed from merely being able to see into time. At first it was limited to a point in time that had a fixed position, it acted like an anchor for them. Now they were able to transport a highly complex device back over 2,000 years. Not only that, but this device is now sat in my brain communicating with my hosts. I understood that you can't just simply say, let's go back to 1984, you need to have all the correct coordinates. This area of science was the most exciting for them, the initial experiment they performed placed a single grain of sand into a 20cm circumference cup. It was one of the few times that I could detect any external signs of true excitement from them. The alchemy that bent time was based on three coordinates, time, space, and matter.

This ground-breaking experiment was completed in a building they called The Home of Advancement. This building was like a museum, it housed all their history since 1979, every milestone was recorded. I was allowed time to view the various levels within this building that sored higher than I could see. Needless to say, I didn't fully understand any of the science, but they explained what each of the major events were and what they achieved. Space exploration was mind-blowing, and what they had discovered was equally breathtaking. Here's another spoiler, there are no other lifeforms within the universe, well none that we would typically recognise. They had identified planets that had supported life in its past, along with those that will support lifeforms in the future.

Sorry, I digressed from the main topic, it's easily done as I uncover new items and unearth new understanding. As I do, I become as excited as they are. Anyway, a CDT device that needed to act as a carrier would have to travel to a fixed point in time and deploy its priceless cargo. They have no doubt that the technology would follow, although the method of deployment was still unknown. They also had to ensure it was done without unbalancing the anatomical development along with the eco system of the time. There is more on this topic to come, so far, they seemed to resemble myself as they kept finding more questions than they had answers. A section of this science considered a deployment option that would be like the education stimulants that they currently use to great effect. This may solve the problem of sufficient deployment like herd immunity or herd transmission. Crucially, they had to ensure the cell cluster would not be rejected by the new host body. As with section one, there was a high probability that testing would be prohibited as the dangers could be incalculable.

I contemplated, as I am sure they have, deployment will have to be done using either a form of robotics, or manually. Manually, means a <u>person</u> travelling back many thousands of years, to a time that would be wholly inhospitable. There they would deploy a cell structure into, well who knows how many recipients who would likely see them as an aggressor. Once complete, they would need to return to their own time, utilising a reverse form and calculation of time, space and matter.

I learnt from the countless documents and files that I had, that all of these challenges were known and understood. They had plans supported by contingency plans which in turn had hugely complex risk assessments and just as complex approval protocols. At any point in time, any colony member would have full visibility of the progress and advancements of any possible solution. It was highly impressive and illustrated what could be achieved if humanity progressed with a common goal.

There you have it; the first two requirements had been identified and understood. Human DNA would be developed and created that would be pre-programmed to trigger certain events in the history of humanity. Alternatively, external sources may be developed or created that would trigger these events. This modified DNA would be carried in a cell cluster that would multiply to create the brain as we know it today. They understood the risks associated with this and have meticulous plans to safeguard each eventuality. The second requirement concerned the method of transportation and subsequent deployment into this newly identified species. They have begun to master reverse time travel as I can now testify to. I have yet to understand my role in this, but I am sure it is part of their master plan.

The next hurdle for them remains a considerable challenge, as they need to answer the when, where, along with how many. The next section was established to provide the answers.

62.87 THE THIRD COMPONENT:

Identify The Optimum Time For Deployment

This area spawned another new division of science, this one also carried an obscurely named branch, Preceding Human Analysis. It would have to pinpoint the 'how', how many of the species would have to be impregnated. The 'when', when in time will this be, every condition would need to be right to sustain and grow the brain. And the 'where', where geographically does this need to be, this could be in various locations across a given region. Critically, each answer to these relatively simple questions would have to overlap the others.

Regarding the when question, now you may think it would be when a creature of some description first dragged itself from a swamp and began to live on dry land. The world's oldest brain was found in a fossil of a three eyed creature that resembled a prawn. Dating back some 506 million years it had a detectable central nervous system. Every living creature requires a brain, natural selection would have taken care of our development path up to the point of our distinguishable ancestors. Consequently, they knew the point of time would be post 200,000 years when modern humans were identifiable from other similar species. It would also be before 12,000 years ago when intelligent farming was recognised.

There's a significant time span between the two known parameters: 200,000 years and 12,000 years. We also need to note the delicate fragility of the population between these points. Too few and you risk the implantation not taking. Likewise, too high and a population runs similar risks and a further divide between species. This time factor would also be impacted by further peaks and troughs in populations caused by other factors, such as climate and geological changes.

As if creating the human brain wasn't enough of a challenge. This element of science would be just as challenging, and again produced various new forms of science in mathematics and modelling. Parts of this new area of science yielded better results and at a faster pace than others. Computer modelling is easier to substantiate probable quantities when you are dealing with historical facts and human development. Archaeology had long understood more about our ancestors and the world they inhabited. They also showed me advancements in Chrono-Diverse-Transponder technology that was allowing them to map time and events far better.

Some of the rigid locations and time reference points that were essential for CDT travel, would become less rigid as the technology could estimate points to a better degree. This meant that travellers could select points in time between certain dates. This in turn gave them far more flexibility which would speed up the science. I was able to extract files and knowledge from their Home of Advancement, each one served to give them complete assurance that the 62.87 Theory was absolute. Every scientific achievement simply confirmed the statement that humanity's timeline and the birth of the digital age broke every rule set out by Darwin.

On several occasions, I have mentioned that the author of the theories also provided conclusive evidence that supported the claim. Critically, it pointed out that it lay within previously unexplored scientific awareness, and this evidence was already in the public domain. Essentially, it said that the knowledge was always there, it was just that nobody had previously joined the dots up.

The Author Provided Conclusive Proof In The Form Of Previously Unexplored Scientific Awareness

This section is probably <u>the</u> most crucial part of this entire book. It validates the primary position and the cornerstone of the claims made by this unknown author. Proving the one fact will thereby validate everything else claimed. The creation of the human brain was outside the rules of evolution and the improvement logic set out by Charles Darwin. Our own science is continually finding new facts about our brains and stating that we still don't know its full potential.

The key timelines in our evolution have been pointed out several times. Approximately 200,000 years ago when we can be identified as a unique species. 12,000 years ago, when we developed organised farming. And finally, the digital age that occurred during our own generation. If we could transport a computer back in time to these two previously noted times, we would undoubtedly observe the same opinion. There would be a complete lack of appreciation for this box of 'witchcraft'. We understand and appreciate what this technology can do. We probably understand how computers function even if we couldn't write code. Today, our brains have been exposed to computers and related technologies, they are now running free and creating more.

Now here's the piece of evidence that cannot be disputed. If we were to perform an MRI scan on an individual today. Irrespective of education levels, social skills or general brain activity it would appear identical to that of a farmer some 12,000 years ago. However, if we look at our brains mass, today's measurement would stand at 1,350 cubic centimetres. Compare this to our friendly farmer which would boast a superior 1,450 cc.

We are, if you like only just beginning to grow into our brains and understanding its true potential. Critically, our brains mass is reducing, however its performance power is evidently increasing. Was Charles Darwin wrong, it's time for you to decide.

FUTURE INTELLIGENCE NEUROLOGICAL EXPANSION DEVELOPMENT

Just as I was getting to grasp this threefold aspect of science and its implications for our entire existence on this planet, they threw another curved ball into the mix. I mentioned that the 62.87 began as a hypothesis which was then scientifically proven beyond any doubt. The same author added a phase within the theory which they knew science could not currently provide. Now you could argue that every part of the theory and what they were trying to develop was beyond their current capabilities.

This added phase took everything to the next level, Future Intelligence Neurological Expansion Development, okay this one was a little catchier, and I had to smile FINED. No one knew or understood if this was speculation or an instruction. It seems that it was never questioned and accepted by some who pushed ahead regardless of the potential consequences.

This section of the theory stated that at some future point they would hold the science and technology along with the opportunity to create an improved intelligence. It stated that humanity held the key to improve itself. I could see how they bought into this instantly; it was all about building Better Today for a Better Tomorrow. They knew they would never see this vision of a perfect human species, but they knew it would benefit future generations. They took delight and satisfaction in the altruism that defined their era of humanity. If they were successful at this, it would be a legacy for the benefit of the entire universe. That's a wild claim, but later I would see what they truly meant by this and how I played a small part.

Just as with the other fields of science, this too created a new field of advanced mathematics. What they searched for was the perfect set of algorithms that would define the perfect species. It took a while for me to get anywhere comfortable with this concept. Here it goes, if you could analyse every unique characteristic of what makes us human, where would you begin. It's that question alone that triggered the first wave of experiments. We know that our DNA defines us, it's the building blocks and the structure for our purpose and our personalities. The question was for each unique characteristic we possess, where must you begin, what would be the starting point.

They sought to answer these questions by analysing tens of thousands of specimens to create the base level. Each set of results are dependent on the situation they faced. If you select just one of your characteristics and mathematically modelled it, each time you measured it, in a different setting with both internal and external factors you would obtain a different set of result.

If that wasn't enough, they then had to factor in the improvement increase or decrease depending on the characteristic they were evaluating. Allow me to attempt an explanation. If you were to isolate any one of your traits or characteristics, and then scientifically and mathematically define it, what reading would you expect. The result would simply alter dependent on the setting or condition. For example, let's identify and measure anxiety levels. An individual's reaction of their anxiety level would adjust dependent if they were in a quiet cinema or on a crowded staircase. Once its base measurement was known, they were trying to calculate both its worth and its optimum score. This defined score, would then determine the level given to this new superhuman. Either improving its worth or enhancing its performance. Alternatively, they may look to eradicated or downgrade a characteristic.

I understood the modelling alone created a completely new type of 1878 level re-hyper-base computer. It was able to take all the individual measurements, it was then ready to factor in the critical time measurement. This time element mapped what would happen from inception through tens, hundreds, thousands and even millions of years forward. They also had to factor in the development of the brain, and the final crucial part of the jigsaw, which is our bodies made of fragile bones and tissues. Reprogramming our DNA would also have to equip itself for the journey ahead. Further in the book I will expand on this and the type of experiments they are conducting.

One last note concerning the theory, this philosophy of building a better tomorrow for future generations free from the imperfection of their ancestors. If you haven't worked it out yet, what this means quite simply, is that we are the first incarnation of humanity to inhabit Earth. We are their ancestors who got it spectacularly wrong and very nearly fucked it up for ever. In a roundabout way this proves Darwin's theory of evolution is correct. At some future point, future science and technology will enable humanity to track back in time and remedy the faults and flaws we currently have. I felt there was more to this, more to discover and my journey had only just begun.

62.87 Evolution

There you have it, that's the 62.87 Theory, and in the best form I can explain it, that is, at this particular moment. The theory was formulated to explain, predict, and understand phenomena, and, in all cases, to challenge and extend existing knowledge within the limits of critically bounding assumptions. The theory proposed a solution, science then proved the theory, and the theory then became a way of life and a direction for humanity. Eventually, our 'future beings' knew they were entrusted to recreate the evolutionary path for our species, by this, evolution was re-engineered to suit its new purpose. The charter was created to protect humanity from the science and the advancements it would bring. Without a set of rules, they could not constrain the advancement of science and technology that had the potential to cause harm in certain circumstances.

I hope you now want to hear more about the world I saw, how humanity had finally solved all the problems we must endure today. I have mentioned a couple of times The Gifts I was given, sometimes I wish I had never asked about it, but now I own it. I am unable to switch it off. I smile to myself when I think how I was also shown the path humanity eventually took. How we changed our ways as a global society. How we finally came together with a common goal, I believe the result was absolute perfection. This evolutionary path could not have been predicted by Darwin, it was unchartered, although with a shared objective it showed what humanity is capable of.

I sit here now with a coffee in one hand, a smirk on my face, but with an uncertain future. I have the answers, the question is will anyone ever listen.

Reverse Time Travel

I mentioned earlier in this chapter that I would explain in more detail reverse time travel. It should also be a further piece of evidence that substantiates its neighbouring claim.

Place your hand in front of your face approximately 12 inches away. As you do this make a note of exactly where you are in the world, start with the country, then town or city, drill down further to your home, office, shop etc. Continue even further to the chair you are sat, the bed you are laying in and even what position you are. Now add the material things around you, especially electronic devices such as phones, tablets, laptops and even TV screens. Now make a mental note of the precise time, down to the second and even millisecond. What you have just created is a complete snapshot of that precise moment in time, it's absolutely 100% unique. It will never happen again in the history of our planet and the universe. For me, it was on the 7 June 2018 at 15:31:55, I was sat in my home office which is just the posh name for our spare bedroom. I was at home in Warrington in the county of Cheshire in the UK. I had just pressed send on an email I was typing; it was the first draft of an article for a magazine. Obviously, my hands were on the keyboard as I sat there at that unique moment in time.

Every molecule, every atom no matter what type and in whatever state it may be in, it can only exist in one place and at one moment in time, it's all unique. Science including cosmology and theoretical physics had established that these instances leave a trail. Just as you can leave a trail of crumbs to find your way back home. Similarly, we can navigate to an unknown destination using a route of commands generated by a sat nav. Overlaying those commands or navigation points with time merely adds the missing dimension. Space and time can be navigated in the same way we use super telescopes like Hubble and Webb. They can see what the universe looked like around a quarter of a billion years after the big bang, when the first stars and galaxies started to form. We have known about the existence of dark matter; we just didn't know its reason.

Scientists in the future have figured out that you can follow each of those molecules and atoms through time to a predefined point. Now if you know exactly where you want to get to, following the trail of crumbs you can identify a place in time and return to it. Science then expanded this treasure hunt and allowed them to place an object alongside other matter, other molecules at that unique point in time. When you bring all three elements together, you have the coordinates required to map this exact. Those three elements are space, time, and matter.

On 7 June 2018 at 15:31:55, a communication device entered a vein in my neck, later I remembered a very small sting, but didn't think any more about it. I was later told that this device is called a Chrono-Diverse-Transponder CDT. They very proudly told me that it's currently the most advanced machine of its type. It also explains why they are a very long way from being able to implant a cell cluster that contains pre-programmed DNA into our earliest ancestors. This device entered through this vein and was able to navigate itself to a part of my brain. Once there, it allowed them to communicate directly with me. Although it wasn't just communications, they were also able somehow to show me the world as it will be 2,034 years from now. I know by now you are not just thinking he's gone a bit too heavy on the non-prescription medications, you are 100% sure of it.

The next part of their explanation seemed to pull everything together for me, it relates to their ability for communication. I mentioned earlier that they expressly told me they couldn't travel forward in time, I thought I was justified in asking, isn't that what I am doing. Well, no, not quite and here's their explanation. The CDT device communicated through a basic website they had previously created, apparently data is easy for them to infiltrate. What they had done was to use a low use website that existed today and placed data transponders within the code of the site. Through this code they could communicate with the CDT thing that now sat in my brain. My next logical question had to be, why me.

Here's their rebut to this simple question. To be accurate, there are two reasons why. The first made me laugh as it's amazingly absurd, it's all down to the fact that we have a very fast broadband router. Here's a special thank you to my broadband provider who are currently charging me £95 per month for the privilege. The second reason they told me stopped that loud laughing in a heartbeat. Because I have 'defects' in my brain, to give them their proper name, which are lesions or scars, Multiple Sclerosis means many scars. These are caused when the immune system gets things wrong, when it should be fighting an infection, it's actually attacking the myelin which is the protective sheath that surrounds the nerves. Due to these lesions, they are able to traverse to the required part of my brain which allows communication for both parties. With a further thanks to my 600Gb router, they can communicate and provide me with a view no one else has ever seen.

You now have the option, continue reading the next chapters where I explain in detail a world that is perfect in every way. Or like me you can be sceptical of perfection, and seek the answer to my recurring question, what do they really want from me. With their superior intelligence and advanced technology why would they want to communicate with a middle-aged guy with a neurological condition. There are many questions I have, okay they allowed me to see the future but why do that, what were they hoping to achieve. I started to question them, what I found brought my life to a shuddering halt. The Gifts I was given allowed me to see more, question more and probe more. Alternatively, you can write off the past couple of hours as a waste of time and continue your life with the blindfold comfortably in place until you finally die…your choice. If you jumped to read this chapter from the main story please head back to chapter 2 and follow the story that brought me to this point.

"However much you deny the truth, the truth goes on existing."

George Orwell

Chapter 10
The Enormity of the Challenge

I found it hard to believe, Friday 22nd of June had arrived so quickly, it seemed I had merely blinked, and June 2018 had almost come and gone. Despite my reservations and usual scepticism, England were looking quite good, their final game of the group stages was on Sunday. England vs Panama was the afternoon game, and while I know Toni would go with the flow and allow me to watch it, Jane would undoubtedly have other ideas. That Friday evening, I simply closed my eyes after we had eaten, Jane thought I was asleep, the truth couldn't have been further from that. With my newfound archive of incredible information and ability to access it, I couldn't wait to try it out. What you have just read in the previous chapter is how I understood it. There was a vastness to the information, records, and data, but as Helena said don't try and read anything, simply look to understand it.

This new ability took some getting used to, it's counterintuitive, and I must admit that it actually hurt at the beginning. Once I had tried and failed a couple of times, it became increasingly easier and faster. As I gained the understanding, I knew that I could access the supporting data at any time, but it wasn't about reading it for later recall, it was simply knowing and understanding. What you have just read is extracts from both the data, and my interpretation of the facts and evidence seen. As humans we are mainly programmed to learn this in the opposite direction, we read and consume the information to understand the problem and associated solutions. This is why I am reluctant to produce academic writing, there it's proving you have read it, not that you understand it. I also had the added ability to rapidly access this information when it was needed. I found that I could mentally sort it, and hopefully articulate it as I tried previously with the 62.87 Theory. They downloaded an incredible amount of information, it took some time for it to fully sink in, and with the enormous weight that would accompany the tangled web of consequences. As I revisited the files, it all became clearer with time.

Essentially, they are trying to create human DNA, and all the engineering that is contained within the incredibly complex sequencing. This fully reprogrammed DNA will then go on to create the complicated human brain as we know it today. However, they are not satisfied with that alone, it must also have inbuilt triggers that will stimulate this organ at key points. Now wait for it, there's more, they then need to create the technology that will deliver this pre-programmed DNA, which will be contained within cell clusters. This technology must ensure these cell clusters will not be rejected by the host, which will go on to multiply within the chosen species. Slide into this the technology that allows them to travel back in time and deliver this successfully. And to top all that, the third part of this hugely complex equation means they must find the exact point in history to implant DNA into the correct number of humans. When you look at it this way, you can see why it took many years for the whole of the scientific community to agree with the findings.

Around 2,000 years from now exist technology that is truly mindboggling. This advanced technology allows items to travel backwards through time. What I glimpsed with my own eyes, was a world dedicated to finding the solutions that lay within the claims of the 62.87 Theory. Time travel using space, time and matter has also revealed that the universe we know and can see today is in its second series of life. Humanity has found the answer to our existence, it's not a god, the truth is far stranger. As I sat there with my eyes closed, I could see how each of the claims within the theory were rigorously tested and eventually ratified. There were no gaps, everything had an answer, even if I didn't have a question that supported it, weird I know.

I also understood better the information Olin gave me about the ripple effect, ownership & responsibility along with the unified use of language. What all this had finally given humanity was a common goal. The by-product was a utopian lifestyle where all the depravity, cruelty, greed, malice, and corruption were all a thing of the past. Whether the goal they seek is correct, which it obviously is, humanity has finally won, it is now living in harmony with the planet along with every other living creature. While all the answers we have ever craved opened up to me, the football was suitably dull in comparison. Brazil beat Costa Rica two nil, Iceland regained their winning style beating Nigeria by the same result. In the other game Serbia lost again to Switzerland one to two.

Saturday morning gave me the opportunity to complete a detailed vlog of the previous day. This was courtesy of Jane's sister who agreed to go shopping with her for a selection of vegetarian food. When they returned there was enough to sink a ship, 'figuratively speaking'. The afternoon was spent cleaning in preparation for the 'Royal' visit the following day. The house was clean as it always is, but Toni's room was given clean bedding, and a 'proper' clean as Jane described it. This gave me the opportunity to make some notes in preparation for my next event whenever that would be. It was done under the guise of me cleaning my study, which mirrored the rest of the house as always being clean. This list obviously started with 'why me', this was an enormous question, and I needed to know the answer. I know the CDT device operated on the basis that I had a high-speed router and the fact that I had a neurological condition, but in reality, they will have had millions of options. I am sure there would have been better candidates, ones that would utilise these skills and knowledge better than me.

This led to the next associated question, what am I supposed to do with this newfound knowledge. Do they expect people to listen to me, to hear what I have got to say. Add to this, my MS limits what

I can do which I am sure they know. Maybe they don't want me to do anything, if this is the case then why give it to me. Very quickly I was talking myself into knots, and everything that I had gained in the past 24 hours was driving me insane. The next topic I wanted to know about, could possibly be the most important, I needed to know more about their lives, and how humanity finally got it right. I envisaged this taking months' worth of CDT events, and I am not sure my sanity could take that. Speaking of which, are these events and the skills I now have likely to damage my health, and especially my mental health. The final overriding question, and one that can be coupled to, why me, is simply, what else do they want from me. The questions they have asked up to now have been strange, all this information would be easily accessed from data archives.

Making Plans For Nigel

Saturday evening followed our normal routine to a point, Jane forgot something on her earlier shopping trip which meant we had to venture out to our local Sainsbury's. Once again, my stress levels were tested as we parked in the blue badge area only to be joined by someone who merely wanted the convenience it gave them. It would be interesting to see if the cashpoint machines were positioned elsewhere, would the shorter distance or the added width within the carpark space win over. Bearing in mind that some people seem to care more for their precious cars than they do for their children, what decisions would they make. The normal routine was further shattered during a very nice meal that we had, Jane <u>only</u> had a couple of glasses of wine. It was one of the only meals that I can make successfully on my own, chicken stir fry, 'Danny' style. I marinade the meat for about three hours in Sesame Oil, Soy Sauce, Salt, and Pepper with a good kick of Chili Flakes, and a bold hit of Garlic.

I managed to watch the evening game where Germany beat Sweden two one, it was an enjoyable game although it didn't stop my mind from racing once more. In the earlier games Belgium beat

Tunisia five two, I only watched bits of this game as Jane had me moving furniture for some unknown reason. In the other afternoon game, South Korea lost two one to Mexico. In the TV programmes they were all building up to the England game the next day, I know Jane saw my interest, but would I be allowed to watch it. That night in bed, Jane was telling me of her plans for Monday, amongst other things, they were going shopping in Liverpool. It sounded exhausting, a decision was made that I wouldn't attend, although it would have been nice to be consulted. This news was greeted with a soft cheer on my behalf, it meant a CDT event could still be possible.

Sunday started with a hurried breakfast, Toni phoned at 8:30, and gave her position and scheduled arrival which would be around 10:00. Jane was bubbling with excitement; I tried to chill with a coffee while also trying to clear my mind. At 10:10 her little VW Beetle in lime green pulled up outside, as she exited from the driver's seat, a tall wiry man got out of the passenger seat and gave a nervous smile which accompanied a sheepish wave. Jane seemed unsurprised, which let the cat out of the bag that this was all planned behind my back. I didn't care in the slightest as I trusted her choice in partners 100%, just as everything in life. They brought in a few bags, and I was formally introduced to Nigel, instantly his name kicked off the brilliant XTC song in my mind. Anyway, Pleasantries were exchanged, and we had the chance to interrogate the new couple over tea/coffee and some biscuits. He was great, very funny and a newly qualified GP who had ambitions to do more. Toni clung on to his arm throughout this initial encounter. It was only interrupted by Toni who insisted she needed more mega-hugs with me and Jane. This made both of us the happiest and most contented people on the planet, they ended in all three of us wiping tears away. I caught a glimpse of Nigel beaming a very large smile, but it was far too early to be asked to join in.

Over Sunday lunch, which was a very tasty nut roast, which accompanied a selection of even more vegetables cooked in various ways. Jane managed to hide all the pre-packed items before they arrived, but I think they both knew they were M&S finest. Nigel commented politely about eating healthier for both my MS and the planet. I was saved on several occasions by Jane who wanted to know where Toni was going to, once she qualified. She was unable to provide a definitive answer, it seemed it may well coincide with Nigel's plans, don't or you'll have me singing in my head again. Nigel also ticked the box for his love of sport although cricket and rugby outtrumped football. Lunch was curtailed early to allow the 'men' to watch the England game while Jane and Toni sat within earshot in the kitchen. Soon enough as the goals started popping in, they joined us to watch a six one thrashing of Panama. If it was anyone other than a third-rate pub team, I may have got on the bandwagon that, 'this was our time', and the three lions' song would have to change forever.

Later in the evening Nigel agreed to go on the shopping expedition to Liverpool the following day. He had never visited the beautiful city of my upbringing, although I explained that it had all changed enormously since 2008 when a huge investment was made. It's only as we look back, we can see that, for once it was actually spent correctly. This gave me most of Monday to myself and hopefully the next event. Later that evening over a couple of drinks we had the opportunity to discuss religion among many other topics. Nigel was brought up in a religious household, although never bought into the god aspect and all the nonsense that goes with it.

Understandably, I was feeling very tired as the evening drew on, I went to bed before the others, this saved the possible embarrassment of the couple sharing Toni's room. My thoughts would have been solely focused and remembering her growing up in that room, however, that job was done, and times move on. I had a fantastic sleep that night, we were a family once more and under the same roof. But times progress, and I knew one day that our family would morph and inevitably grow, although with this also comes enforced distances. During this short visit Jane was stockpiling an arsenal of stories to tell our family and friends. She fell asleep that night with a warm inward feeling and several tears of joy. As my hand was squeezed tightly, I knew this was a period she would never forget.

So, She's The Boss!

Monday began with a relaxed family breakfast, it was filled with laughter and embarrassing tales of when Toni was young, and the inside story of how competitive she was… at everything. They left for Liverpool about 11:00, I almost felt sorry for my newfound friend in Nigel, as he should have taken ear-defenders with him. With the house to myself once more, I had the opportunity to delve into the abundant archive I now had, but it wasn't the same. I found I could indeed understand more about the 62.87 Theory, although answering other questions seemed like there was a glass wall. My usual routine slipped into place quickly, I had lunch, and a thought came rushing in. I obviously couldn't look into the future, whereas those within the events, Helena, Olin, and the others had the ability to search their past. They would be able to tell me many things, they could enlighten me with riches of what the future will bring. As I considered this complex outcome further, I quickly decided that I didn't want to know my future. Imagine having that knowledge, it's frightening to think that your future is laid out, and no matter what you do, it's already there. Further thoughts corrected this initial assumption, even if you were told what your future had in store, surely, that can be changed by your actions. This was something else I would need to discuss with my all-knowing hosts.

Sure enough, at 13:23 I glanced down at my phone and felt a rush of warmth still air penetrate my body. This was intermingled with a tingle of electrical pulses that danced over my skin. As the uplifting sensation took hold, it was interrupted slightly by the odd feeling of tremors that shuddered through my entire being. They lasted only seconds, but I thought for a moment they may wake me. The ripples from this vibrated through my body, fortunately the sensation soon passed without further consequences. All of this distracted me for an instance before the piercing light, which seemed more intense than during any other previous event. The pain was extreme and almost indescribable, I couldn't find an easy comparison. This was primarily due to the fact it was all in my mind, it wasn't real, but that didn't matter.

I blinked furiously over and over until I could see the outline of three people. Helena who repeatedly said, "Danny, blink more and it will soon pass", clearly sat in the middle. This time she was joined by Xendar who looked up and gave me a partial smile in the way of acknowledgment. She then introduced me to only the second female I had met, "This is Jacron-63-Snel", she said. As she did, I thought here was a name that would be shortened easily to 'Jacron'. The introduction brought two predictable actions, she stood and smiled, but this was a proper smile that seemed uncommon with some of the others. As she sat again, my lower peripheral vision pinged to life once more. Jacron is 67 years old and 2 days, her position is Director Psychoanalyst also with the Try-neural Evaluation team, and overall Principal coordinator with the 62.87 Ethics Mandate P211 Team. This made her their superior, it was also given away as she wore a pale-yellow uniform with two thin purple rings around the top of both long-sleeved arms. As with everyone else I met, she didn't look her age, she had mousy brown hair that was also short but slightly longer than Helena's. Her complexion was flawless, and I noticed she had green eyes, there was not a sign of makeup on either of the females. Before they started, I wished Jacron-63-Snel a belated happy birthday, and hoped she had a nice time. She smiled, thanked me, and said she did have a nice day as she met up with friends and family. At least I have established that they still celebrate birthdays in the future. I had to look again and with greater intense, she had really pretty green eyes that shone and twinkled.

I am sure Jacron interrupted Helena as she stood up suddenly, she made probably the understatement of the millennium, when she declared, "You will no doubt have many questions following what you now know", what else could I do, I merely nodded. She then told me that she has the authority to answer any questions that warrant an answer, but there will be some that they couldn't answer, and for those I will understand why. If it was their aim to confuse me, well they had achieved this with outstanding clarity. What I knew now was that she was in charge and if I was going to get any answers it would be today. Just as I was ready to fire into my first one, Helena stood up and asked if it would be alright if they could ask me three questions first.

The first of her questions was not what I expected, as she asked a well prepared and considered, "You told us that your previous employer terminated your employment not long after you were diagnosed, what did that feel like?" I paused for a moment before I began, and without giving it much prior thought I started. The best explanation I could give was it felt almost like betrayal, quickly I clarified this. I told them I had given so much, and sacrificed a lot of time with my family that I will never get back. Now here's a thing, I knew using the word 'sacrifice', in this term was abstract from the now commonly associated secular meaning. Don't ask me how, I just knew it. Anyway, back to my response, the company just asked more of me, and I gave it readily in the belief that I was helping to build a better future for myself, Jane, and Toni. I spent a ridiculous amount of time travelling all over the place. I would spend as much time at home preparing for meetings, and making sure each client we had was well looked after.

I fought very hard to keep my role within the company, but it seemed they had an agenda to get rid of me without understanding my capabilities. In fairness, I didn't know my true capabilities and if I did, I would have probably underestimated them at the beginning. I felt discarded far too early, especially by one of the Managing Directors who was dealing with my return. It was a little strange to have two MDs, and the one I was dealing with didn't have a clue about the business or what we actually did for our clients. If he was involved in a meeting, we use to joke afterwards that we would have to draw him pictures so that he could understand it. That was the company's decision, and once it was made, there was nothing I could do, no matter how outrageously unfair it was. I summed up by saying it felt painful to have been thrown on the scrapheap without a care. What I think they failed to appreciate was it was ending my working career, my working life, and at that point I had no idea what came next.

James My Hero

As I concluded my answer, Helena looked backwards to catch the eye of Jacron, who gave a slight nod of approval. With that Helena and Jacron swapped places, and as Jacron stood up she took a few more steps closer, they were the prettiest eyes I had ever seen, although maybe on par with the doctor from my local surgery. The second question was delivered with the same amount of thought, "Tell me Danny, how did you try and retain your position within the company, and why do you believe they tried to manufacture your exit?", said Jacron in a calm and steady voice. As with every other response, I learnt to take a deep breath and simply speak. If I thought too much about what I was going to say, I was in danger of tripping myself up, or what could be worse they may read both, thought and speech.

To begin with, I wasn't aware there was an agenda, I told them. We had several meetings where they said they wanted to seek an understanding of my capabilities and what adjustments could be made. By this time, I had met James Walsh, he was a specialist employment solicitor. My sister Georgina introduced us, her next-door neighbour had used him in an employment tribunal against the inland revenue, and more importantly, he won. That's a proud badge to wear, although when I first met him, you wouldn't have guessed it. He wore a long trench coat, with an ill-fitting suit and a tie that had seen better days. His glasses kept slipping down, but he had something about him I liked.

Before their strategy to have me removed kicked in, James and I attended three meetings arranged by them. Philip, the 'director without portfolio' and Sharon their Human Resources manager travelled up to Warrington for each one. Philip had a nickname he really hated which was 'Pip', for a bit of fun we used to try and use the word pip during meetings. I am glad to say he always found it funny, and admired the ingenuity involved. Each meeting was held in a hotel of my choice; therefore, I picked the most expensive I could find as I knew the coffee and refreshments would be top notch. Each meeting followed the same script, Sharon would begin by reading the minutes from the previous meeting. This gave James the opportunity to disagree with most of them, more often than not, they omitted vital parts, or the wording would be incorrect. It was evident that we could not agree a common ground for my return, although I was keen to be doing something. In the end, I wrote a revised job description for the role I knew I could do, which would also see my immediate return. When I sent this to them following a review by James, their only response was to ask me to attend a medical which would assess my abilities.

Around two weeks later, I attended a medical which took place in an office in Liverpool, I knew the building chosen, and thought it was a strange place for such a review. Prior to this, I had emailed Sharon to ensure that the person undertaking the medical had knowledge of my neurological condition. I also wanted to ensure they had all my medical notes, when Sharon arranged the meeting, I was asked to sign a release form. Guess what, unsurprisingly I didn't receive a response. Anyway, I attended this fictitious 'assessment', which was an absolute joke, I was in there for less than 15 minutes. I asked the two key questions which developed into four. No surprise this retired GP wasn't anything close to being a specialist, he didn't have my medical records, he didn't know what my profession was, or even, and wait for it… what my diagnosis was. This person, who was evidently not qualified, held my future in his inadequate hands. I was completely shell shocked as I left the building, I phoned James, and his advice was not to worry and to make detailed notes.

What happened next shocked even James, and almost destroyed me. A week later, I received a letter from Philip on behalf of the company, it politely informed me that my employment had been terminated based on health grounds. He kindly attached a copy of the health practitioners report, which was all of 11 lines. I remember vividly when I received this, I just sat for about half an hour with my head in my hands as I thought, how do I begin to tell Jane and Toni. I must admit, I cried like I have never cried before, my life was in ruins, it had been thrown away by people who simply didn't care. I called James who was gobsmacked, he declared that he had never seen anything like this in over 30 years of practice. That evening I sat Jane and Toni down, I told them in graphic detail what had happened, they both held it together and gave me the determined spirit to fight this no matter what.

As I concluded my response, I could feel my heart racing and the tears welling up once more in my eyes. Throughout this time, I could see the frantic twitching of fingers that belonged to Helena and Xendar, their eyes also scanned semi-transparent screens. I also detected a faint smile on their faces, which I found strange.

Normally, you can read people's faces to interpret their reactions, here though, I found that difficult. I looked straight at Jacron and asked her if this answered her question. She replied with a firm, "Yes", and she thanked me for sharing this difficult time with them. I just found it strange that they wanted more information about this period of my life. Jacron politely asked if it would be alright to ask more about this again. I simply nodded without giving it any further thought.

Before I could launch into my questions, Jacron took a couple of steps closer and said, "What you now understand about the 62.87 Theory, is correct in every detail." Rather than asking a question and waiting for an answer, Jacron offered this up as though it was in normal conversation. I told her that I couldn't get over the enormity of the challenge they faced, and what they were trying to achieve. Somehow, she knew I understood the theory without me asking, previously this would have had me worried, but nothing surprises me now. We then discussed how they knew the human brain could not have evolved in accordance with the rules of Darwin. A screen appeared as it had done before, and a graph showed the timeline since humans were identified as a unique species. Several significant events were pinpointed to illustrate this further; it merely emphasised the incredible short space of time before we created the digital age. This timeline extended to 5 million years and then to 3.82 billion years, this is what you must remember, we are at the very beginning of our 'first' existence.

They knew, without a shadow of doubt, that one day science and technology would be able to achieve the objectives of the 62.87 Theory. It is this theory that gave them the plan for the re-engineering of our species and set of rules to live by. They value life in every sense of the word, every achievement is one step closer towards conquering their objective. Build Today for a Better Tomorrow drives them onwards and upwards, and from what I have seen till now, it most definitely works. It is the perfect utopian lifestyle, free from the superstitions and wasted time many endure today in a false and stupid belief, of a better life once this one has ended. The stark truth is that 'this is it', we have a short period of time on this beautiful planet which is the place I love. She told me during their 30 years of Fulfilment they explore Earth and all the wonders it has to offer. From incredible mountain rangers and rivers, stunning waterfalls to breathtaking beaches with beautiful coastlines, valleys, caves, and much more. They can travel through space to see galaxies and phenomena that we are yet to discover. It's the richest of lives, and only attained because they saw the value in working together.

This led me on to my next enormous question, which was probably the most important I could ask. I cleared my throat and asked, "How do we get from the complete mess I see around me in 2018, to what you now have?" I was expecting a partial answer, I mean, how do you begin to put together such a complex summary of over 2,000 years. Instead, Xendar stood up and asked me to close my eyes, and not to be fearful. An immediate thought hit me; this is how they previously downloaded the theory. Sure enough, as soon as my eyes were theoretically closed, there came a rush of wind which accompanied a warmth that touched every living tissue within my body. Once more, electricity pinged and surged over my skin, although this seemed short-lived. Then, a storm of incredibly vivid coloured lights headed towards me at the most phenomenal speeds. They blended in the back of my eyes, and the inner peace that I had obtained previously, seemed more intense. The knowledge of 'everything' I ever wanted was now mine, I felt empowered, and a feeling of refreshment and rejuvenation gave me an inner warmth. It annoyed me that I couldn't explain the feeling I had, the warmth felt like being hugged by Toni from the inside of my core, and then outward to every cell of my body.

This wonderful feeling was then shattered alarmingly as Jacron stood up very quickly. Hastily, she told me the event would have to stop immediately. The next thing I saw was Jane standing over me shouting, "Danny, Danny, wake up!" As I opened my eyes, and my consciousness started to adjust once more to my surroundings, I realised that Jane, Toni, and Nigel were standing over me. It looked like Nigel was ready to jump in and check my vital signs, he seemed eager to start heart compressions. Jane explained that they couldn't wake me despite shaking me and calling my name. I tried to laugh it off by saying I was just very tired. Jokingly, I blamed it on the fact that I had been watching too much football recently.

I looked at the clock on the wall, I knew the concept of time was somehow distorted within a CDT event, this was further proved at it was 17:00. The moment I awake from an event, this distortion always seems magnified, however I manage to recall more with the progress of time. This particular event had been the longest, excitedly I looked forward to revealing more later. Jane and Toni eventually released me from their clutches, and they began to tell me about the mega shopping trip.

Over our evening meal the conversation didn't ease, Nigel had fallen in love with Liverpool and declared the architecture was without doubt precious, he could see why much of it was protected under the world heritage scheme. I explained how completely different it was when I was growing up. Stories of my childhood and teenage years soon flowed, I was proud to be a scouser I told him.

Nigel was impressed that I had remained very good friends with a school colleague, I explained that we were mates and how we were described once as being as thick as thieves. While my scouse accent may have faded over the years, my love of the place never would. It is beautiful and I always loved to be in the city, the waterfront with the three graces is recognisable the world over. There is more than

The Beatles and the magnificent football club we have, note I used the singular there.

As we relaxed over a few drinks the conversation turned more to the future for Toni and indeed Nigel. I maintained the stance that it was entirely Toni's choice where she wanted to go after graduating. Jane had obviously been doing her homework and research. She laboured the benefits of Leahurst, coincidently it's located on the Wirral, which is just a 30-minute drive away. Leahurst is an extension of the University of Liverpool and has both a small animal facility along with an equine and large animal centre. All of this would be ideal if Toni wanted to continue her studies or enter lecturing. A few nifty manoeuvres by Jane moved the conversation towards the future for Toni and Nigel, she was told clearly it was still early days. I could see the pair were outnumbered; carefully I moved in to steer the conversation 180^0 degrees in favour of his family.

It was good being mentally occupied, I was unable to think about what had happened during the earlier CDT event. I went to bed around 22:00, I was tired, although my going to bed first did save any awkwardness regarding sleeping arrangements for Toni. The two were setting off around 9:00 the following morning, they planned a quick breakfast before leaving. Jane came to bed around 23:00, she did her best not to disturb me. As I lay there in the moments before falling asleep my brain wanted to go into overdrive again, I did my best to avoid accessing any of the newly downloaded files. These files will undoubtedly provide more answers and allow me to understand further. The anticipation of what was to come, had me as excited as the nine-year-old version of me, eagerly waiting for the Airfix model of the Spitfire, on Christmas morning.

Chapter 11
Surely That Can't Happen?

The following morning of the state visit began extremely early. Understandably, there was a queue for the bathroom, needless to say I was last in line. Breakfast consisted of several cups of tea; Jane made a stack of toast that was gradually getting higher no matter how many people ate. Then came the farewell hugs, and without tears was the order from Toni. There was a procession of people and carrier bags that slowly filled her tiny car, miraculously, there was three times as many bags as when they arrived just days before. For the final time there was a three-way mega-hug, Nigel knew not to join in, it's still far too early for that. He received a manly handshake and shoulder bump, which I found very uncomfortable, and, in my opinion, these should be left entirely to the younger generation. Jane was certainly comfortable to give Nigel a huge hug and a kiss on the cheek, that alone was a welcome to the family.

We returned inside to the stark quietness of our home, it immediately felt empty again. Jane informed me that following a quick tidy-up she was going out to meet her sister and some friends for coffee and a bit of lunch. If the universe is a vacuum with zero air/oxygen, then the same would happen later for anyone entering a 10-feet radius of them all talking. Jane had an entirely new catalogue of stories to tell, what Toni is up to and what we think of her new man Nigel. Who, in her opinion and description is… 'Such a lovely man'.

As soon as Jane left, I hurried to record the latest vlog and vigorously make notes. Once that task was complete, I was free to make a coffee. I ensured that I was sitting comfortably and ready to begin my understanding of the journey of how humanity developed. It took a while for me to sort through the vast amount of information they imparted to me within the myriad of files. Initially, I couldn't get my head around the sorting of everything, I could access folders either by category or by timeline. I wasn't sure whether this was down to me or the way they had been catalogued. I finally established a method, although I tended to mix them up in my understanding of each one. I then thought this could be the answer, and how I was meant to understand the filing system. Before I continued, I had to make a note of the questions I wanted to ask during the next event.

The easiest way I found to understand the information, was by category, although some of these overlapped. The first category I looked for was an unusual starting point, but an important one. Law and order were relatively easy to locate, although what I found can only be describe as, harsh but necessary. As humanity developed, I could see that the penal system was run and operated on a points system. The most serious of crimes would automatically receive the maximum points. Let me pause here because there were three very important changes that effected this entire system.

Firstly, the complete war on illegal drugs across the world had been eradicated by the introduction of system, or government owned and controlled drugs. I know this sounds weird, but here's how I understood it. These drugs were non addictive and produced the same 'high', or reaction that the user wanted. They left the user's blood stream in a matter of hours, meaning there was no long-term damage or counter-productive reaction. All illegal drugs had been permanently destroyed, additionally, there was no call for them as the system-owned drugs fulfilled every need. As time passed, people no longer craved the original high. What they wanted was the benefits of creativity, and the production of enhanced thought.

Secondly, the education system had long benefited from the use of education stimulants, here's another one that requires explanation. These stimulants increased both the learning power, memory retention, and the unending desire to learn more. It took many years and generations for this to be completely rolled out, but the impact was revolutionary. The structure of the colony system aided this with its fairness, and mentoring system. Providing a class-leading education to everyone was a priority, and the benefits to humanity were easily measured. As part of the entry system into the colony structure, every person had to have a certain level of understanding and agree to abide by the laws for entry. This was the first time I had discovered there was an entry system. I made myself a note to research this further and explore each of the rules and why they are in place.

The third change was the most controversial by far, and like the other two important factors, they were introduced even before the creation of the colony system. CCTV as we know it today had morphed and improved, this meant every public, and publicly used space was monitored constantly with sophisticated AI recognition software. We may view this as extreme today, along with the next seismic change. Everyone was tagged with a microchip at birth, these chips did more than just help to eradicate crime, they were seen as a vital aid to help protect us. Whether this be in a medical emergency or a point of need. Initially, they provided the most basic of functions. Although, as they developed, they were seen and respected as a vital part of our overall development. Today many of us use smart watches that monitor an array of things from heart rates to sleep patterns. Imagine what the future holds, then link this to public security and wellbeing.

When you improve all these individual parts, it's society and humanity that benefits. Vital resources can be used where they are needed, over time society changed for the better, and it soon forgot the shackles that had held it back. I was also reminded that the World Change Movement was gathering pace throughout its time in history, and finally common sense was winning over. Just to return quickly to the points that were in place in relation to the penal system. For the most serious of crimes or for those who would not change and repeatedly reoffend, they were offered euthanasia or spend significant amounts of time in controlled rehabilitation. The other option was to spend the whole of their lives incarcerated without ever seeing another human being. I did say it was harsh, but it's up to you to make your own judgement. As you do so, also consider the result, which led to the complete utopian lifestyle that I witnessed.

Replace The Stick With A Carrot

I mentioned earlier that the World Change Movement gathered pace before the first colony was born. This was in a large part due to its stance and commitment to provide free energy for all. In accessing the vast database of information, I was now able to understand clearly how this was achieved. Sustainable energy supply is talked about a lot at the moment, and we recognise the need to reduce our reliance on carbon-based fuels. This is as much to save us choking the planet and adding to the greenhouse gasses. We all recognise the dangers, it's our generation with its throw away culture that has driven this to incredibly dangerous levels. Well, I can be the custodian of good news, in that we must have fixed our individual cultures, otherwise I would not be writing this. And for those who are totting up, there's another fact.

Saving the planet must be our overwhelming priority. We are beginning to accept this, although at the moment many countries are reluctant to take responsibility and adopt measures to change this for future generations. Here again, we can see the negative impact of the ripple effect and the devastation caused by the lack of ownership and responsibility. As a remedy, I liken this to use of the carrot and stick analogy, it's a perfect way to explain this. Now some governments and associated organizations are using the stick approach as a threat; that, if we don't resolve this then future generations will pay the price. Sadly, for many of us, even though we say we will do anything for our children, this monumental message doesn't register. Also, some nations are screaming that climate change is causing havoc within their own countries, yet they need fossil fuels to compete within the global markets. It's a spinning wheel of negatives that is easily broken and once done they will be the real winners.

I learnt, or more importantly, understood that none of the colony systems were built where it is not conducive for human life. Currently, we see our future energy needs being supplied by alternatives such as solar, wind or within the tidal movements of seas and oceans. Yes, using these power sources we can restore the eco systems that have been damaged. Once more we can free the lungs of the world, the rainforests will revitalise Earth while restoring the very fine balance that exists. Although, for an energy source that provides the ultimate goal of free energy for all, we need to consult and trust science. As the 62.87 Theory sets out, we need to stop thinking in terms of decades or just a few generations and open our eyes and minds to an altruistic state. Considering the mindset induced by the motto BTBT, we are not going to see the fruits of our efforts, but future generations will, and for generations beyond what we currently contemplate. These temporary and short-term alternatives that rely on nature will be adopted, they will change the tide in our favour, although nuclear fusion is where our future lies.

Nuclear fusion is a nuclear reaction that combines two atoms to create one or more new atoms with slightly less total mass. The difference in mass is released as energy, as described by Einstein's famous equation, $E=mc^2$, where energy equals mass times the speed of light squared. I know that doesn't make it any easier to understand, but I just like to quote Einstein, also because I can now, somehow understand all of this. Rather than using a source to generate the energy, like fossil fuels which obviously produce unwanted gases, nuclear fusions source is simply hydrogen… yep water. Energy is gained when two atoms of a light element such as hydrogen are heated and combined. This process forms a single heavier element, such as helium. The nuclear reaction of this produces a massive amount of energy which can be captured and turned into usable energy. It's clean, green and unlike nuclear fission the waste is much safer and easier to handle, and store.

Amazingly, I was shown how this works for them. In one of the many charts and presentations, key information along with a torrent of designs and schematics gave precise workings. Now, crucially, I understood how humanity arrived there. On one small piece of wasteland desert sits their power plant that produces the energy needs for every colony. It's transmitted seamlessly all around the world by incredibly thin fibres. This innocuous domed building pulls energy from the sun through millions of almost invisible light sensitive panes, they are then focused through a myriad of lenses. The fusion runs constantly without the need for maintenance or any human involvement. It's completely free, 100% safe, and with an endless supply of easily accessible fuel. The primary question for me to resolve next, is what journey we must take to get there.

To Begin with we must simply replace the stick with a carrot, what I mean is that we need to utilise the abundant free energy supply we currently have, to its most effective form. With the right planning and investment, energy firms need to be forced to present a deadline date when energy to its users becomes free. Add to these, intermittent breaks need to be known where they will hit certain reduction guarantees. I know that's going to be very difficult as, 'the people', will be asking the existing energy suppliers to create their own demise. We know this can be done, we must force it to be done, otherwise we will never progress.

I can hear the timid response from here, 'but who can force them'. Please take a deep breath, that's going to be down to the likes of you and I, along with governments who are elected to make it happen. We should remember the act of altruism summed up within those four letters BTBT, you and I will not see this, our grandchildren may or even their grandchildren, but somewhere along the line it must happen. It's this level of altruism that we must engage, and it was the World Change Movement and the initial 36 who stood up and made it happen.

The key to this happening is investment, and this must be contributed by the energy firms who will be at the forefront of the research, and from its customers. We need to dip into our own pockets now, to reap the rewards later. There are 28 million electricity, and 23 million gas customers in the UK, of course some will be business users. If each domestic user contributed just £0.50 per month, with each commercial one contributing £2.50 per month. This would be matched by the government also contributing £2.50 each month per household. And finally, the energy firms who will all contribute £10.00 per month for each customer. Energy firms will have to diversify to survive, until however, eventually they too will demise. The revenue sourced by this activity will easily top £18 billion per annum.

This would be dedicated to creating free energy by means of nuclear fusion. Remember this is just the UK, if you replicate this across North America and Europe, and prove to the world that it is achievable, what a legacy that would be. It's also important to remember that the money raised will be used entirely for research and implementation. Careful controls will be in place to ensure this, and a separate organization will scrutinise all elements of the various projects.

Once the world achieves this target and energy is free for all, it will change everything, and that's a bold claim. Energy will be free for our homes and all forms of transport. Business and manufacturing will probably be the greatest winners, providing they pass on the cost savings. I saw that our lives will also be unrecognisable, as we will no longer have to work as many hours to pay for energy, or the elements of this cost, the things we need. Our working lives will change but it's not just energy that will become zero cost, World Change set out plans to make food zero cost in exactly the same way.

Walls Come Tumbling Down

Just as my mind was going into overdrive with the newfound knowledge and understanding I had, coupled with the ability to quickly problem solve, I could see the dangers for me and how it may consume my every hour. I was saved by Ian and Eddie who called in on one of their daily walks. It could have been for the free coffee and treats that are readily available, for clarification Eddie has the dog treats. I enjoyed the break and relaxed conversation. The world cup featured heavily, it was during this hour that I realised I had lost all my focus, or rather all my focus was now on each of the events along with the knowledge and abilities I had been given. If nothing else, I vowed to rectify this for my own mental health. Prior to Ian knocking, I was just thinking about the work life balance, and how important it is. I had completely forgotten my plans for 1 November and seeking revenge the only way I could or thought I could.

After a bit of lunch, I tried to keep my mind busy on something other than the events. I had recorded the football highlights last night, so I took the opportunity to catch up with the games. Saudia Arabia beat Egypt two one, which brought a smile as the Egyptian's star player was probably going home. The laughter continued as Uruguay beat Russia three nil, which probably meant the Russian players would be off to somewhere much colder. Iran was having a fantastic tournament, which didn't stop as they managed a one-one draw against Portugal, there's another overpaid haircut on his way home. Spain's worries continued as they could only manage a two-two draw with Morocco.

After this, I decided to watch the Denmark vs France game at 15:00, there were four games per day now, I decided on this one, although I was disappointed by a frustrating nil-nil draw. I also managed to change my direction of thought onto the game, but this caused its own problems as I was able to dissect the individual performances of each player, along with the tactics and strategies of each team. Well, if nothing else a career in football management or sports psychology could await me. Jane returned home around 17:00, I shocked her by suggesting that we go out for a meal that evening. I tried to relax and enjoy the evening, although she continually grilled me as to why I had changed recently. She blamed the fact that I never switched off and my mind never stops, how right she was.

We returned home, content with the meal and my promise to relax more and try to switch my brain off. That promise lasted about 20 minutes, as I sat down to watch the highlights of the games my mind went ballistic and raced once more. I satisfied myself that, if I understood the various elements of the 'how we got there', I would be able to relax more. This next element kept throwing itself forwards, and I felt its importance. They showed me that everyone was equal without exception, everyone in the colony had everything they could possibly need. Considering this there is no rank or status, all decisions are made by whoever had an interest or stake in that matter under debate. If you think about it governments are there to make decisions on behalf of the people.

Progressing to a society and state that no longer requires a body to make those decisions, politics and politicians become redundant. But how do you enable the people to decide, well firstly the quantity of decisions reduce, as society develops and provides more for everyone. It started with free energy which had a knock-on effect for all other goods we wanted or needed. It may be a good time to distinguish between those two, 'want and need'. A 'need' is something that is needed to survive, here there are really only three, food, water, and shelter. A 'want' is something that an individual desires, but would be able to live without, such as that designer handbag. I use 'want and need' a lot in my explanations for marketing and sales. If society has everything it needs and in abundance, we have thereby taken a huge stride towards a stateless society. A society where everyone is equal, there is no hierarchy or privilege, I mentioned at the very beginning this could be your idea of utopia or anarchy.

It was a simple step that enabled people to vote and have their say on items of varying importance. Technology and the sharing of information such as we have today, is not too far away from this. Although, those in power and with wealth will cling on to this for as long as possible. Imagine something as simple as the UK referendum on 23 June 2016, in which 51.89% voted in favour of leaving the EU, 48.11% voted to remain a member. Whether you agree with the decision or the way it was presented at the time, the important thing is that people were given the vote. All other decisions are made by people who are elected to represent us, however, it's that individual and their views that persuade their vote for or against something. Whichever way you look at this, the people have relinquished their rights and ability to make decisions.

There were potentially too many things I could understand, too many problems that I could resolve. I knew that I had to draw a line under what I investigated, otherwise I would lose myself in thought. I slept well that night and wondered if I would be called to take part in another event.

Astounded In Ways I Never Thought Possible

As we both decided not to set our alarms, Wednesday morning started later than usual. It also started with some excellent news as Jane announced she was helping her sister choose some wallpaper. I knew that a shopping trip like this would keep her out for most of the day. As we lay there in bed before getting up, Jane scrolled through either word games on her phone or being nosey on Facebook. For me it was a chance to stare at my favourite spot on the ceiling, I allowed myself to simply contemplate what had happened to me over the past couple of weeks. I had evolved from detailed planning and execution of my plans for 1 November, to eagerly awaiting my next event, and delving into the enormous knowledge I had been given about humanity's future. This expanded into the truth about our creation, and the potential path we are now on. It's enough to drive anyone over the edge, and into absolute insanity. I am glad I had taken the time to consider what all this meant, and what it could be doing to me.

As Jane left around 11:00, I made my way onto my computer to check and respond to a few emails, one of which offered me some much-needed consultancy work. I needed this for the obvious income, but also as an added distraction. The correspondence took till around 12:30 when, I eagerly awaited a lunch break and hopefully the next event. Presumably, Jacron knew that I was being woken or my semi-conscious state was being interrupted, therefore we had to end the last session abruptly. Whichever it was, I managed to gain my senses quickly enough, and not call out Helena or Jacron, which would have been a bit difficult to explain to Jane.

At 13:13 just after a bit of lunch, I closed my eyes readily, within no time I was greeted by a voice other than Helena's. I grew to find a comfort in her voice, that is before the onset of pain. This time it was Jacron calling my name and uselessly telling me to blink. I enjoyed the uplifting feeling that covered my entire body along with the tingling electricity that accompanied it. It made random patterns over my skin, and once again they tracked downwards from my shoulders. This was shattered again by the intense light; this time it seemed even worse. Eventually, the intense pain subsided, it was replaced by an annoying sting until my eyes finally found their focus. As my vision restored, I could see the figures of two people. It was Jacron and Olin who looked different as they sat behind a rigid floating desk come console. It wasn't translucent as they had been previously, and I couldn't see the back of any displays.

They both greeted me and asked how I had been, Jacron explained that they detected movement of my body, consequently and as a safety measure the previous session was ended. Pouncing on the opportunity, I quickly announced that I had some questions which had worried me for some time. Both said they would be happy to answer any questions they could, and if they were able to at this time. This didn't fill me with enormous confidence, conscious of this, I didn't want them to pick up on any nervousness. The large intrusive elephant was back in the room and demanding attention. A reluctant cough cleared my throat sufficiently, I attacked head-on my most recurring worry. "Why me?", came out softly, it was soon followed by a more assertive fully structured question. "Why have I been selected?". Olin looked puzzled and quickly told me that Xander had already answered this. It was only when I clarified what I wanted further and tied it with other concerns I had. The necessary and additional items wrapped everything up neatly. Firstly, what am I supposed to do with this knowledge and information. Secondly, can they satisfy my need to want to know more about their lives and how they arrived at this beautiful and perfect place. Next, will this knowledge and what's now deep within my brain damage my health, and more importantly my mental health. Finally, and most importantly, what else do they want from me.

Olin went first and said something which I am sure I had seen before, "The best teachers are those who show you where to look, but don't tell you what to see". As he did, he sort of looked as if I should have known this, he continued to tell me that great wisdom will come with this knowledge, I would, in time figure out what I am supposed to do with it. It was the word 'wisdom' that intrigued me, with a measure of reluctancy I was happy to leave this one undone. It reminded me of something that would be said in Star Wars or that genre. As for the potential damage to my health and mental health, Olin went to great lengths to reassure me that they would never risk my wellbeing. Within his total response he used the word 'valuable' to describe me along with 'risk'. He did reassure me, but I was soon to find out what they meant by this.

Jacron then took the floor for the next response, regarding the need to know more and could they satisfy my need. I recall exactly what she said as it was exceptionally powerful, "That's what we are here for, to give you the knowledge and answer your questions". She went on to tell me that I had all the answers, but they would continue to guide me. Here again there came a phrase I wasn't expecting, 'guide me', she also tied a lot of what she was telling me to Olin's first response. Jacron announced, 'they would not be providing any additional information in the way that they had'. I had everything I needed; it was all there. Think about that for a moment, during two incredible downloads they had installed within my brain everything I could possibly need to untangle the utopia I now crave. All the information I needed was there, I just had to access it. As for what else do they want from me, well here it gets even more bizarre.

Olin then joined Jacron as she began to answer my final question, "Do you remember we told you some contributors had been given greater access, and that we wanted to evaluate certain traits", I nodded and softly said, "Yes". What came next surprised me, well, more like shocked me, and gave me a further piece of the jigsaw. She walked me through elements of the 62.87 Theory that I had explored the other day, but I knew I had only begun to scratch the surface of it. There was a crucial part of this which added a phrase called, Future Intelligence Neurological Expansion Development or FINED. I understood this section stated that at some future point they would hold the science and technology, along with the opportunity to create an improved intelligence. Olin then joined in as a display screen appeared to their side. He showed me through various visuals and graphs, although they meant little to me, but what was delivered next did. Jacron announced in a bullishly proud voice, "We are now at the stage to act upon the evaluated baseline DNA characteristics".

They both smiled as she declared that science and technology had now given them the ability to replicate 'staged improvements' in a laboratory setting. What they needed was specific DNA samples, that matched a certain criterion. Here it comes…they believed my DNA and personality traits could meet this benchmark. In short, I was going to be a guinea pig for their experiments, they wanted to sample my DNA and personality traits, and in turn this would allow them to create an improved species. In return I was given morsels or crumbs of information and views of what they wish to create. I thought about that later and for a long time after, it astounded me in ways that I had never thought possible. A part of me, granted a very small part could be used to build a completely improved species. Olin told me that they still needed to gather data and not to adjust any of my answers. As I wasn't told or sure of what part of me, or what they were looking for, this was made easier.

Tell Me More / The Plan

As they concluded their responses, they didn't ask me if I had any questions. I tried not to think about this at the time, but it did seem strange. By now, they were itching to ask me their questions and on cue they were ready. Courteously, Jacron asked if they could ask me a couple of questions, I simply nodded my approval and, in my mind, said yes. I braced myself for carefully crafted questions that would expose my personality traits, instead she delivered the simplest one yet. The question she asked was not what I expected, as she said, "Can you please tell us what happened next for you and James regarding your dismissal from the employment you clearly enjoyed?" In order that I could provide the correct response, I had to recall what I had previously told her along with Helena and Xendar. After a few quiet moments I asked, "You mean after I received the letter from Philip?", Jacron nodded.

Following a deep breath I began; I told her that you must also remember when this bombshell was received. It landed around two weeks before Christmas, all I could think of at the time was how it would ruin everything for all my family. Jane was extremely strong and carried me throughout that horrendous period. Despite everyone's best efforts, I simply couldn't get it out of my mind. Jane knew to leave me to come to terms with it in my own time. Toni was at the age when toys were out, perfume and handbags were in along with vouchers to spend in her favourite clothes shops. I must admit it was an enjoyable time as she reminded me what it was like, obviously not perfumes but albums, clothes that had to include Fred Perry and Ben Sherman. Both Jane and Toni, along with Georgina helped me take on board what had happened, not to simply accept it, but to rebuild and find a way to fight back.

James and I agreed to meet up in the new year, I had no idea what the next steps would be. This is where he stood strong, in that first meeting we both expressed how we were left speechless upon receiving the letter, but more importantly the starkness of the medical report. James said in all his years of practice he had never seen such emptiness, especially when a large amount of information was available should they have asked for it. He wanted me to walk him through that medical examination, my notes were then shown, and he congratulated me on the precise detail. He had several questions and throughout he made almost illegible notes in an A4 lined book, that had clearly seen better days. Everything about James had seen better days, his shirt whilst clean looked like it was at least 10 years old. His tie was tied shabbily and there was years' worth of stains etched into the fabric. During all the time I knew him, I think I only ever saw two different suits. Personally, I had a collection of at least nine which were recycled for new ones on a regular basis.

James laid out a provisional plan, firstly in scribble form which he said he would post out. James was old-school when it came to his use of technology, he was surprised that I didn't have a fax machine. While I was astonished that he hardly used emails, plus his grasp of attachments later had me laughing. He told me it was due to the licence and professional indemnity he had from the law society or something. The main action was for me to send a letter to the company, we worked through what it should contain, but I was to give him a call and read it through before sending. The next thing for me was to gather every piece of correspondence, file note, communication and build them into a chronological order. This was going to be relatively easy for me, but I wanted to make sure, therefore time and care would be given.

The next couple of actions fell to James, we both believed they wouldn't respond favourably to my rejection letter, which would request a further consultation meeting. We needed a plan whatever the outcome and response would be. This involved preparing a request to ACAS for mediation, although this would only happen once the Tribunal Courts had received a submission of our claim against the firm. This would require him completing the first of what would turn out to be dozens of forms. This first one set out why I was taking the action, and what I would be claiming for. Before all this, James needed to ask me the awkward question of his fees. Later

I would discover this would inadvertently be the best bit of business I have ever done. As I was more than capable of corresponding and gathering all the required documents, he said this should be a straightforward case. Considering this, he was happy to work on a fixed fee of £4,500 plus expenses, which he also agreed would only be court costs.

There it was, and there it will be. Inadvertently, my life to a degree was no longer in my hands. Once on the treadmill there was no stopping it or even slowing down. A few weeks later their response was received, I had arranged to meet with James again to prepare the Tribunal claim form. My initial letter asking them to reconsider, and for further clarity was rejected based on the contents of the medical examination report, which they claimed was prepared independently. It may have been independent, but it was still woefully inadequate and more of a copout. The Tribunal claim was around 50% completed by James, it simply required some dates and a few additions from me, and it was ready. We were claiming that I had been sacked from my position on unfair grounds and disability discrimination. It was that part that normally sends shivers down the spines of most employers, that is if you had a spine to begin with.

James also asked me to gather pay slips and personal tax records, this was the first time he had asked me what my annual salary was. I wasn't sure if the look on his face was pure amazement of what the settlement amount could be, or the fact that he had agreed to take the case on a fixed cost. During a pause on my behalf, Olin ceased the opportunity and asked how I felt during this time in my life. The main feeling I told him was confusion, it felt like I was entering a whirlwind in somebody else's body. Not within my wildest dreams did I think this would ever happen to me, and here I was living it. Jane was very supportive, from that moment forward I referred to her as 'my rock'. She seemed to know when to ask questions and when to leave me alone with my thoughts. She was understandably angry with everything, my diagnosis, the way I was treated by my employer, and now what I was having to deal with. I remember her saying in those early days that they won't get away with it and they will not take anything away from us, to which I replied, "They have already taken my sense of humour". We laughed almost uncontrollably and for what seemed like an age, when she instantly came back with, "They can have it".

As I finished this section of my response, it immediately felt like the plug had been taken out and all my energy had dissolved away. I had never wanted to end an event early, that was until now. This was explained to Olin and Jacron, fortunately they completely understood. I instantly woke up and saw it was 15:15. It felt to me that it should have been much later, we had talked about loads of things and in such a small amount of time. As I sat there, I could hardly move any part of my body, it was like heavy weights had been placed within every muscle. My eye lids fought to open but very soon they lost their battle.

Jane returned home all excited and bubbly only to find me unable to move and share in it. I explained that I had done nothing for most of the day and she immediately put this down to the excitement of seeing Toni again. Then came the lecture of working too much, not resting enough, and not telling her when I felt tired. By the time she had unpacked the shopping and told me story after story we finally had something to eat around 19:00. It was with this fuel and much needed rest that my brain began to work through everything I had gained from the earlier event. I knew I had to regulate these thoughts, otherwise I was in danger of burning out.

Chapter 12
Understanding From Knowledge Does Not Replace Experience

Wednesday gave way to Thursday, and in the early hours I found myself wide awake and contemplating the CDT event that occurred only hours before. It was the implications, and the complex outcomes that woke me. No wonder my brain feels like it's being turned into spaghetti, every other day I am given more information, and more knowledge, which only produces more questions. I have no outlet, no one to share this with, and even if I did, I doubt they would believe me despite how compelling I would be. As the hours passed, daylight and the dawn chorus allowed me to focus on my 'comfort' spot on the ceiling. With this further awakening, comes a clarity and defined recollection on some of what was said yesterday. They used the words 'Benefit the entire universe', I have learnt that they are extremely careful in what they say. How could they benefit everything that exists through the work they are doing now. Maybe as Jacron said, 'I have all the answers', I just need guidance to uncover them. I know this is not a question I could ask them directly.

I guess this extends to my recurring question, what am I supposed to do with this information and understanding I now have. Add to this, the gift I seem to have been given to resolve problems easily and quickly. It is this question that worries me more than any other. They would not have given me this if there wasn't a plan, and an objective. What I must do is decipher and untangle this in conjunction with many other things. Maybe if I adjust my questions, I may be able to obtain more meaningful answers. Surely, anything I do in 2018 onwards would have a direct impact, either in a positive or negative way on the future they exist in. When you contemplate it in this way, the plan of my existence must already have been decided. Because of this, whatever I do it makes no difference to the future for Olin, Helena, Jacron and indeed everyone and everything else in the year 2073. Their existence could or could not depend on my actions. If I decide to complete my suicide plans for 1 November, then all of what I have now obtained means nothing, and it will have all been wasted. I dislike the word and concept of a person's 'destiny', although they did select me from a choice of 7 billion others. Maybe I just haven't discovered the knowledge or understanding which will answer all of this for me.

I was also troubled by the long-term affect of what they were doing and wanted to achieve. Within the 62.87 Theory and the section covering FINED, they're looking to create a superior intelligence, and thereby an improved species. They acknowledge the importance to ensure whatever they do; it will not have a negative effect on the future for humanity. Throughout this theory it regularly referred to the laws of Darwin stating correctly that any species will develop, and it will 'descent with modification'. Simply, this means that any creature will develop on its merits and at its own pace, typically in line with other species and the environment it inhabits. That is except for humans, who it proved developed at an exaggerated rate through intervention, and only in this way. Even their own Charter states that 'Science must never be used to create new lifeforms or recreate extinct lifeforms'. With the power they now have, they can create a new species of humans which are clearly outside the laws set out by Darwin. Just because they can do this, does not give them the right to do it.

Maybe I have been given this knowledge so that I can make the decision, if this is the case then that's an incredible power, and surely too much for one person. There is an equally incredible flipside to this conundrum. I have been able to bear witness to a future that is perfect, and which rips my emotions to pieces. Humanity had finally fixed all its wrongs; it was eventually restoring the planet to its original state. Already, I see the huge potential for good contained within the information given to me. I just need to unlock the knowledge held within the two downloads; this could be easier said than done.

A Confidante

Eventually, my usual routine resumed as Jane sprang into action at 05:15 when her alarm pierced the silence that preceded it. After all the rushing around, I finally managed to sit and have a quiet coffee around 08:30. I remembered that my old school friend Dave was going to be in Liverpool visiting some family. Chancing a phone call, to my relief he had some free time just before lunch. We met up in a Costa of my choosing, which was just off the motorway and halfway between Liverpool and Warrington. Following this he was heading back to Liverpool to pick up his wife Linda and head back to Cumbria. I think he could tell I was troubled or worried about something, after knowing someone for over 40 years I guess it's hard to hide.

Over a delightful latte or two we chatted about all manner of things, the world cup, what music we were currently listening to and of course our families. Eventually, we got to the awkward part of the conversation, even though I have shared almost everything with Dave about my illness and my feelings. Despite this, and despite our close friendship, I couldn't tell him too much about what had been happening. I did tell him something was going on, but it wasn't anything that would put me in harm or danger in any way. Instead of this, perhaps some good would come out of it, but once again I couldn't expand on it. He simply leaned over the table and put his hand on my forearm and said, "I am always here if you need me, no matter what it is". As he looked straight into my eyes, I had to do everything to stop the tears. I held it together and simply said, "I know mate". Remember, it's that word mate that takes us back to our school days, and where we would defend each other at all costs.

We parted with a simple handshake, and of course no manly shoulder-bump, we both said at the same time, "See you soon". That was enough for me, I had not unloaded anything really, but I felt I had shared enough and all that I could. Dave knew that something was happening to me, if I had shared any detail with him, I probably wouldn't have known where to stop. Obviously, I didn't want to jeopardise any further CDT events from taking place. Returning home, it felt like a weight had been lifted. That feeling must have stayed with me as later that night Jane commented that I looked more chilled. As usual Dave was given all the credit for his achievement, he had done nothing apart from put his hand on my arm, but I knew he was there to listen and not judge. In the afternoon I was inspired by their notion to reset their year count, starting from the birth of the digital age. I decided to focus some of my energy into creating the ten best songs of each year, starting with 1979. This was fortunate for me as it was a brilliant starting point.

Thursday evening brought me back to my love of football and focus on the world cup again. It was England's last game in the group matches and our toughest yet as we met Belgium. Predictably, we got beat one nil which set us up nicely in the last 16 knockout round against Columbia on 3 July. This is the part most fans like as it's…'do or die, win or lose'. One of the tastiest games was going to be France v Argentina, while Brazil can look forward to Mexico and Belgium would face Japan. You could see the overall winner coming from one of these games.

In the other games, Senegal lost to Columbia zero to one, also as predictable, Japan lost to Poland by the same score. In the remaining game Panama lost to Tunisia one to two. On the highlights programme I caught the other games from the day before which were Mexico who lost three nil to Sweden, Switzerland could only manage a two-two draw against Costa Rica. I also impressed myself with my ability to switch my brain off in an attempt to win back the balance in my favour. Thinking less and not trying to access the files to understand more would certainly help with my sleep.

Now I Understand

Friday began with its normal routine of Jane wishing it was 17:00 as she got ready for work at 05:15. I was savouring every minute of the day as I had already planned every activity I wanted to get through. You could be excused for thinking that having a disease which can be as debilitating would make us want the opposite, but I have always worked best when having a plan. With the assistance of my ceiling, a plan was formed. It would begin with my morning ritual of a shower, followed by a very quick breakfast while I take my medication. This would be immediately followed by a drive to the railway station to drop Jane off, and a more leisurely drive back with a slight detour to my local favourite café. With the help of a latte, I would have the chance to decide upon the course of my questions for the CDT event later. Returning home, I would complete my vlog which I had already prepared in my mind. In real life, this overrun as I found it difficult to draw a line under what had happened and my opinion regarding each part. External demands would interrupt my planning momentarily, I needed to respond to the opportunity for some consultancy. Fortunately, they had already provided a scope for the work via a form I had previously sent them, which provided an outline for what they required. To my surprise and amazement my mind went into overdrive, and I returned to them the most comprehensive reply. It included everything they needed to do with a costed timescale, imagery templates, you name it, it was there in perfect detail, even if I do say so myself.

Lunch came as a relief, while I should have been resting in preparation for the afternoon, I simply couldn't help myself. After a spot of lunch which was spent asking Alexa to play various songs from 1979, I inevitably closed my eyes. Oliver's Army by Elvis Costello & The Attractions was playing, this was a dead certainty to be included in any worthwhile list. As the song faded in my ears, it was replaced by the calling of my name, it was repeatedly called until I acknowledged it with a facial movement. Then began the phases of the CDT device preparing our connection. It started with a comforting warm and uplifting feeling that suspended my entire weight. My focus and attention were snapped back to reality as the lights began to sting and burn. I tried my best to disregard the pain, continually telling myself it wasn't real. Thankfully, this was interrupted by a voice asking me to open my eyes. The pain started to relax into an annoying discomfort as I blinked rapidly as instructed. Eventually, I was able to recognise the voice as Jacron'. My blinking was beginning to pay dividends. Slowly, I established the slightly distorted outlines of Helena and Trynes. Jacron made the usual polite introductions as usual, then, quite sternly she asked if I was feeling up to talking today. I confirmed this via a simple nod of my head.

Before the interrogation on each part could begin, I fired a friendly question as I was genuinely confused. "It's nice to see different people here, but why are there changes each time?", I asked in a soft questioning voice. Jacron initially corrected me as there have been occasions were this hasn't happened. She continued to tell me that each person has a specific role, although the main researchers were Helena and Trynes, therefore, it was only right that they should attend where it was applicable. As she told me this, Helena tried her best not to smile, although without complete success which was nice to see.

While the floor seemed to be mine, I fired another question, this time I rolled into the conversation that I was beginning to access the files better. Although as I began to understand what was contained, it drove me to question it. To explain this further, I said confidently, "Simply understanding something from knowledge does not replace the experience of learning it in life". Jacron simply smiled, and said,

"That's how it should be". I wanted to disagree and quote examples where education clearly fails when these steps are not followed. Cautiously, I pulled myself back thinking it may derail the conversation, and I was beginning to value the time more.

Jacron stood up and took a couple of steps forward, without any gesture or outward communication Helena did the same. Consciously, they left a 5-foot gap between them, this allowed a display screen to appear, it hovered neatly between the two. Jacron stated, "Accessing the information in order to understand sections can be confusing". Here was another gigantic and monumental underestimation of the facts, although they assumed I should already have known this. Hundreds of images then lit up the screen as they overlapped, they fought for superiority, this emergence was useless as hundreds more were propelled into my eyeline. As she explained further, these images began to illustrate factual depictions of events that happened. She knew that I wanted to understand the journey between 2018 and 'now'. In rapid succession images flowed and somehow even without dates or descriptions, I was able to make the thread between them. As I was able to see each part, I understood the resulting journey better. What I had to do was train myself to dig further into the archives. All of this, I began to see was contained within the download I had been given. Crucially, as I began to question each result further, evidence of the journey would reveal itself. Helena then seemed ready to give me an example as I interrupted, "Now I see", to which Jacron replied in a matter-of-fact manner, "We knew you would".

I wanted to ask a dozen more questions, but I thought if I ask now, they may be contained within the knowledge I have, therefore, I will just look dumb. I had to fight hard to halt my mind from racing out of control and wanting to delve into the download. This deep abundance of yet untapped knowledge is there waiting for me to dive into and extract a meaningful understanding. Jacron ended this brief, but crucial conversation with a simple line which I will never forget, "We are here to help guide you, and you will find what you are looking for, it will all come to you soon". By this, she knew that I instantly understood this also meant the direction I would have to take once all the CDT events had finished. Jacron took the opportunity to complete her sentence, "don't forget the tools and skills that you now have." As she said this the screen displayed the following words, it was only brief, but finally seemed to bring everything together. It was the added knowledge given to me by Olin, Vans-tem6, and Staten44, this was just before Helena downloaded the 62.87 Theory directly into my brain. They appeared as simple black text on a perfect white background.

The Ripple Effect

Ownership & Responsibility

Language

These letters and words slowly faded and morphed into new ones...

62.87 Theory

Solutions/Resolution

Understanding

The Journey

Taking all the time I was given, I looked at each of the words, their gravitas grew ever stronger, and I realised the enormous powers I had been given. I knew that each one came with a huge responsibility and immense privilege. Eventually, I was beginning to see their importance and how they were intrinsically linked to each other. It was the first time that the remaining skill had been given a formal name, Solutions/Resolution made complete sense. I could easily see and understand a problem, and just as easily and with astonishing speed develop a solution or resolution to meet that need. With all these skills and knowledge, I could see I now had to respect each one in its individual state but also as a whole. As yet, I didn't know why I had been selected or given this trust, although I had a feeling I would find out and it would all become apparent. For now, I had to hold back my thinking as an uncontrollable number of questions would risk derailing all that I had been told.

As I allowed all of this to sink in, I made visual screenshots to aid my recall, I could see that Helena was keen to continue her explanation, or example. Jacron took a small step backwards as if to hand over the reins to Helena. Somewhat sheepishly, Jacron retook her seat. Space Exploration as a heading appeared on the screen, I was shown a strange looking spaceship. It resembled a cylinder that narrowed towards what looked like its rear. Along its matt black sides were rows of intermittently broken white lights that pulsed from left to right. On the top sat a long oval disk shape that also had rows of lights along its sides and top. As Helena began to speak, rapid schematic diagrams and charts told me of the ship's abilities and functions. Proudly she said, "This, our EX11>453 edition deep space vessel, can reach to the outskirts of the known universe in under 50 years." This was said, and I heard it correctly, 'known universe'. Incredibly, this means in over 2,000 years they are still unable to define the true size of the universe.

The images smoothly changed to what had to be a solar system filled with planets and strange looking clouds of pale blues and purples. I was told that this deep space vessel uses their latest EX11 Matter Propulsion System, at which point the display screen illustrated this. It was incredible in that space or matter is moved along the inside of the cylinder. It seemed to grab sections of space matter from the front nose of the ship and force it at a speed of 7.23 matter pulses per second. I presumed this was an achievement as they both smiled at this fact. These vessels are unmanned, but they allow them to understand matter and map structures throughout the universe. Their aim is to map these invisible forces to one day allow space travel, just as they are now able to reverse time travel with CDT technology. These words landed on me with the weight they were intended. Helena said, "With this intense mapping knowledge, it will one day allow us to use CDT technology to send solid matter to planets for even closer evaluation. Our goal is to send humans to these places using this technology, thereby eradicating the need for physical transportation."

In her monotone style she continued telling me that once our science understands and utilizes the tracks that matter has left behind since Evantis246. This being the mega black hole that created our universe as we know it today. It opens up everything, it's this fourth dimension that brings together time, space, and matter, essentially the reason we are here today, it holds the key to everything. Without either of them saying anything, I immediately knew they were using this technology to understand the future for our universe. That's an amazing thought right there, what, and how our universe will look like in the future. I have learnt recently that they have an immense hunger for knowledge, I know it drives everything they do and everything they stand for. The 62.87 Theory was the seed that germinated from the brain of a single philosopher, come scientist, come visionary into a force that would define the disturbance that readjusted evolution. Such power, such trust and to be held in the pen of a single person. It's incredible to see what's been spawned from that theory and the story it told and opened.

Okay, at this point my head was officially about to explode or implode I wasn't sure which. I was a simple boy about town one day and here we are at half time, and I am looking 2,034 years into the future. The display screen hurled thousands of images showing the technological steps we will take, with each one I was given diagrams and charts for each. Helena told me that all this information can be unlocked by me, I have the tools and the ability to track humanity's progression path for whatever topic I wish to investigate. It was all beginning to make sense, but I knew I would need time to digest this and work through a process in my own time. All of this, this vast expanse of information is now readily available to me. This was not them showing off, instead it was them showing me how to learn and understand. Sometimes, to find the answers we need to start at the end point rather than at the beginning.

Everyone has their own learning style, and for me it's through learning to unlock the pieces and given time to understand how everything works. At the end of this visual onslaught of information, I think Jacron could see it was beginning to overload me, she jumped in and asked if it would be alright to move on. I nodded and the screen quickly vanished, at the same time Helena returned to her seat. As she did a transparent screen and desk morphed in front of each person. For some reason a feeling came over me and, in my head, I spoke the words, 'Now I Understand'. Jacron looked directly at me and gave a soft all-knowing smile.

"The wise man is one who knows what he does not know."

Lao Tzu

Paint A Full Picture

I could see that Jacron was keen to have their chance to continue the questioning, possibly before I burnt out again. As before, she hit me with a crafted question, "Last time you told us how James helped you to prepare, what happened next and how did this affect you?" There it was again, a couple of words that probed deeper than just telling my side of the story, and how was I affected. I shuffled as if to find a comfortable position as I began to tell my recollections. James was always available, either on the phone or ready to meet in person. It was a level of service I didn't expect, and I was always conscious not to take advantage of his time. A letter was received which blatantly rejected my request for them to reconsider their decision. Upon receipt of this, James was ready to step up a gear. The tribunal papers were submitted, along with the fees, which I was happy to pay. Everything seemed to operate on 'Maximum times to respond'. For example, upon receipt of this, the other side had 28 days to respond with a counterclaim if they wished to defend it.

During this time, I remember that James and I met to review the file of correspondence I had collated since I had been diagnosed. He seemed impressed with my attention to detail, and that I had presented them in chronological order. He also wanted a copy of my contract of employment, I made detailed notes on tasks I was given. He then asked me to talk him through the events that brought me to the point of contacting him. As I did, he made hurried scribbles in the same tatty notebook. I skipped the events of my diagnosis to the point that Jane initially contacted Philip to say that I had been taken into hospital, and it looked serious. She knew I had no time for him outside of work, although the call had to be made from a business perspective. Jane later told me that he simply didn't know what to say apart from, 'Do you know when he will be back?' There was little sympathy, I don't think he knew how to portray his feelings apart from how it would impact him and the business.

Jane sent in the doctor's note which signed me off work for three months, these are technically called 'Fit notes, or fitness to work note'. The GP simply ticks whether you are deemed fit to work, and in my case I clearly wasn't. Around four weeks later I felt fit enough to give Philip a call, he nervously asked me how I was doing. He was never what you would call a 'people person', generally he didn't know how to manage the people around him, and more often reverted to shouting and bullying. During this initial phone call, I gave him an open invitation to visit at any time, and he gave me reassurance that there would always be a position for me.

Around three weeks later he visited, it was plain to see he constantly wished he could be anywhere else. James told me that was immaterial, which I had figured out at the time. On another occasion Sharon arranged to call and see me, she told me about the due process they needed to follow. The key part to this, which they never seemed to follow was to find 'Reasonable Adjustments'. This involved the company looking to see what adjustments they could make to facilitate my return to the role I had. I told James of the frequent correspondence between myself and Phillip/Sharon, in which I was continually asking for progress updates. After around six months of inactivity, I took matters into my own hands and developed a method of working. Essentially, this would ensure that I remained productive and of value to the firm. Shortly after this I was offered a new contract, although this was best described as laughable. I showed James a copy of this, essentially it offered me a position on a three-month rolling basis, with a fraction of the salary I had before, it also removed all the benefits I previously enjoyed.

I could feel myself being wound up again, my heart was beginning to speed up and the palms of my hands were getting sweaty. At this point I looked over at Jacron as she leaned forward as if to want more, I could also see Helena's fingertips frantically twitching. Whilst I was delivering my answer, I was trying best not to question why they wanted such detail about this part of my life. I parked that thought and continued where I left off. James smiled when he viewed these particular documents, he told me these were excellent and very much in our favour. It was shortly after this that I was put in contact with James as the company wanted to conduct a health assessment.

I paused for a moment and told them what James said to me, 'The company must follow a process to evaluate my capacity to return to work'. He also said, 'this assessment should also guide them as to what adjustments they need to consider'. This is all covered in the UK by the equality act 2010, he told me it's a guide but also a legal requirement. As you can probably gather there were a few things that didn't seem right. As they had then terminated my contract, I was able to take them to an employment tribunal. The next part was for both parties to try and come to an agreement without the cost of a court case. James and I soon discovered they had no interest in mediation, in the end, they stopped all forms of communication.

Complete Devastation

I recall the first session in court, I looked directly at Jacron and told her that you need to remember, this was the first time I had ever set foot in a court. Everything was alien to me, but James talked me through each step and told me what would happen. The court building was relatively new, and the scene was set as we had to pass through airport style security as we entered. As we waited to be called into the court room my heart raced, it was the same for every occasion after this. James pointed to a lady sat on the other side of a busy holding area. Her clothes were a bit scruffy, and her grey hair looked like it needed sorting out, as Jane would say. She had a small luggage case on wheels, a laptop case and a briefcase with papers sticking out of it. James told me she was a barrister; it was almost unheard of to use a barrister, and certainly not at such an early stage. As we were called into the courtroom, I noticed how cold it was compared to the waiting area. We all sat in front of a raised area, a court clerk said, 'please rise'. A smartly dressed man, probably in his late 60's walked in and sat in the middle seat of this raised area. He gestured for us to all be seated, as we sat facing the judge the court clerk sat to my right making notes.

I don't know why I was giving them as much detail, I thought this would all be unknown to them, therefore I had better paint a full picture. Anyway, he asked if we were all present and he announced how the tribunal would progress. To begin with he asked both parties why mediation hadn't resolved the dispute. This was the first opportunity for James to really put the boot in, he stated that the other side displayed no interest. I put that down as an early goal for us, or an early yellow card for them. The judge told their barrister as the defence, that it was their responsibility to collate a chronological file, each side would disclose evidence they wished to use. Suddenly, it was all starting to feel very serious, and James began to pull a lot of legal jargon as to what he expected. I noticed how this was annoying her as he pushed more and more on to her shoulders. The judge did ask the question if she would be attending all the pre-hearings. As she answered, 'Yes', he couldn't hide his disbelief and amazement. And that was it, as the judge stood up, we followed as a sign of respect, and we made our way out of room 12.

James and I walked out and headed for a coffee shop just over the road, he took time to debrief me on the events that had happened. The next hearing was set for six weeks, and it was their responsibility to present the bundle of evidence. Ahead of this James would get an advanced copy and we agreed to meet up again once this was received. Around three weeks after our first court appearance, I received word from a fellow employee that the business had ceased trading. On top of everything else this news couldn't have come at a worse time. I was having my third relapse in the past 12 months and with this news it could only be described as complete devastation.

How do you describe a relapse, well my best effort was that it's like the worst hangover you have ever endured, whilst still being extremely drunk. For me it seemed as though my whole body was uncontrollable, I couldn't walk without falling over, this was due to my balance resembling a two-year-old child. I had a constant headache and the fatigue I normally experienced had been dialled up to maximum, as a result I craved sleep all the time. When an MS sufferer has a relapse, it's important to act fast and get steroids within the first few days. You will see how frustrating this is when you need to speak to an MS nurse or consultant. The process then was to phone the support line, only to hear a recorded message informing you that someone would respond within 3 days. Inevitably, I would be asked to attend a specialist hospital in Liverpool, where they would perform an MRI scan to confirm if there was evidence of new lesions within the brain or spinal cord. Once confirmed you would be given Intravenous (IV) Steroids over three days. These were intended to reduce the lesions which were caused by an infection somewhere in the body. During the three days of the injections, I could never sleep, and my brain rushed like a racehorse on speed, just a nice side effect of the steroids.

This devastating news left me shellshocked, although I was also reminded that the firm had used an outsourced HR function. Once I was able, I began to research Stowama2, this was the firm used by my ex-employers. My research uncovered just how large they are, although, more importantly Stowama2 HR PLC to give them their full name, also provide insurance should one of their clients require aid in an employment tribunal claim. This was a game changer, but before I gave this information to James, I wanted to have a perfectly clear grasp on what this meant for us. It was a good job I did, Stowama2 sold my employers an insurance package which provided full legal support with up to £1million worth of cover. I could see the faces of Jacron, and Helena lighten slightly as I told them this news, it proved nearly impossible to get a full-blown smile, but I would continue to try. The relief didn't end there, although the next discovery was tarnished with an equally devastating kick in the balls. Stowama2 used another firm who provided the underwriting of this insurance, they were called Calder Insurance PLC.

Now wait for it as that kick in the balls just got harder, and with more intent. It was Calder Insurance PLC who provided the 'health practitioner', and it was them who provided the 'independent' medical report. Remember, it was this flaky report that stated I was unable to return to my role within the firm due to my health. I was thrown on the scrapheap because of this pathetic report. It was prepared by someone who probably knew very little about MS, and I later discovered they had not even bothered to request my health records. As I delivered this part of my response, I could feel my hands getting sweatier and my heart rate was beating faster and faster until the point I thought it was going to burst. My focus then returned to Helena first and then to Jacron, I apologised for the vivid descriptions I had used. Jacron told me not to worry, they had referenced my use of language and understood the point I was making.

I stopped at this point and asked them if this was helping them in some way. Jacron told me it was of interest to them, and they were keen to understand how I was feeling during this period. I responded by simply saying it pulled at every emotion I had. I was very ill during this time, but I had no time to rest, every ounce of my being was focused on the tribunal. I would be left with nothing if James wasn't able to continue with my claim against the firm, especially with them having ceased trading. I was physically and mentally drained all the time, it's difficult to describe how bad it was. This is when Jane picked me up from the floor time after time. With every knock she was there to help me, I would need to gather myself together and go again time after time. She never gave up, she gave me unbelievable strength and belief that I was right, and that one day we would see victory.

At this point Jacron told me they would end the CDT event now; they both thanked me for reliving this period of my life. For the first time they stood in front of me with their feet together and their arms drawn in behind their backs. They both nodded in a gesture of what looked like gratitude, and for the first time I felt I was on an equal footing with them. As I woke, I slowly picked up my phone to observe the time, although before I had even unlocked it with my fingerprint, I knew it was 16:30. I registered the bright sunlight and the warmth coming through the window. An extreme feeling of happiness along with contentment filled my waking body. It may not sound much, but it's rare that this happens to me.

Taking a moment to register all that had happened, my head should be scrambled, and I know that feeling will come soon enough, but for now I could relax in the glow of complete satisfaction. Then the questioning and interrogation began, although even this was in a relaxed manner. I had to ask myself the question, what were they probing for, how could they benefit from all this information. The employment tribunal was a time of deep destress for me, my feelings were constantly being tested and I could see they were picking up on this. How could this possibly help them, what was it they were seeking. I now possessed the power to understand and resolve solutions, but I was unable to figure this out. They had disclosed their desire to create a superior intelligence contained within an enhanced lifeform, my question remains, just how do I fit in with all these plans.

"I learned very early the difference between knowing the name of something and knowing something."

Richard Feynman

Chapter 13
Lose Interest, Run Out Of Money, Or Die

Saturday morning began with a clarity and focus that had been missing from my life for too long. Following the CDT event yesterday, the remainder of my day passed in a drunken haze, which was an interesting use of a metaphor as these days, I don't drink alcohol. It seemed as though I was on autopilot, I picked Jane up from the station as normal, and we got our customary takeaway on the return journey home. Jane told me about her day, and how glad she was the week was over and how much she really needed the weekend. Although we both knew this would be far too short, and no doubt be wasted on trivial and mundane tasks. That semi-drunken haze allowed me time, not to dive headfirst into the downloaded files, but to spend further time evaluating what I now have. I also considered the most effective use of my time, by this I meant time extracting the understanding of humanity's progression, this would then allow me time within the remaining CDT events to question their validity.

Our Saturday morning routine included grocery shopping which meant a trip to our local Sainsbury's store. This had my anger level turned up to full volume once more. I would have to observe the blatant misuse of the disabled carpark by 4x4 drivers of top end, overpriced, overvalued, overwide vehicles. Their owners feeling justified in taking these spaces simply because it gave them extra width for their pride and joy. Typically, this first supermarket didn't have everything we required, which meant an onward trip to a second outlet which happened to contain a Costa coffee, by this time it was certainly required. As Jane whizzed around picking up the other non-essentials, I made my way for a much-deserved latte. While there, I decided I had to understand how Nations laid down their arms and we simply stopped fighting each other. As I thought about this topic, I knew it would have many other benefits for humanity and surely the planet.

Jane re-joined me, and over a second coffee she told me we had previously agreed to meet Georgina and the family on Sunday. A 'nice' family breakfast had been arranged for us at my favourite café in the village. I have noticed in recent years that our lifestyles have modified, brunch is now a thing as is the mandatory coffee while out shopping. Sundays are given over to retail therapy in huge out of town overcrowded carparks. Even our Saturday evening entertainment is blocked with mindless celebrity dancing shows or wannabe singers who crave a glamorous lifestyle. The odd quiz show is thrown in with a smattering of Z list celebrities, these either try to regain their comedy brand, or others who have become celeb's just for being incredibly stupid.

Back to this family breakfast, for an easy life I accepted the blame for forgetting that Jane <u>had</u> previously told me about this event. While Jane pottered in the garden, it gave me the excuse to rest unencumbered by any distractions. This is where Jane is most happy, and I must admit she does keep it looking in fantastic colour throughout the spring and summer. My afternoon was spent appearing to fall asleep in front of the TV while watching sport, instead I unlocked the first deep dive into humanity's progression. As suggested, I began with looking at both ends of the spectrum, first in visual form which would then reveal the data to support each image. Tens of thousands of images then flashed before my eyes. As they continued to come, each one jockeyed for prime position. I soon learnt that I could easily control their flow, just like a tap I could allow more to appear or even drip feed them one by one. As my focus homed in on a single image, I could easily access the data or information that supported it.

I had an encyclopedic sum of information available through merely concentrating on a topic. But now it was more than just the ability to access it, now I was able to begin the task of understanding it. Without much surprise, the future offered a tranquil and harmonious place, people moved freely across the colonies and across the planet. I could also see there was a single common language and of course a common goal, which I knew was the 62.87 Evolution. There were no borders and no defined countries, therefore, there was freedom of movement. Humanity with their single colony structure had built and gained a great deal. Seamless and rapid transport across the world meant their three phases of life could be conducted anywhere. People didn't just live near their place of birth as many of us do today. Well, technically they did, however, this single location was Earth, and the great colony complex they had created. Although even this wasn't strictly true as outreaches on other remote planets was also an option. I could see everything clearly, even on other planets within the universe they had developed research centres. It was incredible, but I had to park this and refocus. It was only when I dug deeper, I found the great colony had a name, Angkor-Dos-Poi-4 and it was often referred to as simply Angkor. Even this revelation had me wanting to know more, was it named after a person or maybe a place.

It became apparent that as I understood more, the more questions I had, rapid transport, outreach colonies, and even the name. I had to stop myself going down different routes, I could quickly see the danger in this. I began with my own brief which was to understand how humanity ended all wars and the production of weapons. My first parallel understanding was how humanity also benefited from the use of a single language. The concept of war which could be defined simply as fighting, is completely alien to them, although they understood what caused people and countries to fight, both pre and post the digital age. What I wanted to know is what was the catalyst for change. For this I knew I had to understand the problem in the first instance, and as completely as possible.

As my mind cleared, images by their thousands rushed in of incredible weapons and infrastructure all designed to strike at a moment's notice and wipe out millions of lives. I could also see the responsibility for releasing these lay with a single person. This visualisation of one man, and it is inevitably a man, who has their finger hovering over the button, was evident in many cases. Clarity came headlong towards me and illustrated what I already thought, and what I already knew. Often, it's one person who instigates wars and sends thousands, and all too often millions to their premature death. It's the fear of being attacked which results in paranoia on a monumental scale. Combining all of this sends countries into a spiralling state of increased fear, and the need for often unbalanced defence. As my mind sorted through the images, I could see how long-term security was draining the already dwindled resources of many nations.

The UK will spend £35.948 billion on defence in 2017/18, this is up 1.7% on the previous year. This huge chunk of money is equivalent to 2.1% of its GDP. Compare this to its health care spend for the same period which will be £214.4 billion. Now here's a stark comparison, only £700 million was spent on cancer research in the same period. If you examine any other Nation, you will probably find a similar story. For example, in the US their spend in 2018 is set to be $682.49 billion. The global military expenditure has increased a whopping 75% over the past 20 years. This is an eye-watering $1.7 trillion annually since 2009. New nations are adding to this sum every year as they feel the need to join the arms race, for a perceived threat that doesn't need to exist. At the start of 2018 nine states possessed approximately 14,465 nuclear weapons, of which 3,750 were deployed with operational forces. It may worry you to know that these include USA, Russia, UK, France, China, India, Pakistan, Israel and the Democratic People's Republic of Korea (DPRK, or North Korea). All it would take to wipe out the world is for one person in power to press their button, retaliation would take care of the rest.

Power To The People

Sadly, this is not the end of this incredibly insane spending. We need to add to that sum the additional spend by nations on security, including what's conveniently called 'intelligence'. Those eye-watering sums become increasingly more difficult to stomach. I needed to clear my thinking and focus again on the journey humanity took to free itself from this mass stupidity. Almost instantly, I saw again the World Change Organisation logo, but just as quickly I was hit by what various nations spend on things like health, education, infrastructure etc. I must concentrate on one, I remember Helena telling me about an initial 36 visionaries of the World Change Movement WCM, that later became the WCO. It was these visionaries who brought together invaluable skills in engineering, project management and the vast array of sciences, and each one had a common goal. Their initial goal was to also create the first colony and draft the rules for entry. What I can now see must have been what those 36 people originally envisaged. A world of peace with no fear, no greed and humanity living with a common goal. It was very humbling for me as I was probably the only human who was able to view what it eventually became.

Somewhere in these early days the phrase Build Today for a Better Tomorrow BTBT was coined. They had incredible foresight and belief that one day peace would come. They knew that one day humanity would build together and finally find its true purpose. It quickly became clearer the enormity of what these people achieved, but also the challenge they faced. They created a plan for change, alongside creating the plans for the first colony. I then saw how these were somehow intertwined and self-reliant, that alone was astonishing if you think about it. It was shown in the 62.87 Theory that we have difficulty contemplating plans beyond 50 years, this just places it in context.

I found the WCM was not a political party, however, they created a manifesto that showed the path to redemption. When this manifesto was published it became the calling rally for those who demanded change. Conversely, it was seen as a threat to the establishment and the businesses that fuelled it, and conveniently that functioned in the other direction. I was unable to see the exact timeline, for some reason dates were missing or redacted from the data that supported the information I viewed. The data also omitted the names of the 36 who published this manifesto. It was these plans for free energy from nuclear fusion, coupled with a plentiful supply of zero cost food, and a simple clutter free lifestyle that grew the WCM' numbers. Wealthy contributors and their families happily parted their luxury lifestyles and bought into the simple ethos that it would be their future generations who would benefit… one day.

The blueprint for the first colony would be home and a place of work for 17,324,160 people. It would be 100% self-sufficient and provide everything each member needed. Everyone entering Colony 1A would be equal and they would all contribute to the health and wellbeing of the colony. I could see the colony grow, and as more scientists and leading computer engineers were attracted, it flourished and provided further enhanced lifestyles. Throughout this period the remainder of humanity observed from a distance, eventually the WCM and its ever-increasing manifesto for change grew in popularity. Business leaders, politicians and even world leaders began to hunger for a better world. The WCM also sought to undermine the establishment with how nations were run, and people governed. Governments were challenged by the people who demanded change, they began to win through almost invisible protests and peaceful anarchistic actions.

Taxes were no longer given to support the mass paranoia of world leaders; eventually complete disarmament agreements were signed. The WCM' manifesto also highlighted the waste attributed to how people are governed. Governments and those in power are elected to serve the people, they should make decisions that improve our lives. If they are seen to serve their own self-interests rather than making these difficult decisions, they become redundant. 100% self-sufficient colonies that provided fulfilled and rewarding lives were craved by more and more. As science grew, manufacturing techniques improved, and computer systems took more of the strain. All these factors allowed for more sophisticated and larger colonies to be built.

Finally, humanity took over where governments and nations had failed, BTBT meant our resources were channelled into the improvement of our lives. I could also see that other factors also changed during this period of flux, the war on drugs and crime was instrumental. Although, it was the revolutionary changes in education, and the use of science to provide the stimulus that proved to be the game changer. As I sat there in the comfort of my armchair in summer 2018, I could watch the spread of the colonies. I could see how they improved and grew in size; the planet was also being rebuilt and revitalized at the same time. It was a key objective of the early manifesto that resources and efforts would be made to right the abuse of humanity's past. As I looked deeper, I observed how computers developed to be a continual aid to the colonies. Even to the extent that computers would manufacture and erect the growing structures of the colony. It really was a magnificent sight.

We are the only species that has the ability to ask certain probing questions, we have asked science to determine our future and make sense of the universe. I have no idea why I was presented with this information; I was fully involved with seeing the growth and spread of the colony. This is where the 62.87 Theory was presented to the world, I remember being told it took 16 years before it was fully validated and thereby set as their evolutionary purpose. Having seen the theory, or at least bits that I understood, I can see how it may have been divisive. Those 16 years must have thrown the scientific world into turmoil, but eventually all of humanity agreed with the theory. I would have to revisit this entire topic, but for now I was hugely satisfied that I knew how we put down our arms, stopped fighting and eventually had a common goal.

A piece of information that was buried among the multitude of supporting data pointed towards the author of the theory. Each research scientist was given a number to mask their identity and retain anonymity. Therefore, I know it was scientist #62 who produced this work that changed humanity's perception of our development and purpose. I also know that it was this scientist's first submission, the second two digits #87 refer to its time or point of publication. In total there were 75 submissions, although even this information was partially redacted. Now my search has a possible identity for the author, I need to find who is #62. I could also see summaries of the other submissions, who knows maybe a link could be found here. While I could access this important information, it felt different in some way, it was the only information that felt unreal.

Increased Pace

Saturday evening came as a peaceful relief, I tried hard not to delve any further, but I couldn't resist going back to the information and files within the 62.87 Theory. I wanted to see if there was any mention of the time before its publication. What I found replicated what Helena had told me just a few days previously. It was many years after the first colony was incepted when the rules by which everyone lived were agreed, this became their first Charter. Sadly, I couldn't find any events that I would recognise, although this deeper dive only confirmed the importance of the charter and the rules for entry. It was clear to see the charter helped them control science, they were obviously capable of many things and without it who knows what could happen. Additionally, I couldn't find the 'rules' for entry into the colony, I would have to add this to a growing list of questions.

Sunday morning started much earlier than normal as we needed to get ready to meet Georgina and her tribe for breakfast. I am often reminded that this is 'a thing now', and I needed to 'get with it'. We were all meeting at a place called The Farm, and admittedly the food there is very good. We arrived around 15 minutes early which wound Jane up, but it's a symptom of my past life that I now find very hard to change. I was never late for a business meeting, I always had everything I needed for whichever meeting I attended. I know I probably had several nicknames for these traits, but they always served me well and clients knew I was always reliable, and it sent the right message.

Georgina turned up looking casual as always, her hubby called Richard is passionate about football and would talk for hours about tactics along with players strengths and weaknesses. Then came the 'terrible two' as I refer to them in a joking way. They have two daughters, Christine, and Maddison, they both fit well their shortened versions which are Chris(t) and Maddy. They are the complete opposite to Toni in many ways, but nevertheless I love them. As soon as they sat down the banter starts. I am reminded of my youth where insults became an invitation for quick witted exchanges that nobody wanted to lose. Even before the pleasantries and welcomes are complete, it begins, this could be anything from what you were wearing to the sequence taken of those welcomes. They have certainly inherited the Thomas gene for humour and speed of response. Breakfast consisted of roars of laughter as often Georgina and Jane were intertwined with our stories of mishaps and funny incidents. It certainly was a tonic for me, and although breakfast consisted of light-hearted insults and put-downs, I thoroughly enjoyed every moment. By the end, my jaws ached with laughter while the others hardly got a word in, what a result.

On this occasion they were no match for my newfound skills and lightning speed. I often amazed myself at the knowledge and information I could bring into the conversation without a second's thought. Jane was mesmerised by this too, my speech which can often be slow and laboured especially in crowded or noisy places was crisp and precise. I realised on the return journey that I would have to watch this in public. I was also reminded by my youth talking to the girls. I think that's where my friends and I won over others, as Paul Weller wrote in the song Saturday's Kids, 'Saturdays boys live life with insults, drink lots of beer and wait for half time results'. From a young age we continually mocked each other in the form of fun filled banter, and if you weren't quick enough with your response, you run the risk of being subjected to more. How I loved those days.

As we returned home Jane had a list of jobs to do and I was given instructions to stay out of the way. This gave me the freedom to watch the extended highlights of the football from yesterday. France and Argentina gave me a much needed high with a goal-fest and the French winning four three. In the other game Portugal went through with a two one defeat of Uruguay. I managed to stay awake until around 14:00, it was a lovely warm day, I was full from my breakfast which is a recipe for sleep. The next thing I am aware of is the uplifting sensation which began to take my full weight, electrical pulses rippled over my skin once more. This is the enjoyable part before the pain and discomfort of the piercing light. The only advantage is that it opens the doors to another CDT event. For a while now I have craved them, it's nowhere near like an addiction, but the rush of energy satisfies me like nothing else can. Soon after the rush, I began to hear my name being called in the distance. Sharp beams of light hit my eyes, and they seemed to be concentrated to one fixed point. Furious blinking eventually helped my vision to become clearer. Helena's voice greeted me in a comforting and calming way, this was despite the plain monotone consistency. There's also something familiar to it, and it's not just how she pronounces my name.

The surroundings remained the same, they were illuminated from within, but with minimal features, that is apart from a window to my right where I could see people walking by in busied conversations. This time Helena sat on the left of three positions with Olin in the centre. As I scanned across the group, I made eye contact with Olin and we both exchanged a genuine broad smile before he asked me how I had been. He then gestured to his left to introduce the male as Lise-Cross-04. He looked in his early thirties with short blonde hair, I had to say he was very good looking with piercing blue eyes and a chiselled jawline. He was well over six feet tall, and although he wore the same loose-fitting clothes, it was easy to tell he had a muscular physique. My lower peripheral vision presented me with a section of information about him. Surprisingly, is age being in fact 42 years and 102 days. His position was President of the Psychoanalyst section, with oversight of the Try-neural Evaluation/62.87 Ethics Mandate P211 Team. He carried himself well, and his posture demonstrated authority.

He politely said hello in a deep voice and smiled, his next comment registered something worthy of note. He said, "I have heard a lot about you Danny and your potential to help us". There it was again, my significance to help them. Before I could give this too much thought, Olin asked me if I had been able to obtain answers to my questions through the information I had been given. In hurried childlike excitement, I told them that I had been able to understand the progression of humanity in respect to how we lay down our weapons, and how the colony movement was instrumental. He beamed a huge smile and told me they knew I would be able to access the files in such a way. As I began to relay what I had discovered, all three commented about how well I had performed. This wasn't in a condescending way; it was all positive, complementary and encouraging. Most of the encouragement came, reassuringly from Olin

When it came to dates and timelines it was Lise-Cross-04, who I decided to simply call 'Lise', who came out with another memorable line. In a calm and reassuring tone, he said, "What you are seeing are facts, the timeline exists for a version of our history". Immediately, I knew what he meant, they had chosen to interact with me, if they then decide to erase my memory, then all of this would be unaffected. They have taken the incredible decision to potentially alter their history. Alternatively, they already know how I will act, and what I will decide to do. It questions if I do in fact have 'free will', although there is no way they could know what I will do with the information and knowledge I now possess. How could they know, when in all honesty, I don't know myself. Before we continued, I asked why another CDT event was taking place today, from the outset I was told that they would never be back-to-back. Olin replied by telling me they had evaluated the effects on my mind and body, which confirmed it was safe to proceed at an increased pace. I thought it would have been nice to be consulted, it begs you to momentarily question their ripple effect theory.

Utopia

Before hitting them with the question regarding the rules for entry, I asked a bit of a lame question about their names. Olin coughed, smiled, then told me it wasn't what they expected. It was the hyphenated elements and the use of numbers that interested me. He explained that in recognition of outstanding contribution by an individual to the 62.87 Evolution, they are recognised by the addition of a single digit. Future generations are then permitted to increase this by one digit. If two or more digits are added it means multiple generations have been recognised. It is extremely important for us to recognise outstanding efforts to the mantra BTBT. He continued to tell me why some don't have a number and use just a single name without any hyphenated parts, this is because it is that person who has been recognised in this way. He elaborated that they may have had an ancestor of merit, but everyone strives for this distinguished acclaim. Instantly, I felt I was in the presence of important and special individuals, although they do emphasise that everyone is equal.

Then came my opportunity to ask about the rules for entry into the colony, and I may have the opportunity to dig more into the timeline. Helena took a couple of steps forward and good enough the trusty display screen appeared. She asked me if I wanted explanations for each of the rules, I smartly replied, "Please add them if you think it's necessary".

#1 Everyone admitted to the colony will abide by these rules in full and without exception.

As this rule appeared, I thought it was straightforward, however, she explained that anyone failing to comply will be ejected, although they have a right to state their case. She added, these rules have been with us for thousands of years, therefore they only really apply to any outsiders who have chosen to enter. Even before I could ask Helena to clarify this, she continued to tell me, there are people who cling on to outdated beliefs and superstitions and live in the wilds. For thousands of years, they have lived a stark life without good healthcare and often poor nutrition. We do our best for them and offer them anything they need. Although their numbers continue to decline there are still around 19 million of them across the planet. As she told me this, I tried to visualise their lives.

#2 A single language called Enlighten22 is the only language permitted to be used. No alterations, modifications or additions are permitted without consent from the adjudication panel.

Again, without even asking she clarified this rule for me too, but I did incorrectly comment well this is English as I can understand you perfectly. I could see that all three smiled as she explained, Enlighten22 comprises many languages and phrases. She reminded me of the gift Olin had given to me about language and their descriptions, appreciation and measurements that were standardised. They are communicating with me in English, I was told this is in fact a foreign language to them. In an upbeat tone in her voice, she asked, "How are we doing?" I simply replied, "It's alright most of the time". This also explains why they have paused sometimes, I guess it's when they're looking something up. She explained that a lot of the language is based on English, along with other European words, even some Asian ones are used too. What they avoid is the multiple meanings of words and phrases, the main area is the description of measurements, which I had already discovered. Courteously, she gave me some examples of where and why changes have been made.

#3 Every colony member is equal, and their contribution to the colony is valued equally without exception.

I thought this one needed no further explanation, although Helena said the next two rules ensure this one is applied. It started to make me think, is everything they do run by rules and committees. Looking at their job titles suggests this too, surely, somewhere or someone must be responsible for making these decisions.

#4 Every colony member will always treat fellow members with respect and as an equal.

#5 Each colony member will endeavour to improve the colony in everything they do.

Helena was correct, I could see how the rules are intended to protect the individual along with the colony. It's a powerful word 'respect', but if you think about it, you don't need any other rules. Failing to respect an individual, breaks every rule you could possibly have or need. In a society that provides you with everything you could possibly need, it removes 'all' of the failings we currently have engrained into us. I asked them if they had a word in their language for things like jealousy, envy, theft, murder, deceit, deception, cheating and the list could go on and on. The collective answer was simple, she merely said, "No". Olin then stood up and said he was probably better placed to discuss this. What he then told me made complete sense, those words and what they mean and describe are passed down through each generation, and continually taught to us. What the colony structure provided, was a way, and a method to break that cycle. All these acrimonious traits are inbred and as children we see our parents, and society as a whole use them. The colony structure made them redundant and resigned to the archives.

At the beginning of this book, I provided a list of things that had been eradicated such as wars, nations, religion, and disease etc. I then pointed out that these were my observations, and not what I had been told, these things and many of our damaging traits have finally been removed. I am sure you would have to agree that this is a perfect world, a utopia, as I described it. If not, if they are missing something I would love to know specifically what. Given the choice of living in 2018, or two thousand years from now, which would you prefer. 'it's a no-brainer for me'. Helena left me for a moment just as Olin had finished his explanation. I think they could feel and sense my realisation of what I had just understood.

#6 Earth is unique and our home, it is the responsibility of every colony member to respect the planet and care for it whenever possible.

Here again, this one needed no explanation, I think they could see I was still shellshocked from the previous discussion.

#7 Every colony member will live their lives in accordance with the three phases of life.

As this rule appeared on the screen, Helena waited to see if I had a question. Her patience was appreciated as I told them, "I understood the phases, and can see how dividing them in such a way ensures the best for the colony". My question was the most significant I could think of, as I asked, "How do people react to choosing their end of life?" It seemed as though Olin and Lise were ready to answer, but they left it to Helena. She told me, "If you have lived a perfect life, if you had thoroughly enjoyed every day of your time on this planet. If you had given freely towards the 62.87 Evolution, and the concept of BTBT it's easy to also enjoy the end. This is done in the knowledge that future generations may also experience the same quality." It was the two words she used that stood out for me. Having a 'perfect' life and 'enjoyed' every day, while they are just words to us, to actually encounter that scenario, is almost beyond belief. Plus, you would have 30 years of your life to encounter and enjoy anything you wanted. I would certainly jump at the chance, which only makes me more envious of what they have. She paused for a moment and then came another standout phrase, "It's important to make the world a better place for the next generation, it's our mission and we are proud to complete this".

It was at this point that I interrupted Helena with a straight question, "If these rules for entry into the colony were developed when it was first created, how were you able to provide almost everything?", I laboured the point 'everything'. Helena seemed happy for Olin to answer this question, he stood and walked towards me. He said, "Danny, you grasp what we are telling you and you ask the correct questions". I waited for the answer, he just smiled and said, "Danny, we have confidence that you will work it out". I thoroughly enjoy puzzles, but this could be going too far, I didn't respond I just looked at him. Before I could say anything as a response, Olin turned and regained his seat. I was beginning to respect him, but he did seem to like the dramatic parts. I knew the answer must be available within the files, I just needed to figure this out, along with what I am supposed to do next.

#8 Every colony member will seek to benefit from the tools of improvement: Ownership & Responsibility, awareness of the Ripple Effect, and the use of Language.

I must admit, I let this rule appear without comment, I had no suitable questions for Helena. I think she knew that I understood the benefits of each. The next one came in boldly and as it did, I began to grin and nod in appreciation.

#9 All forms of superstition including thought, language and action will not be tolerated.

I expected this to be included in some form or another, it ties in with Ownership & Responsibility in the previous rule. I must admit, since I had learnt about the tools, I have changed my thoughts, words and actions. I also picked Jane up a couple of times when she used something like, 'fingers crossed', and even 'hope so'. I could see she was getting wound up by it, accordingly I would have to tread softly. It's easy to see how pathetic and irrational these superstitions are, and how whatever you touch, cross, wear or say It's not going to change the outcome of any event, yet people persist. As an atheist, I firmly place my trust and belief in science. Simply, this means until science supports the fact that black cats and walking under ladders directly affect events, I will not fear numbers, colours etc.

While I respect the freedom of choice for everyone, I have to question others who do not extend this to their own children. We are all born atheists, I get worried when this is removed, and children are force-fed a particular brand of religion. This single and reinforced view of the world is all too often based on fear. Do this, do that, don't say that, think this, all with the threat of hell and being punished by the devil if you don't conform. This perverted stance is echoed in everything that individual is then exposed to, all their friends and family believe and act the same way. In my opinion it's legalised brainwashing and each religion is guilty to a greater or lesser degree. I heard an argument recently in support of 'faith schools' maintaining that they have very good results in all subjects. When the argument was turned to question this approach, they were asked do they spend an equal amount of time teaching all faiths, or were they biased towards one. Atheists are often asked 'where do you get your morals, if not from religion'. The sweetest reply is that atheists are more likely to believe the morality of an action is based on its consequences, while theists are more inclined to endorse moral values that promote group cohesion. My morals come from a good place, not from fear.

When it comes to language, here again most of the superstitions we have are passed down between generations. It's obviously more a use of lazy language than an actual belief, I am still trying to educate myself, and to stop using things like, 'oh god' in surprise of something or even 'Jesus' when something goes wrong. I once had this out with someone of religious persuasion who tried to argue that people use this in times of trouble or despair. They weren't too happy when I turned it back on them and asked them how many times a god intervenes in these situations.

As Helena finished, she added that the rules were complete, not by adding another rule but with the moto BTBT Build Today for a Better Tomorrow, which is always there. As I thanked her, I commented there is a great deal for me to understand. I can see how they ensure every colony member is protected by these rules, and how the colony and our planet is also cared for. When you think about it these are a simple set of rules compared to the legislation we currently live under. Politicians create laws to safeguard every aspect of our lives. Here the colony provides everything they could possibly need and with no dangers from either internal or external forces, there again it is utopia. I also get how through generational reform and modification humanity improves itself, if Charles Darwin could only see this, or maybe he did.

"The one man who plants trees, knowing he will never sit in their shade, has at least started to understand the meaning of life."
Rabindranath Tagore

When is an 'or else order', not an 'or else order'?

I settled myself ready to be grilled, it was their turn in the driving seat, although before they were able to continue, I tried another question. Proclaiming that I was beginning to understand their lives and a major part of this was the transition between the two. I can see how the rules operate for them, and they provide a perfect life. It sounds perfect, but I would welcome the opportunity to see a typical day. Olin could hardly contain his excitement and enthusiasm, he actually clapped as he announced, "That would be a very good way for you to experience more of Blue-Thia277". Olin thought for a moment and finished, "Lise, would you kindly show Danny a typical day for you?", Lise smiled and nodded to confirm, Olin told me this will happen next time, and he repeated how good it would be, although judging by the body language of Helena and Lise they weren't sure.

Their pre-prepared and crafted questions came, the first from Helena, "Danny, can you please tell us what happened next in the events that changed your life?" My usual intake of breath was extended while I absorbed the question and the wording used, 'Changed your life'. I am pretty certain that I have never used this phrase, and although it is true, I wondered where they were heading with this. Composing myself for a moment, I was ready to continue my debrief about what happened next with the employment tribunal. By the way, I did confirm this is what they meant as it continued as horrifically as it began.

Whilst we established there was an insurance policy in place, one that we could claim against, this made them (their barrister) dig her heels in even further. This involved a planned and simple delaying strategy, part of the problem I found was consistency or lack of. We would attend court; this would involve James and I meeting up a couple of days prior to the date to allow us time to run through what was expected. Even on the morning of the scheduled date we would meet in the café and have a final run through. Part of this was to settle my nerves, we mainly discussed football, he had an encyclopaedic knowledge of 80's and 90's football, which included players, managers and trophies won or nearly won. As each session came and went without much progress, James grew increasingly frustrated. This frustration then turned into controlled anger as it dragged out longer and longer. Their barrister would come up with excuse after excuse of why they weren't ready to proceed. Witness statements were either delayed or had gone missing, witnesses were often not available to attend court on dates that were provided.

The inconsistency problem was reinforced as each time we would get a different judge, who I learnt couldn't be bothered reading through all the previous correspondence. This resulted in the judge simply allowing them more time to get what they needed. The cycle was only broken when ten or eleven months later, when we managed to get a sympathetic judge. This only came about as we had seen the same judge before, about six months earlier. When his name came to light as we waited in the holding area outside the courtrooms, James was delighted. Before this he was busy telling me who played in defence in the 1985 cup final. As we all filed into the courtroom the judge must have seen James's face light up. The usual process would include the judge asking each party to state the current position and what else was needed. On this occasion, I remember their barrister went first and tried painfully to justify why they couldn't proceed just yet. It was like a child quickly thinking of excuses and embarrassingly trying to blame her dog for chewing their homework, and for the sixth time.

When James stood up, he delivered a rant that could have gone down in the history of rants. He exposed every effort she had made, every hole available and without saying it outright, every lie she had used. I remember looking over as she seemed to sink deeper into the chair labelled 'FOOL'. Eventually, the judge managed to shut James up and said that it was unacceptable it had dragged on this long. To James' relief and pleasure the judge issued an 'or else order' for the other party to provide the outstanding information within a set period of time. Typically, it was wrapped up in a load of legal jargon and dates were given by the judge. I could only presume this was a positive thing as their barrister hurriedly threw papers into a case and stormed out ahead of us. As we calmly walked out of the courtroom, James held back explaining what this meant for us until we were securely out of the building. As we sat and enjoyed another coffee, he explained that an 'or else order' is exactly that. In this instance, the defence had 28 days to provide what we needed, and the court had stipulated. James told me he would also get a copy of the information, and that he would see the updates on the court system. James was happy as this meant we were finally getting close to completing all the preliminary stuff, which meant we could finally get a date to hear the case. At the end of each session in court the judge and the clerk would check availability for the next proposed date. Their barrister tried to extend this, but the judge insisted on a date that suited the court and us. So, all we had to do was patiently wait and see what came in, and if it was before the due date.

The next court date arrived and as we sat in the café opposite the courts, James repeated what he had told me only a few days before. He had received nothing, and there were no updates on the court system. Apparently, solicitors could easily login and check the status of a case, this impressed me as in all other things technology related, he resembled a caveman. In eager anticipation we waited outside the courtrooms and eventually their barrister arrived looking as glamorous as ever…'not'. Minutes before we were expecting to go through to the courtroom, the clerk called both over to a glass window where they could receive papers and answer enquiries etc. I could tell James was fuming, his arms were animated and expressive in his disgust. Even from a distance I could hear him, "This is not good enough", and kept repeating, "Unprofessional". As he re-joined me, he explained that they had not been able to complete the requested information within the 'or else order', because she had been ill, and her assistant was unable to help. No wonder he was furious, and I was genuinely worried about his blood pressure.

Around 10 minutes later we were called into the courtroom, James held me back for around a minute before we made our way in. I could only presume this was a ploy to show his disgust. I recall his annoyance hit full volume when we sat down and moments later the judge walked in. James and I were both gobsmacked as it was a different judge, instantly we both glanced sideways to see if our reaction was repeated. I later found out we weren't allowed to question why we had a different judge as they were all supposed to provide the same level of service. James launched into an onslaught of timewasting tactics used by the defence and making a mockery of the tribunal system. This was compounded when the judge told him the defence had submitted a skeleton-argument, whatever that was. Anyway, the judge said they would consider this and would call us back in once a decision had been made. It was now my turn to try and keep him calm, I tried desperately to come up with bizarre knowledge of a football legend, where's Google when you need it.

It took some 20 minutes later before we were called back in. We listened eagerly as the decision was delivered, but first he mumbled something to himself. If the judge agreed that the order had been breached it meant, we had essentially won, and we would move to settlement. This particular judge was what you would expect, he was most definitely in his mid-70's. He was obviously intelligent, but you could tell he wasn't streetwise. He looked over his glasses to read things, he was also constantly rummaging through the papers he had in front of him. The anticipation built, but it soon came crashing down. He gave some pathetic reasons why he was not going to enforce the order. My heart sank and as I looked down, I saw James's hands as he angrily scrunched his notes. He then got to his feet and launched into a load of legal jargon and further abuse towards the defence's efforts to derail the case.

It was all futile, I remember the judge defending his decision over and over and eventually James had no choice but to accept it. Later research informed me this particular judge was a legal consultant to Stowama2 HR PLC. Yep, you heard me correctly, a judge that could be adjudicating over an employment tribunal was a paid consultant to the defendant. It didn't stop there; this same judge was a non-executive director of the insurance company. Get this, directly, or indirectly I was being judged by the same people who had ended my career with a medical report that was woefully insufficient. As the saying goes, 'I know, you couldn't write it', although in my case it wasn't just written it actually happened. This was only the tip of the iceberg when it came to the actions of these firms, but I digress from the CDT event.

Throughout my recollections of the events that changed my life, I didn't make eye contact with any of the people who sat there eagerly awaiting the next part. I was feeling physically drained, but I continued to recall what happened. We were still numb as we got in the lift, returning to the ground floor we walked in a daydream state over the road towards the café, all I kept thinking was how am I going to break this to Jane. I looked at James across the table and his face must have echoed mine, how could this have happened. As he composed himself, he tried his best to reassure me that it was only another setback. He had mentioned a while back that this was becoming personal for him, although I wasn't sure how to consider his next statement when he said, he would now fight fire with fire. As it all began to sink in, I made a comment to James that summed up what we were both feeling. The system and their abuse of it through highly paid barristers had an agenda that continued ever since I was fired. They hope and want you to give up, either through it being too hard, and thereby lose interest, or you run out of money, and the final possible outcome is that you die because it took too long. I then told him that the first two would never happen and I would do my best to avoid the third. Looking up, I told Helena, as I returned home and relayed everything I could recall to Jane, I simply said it's crap, how can an order, given its name, an 'or else order', not be an 'or else order'.

I stopped at this point and looked across my audience to find Olin, Lise, and Helena, each of them seemed to be hanging on my every word. I asked them if they understood everything they were told. Olin told me it was important for them to hear the facts, which I thought odd. Fatigue or simple tiredness was kicking in, I told Olin I was beginning to feel tired, but I was alright to continue. Surprisingly, he suggested we leave it there, although they had one more question. Olin then asked me, "This period of your life obviously had an impact, how did it make you feel?" To be honest,

I thought this would have been evident in the way I relayed my recollections. Let's keep it simple I thought. Considering this, I summed it all up by replying, "Whilst I was getting angry with everything that was happening to me, and not to forget this was all caused by the legal process, my overriding desire was to get justice." I concluded, "what they were doing wasn't fair. Olin seemed happy with this and nodded throughout.

Before we finished, I thanked them for telling me of the rules for entry and I was beginning to understand the chain of events more. I also told them that I could see the importance of the 36 people who had the foresight and ability to create the World Change Movement. It was fascinating for me to understand the individual elements they fought for, and how as a collective they had such drive and force for good. As the room faded into darkness and my eyes opened once more, I knew that I would have to do my best to find the names of the 36. Hopefully, somewhere within the files there would be some mention of them, or links to how they could be found. Throughout this entire experience I have repeatedly asked myself the question, why me, and what am I supposed to do with this knowledge.

Chapter 14
Unfair Dismissal & Disability Discrimination

Monday morning began with me looking over my left shoulder to see what time it was, the green digital display on my clock alarm was slightly blurred but, it confirmed 05:35. You may already be feeling Deja vu as I often do. I had been awake for about an hour but lay there completely motionless with my eyes remaining closed. This time alone with my thoughts allowed me to contemplate, not only the day before but, the entire journey I had encountered. During the past three and a half weeks so much has happened, I have gained an immeasurable amount of information and now knowledge. Increasingly I feel that I have been carefully selected from a choice of billions, if not trillions since 2018 and the 2,000 years in between. They are trying to create a new and improved species of humans. Which to me, breaks the most fundamental laws set out by Darwin and duplicated in their own charter. The questions they have been asking recently are not related to my DNA, they are events that occurred during my life.

Over a quick cuppa, and before we leave the house Jane gives me a list of things to be done this week, fortunately none of them include me. With a busy week planned for Jane, I merely hope for another CDT event today. As I sit in our local Costa, yep, I decided to treat myself as I organized recording two vlogs along with supporting notes. I meticulously recalled each rule along with bullet points to aid my memory later. I also thought more about a phone call I had with an old work colleague named Keith. It has been all of 25 years since we worked together, but we still catch up every couple of months. Life has been really good for him, he worked extremely hard and was very well rewarded, he sold his last company for well over £10 million. He never disclosed the full amount, it never changed his character or our friendship. For many years now I have shared with him my frustrations over the abuse of disabled parking. We always end up laughing about it which often involves him trying to justify the use by these large expensive cars and uncaring owners. Since our last conversation he had given it some thought, he told me to expect something different next Saturday when Jane and I go shopping. He had difficulty speaking by the end of the call as the mix of laughter and trying to keep a straight face was too much for him.

We also had our usual call with Toni, and it seems she is spending more time with Nigel. She sounds extremely happy which is the main thing, the majority of the call was taken up by her telling us about him and his family who visited them in Scotland. Jane was in her element and the two just talked and talked. I had the football on in the background, obviously the sound was muted otherwise my head would have exploded. Toni finished by updating us on her plans for the summer and beyond, oh what it is to be young and in love. The football threw up a near upset, Russia drew one-one with Spain, it ended with penalties which saw Spain go through four to three. In the other game, we also saw a one-one draw between Croatia and Denmark, in the end Croatia won three to two on penalties. The remainder of Sunday evening was spent with both of us dozing off in front of the TV. It ended with an early night and a very peaceful sleep.

As I returned home after my well-earned and relaxing Costa visit. Sorting myself ready to record the vlogs for both Friday and Sunday was now easier after a caffeine hit. They took longer than expected, a great deal had happened, which meant I didn't want to overlook anything. As I sat down again with another coffee, I allowed my mind to begin analysing once more. Understanding the journey to complete independence had many threads which is understandable and evident within the complexity I observed. Each one in isolation is achievable, but collectively, well that's where the challenge rests. We are currently unable to see our way through, unable to plan more than 50 to 100 years ahead. What was apparent, is that this was going to take a long-term approach. It would require both the foresight and cohesive strategy to develop the solution.

I think the most crucial thing I learnt, was that 36 true visionaries were able to apply it all, they knew the results would be seen and felt for many generations. This phrase has never been more pertinent, **'We will not see the results of change, future generations will, therefore, choose wisely'**. Maybe, this was what spurned the BTBT message, although it's aimed squarely at us.

Free power resulting in free energy for all is achievable, we just need to apply the advancements in technology that we know will work, and which are safe. The few that resist this progression have a vested interest in retaining their wealth and power over us. Don't be lulled into thinking this is restricted to the money hungry firms who produce carbon-based fuels. Their taxes oil the cogs that keep governments in place and with their own agendas (sorry about the pun). Free energy will have a knock-on effect to dramatically reduce our working time. The main thing I began to understand, then hit me like a bolt out of the blue. Free energy gives people something money can't buy… TIME!

Stronger law and order reforms maybe difficult to swallow for some, but we need to rebalance the legal scales towards the vast majority. Here again advancements in technology can protect the majority and ensure both safety and fairness for all. The war on drugs has been a constant theme for countless decades, but always without long-term results. A new sterner approach must be taken with one hand, while the other applies science to remedy the two-fold problem. Simply by replacing the harmful effects of drugs, with non-addictive state-controlled versions will provide the missing link in the medium-term. Science will then be deployed in two ways. Firstly, as a fool proof way to end addiction and not simply for drugs. The second requires a global stance to alter and then eradicate the harmful effects of the plants used in the manufacture. Alcohol and other harmful addictions will also benefit from this progression. Here again these contribute massively towards the state, hence we need to be careful who actually resists their introduction.

Improvements for humanity must include everyone, the key to unlock this is education. This will also have a direct and positive impact on the previous two points. Standardised and improved education must be the objective, how we arrive there is through many streams. I learnt about a simple, but highly effective solution, in the future they adopt a three-phase mentoring which develops the child into a person ready for society. Science will be used to help stimulate learning and the thirst for more. Changes in behaviour through Ownership & Responsibility, accountability for the Ripple Effect and the foresight to change our Language are all designed to guide us. Time and a leading hand will enable us to cast aside outdated beliefs and place our trust and faith only in science. Education is the key to unlocking a sizable number of changes and with significant impact. I saw how attitudes to class and structures in society need to be removed. I could follow these changes mapping the effects as they happened, until the result was freedom. Removing these hierarchical structures will only be opposed by the ones who benefit from them.

The World Change Movement were not a political party, yet they produced a manifesto for change that delivered its objective along with many other benefits. The 36 visionaries through forethought were able to see a version of humanity that would benefit from this peaceful revolution. The desire for 'better' delivered through tangible change would bring down governments and rulers, in doing this, it also set free humanity post the digital age. The colony structure embraces these intertwined objectives and provides stability and true happiness for all. Eventually, humanity will find its true purpose and only goal, this is held within the 62.87 Theory. In the future, humanity will hold together this crucial component, it will eventually develop the re-engineered evolutionary path or paths resulting from the evolution disturbance. Where this concludes, I don't yet understand, but I know I possess the knowledge and information to hopefully discover. What a journey of discovery this has been until now; was the realisation that hit me, I need them just as much as they need me.

I was incredibly satisfied that I was able to articulate this to myself, it gathered all those individual strands and allowed me to move forward. There was still more I had to understand concerning our journey, but for now, I was happy to park it. The morning was concluded as I caught up on some emails, while responding at my now rapid speed to three requests for freelance services. It helps pay the bills and means Jane can remain part-time, although currently it is a drain on my energy.

I relaxed once more over lunch, this time accompanied by one of my playlists which Doris, sorry Alexa dutifully played. When The Jam ended in 1982, Paul Weller reincarnated himself into The Style Council, shortly after this Paul Heaton entered my life. First as the Housemartins, then The Beautiful South, and more recently, he has teamed up once more with Jacquie Abbot. His song writing can only be described as brilliant, which are then crafted around tunes that carry each song perfectly. His topics vary from touching love songs to political outrage, and even his relationship with alcohol. You know when you're getting old, it's when current pop music and culture seem distant and makes no sense. One thing I do know is that current music has almost no bite. Weller, Heaton and others of that generation possessed a moral compass, and through their writing stirred something that many felt. They used their platforms to highlight injustice they saw witnessed daily; they moulded them into lyrics that portrayed a powerful message that resonated for many of us. These days song writers have singular topics which are typically attraction based.

A Day In The Life

As the song, 'Look What I Found In My Beer', played from the Quench album, I could feel my eyes softly close. This time the uplifting feeling was more intense than usual; the warmth radiated from my skin and penetrated every muscle and sinew. Simultaneously, beads of electrical pulses randomly sparked over my skin, which twitched and reacted to the stimulation. It seemed as though every cell was reacting, but just as the pleasure reached its maximum the insanely vicious white light sparked forwards. For some unknown reason I was observing more about the start of each CDT event. An unrecognisable voice grew louder, following the third or fourth time of hearing my name I began to overcome the pain. It was no surprise that I didn't recognise the voice, Lise was calling my name and advising me to blink. This time he sat in the middle, Jacron sat to his right and Xendar on the other side. They all smiled, but it was only Jacron who asked how I had been. I replied with the usual pleasantries and that it was nice to see Xendar. I asked him how he had been, funnily he seemed uncomfortable with the question.

Jacron spoke first regarding the last event and asked me if I still wanted to see a typical day for a colony member. I beamed a smile as I told them that I was really looking forward to it. Just then Lise stood and took a couple of steps forward. Before he could start, I told them how I managed to understand and place the crucial events that changed humanity, and in a coherent way. I explained that I needed to achieve this in order to satisfy my inquisitive nature. Jacron told me they completely understood, and they had complete confidence that I would find what I searched for. On multiple occasions they had said this, and I now appreciate the information and knowledge that I have. From this I know my understanding will follow, this surely is the key to unlocking more. I then mentioned again the importance of the 36 visionaries, who also understood the changes that need to happen. It was these visionaries who began the WCM and created the plans for the first colony. Not only this, I know they also pulled these strands together and created the manifesto. I needed to probe further to find out the names of these 36, or at least information about them.

This was now my opportunity to strike with a killer question, I paused for a second and then asked, "Am I right to think that without them, none of this would have happened?" Jacron calmly answered, "What you now see is a version of the future". This had been said to me previously, and I knew if I had pushed it, I wouldn't get much further than, 'You will figure it out'. Whatever my decision is, it will play out to produce the result, that is, the one I now see. It is the ripple effect in action, I am unable to alter the future no matter what I do. Each second of my life, each miniature decision directly effects its future. Just as in a Venn diagram where it crosses each other, varying results will be observed. It's cause and effect illustrated perfectly for all to see. In my mind, I instantly saw a potential Ishikawa diagram which had infinite endings. I could choose to do nothing with the understanding I have, I can resign the past couple of weeks to an event that happened to me. Alternatively, I can tell you and pass the decision forward, what you then do with it is your choice and yours alone. Incredibly, we have infinite possibilities all generated by a single action. Mind-blowing I am sure you will agree, one thing's for sure it has stopped me from taking my own life. Like me, you are now thinking, what would the ripple effect of that look like.

Even if you weren't, you are now. I seemed to be getting more answers, more understanding just by being in their presence. This was interrupted by Lise who stood patiently waiting to show me his typical day. Before I could let him begin, I smiled broadly and announced, "I have it now". It was only Jacron who gave me a knowing look and told me to continue. I asked if the display screen could be used, as I did it appeared to my left with a clear white screen. I have no idea how this result was achieved, but as I simply thought of the content it appeared for all to see.

From

INFORMATION

We can extract

KNOWLEDGE

KNOWLEDGE allows us to gain

UNDERSTANDING

I was even more impressed as it perfectly resembled how I imagined it. Without waiting for an invitation, I launched into my excited explanation. Information could sit collecting dust, whether it's in written form, data or any other. It needs to be consumed or digested if you like, only then does it provide knowledge. Although, knowledge of something and the ability to recall this at any time in whatever form, does not mean you truly understand it. Understanding something meaningfully means you can use that to your benefit and crucially you can educate others. I was quite proud of myself that I was able to articulate this in such a plain and simple way. I also came to rationalise that it's the 'experience element' that I had previously tackled with. It finally all made sense, I was able to fit all the pieces of the jigsaw. My admiration was justified as Jacron quietly said, "We had every confidence that you would figure it out". As these words sank in, I knew this was part of their plan for me. I was now ready for the next challenge.

Lise then asked me politely if I was ready, I was indeed ready, although the method of transportation took me by surprise. The lights slowly dimmed, and as I looked downwards there came two flashes of multicoloured lights. I blinked as the shock of this was really unexpected, then I stood next to Lise, and I could see how tall he was, and I am 5'11", no honestly, I am. It felt fantastically weird, I couldn't feel any sensations, it felt like I was standing, but my feet couldn't feel the pressure of supporting my body's weight. Of course, it couldn't, all of this was playing out in my brain, but it felt incredibly real. Lise then explained we were in his residential pod; it was very stark and brightly lit with a warm glow. Where we would normally have skirting boards, here the floor which was a dark blue-grey colour curved softly into the walls. Overall, the room was airy and spacious measuring all of 60 feet by 30. As my eyes rapidly scanned the room, I could see a sunken seating area in front of a window. Well, I'm presuming it's a window that looked down onto an idyllic green landscape with trees in the far distance. I couldn't see any other rooms unless they were hidden behind concealed doors.

My concentration was broken by Lise who told me to ask as many questions as I wish. The reason I was here was to understand a day in the life, therefore, for now at least I wanted him to give me a guided tour. My feeling of weirdness grew to new heights, as Lise walked forwards, I seemed to float next to him. True enough, there was a door which seamlessly opened to our right. I was told this room, which was much smaller with visible partitions was his private area. We moved inwards and his hand touched a glass wall which was completely invisible one minute, the next it had a seating area and another glass room within it. This is our sleeping area he told me, although there were no signs of a bed. He continued to tell me that GAPS controls their sleep patterns. Essentially, the temperature and our sleeping position is managed by GAPS to provide a perfect and maximum sleep. I was intrigued as he told me the 'bed' if you like suspends their weight in almost weightlessness conditions. With a cheeky smile I told him I could do with one myself.

We then turned 90 degrees and as he stepped forward another door opened. Lise told me this was their hygiene and comfort area; I looked around but could only see more slightly reflective walls. He touched another to reveal a large quarter circular glass-walled unit, this was their 'cleansing section', he announced. Where it differs from any shower we know, is that it also extracts harmful toxins that have built up in the body. Lise told me there are electromagnetic charged elements within the water, and these remove unwanted cells along with body waste that may have accumulated. My mind was already working overtime trying to keep up, we weren't yet out of his residential pod which didn't bode well. He smiled gently as he told me body hair, such as on the face or hair length is controlled by pre-programmed DNA. Without any reaction, he said, "This is all designed to enhance life and maximise efficiencies". Here again, I quickly questioned whether this breaks one of their charter rules. Best not say anything just yet.

As we exited his pod, he told me that wherever he is within the colony, a pod is laid out exactly like this for him. GAPS had already planned his day, this included meetings, social activities, and even personal time. As we walked down a wide corridor, I could see sunlight beaming into an open area at the end. It was truly breathtaking, I almost felt dizzy as my eyes scanned up and down, left to right. The corridor opened onto a platform that surrounded a massive circular hole within an incredibly light building. As I looked up it narrowed so much, I was able to gain some sort of perspective for its height. This view was even more breathtaking than my first exposure only a few days previously. Each floor could be seen until they merged into spherical lines. The same was true of the view below me, while it was very brightly lit, I could make out movement on the floors immediately beneath us. Although, the ground floor was too far for me to register any detail which wasn't helped by the bright lights.

Each floor displayed its role or activity around the inside of the 'polo mint' interior, or core to give it its correct name. I was trying to read as many as I could before we moved on. We walked for a while around the balcony until Lise entered a room which he told me was his current workspace. The room contained around 30 people, it was evident that they couldn't see me, a couple of the people looked up, saw who it was and then continued what they were doing. He then told me that he wouldn't go into much detail here as we would consume too much time. I did ask him what he was currently working on, his reply both fascinated and worried me. They are conducting three phase analysis of data collected during evaluation as part of the Try-neural Evaluation, which in turn is part of the 62.87 Ethics Mandate P211. Yep, I didn't know what all this meant until he explained in simple terms. From a subject, I was presuming me or someone in my position, they were analysing the data gathered from specific responses. They analysed neurological activity, and physical changes along with varying external factors or settings. This means every response to a question is being individually examined for what is said, what neurological or brain activity there is, what physical changes there may be, and finally what surroundings there are.

Lise explained further by telling me that they were currently undertaking analysis of 52,000 people at a live game of Pointspace, which he said is a game of strategy played between two teams. They are simultaneously scanning their neurological activity every millisecond as they react to each move a team makes. Obviously, each set of supporters will be reacting in a positive or negative way depending on the action. Additionally, questions are being posed to each individual during all of this activity. Data derived is then being cross-referenced and patterns sought, along with any identifiable trends. He then told me this is just one of 20,355 other similar experiments. I couldn't help but ask what they were looking for. Well, FINED Future Intelligence Neurological Expansion Development is the project where they are looking to create a perfect species with superior intelligence. The data gathered here will help shape future DNA. I immediately wondered if I was being analysed in the same way, and if my analysis would be used in these experiments.

Each workstation consisted of a bank of screens that somehow overlapped, whilst viewing one, others remained partially visible behind it. They seemed to hang in virtual space, I saw one user moving display screens by simply touching its corner and moving its order or priority. Their seating positions cradled them in a partially horizontal position and their headrest produced a visor which covered their eyes. Hand and arm rests were in a natural position with 'ball' shaped controls for their hands. I could have happily stayed and watched, but we seemed to be against a clock. Leaving his work area, we made our way to a series of escalators that took us to floor 12. My eyes could hardly absorb the deluge of things I was seeing. Plants grew in some unusual places and as we descended through the floors, I could see thousands of people milling about. This really was a spherical city that housed everything they needed for daily living.

Whilst on these moving stairs and connected walkways it became apparent that Lise was not one for small talk. I tried asking if he was married, did he have children, does he go on holiday, but they all failed to get a response. He continued telling me facts and figures about the building we were in. Of course, I was fascinated in all he had to tell me, and I retained all the information for later retrieval, but I wanted to understand what their day-to-day lives were like. Pretty soon, we made our way to what I can only describe as a café/meeting area. Lise sat down and my eye-line lowered as though I had done the same. From a centre opening on the table a drink appeared, it looked like water, but it seemed to have a dull glow radiating from it. Lise was now ready to tell me more about general life within the colony, as with their questions it was pre-prepared.

Days start around 06:00, they shower and have nutrients in the form of plant-based cereals. On their working days which are typically three days per week they start at 09:00, just as we do, they hydrate throughout the day with water, although theirs are fortified with minerals that GAPS knows are needed. Workplaces can vary dependent on many factors; their residential pods are standardised and always within walking distance. A replenishment sleep takes place at 14:00 for one hour, and they conclude work around 18:00. After this he told me, their time is taken up by understanding other research, along with things of interest to them. This time also includes casting votes on issues they are interested in or passionate about, you may have gathered he didn't use these descriptive words.

Family members are very important to them, evenings, and days where they are not working will be spent in a vast array of activities, which he painstakingly went through and which I found captivating. As for his family, he told me that he has been with his chosen partner for 7 years and 56 days. They don't have formal rituals of weddings, although they do mate for life. He has two very young children, proudly he showed me photos of them, but he failed to mention his partner's name. As we sat talking, my eyes were often distracted as people passed by, and others sat talking in groups. I noticed they all wore similar clothing of different colours which obviously signified their work position or seniority. I desperately wanted to meet them and ask them all sorts of questions, but I knew time was annoyingly against us. Whilst in observation mode, I also noticed how tall people were, there wasn't much to use as a gauge, but it echoed what I felt, seeing people during previous CDT events. I also looked to see if I could pick out variants in skin colour and obvious ethnicity. Everyone close by were either white, or mixed race and that mix was wonderful and harmonious. I could see Asian facial traits and what I can only describe as southern European.

The last two questions I had were quite basic but nevertheless, intriguing to me. Firstly, I asked about food, I knew they were 100% self-sufficient in every respect, my question was precise and good enough I obtained a full response. Essentially, they are completely vegan which didn't really surprise me. They can prepare meals themselves, although GAPS can also do this. Additionally, throughout the day GAPS will inform them to top-up on certain nutrients their body needs. Of an evening, Lise told me they gather with friends or family, and they will all eat together. A screen then materialised between us, and he showed me areas of cultivated land which was cared for and operated by hovering machinery. Thousands more images then appeared, each one just as amazing as the first. There were vertical planters that seemed to be housed in massive warehouses. Lise also told me about the computer systems that control their growth and then prepare them into the end product. All the time my lower peripheral vision pinged and popped with information about each one along with schematics and diagrams.

The final question related to entertainment and sports, when he answered this question, he seemed to instantly be more relaxed and his voice less monosyllabic. He went into great detail about both, they are very active and play sports frequently throughout the week. Lise particularly enjoys mountaineering along with ball sports and he is a 'level 32' in NICC's, which is their mental agility game. As for entertainment, they have a rich and varied selection, although everything is performed live, this includes story telling which is apparently very popular. He attempted to explain this and it's nothing like story telling that we would recognise. It involves the storyteller visualising their story through brain and mind signals.

The audience actually see, hear, and feel everything the storyteller imagines. A popular theme relates to what future generations will attain, where they will go, and the future of the universe.

I was delighted to hear that music is still very popular, although they don't create new music, everything they listen to is from their history vaults. I jumped at the chance and gave him a list of bands and albums that I would like him to listen to. Lise promised he would listen to them, although I think this was said to simply please me. As to why they don't create new music, he blankly told me that everything had already been created. Musical creativity is alien to them; can you believe they have everything, bar one of the most important things that sets humanity apart. I couldn't comprehend life without the spark and excitement of creating something. Throughout his explanation, images continued to appear, and my peripheral vision was filled with information relating to everything he told me. I don't know how long we were there chatting, but he suddenly stood up and said that we should now return to the others. I thanked him and told him it was very useful for me, although I had more questions to add to my ever-increasing list. The scene we had slowly darkened and as my vision returned, I could see Jacron and Xendar sitting patiently. We talked for a few minutes about what I had just seen. I told them it was nothing that I expected and far beyond what I imagined, but then again, I shouldn't have been surprised. I knew what was coming next, and true enough Xendar who remained seated, politely asked if it was 'acceptable' for me to continue telling them about my 'ordeal'. I didn't dwell on the wording of his question as it seemed less considered than previous ones.

Before I started, I had one question that I needed to ask them. Recalling that their charter states, 'science must not be used to extend life'. Surely eradicating disease and what I have just witnessed will indeed extend a person's life. Jacron answered this one by telling me that pain and suffering have been eradicated, which any civilisation would do if they had the means. Diseases and infections are a thing of the past, they understand them, although it's not something they need to worry about. DNA and gene modifications have been used to cease hereditary abnormalities, but this was achieved thousands of years before. The other items are there to enhance our lives which is fundamentally different. She told me, as they enhance a person's life, they also improve efficiencies. Additionally, they consider the three phases of life provide a complete and fulfilled life for all colony members. She calmly said, "The balance of our population would be adversely affected should they extend life". I thought this was cold and hard, but I understood how the balance of everything is interconnected. Science and medicine may be used to repair damage to their bodies, but it will never be used to diminish the aging process of organs or bones. GAPS or to be more precise, a subsidiary of it will administer pain relief as required, as a result, growing old is a graceful process. As she stopped, she smiled and asked me if that answered my question. I merely nodded and thanked her.

Lise didn't show frustration as I interrupted once more, I told them I understood they had evaluated me, and considered I was ready to experience more frequent CDT events, but I didn't, not just yet. I explained that I needed time to process everything, and more importantly understand it. I used a selling technique to reinforce this by simply saying, "I know you will appreciate this and understand we both should benefit from each event". It's the phrase, 'I know that', this is important otherwise they would have to argue the point. The other is the word 'benefit', it's in its raw state, but I gambled that it would work. Jacron nodded in agreement, this was accompanied by an understanding smile. The reason I gave was true, but I also required space and time to fully evaluate the previous event or events if they straddled more than one.

Tied In Knots

With a deep breath, accompanied by my shuffling stance, I was ready. I looked straight at Xander and told him that things moved at a snail's pace after the episode where the judge wrote his own rules to allow the defence more time. This only made James more determined, but with each piece of correspondence, and each subsequent visit to court he knew we were getting closer. I think there were three further court attendances and with each one I became more relaxed, and familiar with the surroundings. This may not sound much, but MS can play tricks on my mind and memory. For me it is often the recall of places and especially routes. Asking me to get to a location I have visited many times, can leave me confused. Before each court attendance I would meet up with James, we would review the case along with what had been added or what we still needed. Joyously, the date finally arrived, the bitch of a barrister had run out of moves and I think even the courts were getting fed up with seeing her. We even saw one particular judge three times and they joked, 'was this a roundabout where you have lost the exit?' I remember James launching into a deluge of abuse towards the defence, he knew how to steer perilously close, but without crossing the line.

Surprisingly, I was calm as James and I sat in the café, both randomly looking at our watches as the time drew closer. He told me something as we sat there that I repeated to myself throughout the day. He reminded me that, 'I knew more about the case than anyone else in the courtroom, and that I would be telling the truth'. He also used the opportunity to run through what would happen and what the plan was. It was scheduled to last four days, from the Tuesday until Friday. On the opening day James and their barrister would both open with why the claim had been made. Also, on the first day James would have the opportunity to question Philip, after all the delays he was the only witness being put forward by the defence. I heard on the grapevine, that since the firm had ceased trading, he had reinvented himself as a consultant. I also heard the defence was paying him £850 per day to attend. The second day James would continue with his questions, then the bitch barrister would also question Philip to help strengthen their position. James told me it wouldn't be until the second or third day before I would be called to give evidence. James would then be given the chance to ask me questions. It was at this point the bitch barrister would be given time to cross-examine me. It would conclude by James and the bitch giving their 'summing up'. After all this, the judge and the two lay persons would consider all the evidence along with everything they had heard before making a judgement. Following this the court would decide on the award to be given, I think this was referred to as 'remedy'.

Even though he had told me this before, it didn't stop my head from spinning. For a moment I felt as though it would all be too much for me, I think he picked up on this. Placing his hand on my forearm he looked at me in the eye and said, "Don't worry lad, you'll be fine". James and I sat waiting to be called into the court, our eyes were drawn towards the double doors as Philip and their barrister walked in. He acknowledged my presence with a simple nod of his head and his lips moved slightly. After a few minutes, the court usher announced that we could enter. We walked in and took our normal positions to the far side, and the other two the near side close to the door. We were told to rise, and three gentlemen filed in and took their places. The two people either side of the judge were lay persons, James had previously told me they are not legal representatives, nor were they medically trained. They were there to ensure that the judgment would be fair and balanced. I was happy with this balanced approach, having already been on the wrong side of an unfair decision.

The judge then introduced himself along with the two lay persons. To say they were best described as 'grey' is probably fair. They slotted perfectly into the stereotype for what you may expect, in terms of clothing, age, and character. Each one looked pale, tired and in need of a holiday. As they sat, each one had a red coloured ring-binder folder in front of them. The judge went along the row in front of him and asked each person to confirm their names. And that was it, we were ready to start. Over two and a half years since we filed our claim, we arrived at the point we had tirelessly and with determination strived for. The next four days would decide my future, it was that crucial. I hadn't earned or received any money since they terminated my employment, two attempts to claim benefits had failed as they determined I was strong enough to use a wheelchair.

MS is a hidden disease, no one can see the pain, my use of catheters four times a day fail to be noticed. On bad days Jane would have to help me dress, putting socks on became difficult as the spasms and painful stiffness in my legs made me cry with frustration. Fastening shirt buttons doesn't require strength this is true, but it does require dexterity which abandons me without warning. Days of brain fog and confusion can also descend without warning, agonising lapses of memory loss can leave me standing in a room wondering 'what the hell was I doing' Difficulty with word finding causes embarrassment with long pauses where people are unsure whether to help or not. Indeed yes, winning this tribunal would be the largest achievement of my life and for those around me.

The session began with each representative stating their case and why we were here. James went first and took on a different persona, this was nothing like I had seen before. He didn't refer to his notes at any time, he stated our case brilliantly and in extraordinary detail. It was all placed in a perfect timeline too with no deflections or omissions. I can't remember how long it took as I was mesmerised with the story he laid before them. He spoke about my life and the commitment I gave to the company; this included the senior role I performed and the type of work I specialised in. He took them from my first diagnosis and how the disease was directly affected by stress. He laid down a summary of the events that led up to my dismissal, and crucially how I made every effort to prove I was still of value to the company. He then cast doubt on the validity of their actions along with our belief that they had made their decision to get rid of me, despite everything I had done. Essentially, they were on a mission to sack me no matter what. As I said, I didn't know how long this lasted, James concluded by saying that we would substantiate our claim through evidence and testimonies.

The judge and the two lay persons, who I decided to nickname Waldorf and Statler listened intensely throughout. As James delivered this masterpiece his arm movements and gestures were like a well-choreographed dance. At the end the judge thanked him for such detail and announced that we would break for lunch. We reconvened 90 minutes later, during lunch in a pub around the corner from the courts, James told me excitedly that Dave Reynolds (the judge) was known for his no nonsense approach, but most of all his fairness. It was during the initial introduction of everyone that I found out the full name of their barrister. She somehow suited the name Elizabeth Williamson; I would have put money on her entire family being in the legal profession.

The afternoon session began with her delivering their opening statement, it was pathetic compared to what James had just delivered. It seemed ill prepared and disjointed, her notes were frequently rustled as she endeavoured to find items for reference. Her main point of defence was that they 'meticulously' followed practice, and truly attempted to achieve a resolution. They maintained that I refused an offer of a new contract, therefore, it left them no option but to sack me. She stupidly said they relied on the medical report that confirmed I was unable to work based on my health. I relished the opportunity to rip this apart when I was able.

She completed her statement without a thunderous conclusion as James did, I was sure he would be delighted with her below par performance. It was midway through the afternoon session, and I remember James being asked if he thought he would be able to complete his questioning of Philip in the remaining time. The answer was a strong 'No', but he was happy to begin. Philip then made his way to the witness box; it was to my right and around five feet away. This placed him in close proximity to me. I caught the smell of recently applied deodorant; however, it failed in its attempt to disguise the underlying smell of alcohol. He chose to swear on the Bible, I find it amusing that people swear to tell the truth, with their right hand placed on a book full of lies. Philip looked cocky and confident as he often did in his well-cut suit and garish tie. He was a perfect personification of the people who would abuse the disabled parking areas, that all too often left me flabbergasted. I had to briefly explain what I meant by this to my gathered audience. I could see Xendar's fingers increasingly twitch, presumably searching for the meaning. Jacron smiled, consequently I took this as acceptance and understanding.

James stood up, he looked equally as confident and ready for the fight. From the very beginning, it was evident that Philip was no match for James the rottweiler. He tried varying ways to avoid answering each question. James was relentless, he would phrase questions in such a way that begged a compromising reply. All I could do was sit back and enjoy the show, I rejoiced as he nervously squirmed and shuffled in his seat. James would deliver each question which was perfectly based on documents within the bundle of evidence, each given page numbers to aid reference. James would be content to leave a question partially unanswered and told the judge he would return to it. He would then ask another question which would have him flicking through the pages, now this one could also relate to another previously unanswered question, or worse for Philip, a partially answered one. With each one Philip managed to dig himself further and further into a hole of untruths and avoidance. Eventually, the judge took pity on 'Pip' and wrapped up the afternoon session, we were given a time to return the following morning. Philip looked hot, sweaty, and in need of another stiff drink.

That night, I was like an excited child as I explained everything to Jane. I tried to recall every moment in a blow-by-blow account, and of course how excellent James was. I explained how he had him tied in knots, how he used his questions to show the level of deceit. I knew the next day would bring on more of the same. Judging by where he was within the bundle of evidence, I knew there was a lot more to come. I understood better what James had told me earlier regarding my knowledge of the case, and that I would be truthful. Unfortunately, that knowledge didn't stop me from churning everything over in my head for most of the night. Jane spent the evening making phone calls to Georgina and other family members, bringing them the news of what happened and more crucially how I was doing personally. This was a stressful time for everyone, they knew how important it was for me, and what I had invested in terms of time and effort.

Truthful And Transparent

The next morning began another mini routine, (how I need more) as I met James for a coffee before we went over to the court. He asked how Jane and I were feeling, I never asked him if he was ready or prepared, I always took that as a given. As we waited in the holding area outside the court entrances, I remember going to the toilet, and as I dried my hands Philip walked in. We exchanged eye contact, and he said in an unfamiliar soft voice, "That was interesting, more in-depth than I thought". I told James what had happened on my return, and he commented back, 'if he thought that was something', and left it at that. James was correct, the morning session commenced with even more vigour. For each question, Philip would try to avoid the simple truth by giving a politician's answer. What I mean by that is, no matter what you ask, no matter how it's phrased, the answer remains the same, and it's what they want you to hear. On more than one occasion the judge stopped James mid question and told Philip he should answer the question that was asked, as simple yes or no would suffice. Each time I marked this as a win for us.

I noticed he used a method to phrase a question, it would leave Philip vulnerable no matter what his reply. For example, he would ask, 'Do you think the medical report, which was only 14 lines long and was undertaken without having Mr Thomas's medical records, was sufficient for you to make your decision in which you sacked my client?' Think about it, a yes or no answer would lead into the next question which would simply be 'why?' It was poetry and he did this time after time until Philip looked completely exhausted. Eventually, James called time, although not without a final killer blow. He told the judge he would have to leave his questioning there as he was unable to obtain straightforward answers. This barrage had lasted most of the day with a much shorter break for lunch. Their barrister was given the opportunity to then question Philip which took about 30 minutes. Both sides agreed that their barrister would call me to give evidence in the morning. Predictably, James told me to get a good night's sleep and that the evidence given by Philip was watery at best.

I paused at this point and asked my audience of Lise, Jacron and Xendar if they wanted me to continue. I also questioned if the level of detail was too much. I was given the choice whether to continue, and they assured me the detail was perfect, and exactly what they wanted. I still couldn't fathom why this subject was of interest to them. Okay, let's continue I thought, bizarrely I enjoyed recalling the story and watching their faces as I delivered key parts. Throughout the whole time I watched as their fingers and eyes rapidly switched between me and the transparent screens in front of them. I now understand that everything I say, do, and think is all being analysed in microscopic detail. Every single piece of data is being scanned and scrutinised, looking for patterns and trends that can be watched and valued against others.

The next day arrived; it was difficult to contemplate how monumental this single day could be for me. I did have a few nerves as I said goodbye to Jane. When I arrived at the café James was actually reading a newspaper and looked ultra-relaxed. Maybe this was a ploy to help me feel the same before we made our way over to the court building. As we sat in a row, the judge and the two lay persons marched in, and they all looked different in a way that I couldn't explain. I sat in the witness box which gave me a new perspective on the courtroom. I looked across to James who sat around six feet away from the defendant's section. Philip sat upright with a different shirt and tie; Elizabeth Williamson sat wiping her nose with a well-used tissue. I agreed to affirm to tell the truth rather than swear on the Bible and their barrister stood up. What followed was a shambles when compared to what we had previously witnessed. I was expecting to be grilled about the events that brought us to this point. The truth was, I imagined being questioned and had run over various scenarios for months. All I got was her asking me to verify certain pages within the bundle, each one referring to copy emails or transcripts of meetings or conference calls. At one point, the judge out of frustration asked her if she had any actual questions for Mr Thomas, stating 'we know what's in the file, we have all read them'. I looked over and saw James trying not to crack a smile.

Eventually, there came a few questions, however, each one I saw as an opportunity to take another blow at their defence. She even asked me about the time when I attended the health examiner, despite what she meant to ask, I was able to state my dissatisfaction of how it was handled. Then came the opportunity I had waited and hoped she would ask. When turning to a particular page which was a transcript of a conference call, she asked me to verify that an offer was discussed. The look of surprise on her face was a picture, as I calmly disputed it <u>wasn't</u> a true record. She then said what we had been waiting for, 'Are you calling my client a liar?'. Only days before, during my sixth read through of the file, I noticed something and brought it immediately to the attention of James. He could hardly contain his delight and told me this could break their case completely, although it needed to be handled very carefully. Accordingly, when asked this question my response came, 'Yes', she fell silent as I continued to deliver my well-rehearsed retort. Looking straight at her, I asked her to turn to a particular page, in so doing the judge along with everyone else followed suit. Without any facial expression I said, 'Please note the content of this transcript, you will see that it's a direct copy of the page <u>you</u> referred to'. Later James informed me that the judge along with the two lay persons looked in disbelief and simply shook their heads.

Previously, James had told me this 'find' would completely tarnish and destroy all their evidence. Apparently, it only takes one document to be shown as fraudulent and it taints everything they have. After my delivery she asked a few more timid questions, and then handed me over to James. As expected, he took every opportunity to widen the gap between our case and their attempt to defend it through lies. He exposed their efforts to manufacture my removal no matter what. They completely ignored the revised job description I had proposed. He exposed how pathetic the medical report was, how it was prepared and what it lacked. James concluded his questioning and said the words, 'We rest our case'. I often heard that in movies and wondered if it was ever actually used.

Following this the judge gave each side the opportunity to sum up their case which didn't take too long. Unexpectedly, the judge then announced that, without any further witnesses they would consider their verdict/judgment in the time remaining that day. We were then asked to wait in a side room, the defence were given a separate room opposite ours. James was surprised at this announcement; from memory it was around 16:30 Considering the time, James fully expected this decision would be carried over until the next day. He took this quiet time to congratulate me on my delivery of the torpedo, that hopefully scuppered their defence.

Around 20 minutes later the court usher called us back into the court, we all filed in and resumed our places. We stood when told, and as we did, I tried to observe and read the faces of the three people who would potentially shape the rest of my life. They looked menacingly stern and gave nothing away. The judge then declared they had reached a decision; he went through some legal blurb before getting to the important part. In relation to the unfair dismissal, he said they were in no doubt whatsoever that Mr Thomas was unfairly dismissed, and the court finds in your favour. I tried to contain my joy and quietly said 'Thank you' as the judge looked at me. That was the first part in the bag, but it was the next one I really wanted as it would do tangible damage to the reputation of the directors, and the associated business name.

I remember holding my breath for what felt like an eternity. Everything about the setting seemed quiet and eerily still, unfamiliar yet personal. The judge cleared his voice with a light cough, and began, 'With regards to the disability discrimination', he announced. He then paused, 'we were appalled at the disgusting treatment Mr Thomas had to endure, and at a time in his life when he should have received support from his employers, therefore, here again we find in your favour'. Throughout this James didn't move, he retained his stare forwards, it was only when this final death knell was heard that he slowly lowered his head. He then looked at me, and I will never forget the simple words he said to me, 'Well done lad'. I believe this was the first time that truly deserved praise had been given to me, and the words were perhaps the most heartfelt ever.

The enjoyment didn't stop there for me, as the judge then referred to Philips' defence of the case as entirely unnecessary. He also ripped into him about the evidence he had given in the court. He said he found his answers evasive and himself totally untrustworthy. He continued as he said his arrogance and attitude towards the court would not be tolerated. He even had things to say about Elizabeth the bitch and the way the case had been delayed without understandable reason. The next section is something I will never forget too, the message proved to me that fighting for what you believe in is always right, and justice will eventually support it. It clearly demonstrated that no matter how many hurdles are put in your way, how unfair your opponent is, striving for the truth is a justified fight. The judge then turned to me and said, 'Mr Thomas we found your evidence truthful and transparent, we also found you honest and trustworthy throughout. The court thanks you for the way you have conducted yourself during this case'. During this I could see James's right-hand clench into a fist, there was no further movement, he saved that until we were outside the court.

We were told to reconvene at 10:00 the following day where remedy would be awarded. We held back on our celebration until we were in a pub around the corner. James ordered two large whiskeys, we sat, completely exhausted and trying to absorb everything that had just happened. He placed his hand on my shoulder, and we chatted over what was said and the consequences of this for the award. I phoned Jane while we sat there and with a trembling voice I simply said, 'We won'. James conveniently went to the toilet as he could see I was near to tears. As I delivered the news there was a roar in the background from our family and friends who had gathered. I told her that we won both the unfair dismissal and the disability discrimination, by this point I could hear her crying and simply saying 'Well done, well done'. I was holding back the tears myself; James returned and asked me if Jane would be able to attend the next day when they calculated the settlement. I knew she would be hesitant and nervous, but if it helped our case, I was sure we could count on her.

Without a pause, I continued with my recollections, as I told them, when I returned home, tired and smelling of booze there was a much quieter welcome than you may have expected. These people knew that with all I had been through, I wouldn't want more noise than absolutely necessary. There were plenty of incredible hugs that squeezed me tightly, along with affectionate and tender kisses to match. Everyone was very generous in their congratulations for what had been achieved, and for the effort I had put in over the years. These were also mixed with disgust for the treatment I had suffered, and for the court system which allowed it to happen. The gathered party stayed for tasty finger food that Jane and Georgina had prepared. As usual, there was far too much, and as they left, they did so with bags and boxes of it.

That evening, I relished the deafly silence and the time I had to absorb everything and recall the key parts of the day. Toni was always involved in the events; we chose not to exclude her and answer any questions or concerns she had. I recalled how Toni hugged me that day, she showed maturity beyond her years. We were always proud of her and her achievements. In my view, Toni made me incredibly proud in the way she coped with it all. Jane was surprisingly happy to attend with me the next day. She had taken a few days holiday as she explained that she wouldn't be able to concentrate on mundane work while I was in there.

I took this break in my tale to look up, I have no idea why I found an odd comfort in not obtaining eye contact with my audience of three. I told Lise I was beginning to feel tired, as a result, I suggested we call it a day. Funny enough I had to explain this expression. Lise looked puzzled at this and took it literally, which I found odd, even if it is a foreign language for them. Good enough they agreed, but before the lights dimmed, I wanted to ask one more question. I thanked them for allowing me to follow Lise for a day, although I felt it was somewhat edited. What I really wanted to understand was more about their world in detail. There is so much more I wanted to observe and learn, I want to know everything. Jacron smiled again and said, "You have all this, you just need to search, and you will understand". It was my turn to look puzzled until she clarified her point. You asked the right question when you wanted to understand our journey. She told me the download contains this; I looked at one element and one outcome. As soon as she said this, I felt an overwhelming rush of excitement mixed with an equal measure of stupidity. Jacron then thanked me for the detail I provided today and said something that echoed her previous statements, "It has been extremely useful for us".

Unusually, all three stood and Jacron asked if I was happy to continue in two days. I wanted to make sure they knew I wanted these CDT events to continue for as long as possible. I didn't want to come across as needing them, but it was clear to me that I was hooked. Pretty much all my waking hours are spent either waiting for the next one, considering the previous ones or ransacking the files I had been given. I was benefiting in various ways and these people had changed my life forever. Therefore, I made it clear that I was happy to continue and hoped they felt the same. Immediately, Jacron jumped in to answer that they too wanted to progress, she told me they still had items they wished to explore. The lights dimmed and I could feel a change in temperature as I re-joined 2018. I sat with my eyes closed, alone with my thoughts and strangely content in having the opportunity to retell my story, and to people who were genuinely interested in hearing it.

Later that evening, with a very nice coffee I tried to unwind while watching the football. The results of the games were as predictable as the judge's announcements earlier. Brazil finally found a more fluid style and beat Mexico two nil. I was also delighted as my tip for the tournament, Belgium beat Japan three two. Sleep came easy that night and instead of running over possible scenarios, events, probable conversations and questions I may be asked, I felt a warmth in knowing it was all over. During the next CDT event I will move on to tell them what happened next during the employment tribunal. I would hear what my award would be, I believed that justice would now prevail, and my ex-employers would be made to pay for their wrongs.

IF YOU TELL THE TRUTH, IT BECOMES PART OF YOUR PAST.

BUT, IF YOU LIE, IT BECOMES PART OF YOUR FUTURE.

Chapter 15
Finally, The Question

The storm of emotions I was feeling, coupled with the furious pace of my thinking was beginning to take its toll. On one hand I had unbelievable clarity and speed to problem solve. Whilst on the other, I had the aftermath of trying to rationalise everything I now understood. I was understanding more about another world that seemed to want to give me more and more. All of this raged on relentlessly while being compounded by the questions I couldn't obtain answers for. What did they want me to do with all this, what did they really want from me, and why did they really select me.

It was with enormous relief that Jane declared a day of rest on Tuesday 2 July. There was a recurring anxiety that wouldn't leave me no matter what I tried, not being able to tell Jane was eating me up. Technically, I suppose it wasn't lying to her as I had not been asked a question. But all the same, I wasn't being open and telling her everything, hence technically, I was deceitful. Throughout our lives we choose to tell lies or be deceitful to protect others, which may benefit them in the long run. This was causing me real distress, and I thought, maybe today I would get the opportunity to tell her, or maybe that time had already passed.

This day of rest would have to start mid-morning while Jane showered and got herself ready, I took the opportunity to make key notes on the CDT events of the previous two days. I would have to wait to create the vlogs, but my memory and recall was such that it made this sleeker and speedier. Working smarter, not harder was not just a phrase for me, it was beginning to second nature. It became evident that our perception and interpretation of the word 'rest' was going to be massively different. Although I did enjoy a very relaxing coffee, in a shopping 'mall' about 20 minutes from our home, this gave Jane plenty of time to meander through brightly lit and unnecessarily noisy shops. I have noticed how in the UK we seem very accepting of American terms, customs, events, and celebrations. Black Friday was a retailer's delight, and shopping malls filled with expensive coffee shops and eateries offer us everything we could need.

My day improved enormously after this imposed trip; we continued our journey to a beautiful part of Cheshire. The weather was warm and there was a mild comforting breeze, we enjoyed a stunning lunch by the side of a canal. Young children were fascinated by the swans and ducks as they peacefully made their way to absolutely nowhere. As we returned home later that evening, I felt rejuvenated and totally at peace. During the day we chatted about many things, Toni was a recurring topic and how proud we were of all her achievements. If I had died that day, I would have been happy in the knowledge that my life had meant something. I began to understand the principle of BTBT even more now. Building a better tomorrow is not simply down to material objects, it's about creating a better generation, one that can learn from our mistakes, and those of previous generations. Creating an improved world means caring about every component of it. This is why every member of society matters; we must provide better care for our children and not leave any behind.

I began to feel a twinge of excitement that had been missing the past week. England were playing Colombia in the last 16, this is the knockout stages, consequently it was all or nothing. My enthusiasm was still restrained as I had witnessed too many times the immense disappointment that followed every ounce of optimism. I had a collection of England shirts that had been worn only a handful of times. We would gather to watch games, sing Three Lions while drinking our themed beers, we even bought witty musical bottle openers. Team songs that accompanied tournaments were endured; these were truly an insult to my musically attuned ears. We can now look back at these in wonderment, along with the fashions and dated hairstyles. Early in the second half Kane won a penalty which he cleanly dispatched. Our own Jordan Pickford kept us in the contest with a magnificent save, although he was finally beaten, by of all people Yerry Mina, a fellow Everton star. This took us into extra time and the dreaded penalties, where we eventually saw victory. Our opponents for the quarter final would be Sweden who beat Switzerland one nil. This began to finally spark my belief that maybe, just maybe… but then again, this is England.

Peaceful sleep that night came and went and as Tuesday rolled softly and comfortably into Wednesday, I knew it would be CDT event free for a change. Enhanced productivity allowed me to complete extensive vlogs along with meticulous notes and sketches. I also updated an increasingly detailed spreadsheet which supported everything. Time also allowed me to rattle through five email requests for information, along with issuing a couple of invoices. In the afternoon, we made our way to the garden where Jane tended to her plants, and I listened to various albums I had earmarked for such a day. My first selection is one that I would urge everyone to hear. Wisdom, Laughter, and Lines is the second album by Paul Heaton and Jacqui Abbott. They reformed after Paul folded The Beautiful South; I remember clearly the reason given was due, comically, to musical similarities. I think I made it halfway through my second album before I went to sleep.

A Cultural Vacuum

Jane was up stupidly-early on Thursday morning, and all too quickly the usual merry-go-round started. I contemplated what the day would bring as I once again stared relentlessly at the ceiling. I was sure another CDT event would happen today; I couldn't think they would want much more from me in the way of analysis. I grew to be less surprised at the questions they asked me, and I couldn't figure out their end game. Anyway, my morning routine played out without any variations, although late morning was occupied by time thinking of questions I wanted to ask them. I was still nervous to ask the most important questions, in the end I was happy to start with more trivial and then see if an opportunity presented itself.

Lunch that day was accompanied by my favourite Jam album, Setting Sons was released in 1979. Paul Weller's song writing had hit a new incredible level. He originally conceived this masterpiece as a concept album detailing the lives of three boyhood friends who later reunite as adults after an unspecified war, only to discover they have grown both up and apart. This album is only enhanced by Bruce Foxton's Smithers-Jones, please take a listen to this and you will see how and why it resonates with me now, more than ever. The song was originally released as the B-side to, When You're Young, which was a classic Jam masterpiece.

After this melancholic trip down a short and treacherous path, I slowly began to feel tired. It was warm and still, and my eyes softly closed. The next thing I felt was the thrill as my body entered a slow uplifting period of weightlessness. As before I observed in great detail every element as I entered the CDT event. Even the predictable pain from the intense light seemed more brilliant. My name was being called, instantly I recognised the voice of Helena. It quickly grew louder, "Danny, please open your eyes". Eventually, I could make out the people who sat in front of me, and my eyes fully registered the view as five people greeted me. Helena sat to my far left, and Jacron on the opposite end, in the middle sat the three men who had given me tools for life in a previous event. Olin, Vanstem6, and Staten44 were seated in that order from left to right. This is the first time so many people had greeted me, as a result, I felt a little uneasy which I think Jacron picked up on. She was the first to speak and quickly asked me how I had been. We exchanged some pleasantries as usual, and I told her that I had not delved into the files any further over the past couple of days. She looked puzzled by this until I told her that I need time to rest as the past couple of weeks had been full-on.

Grasping the opportunity, I asked some general questions, Jacron smiled as if they were expecting them, although I don't think they could have anticipated the varied topics. For my first question, I explained that I could see the benefits of a single language but had this also removed regional accents. I mentioned that I had tried to place their accents but couldn't with any degree of confidence. She confirmed a theory I had, this was not an intention, because people move frequently and freely across the colonies, language consistency is vital. A by product is the lack of accent.

Next, moving on to the safety of trusting every aspect of their lives to a computer system. GAPS is designed to manage every detail of their lives, and I wondered how reliable this was. Staten44 stood up and made himself ready to answer this, he had a slightly confused look and stance, he started by clarifying the question. His retort questioned why I doubted its safety and it became clearer as he explained. GAPS is an advanced system that has been completely functional in its current form for 947 years. Enhancements are programmed in by GAPS and it has never failed. He then expanded his explanation by telling me about other things that GAPS controls. It manages the air they breathe, the water they drink and the food they eat. GAPS manages the individual health of every colony member, every minute of the day, both day and night. This single computer system seamlessly manages their day-to-day activities, for children and those in education it tailors every aspect to their individual needs.

GAPS along with their transport system known as MASS, which stands for, Movement and Advanced Scheduler System takes an individual in their own Pod Shell to anywhere across the planet, and within minutes. He added, this is also completely safe. I was delighted as once again my peripheral vision lit up and sparked as information about this flooded in. It contained highly complex diagrams and schematics of both the network and the management systems used. I felt a warming glow as I instinctively knew I would find this fascinating and probably highly challenging to understand. This information also contained diagrams of the Pod Shells that are used, and the technology contained in each one. Although, the main feat of engineering was left to the propulsion system, along with how they are coupled during journeys. Unsurprisingly, the propulsion system uses relatively simple magnets, although it's how they are charged that makes the technology different. I knew I would need time to understand this better.

I then provided background information as to why I asked the question. As I stand here in 2018, computers have already begun to change our lives; as a society we are reluctant to trust computers to anywhere near the same degree. Adding a further observation which balanced the argument on both sides. We have only been living with computers for less than 40 years, and whilst reliability is improving, we still have a distance to travel. Staten44 used our trusty display and rather than thousands of images, this time I was presented with schematics and designs for computer hardware, but more importantly, designs for management systems, flowcharts, diagrams, and illustrations I had never seen before. This time I swapped my usual smile for the beginning of a laugh, coupled with shear excitement.

Staten44 declared that I would understand the development and how trust would be gained in time. I couldn't remove the huge smile from my face and my cheeks began to ache. He asked if I had any further questions on this topic, I used a reply that they had favoured, "No, but I may like to return to this topic again". He nodded in acceptance and returned to his seat, while the floor remained mine, I hit them with a further question. Taking a deep breath, I consciously removed the smile and said, "Returning to the view Lise had provided me, I picked up on a point regarding culture, or potential lack of". This time the look of bemusement passed to the five people opposite me. I continued and expanded by telling them I noticed they all wore the same clothes, they evidently had variations of sport but when it came to music, the arts and individuality there seemed to be a void. Now the baton of explanation passed to Jacron, as she stood, she took a couple of steps forward and the screen became larger. Announcing they understood how individuality was important to us, this was the same for 'culture', which she pronounced as if it were a disease. Furthermore, she described how individual creativity recognises it has a limit. "We know how important music is for you", she said in a sympathetic and almost condescending voice. With this comment I tried not to alter my gaze, continuing to explain, images by their tens of thousands began to appear on the screen. Even now, your fashion, art and culture in general is influenced by what has been previously attained. I nodded in appreciation of the observation, she then concluded, eventually the human well of inspiration and creativity becomes exhausted and eventually becomes repetitive.

You can probably imagine how I absorbed this but maybe not my reaction. I told her and the gathered group that I cannot describe my sadness if this is indeed the case. Your only source of inspiration is what the future holds, and you tell stories of how humanity sees the end of its journey. Music and lyrics stir passions and explain things in a voice that I am unable to muster. I understand that you live in a cultural vacuum which is sanitised from any feelings and emotions. I told them, "I was beginning to fall in love with everything you have". I paused for a moment and then delivered this, "My life is enriched by music and all that we have, emotions either happiness, sadness, anger or love are what makes us human". I took another breath and finished, "I don't think I am ready to leave all this behind, it means too much to me". I wasn't sure what reaction I would receive, and I was taken aback as she looked behind her towards her colleagues for their feedback. Honestly, I don't think she knew how to answer, however, eventually she said, "It is important for us to understand how meaningful this is for you, and we will try to evaluate this further".

This is the first time I had challenged them and put forward a counter argument for our lifetime versus theirs. I thought it best to leave my questions here but hoped I may get a further opportunity. As the screen dimmed Jacron regained her seat and Olin asked if I was happy to continue, I merely nodded. My focus was then drawn to the others who remained seated, their fingers twitched rapidly and for the first time I saw them point to items on the translucent screen they each had in front of them. For a while now I presumed these were measuring my reactions during our discussions. I was then ready to hand the floor to them, ready for their questions.

Imagine

I thought for a moment, there was indeed much to admire about the world they had created and the near utopia it was…

Imagine there's no heaven

It's easy if you try

No hell below us

Above us, only sky

Imagine all the people

Livin' for today

Imagine there's no countries

It isn't hard to do

Nothing to kill or die for

And no religion, too.

The great John Lennon would have indeed loved the peace and harmony, although I doubt, he would have tolerated the complete absence of creativity. It seems that somewhere along their journey they had lost the spark required to inflame creativity, and how it can enrich our lives. Not only that, but they had lost what it gives, it's the meaning and passion of emotion that is the gift to others. Creativity can encapsulate what people want to say, it can be the expression of love or the anger of injustice. The more I thought about it the less appealing it became. John Lennon may have looked in awe at the glory they had created, and then hurried back to New York and the 7 December 1980.

Then, from nowhere I asked, "Are there others like me, others that you have contacted in the same way?" Slowly at first and then like a racehorse on speed, I began to join the dots. Without waiting for a reply, I attempted to answer my own question, bizarrely with another question, "Are there another 35 people with the same knowledge as I have?" Olin smiled and simply said, "Now you are asking the correct questions". I had heard them say this before, which was usually followed by 'You will figure it out'. Although this time he elaborated a bit further, "We cannot command you to do anything, you have free choice along with everyone else, what you do with this choice is for you to decide". With this riddle he didn't answer with a simple yes or no, but I understood where he was going with this. If there are a further 35 with the same knowledge, they will also have the same choice to make. The future I have witnessed is based on 36 visionaries forming the future for humanity. Well to be accurate one possible outcome. Should any of the people with the knowledge decide this future is not worth pursuing then it will fail. That is an immense responsibility to put on my shoulders, but one thing remains outstanding, why have they chosen me.

My speed to diagnose a situation, and then dissect the elements until I could fathom a solution hadn't failed me. If any of the chosen 36 failed to act, then the future I had seen would not exist, therefore, I am sure they will have factored this into their calculations. Personally, I don't yet know what to do, although to be a pivotal part of the 'beginning', is highly tempting. I would then have to question my ability to be a part of something incredibly crucial, yet at the same time divisive on an unimaginable scale. As my mind worked through potential outcomes, along with possible effects, the penny finally dropped. When I say dropped, it was with the same devastating force as a dam being burst. Locked away in my brain is the future for humanity, not just for the next couple of decades, nor for thousands of years, but potentially millions. The 62.87 Theory is held securely within files that are locked away in my brain. I only understand a very small percentage of what's there, possibly enough to explain it, but it's there, and able to be unlocked.

Question, if the other 35 have the same files with the ability to access them, then as a collective there is a chance. Although, if I am the only one who possesses them… does that make me the author. There must have been a look of absolute shock on my face as this potential outcome came into stark focus. Almost instantly, Olin said those immortal words, "Don't worry Danny, you will figure it out". I felt some sort of solace in those words and knew I would return to this puzzle later. I took a further moment of thought and told him I had no doubt I would. As my eyes scanned the other four people, they remained emotionless, although I could see that Helena seemed a little uneasy by this brief exchange. I couldn't sense emotion as such, but she did look uncomfortable and rocked slightly in her seat.

Imagine for a moment the choices I have, and the decisions I must make. I am unable to discuss this with anyone, I cannot ask for help or assistance. If I make the wrong choice now, then a potential future that is perfect, well almost perfect, could be lost forever. I was told that the 36 visionaries possessed the skills and ability to design the future. If I look at myself, I must acknowledge that I wouldn't bring anything to the party. I am not an architect or a scientist, I don't have access to riches or people I can influence. I have no skills to offer, therefore, I must factor my inabilities into the equation. This made me a little anxious, turning a spotlight on yourself and not being able to find any benefits is difficult to swallow.

"The highest purpose of art is to inspire. What else can you do for anyone but inspire them?"

Bob Dylan

Only We Can Be Too Honest

My daydream-like state was finally broken as Olin delivered his first question, as predicted it was well structured and calculated. In a very calm tone he asked, "During the previous CDT event, you told us about your satisfaction due to the outcome of the employment tribunal, although it didn't end there, please continue". I gave a brief sarcastic laugh as I told him, personally I wouldn't use the phrase 'satisfaction' as it was a victory. We had endured significantly more than we should have over the years; we had battled through every obstacle and delaying tactic they placed in front of us. We never tired and always had the belief that it was worth fighting for. Throughout the battle it was never about the financial gain, it was to prove that what they did, or tried to do was simply wrong. During the last few hours there, my attention had moved towards the financial aspect, whatever the award was going to be, it was hardly going to equate to the hours that James and I had spent on achieving justice. I must have altered the tone of my voice as Olin seemed surprised at my correction of his phrasing.

I took a deep breath as I began to tell them about the following day, I reminded them that James had asked if Jane would attend, as it may benefit the award. This final day would be crucial as it would determine how much the insurance company would have to pay. Obviously, this would determine how much Jane, and I would have as a cushion or safety net for the future. I wasn't working at the time due to several MS relapses and recurring infections that were all taking a toll on my body and mind. The next day began early, Jane asked me several times for both reassurance that she wouldn't say the wrong thing, coupled with choosing a suitable outfit. Anyway, she settled on a grey jacket and skirt with a blue blouse, I repeatedly told her that she couldn't say anything wrong now. We met up with James in the café and we sat at a table near the window that began to feel owned. It would be easy to just sit there and watch life from this window. Anyway, James ran through what would happen and told us to remain calm as the hard work had already been done. Jane would take a lot of convincing to remain calm, I held her hand and cupped it with my other hand in a sign of comfort and support.

As we entered the courts and passed through the airport-style security. Jane's hands were visibly shaking as she took her keys and phone from her bag and placed them onto a small plastic tray. I continued to hold her hand as we eventually made our way into the court room. Jane turned to me and whispered, "Is this it? I was expecting it to be much bigger". I simply smiled and I could see her shoulders drop, it was the fear of the unknown that scared her. Once she understood her surroundings it was easier to control and navigate in her mind. Following the ritual of standing, the judge flanked by Waldorf and Stadler entered the room, and we all sat. The judge then did something unexpected; he looked at Jane and politely asked her name. He welcomed her to the tribunal courts and told her not to be anxious about anything, he had done this plenty of times before. It worked as she smiled and visibly looked more relaxed.

For the first couple of hours James and the BBB, 'beaten barrister bitch', presented figures and legal arguments based on previous case law. Once again James played it perfectly, he was calm and calculated and seemed to know how and when to antagonise her for the best effect. This took us neatly up to lunch when we broke for 90 minutes. Jane was surprised at how little seemed to be done and asked me if the previous days had been the same. Over lunch James told us that the afternoon would be given over to us, it was our opportunity to provide details of how we had been affected. It had taken years to get to this point, during this time my emotions had been pulled and stretched in every direction imaginable. There had been very few highs, and the odd exception had been overshadowed by unbelievable frustration. Should I mention the 'or else order', that never was, and how a spineless judge aided them to delay us getting to this point. Should I state aloud my theory that I believe their intention, or hope was that I would simply give up, run out of money, or die. Anyway, I am proud of our resilience to get to this point, and the victory we had fought for.

Throughout the years leading up to this, James had always made sure I was prepared, and able to sort things in my own mind. This was short notice for me, and no doubt for Jane. We had very little time to consider what could be asked, and what we wanted to say. I could feel my fist beginning to clench more tightly, I looked up at Olin and the others as they listened intensely to my every word. I then continued my tale as I told them, as we entered the afternoon session, I was the first to be asked to take the stand once more. This time, the judge asked me questions, he began by wanting to know what impact the dismissal had on me. As I said, I wasn't prepared sufficiently for this, and I remember not being able to accurately describe the impact. I did emphasise how the associated stress had a knock-on effect with my MS, but I didn't portray how it made me feel. His questions continued along this vane; I became more frustrated with myself for not answering them as plainly as he wanted.

The judge thanked me for my candid and transparent answers, it was then Jane's turn. As we swapped places, I touched the back of her hand and winked as a visible sign to say, 'it will be alright'. It was a similar experience for Jane, the judge asked her questions about how events had impacted on her and the family. Jane was less prepared than I was, and she fumbled her way through answers. Her most common expression was, 'I don't know'. The judge did his best to help relax her, but I think he could see that we were both unprepared and tried to answer his questions. It was immensely difficult for us to sum up our emotions in a simple answer.

Since my diagnosis we have been forced to deal with things that we were unprepared for. I once described my life as being like a snow-globe, shake it and the pieces that once looked picturesque and tranquil would fly uncontrollably and settle randomly in completely different patterns. Each of those pieces represented a part of my life. I could only watch as the randomness took its new place, and eventually each one settled again, only to be disturbed by another event that we had no control over. I think James could see how badly things had gone, he didn't say anything apart from, "Well that's over for the both of you". After this ordeal we both sat, in a shocked and numb state waiting for the next action. The judge asked James if he had anything further to add, I remember him saying to the judge that he had nothing, although he did specifically mention that it was evident in our answers, we are honest, respectable and hard-working people. We were then dismissed while the judge considered everything that had been provided and would call us back shortly.

It must have been around a 20-minute wait, although it felt more like 20 hours, James attempted to defuse the apparent atmosphere by talking about football. My palms became sweaty as we were called back into the courtroom, the judge then summed up how the remedy had been calculated. Before he gave us the values, he made a specific point that he 'valued our honesty until the very end'. I later realised that this meant we had failed to make the most of the suffering we had evidently endured since my diagnosis, and my subsequent dismissal. If we'd have expanded on our feelings and even shed a tear, the compensation element would have been higher. Hindsight is a wonderful thing once it's pointed out at a later date, in this instance it was like rubbing salt into a wound.

I braced myself in readiness for the monetary award as the judge looked in our direction. These next few moments would determine how the rest of our lives would be played out. As previously mentioned, no matter what this would be, it wouldn't really compensate us for everything we had been through, and what we still had to face. He looked down at his papers, and with a cough to clear his throat, he began to reveal his decision. Firstly, he told us the sum would be split into two parts. For the unfair dismissal, there was a standard calculation based on my salary and how long I had worked for the company. The second part was the most substantial as it considered the impact on our lives. As he gave us the award for the disability discrimination, I instantly gave a sigh of some relief. Both values took the award above the £100,000. I didn't have a target figure in mind, although I knew this would make our lives slightly easier. It wouldn't mean flash holidays, or an extravagant lifestyle, it would simply provide us with a cushion and allow long-term planning. I looked again at my audience of five and said, "I know the value of money won't mean that much to you, but you have to put this in context". I could see they were a little confused until I broke it down for them. I told them the case had taken several years to arrive at this point, additionally, our lives will never be the same again. My employer had removed my opportunity to work, since my wrongful dismissal my health had declined, and I had to acknowledge that I would never be able to earn the money I once had. To evaluate this, we must divide that figure by the years already sacrificed, along with how many years are potentially ahead of me, and it becomes diluted and diminished very quickly. Olin broke my train of thought by announcing their delight that the ordeal was finally over for me and Jane at this point.

Not Quite The End

I got the feeling they were happy to wrap up my answer and move on until I told them unfortunately, this wasn't the happy fairy-tale ending you may think. Olin looked decidedly confused by my remark, but I continued, although I told them I would give the edited version of events. Essentially, the courts allow them 28 days to either appeal the judgement along with the award or pay the sum. Predictably neither happened, James was able to check online to see if any communication had been received into the courts. There was nothing and no payments had been made. James then issued a very stern letter to them announcing they were in breach of the court's judgement. I had a feeling they wouldn't cooperate, to them I was merely a row on a spreadsheet which illustrated a red negative value, and one they didn't want to lose. Despite the firm and the two owners being billionaires, they must have bred an ethos not to give anything away.

Sadly, James declared that any action beyond this point was not within his area of expertise and introduced me to another firm of solicitors. Within a very short period, I could see the gaping divide between James who genuinely cared about winning and this other firm who ensured their invoice followed any correspondence. Eventually, we received a pathetic response that claimed their insurance policy did not cover claims relating to disability discrimination. Rather than the new solicitors checking out their claims I remembered what James had said to me, 'you know more about this claim than anyone else', therefore, I went into detective mode. Within a batch of information I had been given by my ex-employers, there was a URL hyperlink to the HR services they procured. It was a gamble that should have paid off, good enough hidden within the reems of information there was a section that stated what the policy covered. Incredibly, it mentioned disability discrimination was included, but it didn't provide an insured value. I then contacted someone I knew well, who used to work in that department, it took a high degree of sweet-talking, but eventually I obtained a copy of the policy they had been given.

I mentioned the gamble should have paid off, in their attempt to defend its position Calder Insurance provided a copy of the policy, they claimed was in place. This copy conveniently had no date included, it was a disgusting attempt to simply try and con us. When I was ready, I presented all my findings and evidence to the new firm of solicitors. Instead of being delighted with this new evidence, they merely put further obstacles in my way. I looked at the faces of Olin and the others to ensure they were still following the chain of events. We must remember that honesty is a 'given' trait for them and dishonesty is completely alien. Whilst we can place ourselves in both positions it is much harder for them to grasp the concept. Anyway, I obtained a nod of confidence which allowed me to continue. This battle dragged on and on, weeks turned into months and costs continued to climb.

As we got to a climax of events my solicitors announced that the only way to achieve a conclusion was to issue proceedings against Calder Insurance. This would involve a barrister being appointed, I know what you're thinking, and you are right to do so. This drip called Clive Windsor was the most unlikeable person you could ever have the misfortune to meet. In a meeting arranged to talk through the options and despite me being sat at the same table he managed to talk about me as though I wasn't even present. I disliked him then, and when it came down to the final act, an offer was received to settle my claim. Despite the mountain of evidence, in which it proved Calder Insurance's directors had presented false evidence, Clive Windsor told me to accept the offer. It equated to around 60% of the award made 18 months earlier by the court, and with the added costs would leave me with less than 50%. I was battered and left bleeding by everything that had happened. Although there was a final kick as they refused to pay my costs.

A few weeks later the funds were deposited into our account and instead of planning a little celebration, I was instead looking to secure clients to help pay the bills. Finally free from solicitors and the legal profession in which I had witnessed the very best and worst, I decided to take matters into my own hands. I began a barrage on three directors of Calder Insurance who interestingly also held positions within Stowama2 HR PLC. A steady stream of emails would be issued asking awkward and penetrating questions of them and their practices. I also created a website where I posted my findings and the evidence I had obtained. I was regularly threatened by their digital reputation management, however, they always refrained from threatening legal action. Months down the line I finally received an offer to pay my costs, although it came with a tangle of attached strings. This main clause involved me taking down all material along with an agreement never to contact them again. In turn I added my own condition in which I asked them to make a voluntary donation to an MS charity. A few weeks later I was paid the costs which remained significantly less than the initial award. I later found out that the charity received the grand sum of £100. With this, I rest my case.

Incessant Reverse Sequential Advancement

I gave my audience a moment or two to digest what I had added. Olin thanked me on behalf of the people gathered here, but also on behalf of the 'greater good of humanity'. Olin was then joined by Jacron who stood either side which allowed those seated to be framed by them. Olin crossed his hands in front of him and Jacron announced that they had an important thing to ask me. I felt they were a little uneasy, or unsure how to ask this, therefore I thought I would help by telling them that they were fine to ask anything of me, as they had given me so much. What Jacron then delivered took me totally by surprise. I can recall every word clearly, "You are aware that we have been asking you many questions over the past weeks, and you have been incredibly cooperative in your support". I felt this was different from the other questions they had asked because it was unscripted.

A moment further on, she continued with precision, "We have been monitoring and analysing your responses and they meet our criteria perfectly". I must have altered my expression as it seemed to hurry her along. "You are beginning to understand the 62.87 Theory, and what drives us to find the answers and deliver what previous generations have strived for". Taking a further deep breath and moving her body nervously, she continued, with a noticeable calmness to her voice she said, "You are also beginning to understand our endeavours to create a superior species which will help take humanity forward. A part of this requires us to revise the species and enhance its principal traits". Jacron then wound up to hit me as she continued, "We believe a part of your DNA will help this advancement".

Olin must have detected my shock and attempted to retrieve the situation. In a calm and reassuring manner, he told me about their goal to identify certain characteristics and traits within humanity from our age. Initially he didn't clarify why our age had been selected, but I later joined the dots. Firstly, they needed to access our permanent consciousness through CTD technology, and then deliver the question, 'can we use part of your DNA?' Now, remember earlier on I said you required an open mind to understand and appreciate the 62.87 Theory, well this next part needs the same. They are on a mission to identify and locate certain generic DNA traits that exemplify the goodness humanity has. These elements of DNA will then be combined to develop a superior species. This cocktail will not only go on to achieve great things in the future. Just as the 62.87 Theory proves that the human brain as we know it today can only exist because it was created by future generations, this amazing mixture of perfection will be used by future generations to improve their past.

It's okay to be confused here, it took time for this to fully register with me. Let's break it down into the process and what this means.

The first step involves their generation, which exists 2,034 years from now collating sample DNA with the 'perfect' elements or characteristics. Here they have selected mine, I will come onto the reason in a short while.

The second step requires them to merge these 'perfect' DNA elements along with their own sophisticated and improved DNA.

The next step relies upon them developing their science and technology to implant this 'improvement' into the new and improved human species they have been tasked to create.

The consequence of this will result in a future that will undoubtedly yield a super species. And it is this future that will use CDT technology and future science which will enable them to complete the next step.

The final step according to their logic is yet to be completed. With this improved DNA, containing all the required elements, it will eventually go on to be implanted into the earlier species (us).

Here's a further explanation if needed, and trust me, I needed it in my own mind. Crucially, we need to remember that we are part of their first cycle or manifestation of humanity.

- In the year 2073 PD they collected sample DNA.

- At a future point they will develop the science and technology to merge this into one new DNA string.

- At a further future point they will develop the science and technology to travel back using more advanced CDT technology.

- This improved DNA will then be implanted into humanity prior to their own time of 2073 PD.

- This means the work they are doing now will eventually go on to benefit them in their own future.

- Incessant Reverse Sequential Advancement is a beautiful belief and builds perfectly on their BTBT ethos.

- Subsequent generations post 2073 PD will develop their own further improvements, thereby the cycle will always continue, further improvements will always benefit future generations, which will create further improvement, and the cycle continues.

This IRSA became a bedrock of their development, and I remember seeing a huge section of this within the temple to technology and advancement. They are at the beginning of an improvement cycle without knowing the end result. It's almost like human advancement on steroids. I can only hope they have factored in potential side effects.

Returning to Jacron and the request to use or sample my DNA for the future improvement of humanity. My immediate question was why me and what had they witnessed or analysed to want something I had. Jacron answered this quite simply, all of their questions led them to believe that my sense of justice, and unending belief that justice was worth fighting for, set me apart. I was both flattered and concerned. My first response was to reiterate that I did not fight alone, James was by my side throughout this ordeal along with my family. She explained that their analysis proved categorically that I have always strived for justice wherever it is required. I have never thought about this, I knew from an early age that injustice annoyed me, but I never examined it further.

Without doubt I was taken aback by their disclosure, and I knew it would take time to register completely. Olin told me to take time as it was an important decision. I was obviously thankful that they had asked me, I was sure they had the ability to sample this without my approval. He went on to tell me what would be involved in my providing this. Essentially, I didn't need to do anything, as the CDT device was lodged in my brain, they were able to dissect a cell to reveal the necessary code. I must admit I felt very humble, and I guess proud that I had been selected.

Without doubt this event had been the most mentally draining for me, Olin picked up on this and declared the event would end now. As the lights dimmed, I became aware once more of the warmth and the sunlight that flooded the room. I took a moment to gather my thoughts, I was thankful for the previous two days of rest, even with this my strength and thinking were left battered and bruised. A couple of minutes passed before I looked at my phone display to see the time and to calculate how long I had been away. Somehow, I instinctively knew it was 15:15, as my eyes cleared and without surprise, it was.

"The man who asks a question is a fool for a minute; the man who does not ask is a fool for life"

Confucius

Chapter 16
The Conspiracy

Thursday evening closed in the predictable nature it began. I collected Jane from the station at my usual time. I then half listened to her complaining about work colleagues who couldn't do their jobs, and how she felt under-valued. Our evening meal was also predictable, after the first glass of wine, Jane finally began to calm down and lose the high-pitched angry tone in her voice. We both finally relaxed in the garden, listening to a random selection of songs that Doris decided to play. It gave me valuable time to reflect on the earlier CDT event. There was plenty to consider now, all the other things I previously wanted to discuss with them, became almost insignificant. My immediate thoughts were too scrambled, and I couldn't focus or concentrate. Where the answers held within the files I had been given, or am I supposed to simply figure it out as they have suggested before. To make progress, I knew I would have to divide the problem in order to find the solution.

They have politely asked me if they can extract a part of my DNA, they believe it contains a certain trait or characteristic they need. They evidently have the ability to obtain this, but they have asked my permission which says a lot. Hang on, they believe I hold a special, or unique desire to obtain justice and root out injustice. Personally, I don't feel special or particularly driven to obtain justice, and certainly no more than anyone else. Of course, they have been analysing and probing me over the past few weeks, which suggests they must have seen something. This led me to consider the debate between nature and nurture. I may have been born with a particular sequence within my DNA, but if my parents hadn't taught me right from wrong. If I hadn't met James, and our paths hadn't obtained the justice we sought, would I still be the same person.

Maybe, it's a combination of both, maybe having the deep desire to seek justice is held within my genetic material.

The next challenge I had to contend with revolves around their need for this, and its intended purpose. A part of my DNA will be used to create the perfect species. That can be described as an honour or a burden, depending on the outcome. What if my part of the 'super DNA sequence' fails, okay I won't be around to see the potential disaster, but I feel some responsibility. The other thing I still couldn't get my head around was Darwin, and the laws by which I believe. It then struck me that maybe humanity is still following the laws of 'descend with modification'. As Darwin viewed nature, the variations he observed and recorded were correct at that time. He stated that a species will adapt and modify based on the conditions it faced. Although, as soon as humans stepped in, we inevitably altered this process and often created an imbalance. We only have to view the world as we see it in the 21st century to bear testimony to this. Charles Darwin would have looked in awe and amazement at the view I have been privileged to see. I am sure he too would have deliberated and questioned the creation of a super species. The rules by which they live states that, 'even though you have the ability to do something, doesn't mean you should'. Maybe, this is the path humanity should take in order to guarantee our success as a species. I have said before that I hate the word, 'destiny', however, in some perverse way, this could be our intended path. If our species, or a modified version of it is to continue its development for many millions of years to come, who knows.

I also had to try and get my head around the fact that a part of me is not just going to go boldly where no man has gone before, it's also going to perform a 'U-Turn'. This no longer baffled me, I understood what was happening, but it still freaked me out. The extracted segment of my DNA will be merged to create this super-DNA. It will then, at some point, be used to develop this super species, who will then return to a time, before 2073 PD, and implant this into the human species. Incredible to think, the work they are undertaking now, will one day benefit them.

It also demonstrates their ethos of BTBT actually works. I can't believe that they haven't factored in every eventual possibility. What I mean is, they must know this mighty experiment is going to work and yield the results they desire. Do they also know how far this will go, again what I mean is, when does this ever stop. If the answer is ambiguous in any way, the answer could be never, therefore, we have infinity. With each advancement in science, the human species will be the beneficiary.

Parking for a moment the utterly wild notion that a part of my DNA will travel forward, then backwards, only to go forward once more. The second gargantuan bombshell they dropped, or more to the point, I figured out was that I am likely to be one of the 36 visionaries. This is almost as absurd as time travel itself. How is a person with very few meaningful skills, in his early fifties, and carrying a progressive disability meant to change the world. It's crazy to even begin to contemplate, but not only that, I could be the author of the 62.87 Theory. They, and I, are going to take some serious convincing that this could happen. I am struggling to find the words to articulate how ridiculous this is. Here again I can't see how, or why I was selected, other than I have a strong Wi-Fi and a brain defect, there's no other tangible reason I can see. The answer to this question could be contained within the downloaded files I have. In a rare positive note, I can now navigate these better, and I have improved speed of thought, but I am still not expecting a solution.

We Don't Know What We Don't Know

That night I slept exceptionally well, and I woke completely refreshed. I knew I would need time to make my vlog and detailed notes on yesterday's event. There was a great deal to record, not just what happened within the event, but also to capture my train of thought. This was proving hard to do as the days and weeks passed, my thought process had been in overdrive for some time now, and as I made more notes, I also made progress in trying to find solutions. One of the downloads showed me how humanity came out of the destructive mire that I am forced to witness every day, to the cleansing sunshine I have glimpsed. If I am to find anything about my path forward it may be found here, that's if I know where to begin. There are many challenges and obstacles to overcome, the more I think about this, the more I am sure they have selected the wrong individual.

Jane had a day free from work and could look forward to a long weekend. Fortunately, I was granted the time I needed as Jane was going to meet up with friends. They will all have their own battles and daily trials to face, but even within this tight-knit group, they can only share so much. Each one may have family issues, money problems, jobs they hate, and even general health and mental health issues. The unfortunate ones will have multiples of them, each one adding weight to already burdened shoulders. We all do, daily we wake up and meander through whatever events are thrown at us. Hopefully, we come out the other end with minimal scars, and maybe lessons learnt. Anyway, it provided the time needed, I also had some work-related emails and problems to solve. The combination of the workload and time taken to complete the vlog took me to a very late lunch. I had plans for the afternoon which involved a promised coffee with Keith ahead of his surprise on Saturday, whatever this could be. Needless to say, a warm day, accompanied by a sandwich and relaxing music curtesy of the magnificent Keane, resulted in me falling asleep. I set an alarm on my phone in anticipation of this possible eventuality.

Within minutes the warm sensation I could feel from the sun intensified, and I slowly felt my body begin to enter a weightlessness zone. My fingers began to tingle, the hairs on the back of my neck raised. With these very early signs, I knew I was entering another CDT event. How could this be, I had previously told them to avoid back-to-back days. Within moments, I felt the warmth penetrate my skin and lift every cell I had upwards, and to a lofty height of bliss. As it did, I could feel pulses of static-like electricity skip over my skin. It wouldn't take long for the pain to follow; I braced myself ready for the onslaught. Sure enough, it did, and with even more venomous anger than before. A piercing light flashed once, and then began the relentless beam of pain that hit the centre-most part of my eye. My only relief came with my name being called, coupled with rapid and intense blinking. Recognising the voice immediately, Helena spoke softly, "Danny, it's fine, just keep blinking". Soon after I was able to steady my focus, and I was greeted by Helena and Lise. Throughout the most recent events, 'more senior' members of the 'welcoming committee' had been there. People like Olin and Jacron seemed to be running events, it felt a little strange for them not to be in attendance.

Once they could see that my focus had been regained, they both stood and took a step forward. Helena asked me how I was doing and apologised for the frequency of these particular events; however, they wanted to talk with me, alone. I was puzzled by the use of language she used but accepted it on face value. Calmly, she said, "We understand that you will probably have many questions following the last CDT event". Well, this was probably the world's most ridiculous statement ever used. I think she read this via the tilt of my head, which accompanied the look of pent-up frustration on my face. She then spelt out what I already knew and by this time understood, or as best that I could. They had selected a characteristic which was linked to a part of my DNA sequence. I was no expert, although I have never heard of the sequence being identified in this way. I seized the opportunity and asked how much nurture affected this, and could they be mistaken. As soon as the last word left my lips, I knew this was a dumb question. Helena went into an automated overdrive, as she explained that all of their analysis authenticated, and substantiated their assumptions. As she did, my peripheral vision sparked into life, line after line of data streamed into my brain for later consumption.

I was unable to argue this, simply because I was unable to reference anything of my own, although what came next totally shocked me. Lise, who had remained quiet up to this point suddenly said, "We are concerned that some evaluations may have been overlooked". I was shocked, principally as I didn't think they were capable of missing something, furthermore, considering what Helena had just defined, it seemed contradictory. I got the impression there was more to come, I knew they were incapable of lying. For them to be 'concerned', possibly meant they were anxious, although, I didn't think this was a feeling or emotion they knew. Lise and Helena looked at each other and almost nervously, Helena said, "A group of members within the Try-neural Evaluation team who liaise with 62.87 Ethics Mandate P211 Team, have discussed the possibility of inconsistencies within certain data profiling". I knew at this point; I would have to decipher and translate what they were trying to say. I then asked, "Does this relate to my data reading alone, or more that are being readied for this new super species?" Direct questions are what was needed, Helena then expanded on their statement by telling me that their objective was to identify characteristics within DNA sequencing. Sometimes they felt other elements within certain sequencing were being overlooked. Their real worry concerned the fact that some members knew this, but they were striding on regardless.

I immediately knew the seriousness of what they were trying to tell me. It was vital that every element of this sequencing was correct. This perfect blend of DNA will be the beginning of the loop, and the potential birth of this super species. This obviously included my own, I had already aired my doubts, and whether the part of me they sought, was actually there. I then asked what they were doing to ensure accuracy and questioned why they were telling me. Lise told me that voting takes place before any decision is made, they have been trying to raise this issue, although, their voices were not being listened to. You can imagine the shock of realisation on my face when the penny dropped. Sternly, I asked, "Are you asking me to decline, and not to allow my DNA to be used?" Helena who was looking down, raised her head and said in a soft voice, "Yes, we are, yours will be an integral part, we require more time to complete further analysis". She told me that further evaluations could be done within four to five days and should confirm their theory. Her answer was actually extremely long and highly complex, but this was the gist of what she meant. I agreed, if the opportunity arose, I would try my best to delay my decision.

Irrespective of this, I told them I would need more time to consider their request regardless of this revelation. They both looked very relieved, and I smiled which gave us all a level of reassurance and comradeship. I didn't want this unity to jeopardise anything else, I couldn't run the risk of Olin, Jacron, and indeed them all from giving me more information. I took the opportunity to ask the big question, "Why do you feel the need to create a new super species?" Helena looked pleased that I had asked the question and reminded me that essentially there are two elements to consider. Firstly, the 62.87 Theory proves that a future intelligence created the human brain and its consciousness. The disturbance that readjusted evolutionary path instructs them to strive forward with the science and technology to enable this.

In conjunction with this, the second part to consider is the improvement of the human species and one that will enable the 62.87.1 theory to be realised. Before she could continue, I put my hand up and stopped her, "Point 1, what is this?" This is the first time anyone had mentioned a further theory. She looked visibly shocked, it was almost like a slip of the tongue, in fact that's what it was. Lise jumped into her rescue, as he said, "Danny, you will shortly hear more about this from Olin". As he did, he gave a hopeful smile, I must have looked more puzzled, but I felt it best to allow Helena to continue. She wrapped up her defence of this, improved species by relying on a weak argument that they should, and I quote her words, "improve with modification and adapt to our surroundings". I knew I would need time to fully understand what she meant by this.

"Excellence is never an accident. It is always the result of high intention, sincere effort, and intelligent execution."

Aristotle

The Code

There were a couple of questions I needed to ask, and I hoped this would be the time to obtain answers. Who was I kidding, I had a thousand questions whirling around my head and at any time these changed in priority. Regarding the 36 visionaries, and the preposterous notion that I could be one of them. I needed them to give me more information and ideally not to talk in riddles or say that I will figure it out. Helena was the first to weave her way through the explanation, but she remained careful not to specifically say that I have been chosen. She reminded me that I have free choice in everything I do, they cannot influence me. This obviously felt like a contradiction, how can they tell me about the future of humanity, and the perfect world they have created, and that it exists only because of the 36 visionaries. I was beginning to appreciate what they started, plus the answers and solutions I now understood. But all of this may not exist if I fail to act.

It's the ultimate dilemma and I couldn't help but think of Catch-22 and the meaning behind it. The written meaning hides its simplicity, 'a problematic situation for which the only solution is denied by a circumstance inherent in the problem or by a rule'. The novel by the American author Joseph Heller is primarily based on an actual army regulation; it stipulates that a soldier's request to be relieved from active duty can be accepted only if he is mentally unfit to fight. Think about it, **by the act of a soldier requesting to be relieved from active duty simply proves he is not mentally unfit**. Like the soldier, I don't see a way that I can win this argument. In my mind, I am facing a similar situation, if I want to see the future come to life, I know that a part of my DNA sequence will live forever. If I do nothing, all of this has merely been a very weird dream.

I probed them to tell me more about my role, and the question I had from the outset, why me. Helena told me it was in my interest not to be told too much; I could argue that too little works the same. Anyway, what she did tell me was the 36 are all from the same period in time, this coincided with them resetting time and the year 0001, in our year 1980. Each of the visionaries would find their role and realise their skills, along with the knowledge they possess. You will appreciate what I have repeatedly stated, in that, I don't believe I possess any beneficial skills. Lise then joined in and told me that each visionary will recognise another by virtue of the code. The code would be given to me by Olin within the next couple of days. Great, something else for me to worry about, although, I was inching my way closer towards possibly understanding more about our mission and my role.

As time moved on, I could sense they were becoming agitated and anxious, each answer they gave was shorter and faster. Helena was about to tell me something else, that was until Lise raised his arm slowly in front of her and she suddenly stopped. In a rare show of true emotion, I could almost detect a tear beginning to form in her eyes as they glazed over. Softly, but sternly Lise simply said, "Not now", Helena nodded in approval. This simply added another issue to the mounting pile of unanswered or unfinished items I had. I knew by their body language I wouldn't get any further with this or other points, with this imposed conclusion I was ready to finish the CDT event. The pair then disclosed the reason for their nervousness, which related to a point I picked up on from the outset, why these two. Helena asked in a distinctly monotone voice, "The request we have made regarding our group, and requiring more time to further analyse the data, should not be disclosed until we have the results". This almost robotic request meant they were here, within this CDT event without the knowledge or potentially the permission of the others. My surprise, coupled with shock, and a degree of confusion, couldn't be hidden from my face. I asked if my involvement could jeopardise future events. Fortunately, Helena comforted me by politely telling me that there would be no negative outcomes.

As the pair stood closer together, their hands crossed in front of them, and they thanked me for my cooperation and involvement. The lights dimmed to a complete blackness before a stronger warmth flushed over me, this was soon joined by natural sunlight hitting my face. I took a moment to get my bearings, the only word I could think of was, wow. Above everything that I had learnt today, I wanted to know what Helena was about to tell me. I felt this was the only time they had shown true emotion, and I felt it was important. My mind then flipped onto the two other critical points that were revealed, but as I did a nagging question returned and it was one, I knew had to be addressed. A revolving question remains unanswered, why me, now couple this with another, why have they shown me this. Irrespective of whether I am one of the 36, or that allowing my DNA to be used could be detrimental to humanity. None of this will matter if tomorrow I close all my notepads, put away the dozens of memory sticks and continue my life as though this was all part of an elaborate hoax.

I have been trying to find the correct description for what I faced, give it a name in order that I may grapple with it later, and in a dim hope that I can find the answers. They have repeatedly told me that I have free choice, but what is the point of free choice, especially if you are scared shitless of the wrong outcome. Is it a parallax effect. This happens when the different elements of a page move at different speeds, thus creating a 3D depth effect. I am presented with billions of pages, images and now knowledge and one day, I hope understanding. What if confirmation bias occurs, this effect can be known as selective recall, confirmatory memory, or access-biased memory. Helena and Lise have already planted a seed in my mind that all may not be well, based on this should I stop now. Really speaking, I must consider both dependent and independent variables.

Maybe, we all face the statement bravely outlined by Donald Rumsfeld, when he said, "…there are known knowns; there are things we know we know. We also know there are known unknowns; that is to say we know there are some things we do not know. But there are also unknown unknowns - the ones we don't know we don't know.". Beautifully put Don, and I think I will be happy to park this one for a while. My deep contemplative thought continued as I turned to the question of finding another 35 people who have received the same message, and who are, within my lifetime. Intrinsically connected to this must be my place or part within this group of visionaries. We should remember too; to now think of me as a visionary is incorrect, I am only armed with this information, knowledge, and partial understanding because they have imparted it to me. Another of the million or so questions must also be around the information I have been given, do they have the same, can they access everything, therefore, do they also have knowledge of the 62.87 Theory.

My mind then wondered into the additional unknown and two further points that merely generated further questions, and without further answers. The first being the code that will enable me to find others with the same experience, and in return they will be able to validate me. The unknowns here can be summed up as, when will this be given to me, and will I be able to crack the code. This initially worried me as my MS can cause issue with this type of thing. It's another part of the cognitive issues that can mean I sometimes struggle to understand things. However, I was then cheered slightly as I thought about my newly acquired skills in this area of problem solving. The problem still remains of how I will find them, although at least this is a starting point, and a way of validation.

Whilst deep in this fissure, and with my mind racing at an unimaginable speed, it turned quickly towards the next ground shaking addition they torpedoed towards me. I now have to contend with there being a new addition to the already mindboggling theory. We now have 62.87.1 to attempt to understand. If the first theory delt with creating the human brain and our consciousness, the theory that set humanity in a single collective direction, then what could be next. I must ask a couple of simple questions, when was this .1 version released, and who was the author. I couldn't think of anything further to be added, although, I should know by now that there are no limits, and no equation is off the table. By now my brain was physically hurting and I knew I needed to stop everything at this point.

As I opened my eyes, the bright sunlight reminded me of my time and place. Before I moved, a realisation began to form in my mind. With everything I now know and understand, as the phase goes, it is impossible to put the genie back in the bottle. That stark realisation means simply that things cannot be undone, I can't go back, I can't simply do nothing. If I want a better and improved world then I act, if I sit on my hands and do nothing then it will all disappear.

Chapter 17
You Can't Reverse The Ripple Effect

It's almost impossible to describe the uncontrollable randomness of my thoughts as they combined with my emotions on Friday evening. Over the past couple of weeks, I have sought to find the most accurate words to express these thoughts, and how my mind was in near constant turmoil. Tonight, it reached a whole new pinnacle as I found myself unable to follow a train of thought for more than a few moments. Normally, no matter how tenuous it may be, I would be able to find a thread that linked the various elements, although even this basic skill had deserted me. In the past, I would have parked my thoughts, but not now, now I was unable to let go until I had found a solution. Olin, Jacron, and now Helena had all given me insights into what might happen, but with each, they had not informed me of my role. In almost every instance they have said that I would figure it out, and they have repeatedly told me I had free choice. Having free choice and evaluating the best decision would normally not have such severe consequences.

Seemingly, unanswerable questions swirled around within my thoughts, each time I recognised one, another fought for importance with the next. Previously, the why me question took superiority; although, this was soon joined with, what am I supposed to do with it. Anyway, these are now seated comfortably next to the question regarding the 36 visionaries, and my role. Linkage between them is clear to see, but no matter what logic I apply, they keep returning unanswered. Even if I were able to park these for a moment, other topics contain their own questions. I now know why they want part of my DNA sequence, but I don't understand why. Amidst all of this chaos, I hadn't lost sight of the crucial difference between, information, knowledge, and understanding. This moment of clarity was soon lost amongst further thoughts about there being a 62.87.1

theory that also exists. Hold that thought, as I raced back to there being a concern raised by Helena and Lise. Covertly, they believe something may have been overlooked within my DNA sequence, but time maybe running out to intervene. And finally, if there is a potential finally, there's something Helena was about to tell me. Above everything else, I felt this was the only element that contained anything close to real emotion.

I only hope you can appreciate what was going through my mind. Furthermore, remember that since some inspired intervention, I am now able to think and find solutions faster than any other human alive today. I was grateful that Friday evening poised no further distractions. I picked Jane up as normal from the station and as tradition dictates, we ordered a takeaway. When it was finally delivered late, it was understandably warm rather than hot, and to top it all, it was incorrect. Fortunately, Jane had already consumed her first glass of wine which helped defuse the situation. Rather than a full-blown tantrum, we merely got a string of abuse and the declaration that we would never use them again. I knew this wouldn't be the case as the food once nuked (microwaved) was still very tasty. As more alcohol was added to brain numbing soaps on TV, we had the opportunity to talk, or should I say, I listened to how bad her week had been.

I have urged you to listen to several songs throughout this book. I believe each one will either help position a feeling or help to explain it. Well, here's another, and this is one I hope you will ask your know-it-all smart speaker to play. Paul Heaton explained our routine embedded approach to the seven-day week in a song titled, 'A Good Day Is Hard to Find'. Jacqui Abbott helps to deliver it with an addictive tune.

The Wake-Up Call

Saturday morning started with a loud dawn chorus of what sounded like a major dispute between warring magpies. I made an observation once when I associated magpies' walking to men wearing women's high heeled shoes. I didn't need to look over my shoulder to obtain the time, somehow, I knew it was 05:15. As I lay there wide awake my focus soon sought out my comforting visual reference point on the ceiling. Quickly, the unanswered questions from the night before came back into clarity and whilst they remained in this state, I wasn't over concerned. I hadn't found the link that I had searched for, but what I did find gave me an insight into understanding them. Over the past few weeks' doors have been opened for me and I have been allowed to view something exceptional. Not only is it exceptional, it's also unique and something only 35 other people will see. As each door opened, I realised it can never be closed. Although, to be more precise, the view I obtained can never be erased once witnessed. Realisation hit me with the understanding that a new timeline begins with each new piece of information we have.

With this new discovery of mine, I quickly assimilated it to what Olin had told me about the ripple effect. Each action will inevitably create a ripple effect, the magnitude and consequences may not be fully understood at the beginning. No matter what we do thereafter to manage the effect, any further action will begin its own new ripple effect. What Olin hadn't told me, or made clear is that once started, it can never be reversed. This greater understanding has given rise to a new quandary, I wonder if they'd completely mapped out the ripple effect of their actions. As they have the whole of humanity working towards the beginning of everything, surely, they will have played out and considered every possible outcome. If this is the case, then no matter what I do, it will be what they had planned. But then you bring in the complete unknown that is called free choice. Free choice could be arrived at through meticulous planning, likewise, it could be decided through a random toss of a coin, and the call between heads or tails.

No matter how many times I considered the options I have, and no matter how much gameplay I planned, I knew I needed more information. I also needed to ask some hard questions of myself regarding my ability to take this forward. The stark reality of the choice I have, will have potentially massive life changing effects on my family and friends. If I reveal everything I now know, and understand, it will be the start of a ripple effect where I can never determine the results. Hence, my decision must consider this and how I must protect and shield those I love. My resources were being drained, and I was unable to think effectively as possible answers and gameplays run frantically in multiple directions.

I hoped Saturday would provide me with sufficient time to recharge my much-depleted batteries. Fortunately, the Saturday routine would, or should, mean that I have time to myself, and I knew I had to create my detailed vlogs today. As a consequence, I had almost forgotten that Keith had something planned. Actually, I had forgotten all about it, I quickly composed myself when I saw him in the carpark, we chatted briefly before he unveiled his surprise. I was parked in the disabled section and Jane faithfully displayed our badge in the windscreen. Typically, this disabled section was busy, although it was relatively easy to spot the legitimate users from the 4x4 all-terrain monsters who craved the additional space provided. Even at this early time the weather was glorious and beginning to warm up. Keith and I sat on a wall, and he urged me to watch carefully, there was no need for careful observation as two clapped out, past their sell-by-date cars entered the carpark. Each driver diligently parked their cars in such a way that they sandwiched two cars neatly into the bays they chose to illegally occupy.

Keith reassured me that neither had displayed a disabled badge, in fact they had been observing the carpark for the past hour or so. He then showed me a video of each vehicle owner as they swiftly jumped out of their cars. The covert filming continued as they both entered a gym that was situated less than 200m from the carpark. We then sat observing the scene as other cars came and went. Around fifteen minutes later the two unwitting participants to the subterfuge returned, they immediately looked in disbelief at somebody's pathetic parking. The look of fury began to rise as the realisation hit them, there was no way of moving their cars. Their beautiful, prized possessions sat gleaming in the mid-morning sunshine. They had been rendered useless by two clapped out bangers that were not worthy to be even close to theirs. As the owners looked around, seemingly trying to find the idiots who couldn't correctly park, an associate of Keith's walked towards them. To everybody's surprise, even shock, they were accompanied with another person filming the events on what looked to be a professional camera. Keith then flicked his mobile phone to an App which showed a live feed from the camera which was recording everything.

He then beckoned me to look closely, and he asked, "Do you recognise him?" It took a moment until I did recognise his face, although I couldn't recall his name. He was a BBC reporter from the local area news, he always struck me as being rather smug and full of his own importance. The look on my face must have been a picture of shock, bemusement which was coupled with a slight snigger, the only words I could find were, "How did you?" The reporter immediately introduced himself to the unsuspecting drivers and indicated the obvious. He directed the pair to witness these spaces were reserved for disabled people with appropriate blue badges. All these merely summarised matters before he asked them if they had a legitimate reason to park here. By this time, a small crowd was beginning to gather, some of them could be seen recording or live streaming on mobile phones. Evidently, everything slotted into place for the pair as they quickly tried to cover their faces and demanded that filming stopped. Of course, this wasn't going to happen, in fact the opposite was true as the reporter hit them with a barrage of short, sharp questions. "You do know these spaces are for people who actually need them?", "Do you think it's right for you to deprive people who have a physical need?", "Are you using these spaces just because they provide more space around the parking area?" Unable to answer, each driver simply, and probably regretfully walked away. The reporter, to my relief didn't follow them, instead he faced the camera and rounded his report up with a message of how people abuse and use these bays incorrectly.

Thankfully, the ordeal was over for the two victims of this demonstration, and to my further relief the reporter and camera operator didn't join Keith and I who continued to watch from a safe distance. Shortly after, the cars were removed by his acquaintances, and I can only presume the other cars were retrieved at some later point. Keith was extremely pleased with himself and could hardly contain his laughter. Triumphantly, he asked me if I was impressed, I answered cautiously that I hoped lessons had been learnt. Perhaps, I approved of the result, although, I was not a fan of dishing out a form of justice in this way. My mind went back to the ripple effect and how this relatively minor divergence would follow these two people. Keith nor I could possibly know what effect this may have on their personal or working lives. In fact, I shudder at the possible thought of how it may also affect their families and friends. Granted, the point will have been made, however, we will never know the full extent of our actions, and I didn't want to begin to explain this to Keith. We sat outside until Jane had finished shopping, before we left, I had a few things I wanted to get. Once I returned with a new notebook and memory sticks, we said goodbye to Keith. Whilst I was in the shop, he took the opportunity to show Jane the recording and boasted how he set everything up. She saw the 'funny' side, but also commented on what this may do to the people involved. Later that day I called Keith and asked him to use his influence to ensure it would never be shown on TV.

Every Life Matters

Earlier in this book I urged people to read this section if they were considering suicide, or perhaps knew someone that needed help. I am not an expert by any means, although I do have first-hand experience of being incredibly and dangerously close to the edge. If events hadn't have happened, and these events didn't change my mind, then everything that I was planning for 1 November 2018 would have resulted in my death by suicide. Over the past couple of weeks, I have learnt an enormous amount, but none more important than understanding the ripple effect. For those who have skipped straight to this page allow me to explain.

Everything we do in our lives matters, granted some things are more important than others and will have a greater or lesser impact. What we don't know and can never truly know is how our actions will affect others. It could be something really simple like bumping into someone as you walked by, or what you may call someone without harmful intent. I was introduced to a way of thinking called the ripple effect, now this is not necessarily something we have to do or act every second of the day. There must be a fair and proportionate measure of how you think and use this knowledge, I am also very new to this, therefore, I am still considering potentially too much. It's obviously easier for the big decisions we need to make, although we don't always give them sufficient consideration. Additionally, I have only just begun to understand that with equal if not greater importance, you can never reverse the ripple effect.

Let's consider our actions that could be considered really minor, or even trivial. We may expect them to have a minimal ripple effect, if any at all. What if we were to simply bump into someone as you walked past them in the street today. Unbeknown to you is what kind of day they are having, and your inconspicuous nudge may be yet another way they perceive the world is against them. Likewise, the ripple effect can have positive outcomes. That nudge could mean you make eye contact for the first time with the partner you end up falling in love with. What makes the potential difference is how we initially react. They say that manners cost nothing, therefore, a polite and meaningful, "Sorry", would potentially alter the effect. What if we crank it up a little bit and add a simple comment into the equation. An observation of somebody's appearance could have similar outcomes, a comment may be unintended to cause upset, although, once said it cannot be reversed. We may simply say that someone has unusually large ears and think nothing of it. Although, to the individual it may bring back a flood of childhood memories of bullying. Personally, I despise something like this which is then followed up by, 'I am only joking'. As if that add-on is going to reverse what has already been said and registered. Now there are those that would argue that we shouldn't take offence by something like this, but we cannot know the impact it may cause. As a child, I remember being told that if you don't have anything nice to say, don't say anything at all.

If we explore the ripple effect further and consider our actions in relation to a larger event in our lives. Before I continue, I would like to stress that this is not about placing a guilt trip on anyone, it's purely about asking us all to think, and think seriously about potential consequences. What I had planned for 1 November 2018 would have seen my life come to an end. I believed that my choice was the correct one, however, I can now view this differently and consider other factors that I had not previously. I was intending to use my suicide as an example, to illustrate to the world that I mattered. I also believed that this would actually be the best thing for those I loved, it would make their lives better in the long term. Now that I understand more about the ripple effect, I can see and appreciate better what this would have caused.

It's important that we do not attach a 'theoretical value' to the impact on those who we believe may be affected by such actions. For example, I may think that Jane and Toni would feel the effects more than others. Next, may be Georgina and her family, and these may be followed by friends. We may be tempted to attach a scale to these, for example, based on how long they have known me, or how much contact we have had recently. Although, this is all complete bullshit, and it is, because I can never know, appreciate, or understand how anyone would be affected, and to what degree. It's correct to say that the act of suicide passes the pain and suffering from one person on to others. What this phrase should say is that it passes the pain to many others and for an indefinite period. What I would never know is the psychological burden it would pass to others. The ripple effect could mean that someone close to me decides upon their own significant action, they may decide not to enter a long-term relationship, or have children as the pain of loss is too much to handle.

Every life matters, everything else I have said in this book can, and probably will be thrown away, but one thing is certain and true. No matter what happens we must value life for as long as we have it. Once we are born, and take our first gasp of air, our clock begins its countdown to zero when the lights go out. Every second we spend is a second that we will never regain. As individuals, we occupy this planet for an insignificant number of years. On face value, it's a blink of an eye, and we may be fooled into thinking it doesn't really matter, nor what we do, or what impact we may have. Having witnessed a future that is intrinsically dependent on the past, and the previous efforts of previous generations, I now understand the value of every life. What we will never know, and what we can only speculate is what our future descendants will go on to achieve. Let's flip back a little and overlay our significant actions with a theoretical ripple effect. My actions to end my life by suicide could seriously impact future generations, those could go on to achieve great things, but all should go on to benefit society and humanity.

For those who may be considering suicide, all I would ask is to think. Please, please, take some time to consider your potential future. You may have reached a similar point to me; I was convinced that my actions were well considered and well thought out. I can now see that I hadn't fully considered the impact they would have on others. I wasn't aware of the ripple effect and how many people would be hurt, and in unknown and immeasurable ways. If you think there's no way out and you have reached the end of the darkest tunnel, please take time for one last moment to reflect. Before you do anything please discuss the ripple effect with one other person. If, by the end of that conversation you still think there's no way forward, no way to rectify whatever you may be going through, then please give me just one day more, one further 24 hours.

If you're unsure what to say or how to say it, please use this context. 'The ripple effect is something we can never fully measure. Recently, I have been considering my own life and the value it has to others. If I wasn't here, if I was to simply disappear tomorrow, can you help me rationalise how that would impact on those around me'. Once you have begun this conversation you should add, 'I am in the position where I cannot see past tomorrow'. I can only hope that whoever you are speaking to will help you realise your true value and how much you mean to those around you.

The next part will take bravery, it's possibly courageousness that you never thought you had. We all have problems some large, some small, but each are personal to us. These problems may have driven us to our darkest point, a point where we cannot see tomorrow. I can assure you there are no problems, no matter their size, complexity, or seriousness that cannot be resolved. To see tomorrow you may need to surrender these problems and share them with others. There are people and organisations that can and will help you see past them. They will help you to remove them so that you can see a day in the future where these problems will appear as they truly are… they are problems to be overcome.

Before you do anything, take 24 hours with a clear mind to consider your own ripple effect. On a piece of paper write down the names of people around you that you know. Along with those names add your relationship to them, don't worry about importance or ranking them, we are only concerned with name and how you know them. Now add to this how long you have known them, it doesn't matter whether it's years, it may only be a few months or even a couple of days. All of these people will have shared time with you, no matter how precious that time, every second will have mattered in some way. What we don't know, and what we can never truly gauge is how much they value us.

Now comes the hard part, for each of those names, consider what their lives will be like without you. You must do this objectively; you must forget what was previously said or done. You need to park any of the 'bad' things, your perception of those bad things will be different from theirs. You may apportion blame on yourself or them for something that has happened, however, once again this can be subjective. We can never truly know how other people react to situations; therefore, events must also be removed from your evaluations. Remember, this is not to apportion blame or to place guilt on you, it's only to provide a clear space to allow us to think.

The ripple effect initially places you at the beginning of events, if those events start with your demise consider how each of those names on your list will be affected. Just like throwing a stone into a lake, or even broken stones, those ripples reduce the further we get from the source, although, they can still be seen and felt. Our actions are rarely felt in the singular, as humans we communicate, we create stories to tell others. Actions felt by one person will often be relayed to several others, and by doing this other ripple effects begin. As we tell these stories we relive the events, and they will either increase or decrease in magnitude or importance. One thing is certain, we can never predict the impact of events on others because they are all subjective.

None of us can see into the future, we cannot know what the future will bring, and as such we are unable to define what will be the ripple effects following our actions. All we can say is that people will be affected by them. The last thing I want to do is hurt or affect my family and friends through my own selfish actions. I know that the problems I have can be overcome, with help I will be able to achieve my goals, and I know how much I am loved no matter what I may be facing. I am not unique, we are all cared for, and every life is important and must be valued now and given to future generations. If you have skipped the bulk of this book to find this section, I sincerely hope it will help. I urge anyone who is contemplating suicide to reach out and ask for help. Talk to someone or just give some time to think about the ripple effects. Organisations that will help can be found through a simple Google search.

BE STRONG

BE BRAVE

SEEK HELP & TALK

Chapter 18
The Code

Following the events organised by Keith in the morning, the remainder of Saturday passed off quietly. The news and several TV programmes focused on England's chances of going all the way in Russia. Yesterday's games could only be viewed as the garlic enhanced starter, and I always look forward to a garlic overload whenever I can. Anyway, Uruguay was beaten by a very strong French team by two goals to nil. In the other game my favoured Belgium team were triumphant over the once mighty Brazil by two goals to one. I admit, I was now ready for the main course with my plate cleaned ready as England took on Sweden. There were fewer flags flapping from upstairs bedrooms, and a distinct lack of mini flags sticking out of car windows. It felt in some ways that the constant let-downs over the years through previous generations had infected this one. As the song said, our '30 years of pain' was continually being extended, and whilst the latest crop of tattoo adorned hairstyles promised much as individuals, as a team we never quite made it.

One look at the TV schedules and Jane was off out for a catch up with friends. I received a very polite request to drop her at the station, to which I obviously agreed and obliged. After lunch I was free to create a very long and detailed vlog for both the recent CDT events, along with capturing my rambling thoughts. My list of questions grew ever longer, and all without definitive answers. While I could add what had become half-educated guesses or theories, I was unable to confirm anything. I felt time was against me, certain things had been said to indicate this. Additionally, I couldn't see that I had much value to them once they had obtained my approval to use a section of my DNA sequence. This obviously raised my concerns, based on the fact that Helena and Lise had distinct reservations about allowing it to be used. Could this indicate a danger to them or me, I had no idea.

Recently, I have compiled lists of things I wanted or needed to ask them, but once in the CDT event I was unable to recall them. Obviously, I cannot take a list with me, I feel I should be able to remember them, maybe I need to find another way. The most important questions relate to my involvement and why have they chosen me. I don't believe it is simply for my 'perfect' DNA sequence or that I have a router with the adequate speed required. I must fit some other criteria, there must be a plan where my participation is required. I am also struggling with the whole, 'free choice' thing. My better understanding of the ripple effect means that they already know what my choices will be. As they have told me on a couple of occasions, they exist in one version of the future. My free choice, therefore, will either result in this, or a completely different one. I know this is very heavy, my brain hurts thinking about it, so I guess yours may be too. Whatever my decision is, it must be the correct one for me, and my future along with those around me. If I am part of the 36 visionaries then either, I find them the other 35, or they will find me. Then, somewhere along the line the 62.87 Theory will be written and the rest, as they say is history.

The creation of the vlogs took much longer than anticipated, they also required the consumption of more coffee than usual. The entire process took around three hours to complete, by the end I was absolutely shattered. To be more accurate my MS fatigue went into meltdown, I really struggled to find the energy to pick up Jane later from the station. She was in a really buoyant mood when she returned. Toni had called her to say her, and Nigel were coming down next weekend, as a result Sunday would be spent cleaning and making sure everything was ready. I was ordered to take it easy for the remainder of the day, there was never going to be an argument, I just hoped I could stay awake. To my surprise and probable shock

England were victorious, Harry Maguire fired in a bullet of a header after 30 minutes. We then went two up with another header from Deli Alli, meanwhile, our own Jordan Pickford made some excellent saves and regularly kept us in the game. Elsewhere, Croatia knocked out Russia which set us up a semi-final with them on 11 July.

As expected, Sunday came and went, I managed to keep my distance from Jane's impression of a hurricane as she cleaned the entire house. Fresh carnations were placed in Toni's room, I was even given a carnation in a small vase for the table next to my chair. Even though I had either slept or rested the entire day, I still managed a full night's sleep on Sunday. I would like to say that I awoke fully refreshed and ready to go on Monday morning, but that would be far from the truth. I managed to drive to the station, although Jane was insistent on walking to get the bus. This would add a further 45 minutes to her journey, this would be compounded by the added nightmare of screaming energetic kids with very little manners. I returned home and decided to tackle a few emails that had landed, none of them were important, I just hate leaving them without a reply. During the morning, aided by several strong coffees, I seemed to acquire more energy, although the speed of thought that I recently enjoyed had slowed down noticeably. I took an early break for lunch; music became my go-to form of relaxation and I enjoyed the internal banter with myself to decide who to listen to. An old favourite came out on top, Deacon Blue burst onto the scene with some classic anthems, none less than Dignity. Every time I listen to this it immediately transports me to places where all my cares and worries vanish. It also illustrates that a determined individual can never be broken, even if that individual shows no promise.

A few songs into the random selection offered by Doris and I was asleep once more. Unable to register how much time had lapsed, I could slowly feel the warm and uplifting sensation begin. It was mesmerizingly enjoyable, relaxing and almost like a form of medication. It's difficult to explain how I can feel every cell being manipulated and caressed. The weightlessness is also something that defies explanation. Then came the trickles of charged energy that moved rapidly over my skin, although this time I could feel more than tingles. I heard my name being called over and over, but I was unable to respond. The constant requests to open my eyes registered, although here again I was unable to act. Eventually, I summoned the strength and following several attempts, my eyes open slightly. Rapid blinking allowed me to bear the pain and open my eyes further until I was able to focus.

As my vision focused, I could make out the now unmistakable outline of Olin and Jacron. My blinking became less hurried, and I eventually made eye contact with the pair. Olin greeted me, but instead of the usual pleasantries he asked me how I was feeling in a stern and unusually stark way. He told me how they had detected some unusual readings within my CDT device. I explained that I was feeling more fatigued than usual, but that I had put this down to my MS. I immediately grew concerned for Helena and Lise, fortunately my answer seemed to provide a level of reassurance they needed. Whether it was my explanation, along with their understanding of the disease, but they quickly got down to business as usual.

Jacron began by telling me how much they valued my time, and how all of this must be quite different from what I was used to. I couldn't miss this opportunity to tell them exactly how different it was. I kept my cool as I began my onslaught, "I don't think you fully appreciate how difficult this has been for me", I began. "firstly, yes this is very 'different', as you put it, I have had to deal with so much, and none of this was expected", I began to feel my heart pounding as I continued. "you asked me not to discuss this with anyone else, and this has been very difficult as I have had to hide all of this from

Jane, Toni, plus some of my closest friends". The faces of Jacron and Olin changed, I knew they weren't expecting this, and it really did take them by surprise. Little did they know, I had only just started, "If that wasn't bad enough, I have been given many questions and all without answers, and when I ask for an answer, the pair of you simply tell me, I will figure it out". I was now on a roll, "and, these aren't trivial questions, I am supposed to work out my role in all of this, am I one of the 36 visionaries? If so, how do I find the other 35? Do I place an advert in my local paper, it's almost too much".

By this time, I wish I'd had a camera, "then we include this 62.87 Theory that you have kindly downloaded directly into my brain", I paused for a second, "here again, I have no idea what I am supposed to do with this". As I continued to hurl all the things I had to contend with, I could feel my stress levels rising and it felt good to be able to vent in this way. I then launched into a section where I pointed out that I have never asked anything from them. "I could have asked for the winning numbers to the lottery, I could have asked for the results to certain races or the winning teams in loads of sporting events, but I never have". As I sighed, I finished, "I have entered into this relationship with no care for myself, no axe to grind and no wishes to become rich, I have never once thought of self-gain".

The Future For Humanity

I think Olin had wanted to interrupt my full flow for a while, he finally raised his right hand in an almost apologetic way. To my complete surprise a door towards the rear of the room slid softly open, as it did a man walked in. As he approached the point where the two others sat, a seat metamorphically emerged seamlessly from the floor. Before he sat down, he introduced himself to me, "Hello Danny, it is a privilege to finally meet you, my name is Youglav". His voice was much deeper than any other I had met so far, as he sat my lower peripheral vision sparked to life as is bio was made available to me. His full name was Youglav-Tam18-Madrog, I was delighted by the way he had already abbreviated this for me. His age was 56 years and 136 days, although he could have passed for 40 or even mid 30's easily. Similar to the others, his complexion was radiant, and he was an athletic 6ft 4inches. The next set of data had me wondering what this meant, his position simply read: Director General – 62.87 Evolution Ethics Mandate P211 Team. If I was interpreting their chain of command correctly, this made him the big cheese. His skin tone was far darker than any of the others, he was clean shaven with very short, almost shaven hair.

He then asked me if he could remain seated, as if this made any difference to me. He then made a comment which confirmed he must have been listening to the beginning of my rant from outside. For a moment I wondered if he had observed any CDT events first-hand or waited for a later analysis. "We do understand how much we have asked of you, and you may never know how much we value what you have had to surrender", he told me. It was that word surrender that had my heart beating faster. He then confirmed that I would now be given all of the answers I desired. The relief was almost immeasurable for me, finally I would find out what all of this meant and what is expected of me. "We do have to take this in stages, there is a process", he said. Why does there always seem to be a twist I thought, why can't they just give a simple answer.

Youglav relaxed back in his seat and said that it's best if we take this in stages. The most pressing questions for you and the best place to start will be with the next phase and 62.87.1, he smiled as he announced this. I must have looked either bemused or enthralled as he continued. He took time to clearly reiterate the original theory, it was everything that I had accessed but it was beneficial to hear is explanation. He casually mentioned that there was a revision or addendum to the original theory. I had only heard of this covertly via Helena and Lise, yet he presumed I already knew. Let's see how this plays out, I thought.

As he began, our trusty display screen materialised to my left, and I could feel something in my vision which seemed to be accessing files. His voice had a warmth, and the deepness of his tone made him easy to hear without it being distracting. He told me, the 62.87 Theory stated that humanity's evolution, and the birth of the digital age could not have been achieved without an external force. I understood this now, but only once you factor in the life expectancy of our species, the timeline which will be millions if not billions of years, and to be exact 3.82 billion. We have been fortunate to witness first-hand our birth, and creation of the digital age. The theory demonstrated that connected thought, consciousness, along with the use of language all required programming. Their mission was to develop the science and technology to create the programming required to achieve this. Clearly, I knew all of this, and whilst he was explaining it again the display screen provided further scientific data and analysis. He paused for a moment and asked if I had any questions, I thought before saying, "Please continue and I will ask my questions once you have finished". He seemed to be happy with my reply as he gave a brief and barely noticeable nod. Continuing with his explanation, he reiterated their challenges regarding the means of transporting this cargo and then deployment. Once complete, our species would begin an expediential growth plan beyond the normal rules.

The display screen that now had my full attention continued to present graphs and data to support each statement. I made a bold move to interrupt his flow by saying, "I understand what I am capable of understanding at this time, I appreciate the recap, but can you please tell me how much of this you have achieved?" To my surprise he seemed delighted with my question as he told me progress has been substantial in all areas, although some more than others. The background colour changed on the display screen before it presented a timeline with various dependencies dotted along it. Each area also had a breakdown of subsectors with achievements highlighted and each with its own timeline. The quantity of data was frightening, and as more information flowed through the faster it became. Suddenly it stopped and the screen showed a harsh plain white.

Youglav looked sideways towards Olin and Jacron but said nothing. I broke the silence by thanking him for his 'detailed' explanation. I knew there were items he didn't cover, but I was pleased to let them pass otherwise we could have been here all day. I jokingly said, "I hope you don't expect me to remember all of that". His reply puzzled me, previously they told me no further files would be download into my brain, "We don't expect you to recall them all now, however, in the future they may be called upon", he said calmly. I was careful to phrase my next question correctly, I didn't want another guarded reply. "Regarding the creation of the new super species", as soon as I opened with this statement his eyes seemed to light up, well they did, until I continued, "the third point of your charter states that 'Science must never be used to create new lifeforms or recreate extinct lifeforms', so how do you justify this?" He began his reply without hesitation, I was a little worried because it began with a politician's opening, "I am glad you asked that". Anyway, he gave an answer that I half-expected, they don't see this as a new creation, rather they see this as a natural progression of the human species. He waffled a bit to expand his answer, and when I pointed out that they are looking to modify and improve the DNA of humanity, he gave a faint smile and claimed this reinforced their understanding.

As we were now on this topic, Olin took the opportunity and dived in with the question, 'Have you decided yet?' I explained that I was still trying to appreciate the enormity of the request. I could only hope that they were unaware of my covert and undisclosed CDT event with Helena and Lise. He replied that they were ready to help me and answer any questions or concerns I had, as he told me this, Jacron and Youglav looked like a pair of nodding dogs as they displayed their agreement. I could tell that they were keen to obtain my approval, I had my doubts simply because of what I had been warned about, although this hadn't been confirmed. They excepted my response without pushing back any further, I then saw an opening to continue my investigative approach, and hit them with a very simple follow up, "Please tell me, what is the point of creating a new and improved species?" Youglav looked even more excited, and I waited for a similar politician's line before he replied. Surprisingly, he turned the question back on me, "You should have already arrived at the correct conclusion by now", he said, this time his voice seemed deeper than before and more considered.

I looked straight at Olin, a few seconds later my stare moved towards Jacron, and a few seconds later it returned towards Youglav. My facial muscles tightened; my gaze nervously switched to looking downwards and the absence of anything. I had previously entertained a thought; it was a wild thought which I temporarily discarded due to the lack of credible support. Now the thought had been regerminated, it allowed my brain to rush furiously in several different directions. Recently, I had inadvertently mentioned within one of my vlogs a notion within a single word. As my eyes raised and once more became refocused on my audience, I was ready to explain my theory. I started by stating my understanding that the earth and our sun is currently in its most stable state. We know that the sun will eventually have consumed its full source of hydrogen in around 5 billion years. If humanity is to survive then an alternative home will be required. The gang of three hung on my every word as I continued to explain my interpretation of a theory. The super species which is now being created will undoubtedly be just the first re-creation of the human form. Each new reincarnation or generation will contain further intelligence, intelligence that we can't even begin to imagine. I could see how my explanation excited them, Olin then urged me to continue by simply saying, "And". As soon as this registered, I knew there was more, I just had to allow the thoughts to expand further. "It's not just to find a new home, it's to", my words stopped at this point. It was like a thousand lightbulbs exploding due to a powerful surge of energy, my mouth moved, but no sound was made. I tried again, eventually the word came out, "Universe". I repeated the sentence in full, "Humanity is looking to survive the ending of this universe and continue to the next".

One day, the universe as we know it will end when a super black hole consumes everything. Every galaxy, every star, planet, molecule, and atom will be pulled and crushed through immense forces. We are unable to imagine or measure the density of this mass which has no regards for what was there before. Evantis246's generation will die, eventually a new universe will come from another singularity moment. 62.87.1 calculates when this will be, and it provides the first line of the blueprint for the future for humanity. Wow, what a theory, and what a journey. Youglav looked immensely proud of my achievement, it felt like I had created or given birth to the theory. He then expanded on my statement and provided more substance which merely theorised the concept further. I was surprised by the absence of any supporting data, charts or plans that normally accompanies a powerful presentation. Although, he did expand on this theory and how future advancements will create further levels of intelligence. Creation or an advancement of the Evolution Disturbance will give birth to a self-perpetuating model of increased intelligence, a superior level far beyond our realms of understanding. An amazing thought washed over me; a part of my DNA sequence could be used to kickstart this new adventure. Helena may find a valid reason for me to reject its use, I am hoping that won't be the case.

…AND YOU LIKE TO THINK YOU'RE A KING BUT YOU'RE REALLY A PAWN!

My achievement seemed to hurry things along with them, in fact Olin respectfully interrupted the excitable Youglav by saying, "I am sure Danny will give this more thought". I was also keen to continue, whilst I was enjoying the conversation and learning new things, I had an agenda here. I swiftly took the opportunity to move onto 'why me'. I was careful how I phrased my next question; I had to avoid a vague reply. I addressed the three of them, "You have opened my thoughts to being involved in some way with the 36 visionaries, but I am unable to figure out my true role without understanding theirs". Olin sat back in his seat while the other two leaned forwards, "Before I can accept any challenge, I need to be satisfied that I can deliver on it", my tone softened, it almost came across as a plea for help. Olin was the first to break ranks and sympathetically he replied, "We now understand the dilemma we have placed you in, we had to ensure that you were capable of understanding". I looked puzzled and simply replied, "Understanding?" Olin stood up and took a few paces towards me, it was the closest anyone had ever been. If he could have physically touched me, I am sure he would have. He explained how they needed to find individuals who could accept what they had been shown. It was more than simply accept; these individuals would possess the ability to question everything. Just as I have done, these other individuals have developed new skills, new knowledge, and new realisation.

I looked directly into Olin's eyes and told him I understood. Each of the 36 will have been given the same opportunities. They will have been able to access the same files, although as I learnt, information simply provides knowledge and if you're able you may extract understanding. What I wanted to know, what I needed to understand was my role. I felt it would be useless to ask outright for my job description along with its roles and responsibilities, therefore, the questions would have to be carefully delivered. "Have the other 35 understood as much or more than I have?", I asked, although I wasn't hopeful for a revealing answer. Olin seemed flattered by the question and told me in a roundabout way that I had understood everything that was offered to me. I mean, this shouldn't be this hard, what's difficult about getting a direct answer. Suddenly, something clicked in my mind, it comes back to the contentious issue of free choice. I guess they can't be seen to direct me, they want any decision, any choice to remain with the individual. Surely this is a risky attitude as it will only take one of the 36 to decide upon a different route, and all the cards will come tumbling down. I gave a slight smile and said in a soft voice to Olin, "I understand, free choice". In return, Olin answered with a smile, nodded softly, and returned to join the others.

All my life I have felt there should be more to this, certainly not in a religious or spiritual way, just some way that meant I achieved something. I know that I have a great deal to be content with, Toni is amazing, and I know she will go on to have a fruitful and happy life. In that, I feel Jane and I can leave this world in a better place than we entered it. That's an achievement to be proud of, only now I have the opportunity to create something the world has never seen before. I can be the spark of creation, the light that is needed to readjust humanity and set a new course. Thinking in this way helps me rationalise the 'free choice' option, and I wonder if the other visionaries have come to the same conclusion.

I looked once more towards the three and asked my next question, "Have all 36 understood the 62.87 Theory?" I opted for the direct approach, there could not be any ambiguity in this. It was now Jacron's turn to answer, she composed herself and carefully told me, "Not all 36 have had access to the files". She paused, and I waited anxiously for the crucial remainder, "Only those who have understood it sufficiently will be able to articulate it fully to others", she calmly stated. I thought, rather I believed that I understood the theory, but I was unsure if I was able to explain it to others. The files stored within my brain contain a vast amount of information and data, the bulk of this I don't understand, I don't even know how to access it all. Maybe there is another visionary with more ability than I have. As I have stated many times, I am a middle-aged man with a chronic disease, I hope the other 35 are much more capable than I am.

Without prompting, Jacron then announced that I will need to recognise the others. My facial expression must have altered to one of eager delight. She also told me that each person has been given the same code. Those who were unable to access the code would not be suitable, and their participation will have ended. I asked gingerly what ended meant in this situation. Jacron explained that their memories of all prior CDT events will have been erased and all temporary files removed. I don't know if I looked nervous and my voice seemed to be less than confident as I asked, "Do you get more than one attempt?" She giggled and told me they had every confidence in my ability, I was told to relax and look for the code within the code. This seemed to be a strange way to make me relaxed, I closed my eyes, rotated my neck, and said, "OK, I am ready".

A display screen appeared towards my left, it seemed larger than normal, and the background had a 3D effect. It was like looking into a cube, although there was no special parameters or depth. Without warning a random selection of characters and keyboard symbols appeared, from left to right. There was a split second between each character, and as each line filled, the next line began. I didn't know whether to wait until it had stopped or attempt to decipher them line by line. I held my nerve and tried my best to retain my composure. My eyes focused on each character, and I began to look for a link or a method, but this was useless. By now there must have been 15 lines or more, nothing made sense, it was all random, but even within the randomness there seemed no order. Like a machine generating a given sequence, line after line appeared. I began to look intensely at the individual characters they began to fade out of focus and obtain a shuddering ring around their contours. Eventually, the readout stopped, 26 lines of 26 characters stood motionless on the screen. Look for the code within the code she told me. I blinked, and as my eyes opened my logical brain began to search, the speed of thought that I had recently acquired went into comfort mode. Characters became bold and others faded, the code materialised in front of me, I smiled cautiously.

Olin and Youglav stood to their feet in a single sharp movement, then, at the same time Jacron and Olin said, "You have it?" I merely nodded and whispered the words, Jacron leaned forwards, "Again" she urged. With intense confidence I announced the answer, the three of them rejoiced. Olin and Youglav beamed incredibly infectious smiles and shook their heads in disbelief, while Jacron, well she stood stunned and motionless. I must admit, I was pleased with myself, but didn't feel the evident reaction justified the achievement. Laughter coupled with sheer excitement trembled in Youglav's voice as he told, "This was the quickest anyone has ever deciphered the code". Jacron gained her composure again and began to tap her thighs in way of an applause. Youglav continued to heap praises onto me and told me that I was indeed a rare find. I didn't know how to digest this or what it all meant; they were ecstatic. I could only be pleased I had passed their test and waited for the next. All your life you think you're a king only to find out you're a pawn.

For some bizarre reason it turns out that I may actually, well, turn out 'to be someone'.

Variations of this code have been given to 35 others; each one will be able to decipher this one although not in the same speed. Olin began to tell me how I will be able to identify the others. When I am ready, I will be able to search for them and the next step in the formation of everything will begin. I must have looked bewildered again; he attempted to clarify this by saying 'I will figure it out'. How I hate those five words when strung together, so far nobody has told me how I will figure these things. Maybe I was reading too much into the phrasing of what they were telling me, but I got the impression that I would be leading the search in some way. It would be a waste of breath for me to ask if I was the author, although, I was desperate to know my true role.

Below you will find the code; it took me 4.2105 seconds to fathom. Thankfully, I was somehow given the ability to calculate logical problems at insanely fast speeds. My challenge, when the time is right will be to locate 35 others. Some of them will know the path they are intended to take; I will now be able to recognise the others through this code. Some will be unable to decipher the code, for those it will be the end of their journey, their memory of previous CDT events will be erased, and their lives will continue as normal. Each of the chosen ones will bring the necessary skills to create a new world. They will have the foresight and intelligence that is required to set down a manifesto for change. When all 36 are together the dawn of a new chapter in our evolution will begin, before this can happen, I need to make some extremely important decisions regarding my own participation. Well to be more accurate, a part of my DNA sequence may have a role to play.

For the first time in what seems an age, I felt content, I knew there were still tons of unanswered questions, but I felt more confident in my ability to finally figure things out. I also began to appreciate my role going forwards, although I still need to balance this against what will be right for my family and friends. It was time to end this CDT event, I thanked each of them by name and I said to Youglav, "I appreciate what you have given me". He simply nodded, turned, and began to walk away. Olin caught me off guard slightly as he asked me, "You will give our request some serious thought". As I was about to reply the lights dimmed to a complete blackness. My worldly consciousness began to restart, there was a warmth that spread over my exposed skin. Within seconds the blackness faded, and I had to scrunch my eyes to protect them from the direct sunlight. I lay motionless for seconds, but as my thoughts began to clarify, they soon became long minutes. It is painfully slow, I want to know all the answers now, I am starting to understand their inability to furnish every answer, along with every solution until such times as they will no longer impede my decision making. This understanding could only come with time, and experience of communicating with them. Eventually, I opened my eyes and the stark reality of my other life kicked in.

"Wise men speak because they have something to say; fools because they have to say something."

Plato

The Code

D	S	≠	P	b	g	f	H	<	G	4	C	/	T	N	w	d	β	E	5	O	©	b	b	;	L
o	h	1	3	A	=	u	m	#	K	Ω	p	d	≠	e	z	÷	A	h	>	O	f	¥	R	&	±
a	V	e	7	j	V	£	L	∝	M	E	Q	q	]	Y	a	m	c	u	|	4	=	i	4	2	q
;	E	y	*	∞	X	t	v	?	P	D	U	€	s	1	>	~	x	"	|	7	X	D	$	8	7
{	i	±	"	F	}	B	d	2	p	A	÷	Σ	∝	G	U	≤	}	+	9	€	≥	!	M	g	?
c	T	F	<	≤	Y	3	+	β	9	π	3	4	w	;	$	5	X	f	M	3	V	5	B	'	G
C	€	5	f	?	G	8	d	k	F	5	u	P	H	#	∝	C	o	%	x	E	7	M	d	O	*
8	J	A	x	O	Q	4	/	2	R	I	∵	m	G	L	[	6	$	∴	/	T	3	J	$	π	{
Y	*	&	≥	r	∴	%	|	±	3	b	E	=	>	e	(	8	W	:	)	8	v	±	v	A	%
#	=	π	h	7	9	z	q	@	U	k	i	S	*	H	A	b	y	s	∠	F	[	r	@	h	0
>	d	'	p	*	z	÷	6	∠	∞	c	@	g	F	9	r	H	2	2	d	9	#	6	K	2	£
s	s	|	D	g	7	8	8	¥	N	s	=	!	]	≠	B	z	∞	8	7	-	T	U	[	Ω	u
[	q	!	"	9	V	E	A	©	8	#	C	a	v	%	t	3	o	r	±	R	/	*	√	≥	#
$	≥	>	/	R	u	0	/	|	>	d	[	>	L	b	O	b	=	h	^	F	Z	R	M	t	u
c	u	@	Z	Z	£	M	9	~	y	0	∴	Q	7	S	π	∵	3	;	u	A	"	E	H	F	6
4	J	Ω	∝	N	%	n	:	x	3	e	$	{	1	2	K	#	P	n	∝	3	p	#	}	W	]
3	N	£	8	Q	*	π	D	W	≥	9	T	f	f	β	9	%	T	G	P	]	O	v	t	≤	d
u	o	≥	*	d	|	S	D	u	m	*	∞	w	5	&	<	V	j	3	≠	S	B	|	<	o	q
]	L	b	9	∝	E	3	o	V	6	2	A	[	g	!	Q	7	z	=	!	©	~	C	?	4	$
p	β	€	;	p	@	F	%	t	/	1	h	#	J	r	Q	V	x	M	M	<	j	K	€	6	∵
Y	+	4	5	a	<	i	H	x	E	÷	N	±	h	7	s	π	e	(	D	:	a	±	k	y	∵
Z	∠	v	"	A	w	O	≠	≠	a	*	R	V	C	8	Z	W	i	≤	{	£	m	=	)	)	%
c	L	#	g	g	q	G	G	G	J	P	∴	S	U	Y	b	0	i	P	"	m	F	/	T	h	h
8	o	∵	Q	Σ	£	=	X	∞	>	f	;	B	9	H	j	≥	i	P	K	≥	O	"	v	p	X
P	6	K	*	D	%	]	d	0	a	N	!	>	>	?	=	E	x	s	R	±	8	7	V	O	∠
≥	2	(	]	h	M	1	≤	#	[	7	j	?	?	L	o	N	C	s	/	π	H	H	7	2	E

26 lines by 26 columns and without a clue the answer will become obvious to those who can figure it out.

Chapter 19
In The Crowd

It's a very strange thing, I don't remember much of Monday evening or night. I must have been on complete autopilot and simply going through the motions of everyday life. Making a drink, setting the table, picking Jane up from work, meaningless and idle chatter that contributed to the background noise which surrounded us. Eating, drinking, saying yes to questions I didn't hear, watching the news and not eating your tea. All are the mindless routine of routines, these meant less to me now than ever before. This is not a sad or worrying reflection on those around me, more it's a symptom of a troubled mind. My brain can now decipher incredibly complex problems, understand, and resolve solutions faster than anyone alive, yet all I can do now is try and work out what I am supposed to do next.

The only way I can see through the multitude of unanswered questions is to create a list of knowns and unknowns. I can hear the shrieks, not the Donald Rumsfeld quote again, "…there are known knowns" etc. Well, no not quite, but it's a starting point to enable me to rationalise and streamline my thoughts. Here we go folks, another glimpse into my distressed and diseased mind.

It's all about allowing my DNA sequence to be used, I could simply say that I don't care one way or the other. If I do nothing to prematurely curtail my life, it will occur naturally in, well who knows, but it will not exceed, let's say 30 years. What I am contemplating here will not happen for another 2,000 years. If, and it's a very big 'IF', they do happen to use it and the fears of Helena and Lise are correct, well as I have now learnt, that's only one possible outcome of the future. But what if my DNA is a vital piece of the extraordinary jigsaw, then I will be distorting a future that possibly sees humanity's survival far beyond anything we can really comprehend. What I need to do is understand the concerns they have and make a judgement call based on that information.

Moving on to my future role. Thankfully, I have now been told more about the 36 visionaries. If I were to allow my thoughts to run unhindered, they would unearth more questions, more scenarios, some related and some unhelpful. We know that each one, or should I say, each correct one will be able to decipher the code I was given yesterday. It was nice to hear that I also hold the world record for seeing the answer, although, I don't fancy trying to explain that to The Guinness Book of Records. Here again, I have a momentous decision of what to do next. Whatever my actions are, they will inevitably have a direct impact on Jane, Toni, and the rest of my friends and family. If I choose to do nothing, and simply continue with my mundane life, the only consequence will be that I take all this knowledge to the incinerator once I die. The future for the 36 visionaries, the Change Movement and everything I have witnessed will possibly or probably happen via an alternative route. We continually return to the thorny issue of free choice, and it's not just mine, it's the other 35 who have the same choice to make. If I were to locate 34, will the future change. Of course, I know it will, although, we, and that's the collective 'we' would never know how different it would be.

A further question must be aimed at my future ability. In fear of sounding like a record stuck in the groove, I have serious concerns regarding my ability to carry out and continue with anything they think I should do. My recurring question from the outset has been simply, why me. To date, they have not been able to reassure me or provide confidence that they have selected the correct person. It scares me to think how many people will rely on me, it's bad enough that I am currently unable to provide sufficiently for Jane, and to be there should Toni need me.

The next bombshell of a topic revolves around the identity of the author. Through the files that were brutally downloaded into my brain, I am beginning to understand the theory. I was told they didn't know the identity of the author, to be honest I find this highly unusual or even unlikely. This insanely wild theory changed the future of humanity and reset a course for its collective output. Without the 62.87 Theory their future almost becomes redundant. Locked within my brain are the files that will free humanity and provide the truth. Considering all these elements, it only adds weight to the argument that I should set aside my own wishes and proceed with, well whatever the future holds for me. I am constantly reminded of the ripple effect and everything Olin and the boys gave to me. Within an instant, I was able to appreciate the benefits of correct and simplified language, along with accepting responsibility for the outcome of my actions. Understanding the true meaning of understanding will also help me in the future. I know that may sound obscure, although when you accept the order that is required it makes clear sense. This simple yet brilliant definition of understanding should be etched into the minds of children from a very early age. **Information is worthless until it becomes knowledge, but this too is worthless beyond its owner until it is finally developed into understanding. Once we understand something we are able to impart that to others.**

Now I must also discover who is the author of 62.87.1, this just gets deeper. Recently, I was formally told in a really confusing way that the original theory was expanded at some point. Let me clarify the confusing element, Helena and Lise seemed to inadvertently let slip that a further revision was also required. In the most recent CDT event, I was provided with more information and acceptance of my initial understanding of it. Ultimately, these are intrinsically linked, the expansion of the original theory should really be allowed to stand in isolation. The original theory deals with the initial birth and subsequent development of humanity's consciousness and being. The creation of the human form as we recognise it today requires humanity's science to be deployed far in the future. It's a ridiculous notion, and one that will undoubtedly meet stern resistance. When placed in context with our development, and the birth of the digital age it begins to become more recognizable.

I recall now that Youglav provided more information about the complexity of the human brain. There are about 85 billion neurons in a typical adult human brain, and around 100,000,000,000,000 assemblies or synapses between all those neurons. Currently, the human brain can process 11 million bits of information every second, which is indeed an enormous sum, but our conscious minds can handle only 40 to 50 bits of information per second. The super species they are developing will handle 100 times this, and they expect future enhancements to be in the millions. It's this expansion of intelligence that will see the survival of humanity for millions if not billions of years to come. It's that concept that really blows my mind, and to think that I may play a small, but significant part in this journey, and that adds further clarity to my decision. The question remains though, I don't know if the same author penned this or not.

Mounting Evidence

I had to process all of this along with more scenarios, more outcomes, all of which I am unable to articulate at this time. It was 08:15 and Jane was beginning to wake and move more around the bed. It was time for me to temporarily take my gaze away from the reliable imperfection on my ceiling and park my thought processing. I knew the normal Tuesday routine will begin once more with us both having a shower, no not together. Although today, I would need to find a very quick explanation. Jane noticed that I had developed a series of unusual marks over my skin. These looked similar to shingles which I had one year before I was diagnosed with Multiple Sclerosis. They resembled shingles in that they seemed to follow tracks of nerves or veins. They were tender but not painful, as soon as I touched them, I realised what they were. During the entrance into a CDT event, I feel random electrical activity that pulses uncontrollably over my skin. This was the first time any noticeable marks had been left.

Quickly, I told Jane they were probably nothing to worry about, and that I would make an appointment with my GP. I had 15 minutes remaining to phone the doctors surgery in an attempt to get an appointment today. After seven attempts and hitting the engaged tone each time, I finally got through. To our amazement, I was offered an appointment at 14:00, this meant my afternoon would be governed by this. Jane offered to come with me, and despite futile attempts to play down the potential implications, she insisted and eventually won this battle of wills.

Fortunately, I managed to get some quiet time in my office to make notes and create a very quick intro vlog. The latest CDT event had my mind rushing everywhere, maybe a day off, a day without taxing my brain would help. We headed into our local village early, it was a beautifully sunny day, not too hot and fortunately low humidity. Humidity coupled with heat is a real aggravator for some of my worst MS symptoms. It's unknown why, but it causes horrible 'brain fog', which has a knock-on effect that causes slowness of speech. We sat in one of our favourite café/bistros and had a lovely lunch. We chatted in a relaxed setting about loads of things, inevitably the subject returned to Toni and what the future holds for her. I really wanted to tell Jane all about what had been happening. I was mildly apprehensive about the upcoming doctor's appointment; I would have to play down the seriousness of these newly developed marks. Jane managed to win the battle and came in with me. The doctor wanted to know if anything could have caused these, confidently, he said they weren't shingles and gave me a course of antihistamines. Before finishing he wanted to check my blood pressure, this is when it all came crashing down. "It's extremely high", he said but in a subdued tone as if to lighten the worry. Jane then jumped in to say, "He has been very stressed recently, he's always on edge and looks very tired". Well, that was the killer blow, more medication to bring down the blood pressure and another to help with anxiety. As if I didn't have enough to worry about, now pile more on

We returned home via a trip to the chemist, Jane went into nurse mode and even plumped up my cushions in my favourite chair. I was ordered to rest, given the TV remote, instead I opted for my headphones and a choice of music. Sleep soon followed, completely undisturbed, I must have been there for around 3 hours. Before Tuesday morphed into Wednesday, I had the first semi-final to look forward to. France vs Belgium was set to be a mouth-watering game. Jane pretty much left me alone for the day, although I was ordered to leave my laptop alone. Honestly, I think I get withdrawal symptoms if I don't see a spreadsheet on a daily basis.

To the football, it was played in Saint Petersburg in glorious sunshine. Belgium had the best of the first 30 minutes with some outstanding performances from their star players. Then a header from a corner saw Umtiti and France take the lead. Despite a valiant effort, my preference for the tournament saw Belgium out with France looking forward to a final. Throughout the game I could see Jane looking sideways towards me making sure I wasn't getting too excited. Of course, my stress levels were high along with my heart rate and associated blood pressure, although it had nothing to do with the game. I tried to tell myself to relax, but it's like telling yourself not to worry about something. This light debate took me back to Olin and the use of language, taking responsibility etc. I know it's useless to worry about the things that I cannot influence, but here there are a magnitude of things that hinge on my decision; therefore, I am probably justified.

I woke with a rare excitement on Wednesday, I had the England game later, although my thoughts were also anticipating another CDT event today. Fortunately, the reddish marks on my skin that were left by the electrical activity had lightened which satisfied Jane, and she thought the tablets were working. Once again, I was under strict instructions to 'take it easy', I defied the 'no laptop rule' under the guise I was waiting for some semi-important emails. Truthfully, I didn't want another CDT event today, the notes and vlogs I needed to make should take priority, plus I had a needle like feeling in the back of my mind that I was missing something. I knew that time, along with the freedom to process my thoughts would find the problem and identify a solution. Jane wanted to stay at home to babysit me, it took a lot of time and effort to convince her that I would be fine. Eventually, she did meet up with Georgina for a catch up which really meant shopping, lunch and a couple of drinks.

I used my time effectively and efficiently; Jane had prepared a sandwich for me which meant I could work without interruption through lunch. The time passed quickly but I managed to produce a very detailed vlog with an enormous number of supporting notes, and of course the all-important code. Either my memory or files that I could access allowed me to create this perfectly. In good time, I completed this and made my way to the living room where I sat in eager anticipation of the next event. While waiting, I allowed my thoughts to assemble, the missing piece, which I felt important seemed insignificant, but it kept on bugging me. It was when they said, 'and', which indicated there was more. I managed to unlock the next part, it's amazing to think that one day, they may possibly create the intelligence to outlive the end of this, outlive our universe. It's crazy, wild, and completely bonkers, however, I now understand that you must consider everything, and in the whole. We struggle to think and plan beyond 50 to 60 years, our generation has given birth to an incredible creation. The digital age will know no boundaries, and when you couple this with the capability that humanity holds, who really knows where it will eventually end. Don't think in terms of 100 years, 1,000 or even a million, if, and it's a big 'if' humanity survives, what will we be capable of in a billion years from now.

I also allowed my thoughts to return to the ripple effect, but this time I attempted to link it to this self-perpetuating cycle of renewal and improvement. I was told that we are currently living out the first generation, future cycles will develop improvements within intelligence and the methods/means to transport and deliver its precious cargo. Just as I witnessed 2,034 years from now, where they are trying to create the birth of intelligence and consciousness which will be transported and implanted into our early species. Future generations will create their own improvements, and by doing this, it will allow the cycle to begin. Where this ends no one could even begin to speculate. I can see how this will operate, however, it can and probably will damage my brain forever if I allow myself to delve into it any further. As the time passed, so did the opportunity for a CDT event today. My mind then began to wonder if there was a reason, although this was short-lived when Jane returned home earlier than expected, she filled the air with chatter and added clutter in the form of shopping bags.

The Charm Offensive

Jane knew that my focus would turn to the football, our evening meal consisted of varied hot and cold nibble food. This meant I could graze whilst watching the build up to the game, uninterrupted by cutlery, I was permitted to vent my frustrations on our performances in previous tournaments. As for the game, we met Croatia in our semi-final which was held in Moscow. Around 10,000 England fans had made the journey, the news was scattered with worries about the potential for crowd trouble, thankfully, that wasn't to be. England took an early lead with a superbly placed free kick by Kieran Trippier, sadly that was to be the highlight of our efforts.

We made few chances after that, and eventually an equaliser came. Regretfully, our own Jordan Pickford was guilty of a few unprovoked goalkeeping errors. Hopes were then raised as a bullet-style header from John Stones was cleared off the line. That moment seemed to signal the end of our hopes as he went from potential hero to zero as his defensive error allowed the winner to be slotted home. The few England flags that remain flapping in the sunshine could now be taken down, once more we came close, but our ever-increasing years of pain would have to continue. Croatia would meet France in the 2018 world cup final on 15 July, the day before that, England would meet Belgium in the third-place playoff. Once more England fans would be left with nothing, a few memories of what might have been. Another replica shirt would be neatly folded and placed on the ever-growing pile of 'not quite good enough' reminders. I once debated that phrase with Dave, we both agreed that's the worst put-down ever. Not that your opponent was better, but simply 'we weren't good enough'. I think it's safe to leave our hopes at the door and enjoy the spectacle for what it is.

I didn't allow my thoughts to resurface during the remainder of Wednesday night. The sound of Jane getting ready the following morning proved that I had slept well and that I was ready for what the day would bring. My usual routine played out as predicted, although a slight detour was injected with a trip to my local Café for an early morning caffeine hit. I pottered around in the morning, roughly translated this meant doing a few chores that I had been avoiding, once done I did feel better and with less clutter, I felt more comfortable. Nervously, lunch time approached, and my excitement built with the anticipation of the next CDT event. My selection of music varied from my normal random trust in Doris and whatever algorithm Amazon used to entertain me. This time I selected a carefully put together playlist I called simply New Wave. It consisted of classic tracks from Ian Dury, The Clash, Blondie, Dr

Feelgood, Elvis Costello, Squeeze, The Undertones, The Police, Boomtown Rats, and Joe Jackson. Of course, The Jam were included with several masterpieces, also on the list was Madness, The Specials, and The Beat for the odd Two Tone anthem.

As the music played and the warmth of the sun relaxed my body, I soon fell asleep. I had no concept of time, but it felt as though the darkness was soon interrupted. Slowly, I could feel my entire body weight becoming as light as a feather. My body didn't move, rather it was everything else simply vanished and I was held in a state of complete helplessness. Like before, in fact like every other event, I could feel every cell being surrounded by the absence of its neighbouring cell. I suppose you could say that each one was held isolated, although they were still connected. Then, pulses of teenage blue coloured ribbons of charged energy made their way randomly over my skin. Helena could be heard repeating my name several times. Eventually, the pain subsided, and I was able to regain a level of sight.

As Helena's voice grew louder, the repeated message stopped, and I was able to blink sufficiently to focus on her and Jacron who were sitting in front of me. Jacron asked if I was alright, I told them I had rested well and had time to consider the most recent information. Jacron wasted no time as she methodically delivered a shock-wave statement, "This will be our penultimate CDT event with you". "OK" was the only reply I could come up with. I wasn't prepared for this, I knew this day would arrive, but I had put no planning into what I wanted to know before the window of opportunity had gone. Again, without wasting any further time and in a play to deflect any questions she said, "This wouldn't have been expected and we will endeavour to answer all of your key questions next time". She continued in a pre-rehearsed way, "We will require your answer and approval to use a sequence of your DNA". Presumably, this is why I have been given Helena and Jacron, I value their company and respect their openness and genuine willingness to help.

I have no real idea where this outburst originated or the timing of it, I demanded they get Olin and Youglav as soon as possible. The exact words I used were, 'Get them here now, please!' It seemed to work as I could see Jacron touch her transparent screen on two occasions, this was followed by her placing her right index finger to her ear. Moments later she said, "They will be here in seven minutes". The stark look of concern on Jacron and Helena concerned me, I told them not to worry, my eagerness was not related to a problem. As soon as I announced this, they both instantly looked relaxed. I had almost forgotten that lies are an unknown entity to them, with me saying this, it was greeted almost as an instruction not to be questioned. The next few minutes seemed to take forever, I didn't want to engage in small talk, and they seemed happy to focus on their display screens the entire time.

A door at the back of the room silently slid open and the two gentlemen entered and calmly walked towards Jacron and Helena. Rather than sitting, Olin asked, "How can we help you Danny, is there something concerning you?" I apologised for disturbing them, explaining that I understood time was now against us and what I had to say was important. Again, I don't really know why I asked this or initially for what benefit. "Can I have use of your display screen?", I asked. As soon as I did it appeared to my left-hand side. With a deep breath and a focused look, I began, "When we discussed the additional section of the theory that explained the reason for the development of a super species, you said one simple word which urged me to continue theorising further. That word, and that word alone opened a door for me". I looked down for a moment and braced myself for what came next. "That word was _and_", I said softly. Olin and Youglav began to smile, as I continued, "What I discovered and understood was the end goal, where intelligence and technology could one day take us. We know that eventually our sun will die and that one day, billions of years from now our universe will also die." I looked straight at Olin for some sort of acknowledgement. As I explained this, the display screen visualised my thoughts in graphic detail.

I was now ready for the finale, "If you expand the theory to its end point, and somehow a form of humanity should survive such a climax where the universe implodes on itself. The rebirth of life will have to begin from scratch." I knew I was on the right lines as my two captees moved closer towards me and their smiles grew wider. I looked behind them, Jacron and Helena were not with me in this brainstorming party, they looked bemused and turned to each other for support. That's it, I was ready, "This theory can also be reversed", as I began, the display screen cleared, it was also ready for what came next. "and it may have already been reversed. Let's take the initial theory first, it states that the human form and its intelligence and consciousness could not have evolved without an external force. You are now seeking to create the brain cells that will evolve and accept the knowledge required to one day create the digital age and everything that evolves from there." The display screen remained with me and illustrated this perfectly. I continued, "now, continue that reversal trajectory further back into our history and evolutionary path. I then allowed the display screen to demonstrate this in high speed, following our roots to find our earliest recognisable ancestors. "We need to go further back to find our source", I demanded.

The display screen went into overdrive, the imagery sped up until it became a blur, we could see the effects of the ice age and movement of the tectonic plates. Eventually, our camera view submerged into the oceans and began to slow its pace. Unrecognisable to us, we were then able to see the earliest forms of marine life. But we weren't there yet, we needed to go further back.

This view remained static and almost black; the stillness was a respite for our eyes. Our image whilst relatively still, gave us the undoubtable impression that we were dropping deeper and deeper. In the distance we could see faint beams of light which moved in a rhythmic motion. As we grew closer the image sharpened, a human like figure could be seen with an instrument that pierced holes into the sea bedrock. Black gasses and plumes of smoke were emitted from each puncture hole. Each human-like figure, and there was around five of them, were injecting these gasses with something from a canaster. I concluded my explanation with, "The beginnings of any lifeforms on our planet could not have materialized without external measures". My focus was drawn towards Jacron and Helena, with mouths open in astonishment, they were the polar opposite of Olin and Youglav who could hardly contain their joy.

Youglav turned to Olin and said, "May I". He then turned to me and said they can only applaud me for my explanation, and expansion of the theory to its end conclusion. Apparently, this continuation of the theory is not widely known or accepted. I enjoyed the open discussion that ensued once this window of opportunity had presented itself. They have given this hypothesis a working name; Intellectual Based Evolutionary Recurrence Hypothesis or IBERH. It essentially states that the end of time revolves into the beginning of time, and the evolution of everything can only happen through selective intelligence. They were beside themselves with joyfulness, they were incredibly enthusiastic that someone of little intelligence, yes me, could have developed this conclusion. By this time Jacron was smiling too, although she had not developed this conclusion herself, she was delighted that I had. On the other hand, Helena looked unimpressed and unmoved by the excitement that now filled the room. Olin took a couple of steps towards me and with a twinkle in his eye, which may have been a tear, he said, "We hoped you would figure this out, now you will have the confidence to go forward."

I was rightly proud of my achievement, I felt a rush of enthusiasm pump through my body, my heart pounded and with every beat the sensation grew. Confidently, I stated, "I think my role in all of this will become clearer to me now, so far, much of this has washed over me, but now I can begin to see a way forward." Pouncing on the opportunity to leverage more information and to complete some of the other gaps I had, "I have continually questioned how events would play out when we factor in the ripple effect, and free choice. I have absorbed all the information presented to me; while forming my own opinions, I have converted this into knowledge and understanding. Nevertheless, all of this will have been futile should I choose to continue my simple life, unhindered and unobstructed by the choices you expect me to make", I told them. Explaining to them my understanding of the ripple effect and that it cannot be reversed. Hence, the wheels they put in motion, ever since our first CDT event have led to this intersection. I doubt if there is anything more they can do to further inspire me, or add for me to accept the baton, and to complete the final leg to a potential victory. I gave them the opportunity to contribute anything, Olin told me there was nothing more they can add, although they will gladly answer any questions I have.

Revolving Improvements

I returned to the topic of understanding who the author is, and my role to articulate this to others, if indeed that is what is to be expected. I reiterated what I knew, what they had told me from the outset. The author of the 62.87 Theory was never named, the digits referred to the release number. I told them I found all of this to be misleading, with the birth of the digital age, almost every piece of data has been recorded. Elements of my own life will be recorded and available for the rest of time. I am not unique regarding this, medical records, employment records, the taxes I have paid, the purchases made, and probably every email and message ever sent or received. Cookies will undoubtedly track my searches, likes and preferences, in fact my digital footprint will tell you more about me than I could ever remember. To state that a future scientist could publish something of this magnitude without there being a record is incredulous to say the least. Additionally, the future of humanity is now focused on delivering the fruits of this idea. Furthermore, there is an additional piece which sets out a survival path for a future species whose origins began with us 'simple' humans. This super species will endeavour to transition somehow to the next reincarnation of the universe. As I have said before, hold on there's more. From somewhere I have been able to articulate a method by which life was given to our planet, it goes by the catchy name, Intellectual based Evolutionary Recurrence Hypothesis.

What I can't yet figure out, is how the information safely locked away within digital files that are stored somewhere in my brain, can be passed into the future for release by someone without an identity. I knew I would be wasting my time asking the question, and true enough it was. I positioned it as best I could, unsurprisingly, Olin replied, "You will figure it out." As the saying goes, 'If you're confused... welcome to my world'. I learnt recently that the 36 visionaries will be identified by their ability to recognise a code within a random series of characters, digits, and symbols, some being mathematical. I am obviously one of them, and currently, I hold the world record for the fastest time to unscramble this.

One day, I will learn what my role is, although doubts remain, in fact far too many doubts. Speaking of which, these 36 will go on to develop a group that finally brings humanity together with a common goal. A manifesto will be drafted that will show how 'change' must happen and the direction for a better way. Everything I have seen, heard, and recently understood hinges off a simple mantra they have, BTBT Built Today for a Better Tomorrow. Each generation knows and accepts they will never see the end result, unselfishly they give everything they have towards this common goal. All of this was discussed and confirmed with my hosts, for the first time I felt on parr with them and treated as an equal.

We all have a fleeting existence, in reality we are a speck of dust in the form of gathered cells that live and breathe for less than a femtosecond in the scheme of universal time. Just as the ripple effect can't be reversed, our input into the events of time is all critical and proves that every life matters. Whatever I choose to do, whatever your responses are, each one alters the future for us all. We are all linked, by ancestry along with time both past, present along with our future influence on time. During our discussions between equals, I positioned a question regarding getting it right and learning from the past.

I discovered that we are all part of the first phase of life, we, along with my hosts from the future are the same. Get this, somewhere in the future, V0.1 of humanity will figure out a way to iron out the problems humanity has faced or more importantly caused. This potentially means, no wars, no religion etc. In fact, the long list of troubles that were mentioned earlier in the book will be no more.

Please allow me one last indulgence related to this section. Our actions now will all relate to what happens in the future. This all denotes that there is one true reality, the global currency is time, or to be more specific 'your time'. No matter how long we live, every action we take has the potential of starting a ripple effect that can change the future. Every second of your life is a measurement of your increasing demise. It's a currency that you hold, and you choose how to spend. Every advertisement video we watch during the games played on mobile phones are a transactional cost. These are our bank accounts of time, and unfortunately there are no credit cards, finance agreements or overdrafts. One thing is for sure, you cannot be overdrawn. Our time on this planet is not infinite, it's fleeting and over far too soon.

"Talent hits a target no one else can hit. Genius hits a target no one else can see."

Arthur Schopenhauer

My Final Goodbye To Helena

As I eventually wrapped up my fascinating conversation with Olin and Youglav, I thanked them for everything I had learnt. They were equally pleased and concluded with a sentiment I had heard before, 'We hoped you would figure these things, and we have not been disappointed'. The pair of them had genuine smiles throughout, and the sense of excitement was visible in their body language and gestures. Jacron must have felt side-lined by my observations and conclusions, although she didn't show it, she remained quiet for the most part. Anyway, she now took the reins back and asked a direct question, "Have you made a decision yet regarding the use of your DNA sequence?" As I prepared my answer, Helena's arm moved to touch her device that had previously been used to transmit information and files to me. Instantly, I received a message in my lower peripheral vision that said, 'Please do not react'. I tried not to alter my poise or stumble over my reply. Without a further warning, another message came through, 'Please do not announce your decision, read this file first'. This was obviously unusual and unexpected, but I trusted Helena more than any other. Without hesitation I complied, telling Jacron that I had given it a lot of thought, but I have learnt a considerable amount recently, which means I must give careful consideration to every possible outcome. As I spoke, my peripheral vision saw a white circle appear which I presumed was the file.

Olin shifted his position to take a more central stance and eye contact with me. He looked more serious, although still relaxed as he said, "Danny, our time with you must sadly come to an end, we cannot thank you enough for your trust, honesty and most of all for your time". I could only nod in acceptance and allow him to continue, "our next event will be our last. We will be happy to answer any more questions you have; you appreciate that time is not unlimited." I must have changed my facial expression as he quickly added, "Don't worry Danny". His 'prepared' speech continued, "We will then require your decision which we hope will give us approval to replicate a sequence of your DNA."

My focus on Olin didn't change or move, he then delivered his final blow, "I hope you will join us in thanking Helena for her diligence to locate you and her attentiveness during the entire process." I took his pause as an opportunity to pay my own compliments. I looked over towards her, and past Olin's figure, she looked radiant and with a beauty that was more than just in her flawless complexion and perfect cheekbones. She had delicately formed lips, and of course those eyes that would leave anyone speechless. For a moment I couldn't think of exactly what I wanted to say, how I felt, and now with the unknown message, I had to say goodbye. "Olin, you're correct, Helena has been a great help to me, and I understand none of this would have happened without her, I owe her a debt of gratitude." I wasn't sure whether this next subtle message carried the same significance, I winked, smiled and whispered, "Thank you."

I could have taken the opportunity to thank Olin, Jacron and all the others I met along the way, but I thought this would wait. By this time, I was getting tired, I also had the note to read, and my mind was beginning to consider what it could possibly contain. Olin snapped me out of my thoughts as he majestically said, "Helena will not be able to attend the next event, we would like to say thank you from us all". I now understand why she took that opportunity to halt my response, I also know she will not be available for me to question the contents. I wondered for a second if Olin or the others were aware of this, or the covert mission her and Lise had with me. Olin finished by asking me to consider their request, he also said that other answers may come to me once I consider them fully. I took it he was referring to my roles going forward and in relation to the 62.87 Theory and the identity of the author. Thanking them all for their time, I could only say that I looked forward to the next event with mixed emotions. Sad that it will be the final event, but hopefully I will be able to obtain answers for many of the outstanding puzzles I now possess.

As I looked outward, I wanted some time to absorb the image in as much detail as possible. It was plain and sterile, brilliant whilst shockingly simple. Uncluttered and symmetrical, balanced in perfectly defined sections. My hosts were immaculately presented, clean and crisp clothing that always looked new. Hairstyles were neat and unchanged, clean-shaven, and polished which also included Jacron. The lights dimmed to a chilling black, there were no light residues or imprinted images, just complete blackness that was accompanied by a matching silence. My senses began to restart with my hearing which was triggered by the background hum of faint traffic noise, birds, and a couple walking past the house, they weren't talking, rather the sound I heard was of their footsteps and their breathing. Light, and the warmth from the sun on my bare arms were the next to kick in. I wanted to savour my feelings and the emotion of leaving behind a world that amplified perfection, peace, happiness, and contentment. When I opened my eyes, I knew that my own reality would trigger unhelpful thoughts.

Minutes passed before I gathered my strength and courage to view my living room and all that it represented. I instantly smiled as I saw a picture of Toni, it was taken when she was around 12 whilst on holiday in Florida. Our little girl was immensely happy, and seeing the picture reminded me of everything I have here. It's impossible to predict the future for anyone, but with Toni I feel as confident as any of us can be that she will have a very happy and fruitful life. If that's with Nigel then he will be a very lucky man, and I have a feeling he will only add to her enjoyment of life. I will have to give very careful consideration regarding my own 'next steps'. Anything I do will undoubtedly impact her more than anyone else, I will have to figure out a way to protect her innocence at all costs.

My attention was then drawn to the file that Helena had sent me. It's the first telepathic email I have received. Its contents will have a direct bearing on the path I take, thus due consideration must be given to it. I have no option but to open it, taking sufficient time to digest it will be key for my final decision, and all before the next and final CDT event. I decided to access it later that evening, collecting Jane as normal and going through the motions of our normal life would provide the time. The advantage I have is that it's Thursday, this should mean the next event will not happen until Sunday or more likely Monday. I concocted a plan to keep myself busy this weekend and remain active and awake each afternoon. This will give me further time to evaluate the contents of the file and make all the decisions needed.

Chapter 20
The Final

After I awoke from the event, my life seemed to continue in a form of slow motion. I absorbed every aspect that happened, whilst at the same time reliving every microscopic detail of the conversations I had with my hosts. Throughout all this my brain went into maximum output as I considered everything I had learnt. With the knowledge that the next CDT event was going to be my last, I had to ensure I obtained answers to everything. When I say, 'answers to everything', I guess what I really mean is acknowledgment that my understanding of the key issues is accurate. I cannot ask a question that requires a simple yes or no, the answer will invariably be that I should, 'work it out'. Additionally, I must appreciate free choice, and factor this into every consideration so that I can reach a decision that I am happy with. Even free choice has greater importance now. Considering the ripple effect, and how this can impact the lives and futures of those around me is something I may not have previously evaluated correctly. I must also consider my own abilities and what I believe can be achieved.

It's true and fair to say that I have learnt a phenomenal amount in the past few weeks. I have had to examine my own life and, in more detail than I ever thought possible. Gaining new skills and new abilities that set me apart, has either been a triumph or a burden. I must now learn how to use them in a way to improve the journey for humanity. The view of the future I witnessed can only be described as amazing and complete perfection. I have been given the information, the footsteps, and the journey humanity must take, however painful that may be. Although, it remains for me to convert that information into knowledge and then crucially into understanding. Once in this state, I will be able to enthuse others, this will enable them to create their own understanding. Crucially, anyone who wishes to develop and replicate the footsteps for a better future will need to go through this important process. I feel one of the critical mindset changes is to accept the key mantra they use, BTBT Build Today for a Better Tomorrow. Our current drivers are 'need and greed'. Altruism seems to be within the DNA of our descendants which, let's face it is a distant cry from our here and now. They truly embrace the fact that they will never see the fruits of their labour.

I also carry the key to humanity's future in the form of files locked away somewhere in my brain. The 62.87 Theory will forever change our view of creation, both of humanity and potentially the universe and all life within it. Every time I think of this, my uneducated rational self needs to argue against the concept. Yet, 2,034 years from now, this theory drives everything they do. I am beginning to understand how to effectively consider the origins and identity of the author. Although, my mind is currently preoccupied with my role in extracting the files and enabling their safe transportation into the future. I am slowly allowing my mind to also theorise about my role alongside the other 35 visionaries. It will be these enlightened mavericks that will create a charter for change. They will also gather humanity into a single entity without prejudice of any sort. Finally, humanity will come together under the banner of BTBT and seek to establish the first colony. No more fighting, no more greed, no more division, working for a common goal. Free energy and a trust in science and technology will prove that these early steps will pay dividends for all. Remember, the ones who will retaliate against this change are the ones who have most to lose. It will be the people who gain in ways we never thought imaginable.

Telepathic Email

Eventually, whilst in an ocean of uncontrollable thoughts, I found a moment of complete peace and tranquillity. I sat comfortably in the warm sunlight, a coffee by my side, which accompanied zero distractions. It was time to access and read the letter from Helena, although before opening it, I considered what she risked in sending this to me. Her actions though possibly justified and well-intended went against many of the attributes they hold dear. They have no concept or understanding of things like lies and dishonesty. How she advocated this through her own principles must have been an incredible challenge. Anyway, I have it now and I told myself that I should read it with an open mind, and without thoughts of how it had been delivered. I refocused my mind on the white circle, without much effort I was able to expand it to a normal sized document. As I did this, I couldn't help but think of what had been achieved, I was the first recipient of a telepathic document. Here it is, a word for word copy of what she sent to me.

Hello Danny,

I have valued our brief time together; you have provided us with an abundance of information and data which will add enormously to our research. Olin expressed our gratitude, and I can only add my personal thanks for how open and honest you have been. I spent 780 hours researching, sampling, and analysing prospective examples for the Try-neural Evaluation programme, with immediate links to the 62.87 Evolution Ethics Mandate P211. Once I found you, our research became enriched beyond our expectations.

There are three matters I need to explain to you, once you have these, I hope you will see how important your decisions are. The first item concerns why I put you forward, this will be unexpected. We share the same blood line, that is to say, I have tracked my ancestry which traces back to you. As a direct descendant you should be excluded from the programme. I wanted the opportunity to talk to you, I knew you possessed 97.32% of the attributes required for the initial programme. It transpired through our analysis that you were an ideal candidate for the V36H2 trial. At this juncture you now understand the role of those selected for the Visionary Scheme.

The next item concerns your participation and sanctioning for elements of your DNA sequence to be used in the Reclassification Programme, the one you called a 'super species'. This information will also be unexpected, and I would have preferred to inform you about this in person. Lise and I analysed your DNA sequence and genetic profile using historic measures. This form of analysis indicates clearly that you carry a deficiency. This error will be known to you as Autism, for you it is characterized in several displays. I hope you can take this information forward and seek to possibly rectify it. If your DNA sequence is sampled, we know that any attributes or defects will be amplified in the future. My life partner is Lise, and we both urge you to consider the potential impact of allowing foundations of your DNA sequencing to be carried forward.

The final matter relates to your future role. You have repeatedly asked for clarification and guidance as to what is expected of you. Each time we have informed you that it is only you that can decide. With all the information you have been given, along with the advice and skills you now have, we believe you will make the correct choices. Believe and trust in your abilities, I know what you are capable of and that is nothing short of greatness.

My thoughts will be forever with you, Helena.

I pictured Helena's face as I read this, I imagined her compressed emotions, and conversely, I visualised her eyes looking deep into mine. After reading this letter three times, and with each readthrough I picked out more impacting statements. The tone of the letter was also typical of their use of language, very precise and regimented. It could be described as monosyllabic in terms of lacking emotion. I sat dumbstruck and unable to move, my thought process halted as I tried to digest the contents of this life-changing letter. Dissecting each crucial part and analysing each one separately would hopefully provide some answers.

Firstly, the news that Helena is actually a descendant of mine. I have potentially come face to face, in a virtual concept, with my great-great-great, multiplied by who knows how many times, granddaughter. The thorny issue of free choice returns to torment me again, I considered for a fleeting moment that she may only exist if my decisions fall favourably in a certain direction. But why did she search for me in the first place, why did her search through the generations end with me. Various questions zipped through my brain; I found one after the other that spurned even more. I would never understand the reasoning behind her choice, but I now have to live with it and decide how to proceed.

I also thought about declaring it in the next and final CDT event. This would potentially alter the outcome, although I am sure it would also result in Helena and Lise being expelled from the colony. One thought remained with me, it has been with me now for weeks, I believe I was purposely selected. Although Helena thought she was searching her genealogy for personal gains, I feel there was more to this selection, and I will attempt to clarify this with Olin and Jacron. Additionally, they had previously told me that I fulfilled certain criteria for my selection, therefore, Helena's personal choice would have been immaterial. She also told me that, 'I possessed 97.32% of the attributes required', which indicated I was a correct fit.

There was no doubt I would return to every section of this letter, but for now I moved on to her next explosion. Regarding the use of my DNA, I think it's fair to say they have pushed me very hard to provide them with a 'yes'. Now Helena tells me, despite the extraordinary intelligence they have, a blip in my sequence has been overlooked. Her and Lise only detected this because they decided to use historical tools to form a diagnosis. This makes sense to a point, genetic illnesses and alike were irradicated thousands of years before, as a result they may not have searched for it. But it doesn't make sense for them not to have declared this finding to their peers. Instead, they have now placed the burden of responsibility squarely on my shoulders.

I must now begin to understand what this diagnosis means to me, whilst reconciling how it will impact on their programme. She kindly worded this as, 'for you it is characterized in several displays'. People have joked in the past about my attention to detail, although I never thought it was anything more, and certainly it didn't warrant a defined name. Considering our daughter Toni, I don't believe she displays any unusual characteristics, and certainly nothing to worry about. There's a dilemma attached to this though, if there is something, should I tell her. Helena is also worried these will be amplified in the future; the process they intend to use will continually increase intelligence. She is concerned this constant enhancement will increase any unwanted elements too.

And finally, we arrived to discuss the jigsaw with the missing piece, or to be more specific my role going forward. There is one word that turned everything for me, 'greatness'. Something has been stirring in me for a while, although I have been too scared to even allow it time to brew into realised thoughts. It's more than just a fast broadband, and me fitting a certain pass criterion, they have opened doors within my brain and given me a set of skills. It is time for me to take control of the next event and obtain the answers along with confirmation that my understanding is correct. To conclude, I have figured it out, however, they may not be expecting the outcomes I am going to provide to them.

The way Helena signed off her letter really touched me, 'My thoughts will be forever with you, Helena'. It's mind-bending to think that my life will continue with the knowledge that someone related to me, will be thinking of me. Now it's not just anyone, this is a bloodline relation who is living out their life some 2,000+ years in the future. Our lives will run simultaneously for the briefest period. Technology allowed this to happen, and it did so, in order that humanity's future will be placed on the right path.

I am only just beginning to understand this perpetuating cycle of influence and improvement. Future technologies permit humanity to meddle in this way, it comes with a great deal of responsibility. They could irrecoverably charter a disastrous course that could result in their demise. Obviously, I now understand the true impact of the ripple effect, and how even the slightest adjustment to someone's life or behaviour can result in monumental changes that can be far reaching. Personally, I don't think they fully considered this, or, if they did, just how they are able to map out the spider's web of conflicts and variables.

It's A Waiting Game

The letter from Helena didn't indicate when the next CDT event would be, although I somehow knew they would allow me sufficient time to gather my thoughts and consider my options. I now understood so much, and in my own mind I knew what actions I would be taking. Any time given to me now would simply allow me to question everything. This probably isn't a good thing for someone with the complex conditions that I have, and apparently display. It was my most recent diagnosis that was due to worry me the most. If I have lived with this condition for 40 odd years, then I don't see how it should change the way I live now, or my future choices. Instead of allowing this to fester, I turned my focus to the 62.87 Theory and the addition of the appendaged section. This would take care of the evening routine, but now with the added pressure of no football. Jane was evidently tired which resulted in her falling asleep after one and a half glasses of wine while watching mind-numbing soaps. It's funny that, in the absence of religion, soap operas are now designed to teach morality to the masses. They are exceptionally unreal, with unbelievable storylines and amateurish acting, yet they hold millions mesmerised for hours during the typical working week. The gap in believability allows screen time to be shared with mobile phones that hold us in a trans-like state. Our brains engaged in mindless nonsense until we return to the daily routine once more. Is it an intended condition the state utilises for its own benefit, keep them occupied and they will challenge less. I'll let you consider this and develop your own answer.

My mind is now calculating variable solutions for humanity's survival beyond the death of our solar system. Furthermore, I am contemplating the demise of the universe as we know it, and eventually our rebirth into a new one. Not satisfied with this, a section of my brain is concurrently dealing with the challenge of creating life on this planet. A super species with an intelligence level far beyond our comprehension is currently being created. I discussed with my virtual peers how this would be achieved and how the foundations were being created. The original theory describes how intelligence within the human form would have to be created by its descendants. Once accepted it became the force behind everything humanity strived for. Science would hold the key to unlock everything, and technology would be the vessel to deliver it. I am on the verge of being a part of this astonishing voyage of discovery.

I awoke on Saturday with Jane already up and buzzing around various bedrooms. "It's 08:30", she announced in a hurried and stern voice. I suspected a meaning behind this attitude, and I wasn't wrong when she followed up with "Toni and Nigel will be here in a few hours". With everything that revolved within my own little world, I had completely ignored, forgot, or simply bypassed an event within this one. Usually, I would be thinking purely about creating my vlog with supporting notes. Alternatively, I would be contemplating the last event which would inevitably mean overthinking the meaning of each portion, analysing each piece of information, and reconsidering every word spoken.

Today was going to be different though, Toni was coming for the day, she will then be travelling onwards tomorrow to see his brother who lived somewhere, I will have been told where, but it had not registered. Fortunately, Jane reiterated the agenda while putting clean sheets on Toni's bed. I was asked to help, but quickly told how useless I was, and then relegated to make some tea. The plan would begin with settling them in after their journey from Scotland. This would be followed by lunch with Georgina and the gang in a very nice little pub on the outskirts of Chester. Hopefully noise would be kept to a minimum as the day was forecast hot with high humidity. Our return journey would take in the delights of a huge cathedral to shopping, also known as an out of town 'outlet village'. Leading brands were all represented, people would delight in purchasing items festooned with their logos. Once they had purchased one billboard garment they would scuttle off in search of the next bargain. My wish came true as the girls left Nigel and I in a busy overpriced coffee shop, they should rename these establishments, 'The Perfect Man Creche'. It gave us time to sound each other out, also known in some circles as 'bonding'. He has got a very good sense of humour, and I can see why Toni has fallen for him. He is genuinely kind and respectful to others, I can see how they share many interests, but also have a healthy interest in things of difference.

When we returned home, I was allowed time to have a sleep, also known as a 'nana-nap', as my family like to call them. After a hectic day of doing nothing but talk, eat, and drink coffee, it gave me some quiet time to consider a massive decision. In the next couple of days, I will participate in the final CDT event. A chapter of my life will end, the door will close forever on the year 2073 PD. As the saying goes, when one door closes, another door opens. In this case, if I choose to open the new door it will drastically change the lives of those around me. The most important people in my life will soon join me as we sit around a dining table. The monumental decision now facing me is whether to tell them. I could open up and drag them into a world they could never anticipate or probably understand. What would happen if they do accept everything I tell them, but then demand that I do nothing with the knowledge and understanding I hold. I would have to abide by their wishes, I would never force anything upon them. The importance of this can never be fully appreciated. While I must respect their decision whatever, I would hope they understand its importance to the future of humanity.

Sleep eventually came, I was gently woken by Toni who sat on the side of the bed and softly rubbed my shoulder. She asked me if I had slept well and told me she was concerned about me. Concerned can mean many things, I read this as meaning my health. I reassured her I was doing well, there were no new symptoms, I felt well in myself, and generally happy. Jane and Toni will often discuss my health, whilst this is understandable, we don't tend to discuss anything as a family anymore. Even on a bad day, I purposely tell people I am doing well. I mainly do this because I am fed up with my own voice reeling off symptoms and someone saying they understand or even worse relating it to their own aches and pains.

Anyway, we had a really nice meal of varied Chinese dishes which meant a lot of sharing and discussion over favourites. We then sat in total comfort, drinking wine or in my case soft drinks, and reliving embarrassing stories of Toni as she was growing up. These were made doubly worse for Toni as various photo albums were then dragged out. Nigel laughed without a care, he sat with his arm around her, and she was confidently hugging him when some of the stories were too much to bear. The highlight for me was when I asked Doris to play, 'The Mayor Of Simpleton' by XTC.

Immediately, Toni and I bust into spontaneous 'dad-dancing' and singing. It was as if we were transported back to her teenage years when this was our song. I used to disturb her studying with my rendition of the lyrics accompanied with a silly dance. For a moment in time, we were oblivious to our surroundings, Jane was petrified, scared rigid that I was going to fall over or worse. Nigel looked on and laughed as Toni was also lost in the lyrics. As the song ended, we told the tale of how this came about, how this was our special song.

With all of the antics, coupled with copious glasses of wine, the opportunity didn't materialise for me to announce anything, but I think that decision was made earlier when Toni woke me. It felt like we were slowly losing Toni, for several years now her life had been moving at a head turning pace. She was facing some important decisions. With each decision, with each move, her life was evolving, and we could only stand on the touchline and watch.

The Awakening

The next morning saw Jane furiously running around the kitchen, making sure there was sufficient toast and cups of tea. Before we knew it, they were packing up the car, Jane, Toni, and I enjoyed one of our massive three-way mega-hugs. I was even comfortable enough to give Nigel a handshake and semi-awkward hug, Jane on the other hand nearly squeezed the life out of him. And then the silence returned, immediately upon returning into the house it felt empty and deadly still. Toni bred life into our home, it was a short visit, but nevertheless she awakened every part of us, every emotion and sensory organ was lifted. This weekend would prove to be lifechanging for me, there was going to be a critical part of my future that would not affect Toni. Whatever the future brings, whatever doors I open I will never allow them to touch Toni. Understanding the ripple effect now made more sense than ever, and I knew I would be able to fulfil this promise.

The next three days passed by in a way I never thought possible, the normal routine morphed into days of enjoyment. I sought and found pleasure in everything I achieved; every moment spent was with a renewed vigour. My most recent vlog was highly detailed, and my notes summarised all the thoughts I was having. I managed to organize them and found new ways to consider each decision I would have to make. Alongside each option I detailed the impact and ripple effect caused by each one. Although now I was able to map each one in a measurement of lifetimes and generations, rather than by weeks or months as it may have been in the past. Thinking with this much clarity and speed was breath-taking. With each decision and concentrated thought, I felt more alive than I have ever been. Forget drugs, alcohol or any other mind changing influence, this feeling I had was like no other, it felt addictive and intoxicating with only a positive outcome.

Eventually the day arrived, even breaks for lunch over the past few days presented new opportunities. The music I was listening to varied more, instead of a pre-arranged playlist of old favourites, I was now selecting previously ignored albums from artists and bands I liked but I'd never delved deeper. I had lists of recommendations from friends, but I always sort comfort in the ones I knew. This new awakening was broadening my horizons and introducing new delights. Sitting there in the warm sunshine and feeling comfortably numb, my eyes inevitably closed. It began with a tingling sensation in my fingertips which slowly tracked up my arms. Simultaneously my toes, feet and legs rejoiced in the same feeling. For a fleeting moment I paused and savoured the delights, next came the feeling of indescribable weightlessness, bones separated from adjoining muscles and sinews, this parting tracked throughout my body. I could see through everything, through microscopic detail I watched as cells parted, the further I went, the more I viewed. Every cell hung in isolation, each one freely giving itself without question. The pleasure was immensely fulfilling, although it was tainted only because I knew this would never happen again. This fleeting thought was soon eradicated as pulses of neon sparked blue light flickered over my bare skin. The pain intensified as they grew more frequent and deeper within my tissues. A single stream of laser white light signalled the next phase. A distant female voice grew louder, at first it was almost unrecognisable, although after my name was called three or four times, I could place it. Regrettably, it wasn't Helena, Jacron's voice could wait, I wanted to absorb the weightlessness and partial tranquillity for a few moments more.

As I began to open my eyes, the sterling brilliant white light seared and scorched as it penetrated my imaginary visual senses. I blinked to let the odd beam through, all the time Jacron urged me to blink more frequently. Eventually, figures began to materialise as shapes emerged against the brilliance and starkness of blue tinged white light. To my amazement my greeting party consisted of Jacron who stood to my far left, then seated were Olin, Xendar, Staten44, Vans-tem6, and finally Youglav. This array of big hitters would obviously constitute my farewell committee, it was either that or they were to be judges to ensure a fair fight. In turn, each one said hello Danny as my eyes scanned the line from left to right. I merely nodded and said hello in reply. We only required sneezy and grumpy for the full set.

Whilst Jacron remained standing, she confirmed this would be my final CDT event, she did, however, drop an interesting comment when she said, "Using current technology". Was this an indication or suggestion that the door to the future could be opened again, who knows. She padded out her speech by reiterating how delighted they had been, how the data they had obtained was key to their research and how well I had accepted data and information from them. It was during this time I noticed that they were all wearing the same-coloured uniforms. They all looked ultra clean and presentable in their pale grey t-shirts with matching trousers. I was then jolted from this seemingly mundane observation by Olin who's turn it was to stand and address me. "Danny, I have come to value our time together, and I will miss our conversations", he stated in a solemn tone. In a more upbeat version, "Are there any final questions you have for us?" I smiled and replied, "Olin, I cannot thank you enough for the information you have given me, and for the obvious trust you have placed in my hands". I took a deep breath in readiness for the next section, "I have literally hundreds if not thousands of questions, all of which are important in their own right, but the time we have here is far too valuable, therefore, let me state what I understand, and you can try to confirm my assumptions".

It took a few moments before Olin smiled which I took as a form of agreement, it was a shared currency we had. The next section of mine was not rehearsed, but it flowed perfectly as I told them, "I obviously didn't seek this invasion into my brain and especially in the manner it has been done, although it has opened a world to me that few will see. I have been entrusted to carry a message forward, and this message is more important than anyone could ever imagine". Even within this brief opening I could see how attentive they all were. I continued, "even if I were to ask you a direct question regarding my role and what I am expected to do, it would be irrelevant because there is one thing no one can control, and that is free choice. I may well hold the secret to humanity's future, and I may commit to you here that I will accept the challenge". I paused for a moment as I thought of Jane, Toni, and Georgina. Perhaps they could read my facial expression if I indeed had one. Olin seemed to move slightly forward, I finished by saying, "but that could change because of unknown and unseen factors that are beyond my control". Olin simply looked at me and said, "You are correct".

Never-Ending Circle 8

Turning to Youglav, I told him how I understood they wish to use part of my DNA sequence, as I did this, there was a look of excitement beginning to form. Letting him down gently, I told him how I would return to this in a moment. While on this path, I told them how I could question their reasons for the need to create a super species. I also said that I feel this bends or breaks one of their own laws, for me it also breaks the laws of evolution as established by Darwin. It was evident that he wanted desperately to debate this further, but Olin seemed to indicate that he shouldn't. One of my recurring questions has been around the 62.87 Theory, and why I was given access to the files containing everything they had.

Whilst I was beginning to gain access to them, I said, it's evident that I have only a basic understanding of the theory. Then came the crunch piece, "You told me from the outset that the author was never known". Youglav nodded briefly, which allowed me to continue, "parking the question of the 36 visionaries and what information they had been given for a moment. Somewhere the theory has been entrusted with one of us." As I delivered this seemingly unremarkable sentence, Youglav began the faintest of smiles, it was a knowing smile, waiting for me, waiting for me to unlock the next padlock. "One of the visionaries will ultimately identify someone who will continue to care for the theory. It will be passed down through generations until such times that humanity will be ready to accept its findings.", I announced. By the time I had finished this section both Olin and Youglav were beginning to nod in a show of appreciation.

I paused for a moment before summarising my theory. "What I know now, and which will be realised through the passing of time is that the author will never be known. It is 'destiny' that there will simply never be an author." Okay, I know this sounds crazy, and maybe I should have put a, 'keep an open mind' warning at the start of this passage. Anyway, let me continue, "You provided the files to me without genuinely knowing the identity of the author, and I have accepted them on this basis. As they will now begin their journey through time and generations, they will do so in this state, without an author." I had to pause again to gather my own thoughts, I continued, "What's been created here is a perfect never-ending circle that mirrors infinity, similar to a number eight. You don't know the identity of the author; I don't know who it is either, which means neither of us will ever know." The famous Winston Churchill quote came to mind as it could perfectly describe this as 'a riddle, wrapped in a mystery, inside an enigma'.

Addressing Olin and Youglav, I told them it was my understanding that I would play a pivotal role in the formation of things to come. Purposely, I left this ambiguous, if I'd tried to put too much detail here it would have bogged the conversation down. I was happy to keep it vague, as I stated at the start, the aspect of free choice remains in place for everything, it's pointless to be too definitive. Although, I did feel it beneficial to mention the additional section concerning 'Point 1' of the theory. I assumed this section would be added to the main theory during its journey through the annals of time. I gazed across my collected audience, it's truly mind-bending to think of them as future generations, I could only think that somehow humanity was able to drag itself out of the turmoil we now face. Helena told me we shared the same bloodline, when I looked into her eyes, I could imagine how countless generations had contributed, each one adding more to create a better version of the same species. I now stood in front of these people with a monumental journey ahead of me.

My Decision

For my journey to start, I must find the other 35 visionaries, just as they have been told to find me, our paths will cross and begin a single set of footprints into the future. I don't have most of the answers, I don't even know most of the questions, but what I do possess is a set of tools and skills that will undoubtedly help me. With the ripple effect I can plan and consider how the future will be impacted through our actions. Information is fine, although useless until this is transferred into knowledge. Knowledge is not the full article until experience and wisdom relates it to understanding. Once we possess understanding we can truly appreciate its worth and enlighten others. Clarity of language will prove to be invaluable to its owner. I know this all sounds airy-fairy, but it's true and it works.

Locked somewhere in my brain is a vast array of files, I can access them through my own thought, but I need to work out a method to further download them into a more useable format. These files contain an incredible resource of two main topics, the first relates to the 62.87 Theory along with the supporting evidence. I have been able to access parts of this, and I am beginning to understand it, but I will need much more if I am to pass this to others. The other file dump is possibly more interesting and arguably more useful. It demonstrates in amazing detail the path humanity will have to take. Some of the parts I sampled were distinctly unpalatable, they showed a path humanity must take, however difficult they may be. One day it will happen, I am just the messenger, it will be for others to see the steps of change through to completion.

For some inexplicable reason and in some unexplained way, I am able to solve complex problems with unbelievable speed. During the past few weeks, I have tested this out in various situations, it doesn't matter the problem or subject, it's yet to fail me. Put this together with the other information and tools I have been given, means I am ready for the challenges to come. A tear began to form in the corner of my eye, I took a very deep breath and began a statement, it can only be described as coming straight from the heart.

I looked ahead and started my speech, "Recently, I was informed that I carry a flaw within my DNA makeup. You will appreciate the shock of being told this, I don't believe this should ever be defined as such, a flaw, that is. This definition along with similar badges does not in any way tell my story. It must not be allowed to distort your view or indeed prejudice your opinion of my true and full potential. It's far too easy for these badges to blinker you from what is truly there. Ask me what I can do, never dictate to me what I can't. We can all share a heavy load, but it must be equally divided. Celebrate our individuality and embrace our unique skills." I looked for any sort of reaction, but there wasn't a movement of any sort. I knew there was a danger of exposing Helena and Lise, although it was vitally important to state this.

As the floor remained mine, and I felt an air of expectation, I was ready to deliver my decision statement. "Let me tell you this, I now understand more than I ever thought possible. I can see in abundant clarity the path humanity must take, and that it must start here and now. I am not unique, I don't possess any special powers, my life is no more precious than any other. I commend you for everything you have achieved, and for what you will continue to create in the pursuit of perfection. For me, or any other to be a part of this journey is a privilege, what you have asked of me, I will do to the best of my abilities. There are some that see only weakness where true strength and courage prevails. The disease I carry daily will not define me nor will it limit my endurance. There are some that see faults in the differences I display, or how my mind operates. These differences are what makes us unique, they should be celebrated and praised as a benefit to all of humanity." The faces on Olin and Youglav were priceless, eager anticipation mixed with pent up enjoyment.

Mixed emotions soared through my mind, my heart beat faster and faster in what felt like an uncontrollable pace. As my face grew hotter, I could almost feel beads of sweat accumulating on my brow. This was going to be a decision that could help change the outcome for humanity and our onward journey. It felt too critical and too enormous for one being to make alone. Suddenly, I felt exceptionally small in the face of such pressure and expectation. The decision I made was one that came easy in the end and gave me pleasure to announce. For the very last time, I looked into the eyes of everyone and took imaginary snapshots of each. These would help remind me of everything that had happened, every conversation, every piece of information and every discovery that I made.

The time was ready, I took a final deep breath and said calmly, "I was selected by you as I met your criteria in all aspects. I believe you know what path I will take, and how I will go on to complete my challengers. I understand what my role is now, I finally obtained my answers, and with this conclusion, I am ready to provide yours. Based on everything I now understand, along with the information I have provided to you, and the analysis we have both undertaken, there is only one answer I can give".

By this point you could cut the atmosphere with a knife, my final words to them were the only ones that would fit within the context of everything that had happened. Softly, I delivered my final words, each one summed up perfectly the entire experience we had shared, "You will figure it out!", fell gently upon expectant ears. I looked towards my audience; each person's face had a measured degree of confusion. There was only one that stood out as different. Set apart from the others was Olin who looked directly at me and simply smiled.

As my eyes closed a sensation of relief washed over me, it felt as though a heavy weight had been removed from my entire body. Reality began to kick in as I felt the warmth of the sun again and my breathing slowed. I opened my eyes and remained seated and calm, time would be needed to digest everything that had just happened. It would take even longer to fully appreciate and come to terms with everything that the past few weeks had thrown at me. A tinge of sadness was the first emotion I felt as I sat there within my own little bubble. I couldn't help but think, what would their decision be, would they go on to use my DNA. Maybe not knowing would be the best outcome, anyway I knew this would be wasted thought, consequently, it would be parked safely for the moment.

I hadn't yet mapped out or detailed any plans as that was going to take an enormous amount of time, but I knew what my final objective would be. I would be the one person to gather the other 35 visionaries into a group. Each one will have their own set of skills and understanding of their roles and responsibilities. I knew how to recognise each of them, the code will act as my padlock, and their brain power will serve as the key. Together we will form a party and create a manifesto that will change how the world thinks, and how humanity must come together. I have been charged with the safekeeping of the 62.87 Theory, the author will remain unknown rather than anonymous. This will begin its circle through the generations, and at the correct time it will be unveiled. The world of science will go on to prove its validity, the rest is history.

A Turn Of Events

I wanted to take some time to consider my options and focus on the intricate planning that would be required. I enjoyed the final of the world cup on July 15th where France beat Croatia four goals to two. It's certainly a tournament I will never forget. England were as predictable as ever with the pain having to continue. My world turned on its head a few weeks later. It was a typical and ordinary Monday; I dropped Jane at the station but instead of returning home I heard the calling of a coffee. I remember entering my favourite café and engaging in some friendly banter, but that was the last thing I remember. On Monday 13th August I suffered a massive heart attack, I woke up 5 days later on the intensive care ward. It certainly puts things into perspective when you're told that you were clinically dead for nine minutes during furious attempts at revival.

There were no windows on the ward, lights were dimmed, but a glow from the machines that monitored my vital signs bounced a fascinating mix of green, blue, and white. A nurse leaned over me to adjust a control, that hypnotic and mesmerising light twinkled off a cross that hung loosely from her neck. I had to let it go when she said, "It's a miracle you're alive, god must have special plans for you".

----- FIN -----

www.ingramcontent.com/pod-product-compliance
Lightning Source LLC
Chambersburg PA
CBHW071754310726
48976CB00001BA/202